RED JAVELIN

BOOK ONE OF THE RED JAVELIN CHRONICLES

By

ROSS HARRINGWAY

RED JAVELIN

COPYRIGHT © **2015** Ross Harringway

OMEGA PRESS

An imprint of Omega Communications Group, Inc.

For information contact:

Omega Press
5823 N. Mesa, #839
El Paso, Texas 79912

FIRST EDITION

Printed in the United States of America

OTHER BOOKS BY ROSS HARRINGWAY

FROM OMEGA PRESS

The Clovis Legacy Series

The Forbidden Region
Reign of Death
Shadows in the Dark
Weakness is Provacative
Illusion of Freedom
Burdened with Morality

CHAPTER ONE

2533 THE YEAR OF SIKORSKY

"I regret killing you," Janos Janicek mumbled in his sleep. He tossed and turned as his mind fought to avoid another nightmare.

For the last three nights she came to him in his sleep. She never accused him in the visits; he assumed that the woman was haunting him for his past actions which caused his guilt over her death to control his dream. It seemed as if she wanted Janicek to do something, to take action.

His youngest wife slept next to him in their large bed. His other wives were asleep in the other rooms of the massive Presidential Castle located in Prague. About fifteen feet from the foot of the bed was a fireplace that was still lit and three of his solid black affenpinscher dogs were standing up and listening as Janicek continued to talk in his sleep.

Janicek had been one of the highest decorated officers of the Space Command. He had served as a Captain and then Admiral of his own fleet of Battle Cruisers. After twelve years as an Admiral, Janicek elected to retire and enjoy his twilight years with his children and grandchildren. When he returned to the Eastern Europe Province of Old Earth, the citizens begged him to run for President. At first he resisted the calls for him to serve. At the urging of his five wives, Janicek finally agreed and his election was won by a landslide over two lesser known opponents.

After the politics of the campaign were over, Janicek and his family moved into the large castle that had been a tourist attraction before being converted into the Presidential Palace. The castle had ten floors, eighty-seven large bedrooms, eight kitchens, thirty bathrooms with showers and hot tubs, three large dining areas, a few studies and a basement with plenty of space for a wine storage and other rooms. The Janicek family had government employees that would cook their meals and maintain the castle and the grounds outside. They had a manicured lawn, lovely trees and rows of flowers surrounding the brick walkways.

Janicek had served the United Nations of the Eight Solar Systems well and received more awards than any Admiral in the history of the service. He was a brilliant military tactician, skilled pilot and an adept and respected leader. His service in politics, children and numerous grandchildren kept him feeling young as he was constantly active. He tried to write his memoirs each night so that future astronauts and soldiers could learn from his experiences. But the woman that came to him in his subconscious caused him to have what was known as writer's block. He could not bring words to describe the one event that he could never forgive himself for.

Although he had been hailed as one of the greatest commanders in military history, there was one mission that Janicek could not forget. It haunted him, tore at his very soul.

And one of the soldiers that was lost on that mission was visiting him in his dreams. It wasn't nightmares that came to him. It was as if she wanted him to take action, to do something, but he could never get her to tell him what it was that she wanted. He could see her grey blue eyes, full lips and blonde hair as clear as if she were standing right in front of him. She was just as beautiful as she was the first day he had met her on his Battle Cruiser. She came to him each night, wearing her old Marine Corps uniform, with her burgundy colored Spetsnaz beret on her head. She would smile at him as she tried to soothe his guilt. They were standing together surrounded by a white light that was bright but did not hurt Janicek's eyes. It was a place of peace and serenity which Janicek found himself hoping to remain. He wondered if he was with her in Heaven or Valhalla or some other place that the various Gods promised to provide for men and women at their end.

"I don't blame you," Melita Gorski said softly. "You must let go of your guilt so that you can be prepared for what is about to transpire. The eight solar systems will need you. I have seen visions of the future, the weapons that the dictators will bring to force all of humanity to bow before him. You are the one with the experience to fight him. You must be ready to gather your old friends, to convince them that they must fight by your side one last time."

"Tell me what you want," Janicek asked in his dream. He was tossing and turning in his bed. He was perspiring as he had during her last two visits.

"Something horrible is about to happen," she warned him, her voice seemed to echo with dread.

"What is going to happen?"

"Many innocents are about to die."

"You are a ghost, how do you know such things?"

"I see things where I am."

"Please tell me what you want me to do."

She smiled at Janicek, "My husband will soon be in danger as well as my sons. Your family will also be in harm's way."

"How?"

"I see a fire in the sky. I see flesh burning off of the bodies. It is horrible."

"Where is this fire?" Janicek asked her.

"It is everywhere."

"On old Earth?"

"It will consume many worlds. Help my husband. Please. Help my sons."

"How can I help them?"

"You were the greatest Admiral ever."

"Why are you coming to me?"

"Because without you billions will die."

"Billions?"

"My children and yours will die."

Janicek could see the contours of her face. Her eyes seemed to have urgency in them. "How do I help your husband and sons? I don't even know where they are."

"You will know what to do."

"When do I act?"

"When the Calypso returns that will be the sign. When the Queens unite. When the traitor shows the way. The entire population of humanity will witness the events as they transpire. When the fire in the sky erupts, you must begin to act or billions will die without your leadership."

"I don't understand. You are speaking in riddles." Janicek said, speaking out loud in his sleep. For some reason, his wife that was lying next to him in the bed did not hear his words. "How will I know when?"

"You will see the fire in the sky."

"Where will I see it?"

"Everyone will see it. They will return. They have been at peace but they will return."

Janicek noticed that she was beginning to fade away as she had the last two nights. He cried out in his sleep, "Wait! Don't leave! Tell me what is about to happen!"

She looked back at Janicek and smiled. Her image was fading away from him. "I must warn others. I cannot come back to you. This will be our last conversation. Watch for the fire in the sky. It will be the sign to bring you all together. Watch for the fire The Calypso will return. You will see the Queens unite to fight the evil ones. The time is coming."

And then Melita Gorski was gone.

Janicek woke up and gasped for air. Although there was an ample amount of burning wood in a fireplace at the corner of the bedroom, his exhale came out white, as if he were out in the freezing cold. He felt a chill up his spine, as if there were someone or something in the room with him, watching his every move. He sat up quickly and saw that his wife was still asleep. His three dark affenpinscher dogs were staring at him, sitting at the grey stone arched doorway. One of them was moving his head from side to side as if trying to figure out what was wrong.

Janicek decided that he needed a strong drink. He walked down a winding staircase of stone steps surrounded by a grey stone wall to the first floor of the castle. The way was lighted by burning torches that were hanging at an angle from the walls. His hands were shaking as he took each step, his eyes on his shadow that seemed to move in awkward positions due to the flames. He walked across the stone floor that was covered with several expensive placement carpets of multiple color schemes. There were several couches to his right and a large fireplace that was burning bright. To the left of the fireplace was a dark wood and metal bar that had his favorite whiskey stocked. He found a small glass and poured himself a triple shot before he sat down on one of the several comfortable couches. His hands were trembling due to the fear he felt from the apparition of Melita Gorski visiting him so often in his dreams. He would not sleep again for the rest of the night as he sipped on a whiskey and water in front of his fireplace.

"The fire in the sky," he kept repeating the phrase to himself.

What the hell did she mean by that? He took a full shot of his drink and coughed as the liquor burned his throat. He stood up and walked over to the bar, poured himself another drink. He reflected on his many years of service with the Space Command. He had been a pilot, a captain of a Battle Cruiser and then an Admiral of an entire fleet. He had defended humanity from threats foreign and domestic. He had led men and women into combat many times. He knew of warfare and suffering. He had also faced fear on many occasions in numerous theaters, risking his life for the Glorious Leader and the expansion of humanity. But never had he felt fear as he did now. Her words sounded so ominous and full of dread of what she believed was to come. She had him believing her words, which had his hands shaking. She showed him visions of people burning alive, space craft melting in deep space from some unseen power.

She had his attention. He downed another large gulp of the liquor and sat down on the couch, happy to see that one of his loyal affenpinscher dogs had joined him by the fireplace. What he had seen was not just some average nightmare. The visions that he saw seemed so real, as if the events were happening right before his eyes. He shuddered as he thought of the words that were spoken to him by a woman he had personally ordered killed. She sounded so sure that the fire was coming. The fact that she mentioned the historical science exploration space craft named the Calypso had him thinking of her assertions that the ship would return. He recalled that the history data bases recorded the Calypso as destroyed during the war over Akarzdamedia. He wondered if she was referring to that specific ship or another with the same name.

What Janicek did not know was that he and the rest of the world would soon witness a fire in the sky. The entire human race would soon see the largest explosion in their history and it would be an event that would bring about a war that would be costly in lives and weaponry. It would be a war that Janos Janicek had been destined to play a significant part. She told him to find his friends to help him. Janicek began to mull over in his mind the locations of his former crew members. He called upon his personal computer to begin compiling a list of those he had once served with.

CHAPTER TWO

In the aftermath of the so-called "Blood Moon Incident" the people of the Earth Empire began to ask probing questions. The news media had produced several thousand live interviews with the survivors of the incident. There were several times more productions released with interviews of the family members of the survivors and the victims. Within a few months of the victory on the Blood Moon by the Newton and Clovis Academy cadets, there were over a million written articles and opinion pieces sent out over the entire computerized broadcast system. And each article spawned thousands of comments from the readers.

The Rosenburg family had been accused and indicted as the perpetrators of the many deaths of the young cadets and the retired men and women that were the Judges on the Moon orbiting planet Semiramis. The Rosenburg's were descendants of Vladimir Sikorsky which had major implications for the citizens of Earth, all of her settlements and colonies. Many of the families of the victims demanded investigations into the family ties between the Rosenburg's and the Sikorsky's.

The public attention to the events was an unwanted outcome by the perpetrators. They had been outsmarted by Cadet Yuri Gorski and his fellow students from Clovis Academy. Many of the cadets survived the ambush on that moon due to the leadership that Gorski provided and his never say die attitude.

And the human population that was spread out over eight solar systems witnessed the majority of the events. The individuals involved in the illegal acts had nowhere to hide. Their identities were well known. The majority had been arrested or killed. One of the assassins, Dell Ragnarsson, had never been found but was presumed dead.

Vladimir Sikorsky, the Glorious Leader and Secretary General of the United Nations of Earth, was taken by surprise regarding the reaction of the civilian population in the aftermath of the Blood Moon Incident. Although Sikorsky had publicly disavowed any knowledge or involvement in the deaths of the cadets, many chose to believe the conspiracy theories that were being floated around that the Sikorsky family had been a major player in the event. The rumors spread by word of mouth and by use of satellite broadcast from planet to planet, from moon to moon, from space station to space station, from battle cruiser to battle cruiser. Some of the colonies on other worlds began to march in the streets and protest the two hundred year rule of Sikorsky and his children, grand-children, great grand-children and great great grand-children. Sikorsky refused to accept the numerous calls for his resignation as Glorious Leader.

Sikorsky gave several speeches to remind humanity of all the good he has done for them. He reminisced openly regarding the fact he was the hero that saved Earth two hundred years ago against the invading alien race called the Akarzdamedians. He called upon historians to speak out so that the masses would be reminded of the expansion of humanity across several solar systems under his rule and leadership. The propaganda ministry of the United Nations sent out numerous press releases in support of the Glorious Leader.

But despite all of those efforts, the protests continued.

Vladimir Sikorsky determined that examples must be made. He called upon his ranking officers and ordered that they select one of the colonies to show the rest of humanity that insurrection would be dealt with sternly and without remorse. Sikorsky's sons and daughters on Sikorsky's Planet analyzed each of the rebellious outbreaks. Several of the nation states on old Earth were rioting. Ireland, Spain, the Nevada Territory of what had been known as the United States and Japan had thousands of civilians calling for a change in leadership. The Earth's Moon had two colonies. Both were declaring independence from the current governmental structure. The Martian colonies were also joining in on the demands to replace Sikorsky and his family.

And there was the rebellion on the terra-formed moon named Chronos that was orbiting the gas planet Osiris. Chronos had taken four years of difficult effort to produce a breathable atmosphere for humans to live on her surface. The moon was rich in lithium, silver, iron, tungsten, titanium, bauxite and coal. To extract these elements and transport them, the Space Command established mining communities on Chronos. Those settlements grew as other people determined they could colonize the moon and profit by opening restaurants, bars and other service oriented businesses.

Over the years, the population grew to eight hundred thousand twenty-seven people. As the events unfolded on the Blood Moon, the people of Chronos began to demand change. The people were inspired by the speech given by Les Gillis and the heroic battle of twenty-four small Allen Fighter space ships against four. They were encouraged by the bravery and selfless acts that Gorski and his friends demonstrated in that conflict. The mining employees felt they deserved better working conditions and fairer wages and were no longer afraid to state their demands. The demands turned into riots when the Glorious Leader told them to be happy that they had a job. The riots grew into a successful overthrow of the government. The civilians arrested Karl Sikorsky, the Secretary General of Chronos and grandson of the Glorious Leader. The colonists did not stop there. They apprehended the entire support staff of Karl Sikorsky. The majority of the high ranking staff were also descendants of the Glorious Leader. Each were given swift trials and then executed by the screaming mobs. It was a bloody replay of the French Revolution. Hundreds died in the purge.

One of the leaders of the Chronos rebellion was a man named Enrique Ortiz. At first glance he would not have been a person that others would look to for leadership in a time of political turmoil. Ortiz was short, overweight, average looking, not very articulate and was an owner of a bar named Dos Gueros Muertos. Ortiz had been a member of a large extended family that had spread out over the eight solar systems. The Ortiz clan opened bars and restaurants on several planets, moons and space stations and even began to sell franchises to other investors. Business was good for the Ortiz family.

Enrique Ortiz brought his wife and three children to Chronos to establish a presence on that moon and begin to profit from the settlers and those that would come and go. But as the Blood Moon Incident occurred, a miracle happened for the Ortiz family. A few years earlier a young girl named Karla Ortiz had been kidnaped. Despite herculean efforts, the Ortiz family could not locate her. They hired investigators and appealed to law enforcement and higher authorities to help them. But she was gone and no clues of her whereabouts could be located.

Until the day that the cadets from Clovis Academy fought back against the Rosenburg killers on the Blood Moon. When Cadet Drew Harrison stabbed the flame dart into David Rosenburg's arm and caused his death, he set in motion events that he did not know would ripple from his simple act of self-defense. David Rosenburg had taken several slave girls and forced them to marry him. One of those unfortunate girls was Karla Ortiz. With the death of David, Karla was free to leave the Rosenburg Ranch and reunite with her family. She first stopped on Chronos when she had learned her uncle was living there. She spent three days with her nieces, aunt and uncle before leaving on a space craft transport to reunite with her father and siblings. She told her story to Enrique Ortiz before she left. She showed him the scars on her back from the whippings she received from the cruel Rosenburg family.

Enrique Ortiz was enraged by the treatment that his niece had endured at the hands of the barbaric Rosenburg family. He began to spread the word to his neighbors as to what he learned from Karla. And the people on Chronos listened. The negative actions of the Rosenburg family became a rallying cry for the people to stand up and fight. Ortiz reluctantly became the de facto leader of the rebellion on that terra formed moon. The people fought and first stormed the Military Intelligence building located in the capital city named Mount Olympus. Using laser rifles and pistols, the soldiers killed several hundred civilians that were armed with steak knives and wooden sticks. But the people overwhelmed the soldiers and killed them all. They took their laser weapons for themselves and moved in to take the Space Command landing strip located nearby the capital.

The battle went better for the civilians since they were now armed with state of the art weaponry. Most of the pilots stationed there surrendered to the mob and were spared. They joined the rebellion and willingly provided air coverage for the civilians led by Ortiz as they attacked the governmental offices which housed several Royal Family members. After two days of fighting, Ortiz and the civilian rebels took complete control of the government. They freed the political prisoners that were awaiting trial.

For the cruel and twisted treatment of his niece, Ortiz had all of the Royal Family on Chronos executed by hanging. He allowed the news media to broadcast the events knowing all too well that Vladimir Sikorsky himself would view the deaths.

As Ortiz predicted, the news of the executions of the descendants of the Glorious Leader reached the other colonies of the Earth Empire.

After consulting with his sons and daughters, who were his most trusted advisors, Vladimir Sikorsky determined that swift action was necessary. The family could not afford for other colonies or planets to rebel. Accordingly, Sikorsky ordered the moon of Chronos to be the example of what would happen to those that would dissent or question his dominion over them. The Glorious Leader calmly marched from his Royal Palace of over one hundred twenty floors to the nearby Sikorsky's Planet Academy. Rarely would the Glorious Leader, a man of over two hundred forty years of age, venture out of the protective confines of his Palace. But Sikorsky was driven by the knowledge that his seed had been intentionally targeted. His grandchild, great grandchildren and great great grandchildren had been murdered. The entire population of Chronos had to be punished. The rest of humanity had to be witnesses to the swift destruction that would come to those that committed such acts against the Royal Family of Sikorsky.

The Glorious Leader arranged a meeting with one of his closest allies, a Professor of Metallurgy and Weaponry. His name was Professor Andrew Brey O'Connell. Sikorsky met with O'Connell in his seventh floor office at the University building for Weapons Design.   The office was about thirty square feet wide and had a nice metal desk in the back wall with a black leather rolling chair for O'Connell to relax in. There were several guest chairs made of the same leather in front of his desk. O'Connell had intentionally left three of his four walls bare so that he could use the latest three dimensional holographic computer technology in the solitude and privacy of his larger than average space.

O'Connell was in his late forties and had spent the last several years away from his home on old Earth to build a massive facility and develop weapons for humanity. He was an expert in nuclear weaponry and metallurgy and had been published in many periodicals on issues of new advancements in weaponry. He was over six feet tall, in good physical conditioning and dressed in the latest fashions. His brown hair and green eyes complimented his strong cheek bones and chiseled chin.

He had always proven to be a reliable ally to the Glorious Leader in times of need. Sikorsky had contracted with O'Connell in the past to help with minor skirmishes or rebellions. He was receptive to assisting the Royal family, no matter what the request. He had given them weapons that would eliminate an enemy and the death would seem to be a heart attack or an aneurism. For his work, O'Connell was well paid and provided his own security force. The only concern Sikorsky had regarding O'Connell was that the enemies of the Royal Family would kidnap the man and force him to create weapons to be used against them. O'Connell understood the need for the extra security around him and never complained about it.

O'Connell greeted the Glorious Leader with a hand shake and a smile. The Professor knew that Sikorsky would not come to visit him personally unless the circumstances were dire. His involvement with the Royal Family had been a closely guarded secret. O'Connell had been working on some of the most confidential projects for the Sikorsky's. O'Connell listened silently as Sikorsky directed that he wanted the entire population of Chronos Moon to be eliminated. O'Connell nodded in agreement. Any move by any holding of the United Nations of the Eight Solar Systems to secede must be met with resolute force. Examples must be made to dissuade others with similar ideas of secession in their minds. O'Connell shook Sikorsky's hand and informed him that he would need to take leave of him to launch the attack. Sikorsky thanked the loyal Professor.

Andrew Brey O'Connell spent his childhood in Ireland. He grew up experiencing the tensions of the rising extreme nationalist movement of the past several decades. One of the dynamics of the cry for nationalism was to indoctrinate the young to despise the oppressors. O'Connell had been recruited by the nationalists of his country to learn how to build explosives. At age eleven, O'Connell had become adept at crafting weapons of death to be used against the people of England. By the time he graduated from the equivalent of high school, O'Connell had mastered the art of building explosives. He furthered his knowledge by studying metallurgy and weaponry in college.

After achieving his doctorate in metallurgy, Professor Andrew Brey O'Connell had been employed by the Fenster Corporation as a weapons designer. Later he was offered a position with the Rosenburg Corporation and relocated to the planet named New Edinburgh. As an employee with the Rosenburg Corporation, O'Connell was one of the first to inspect the underground facility built by an alien race called the Danaraja. O'Connell assisted the Rosenburg family in copying the technology and adapting it to suit the desires of the Royal Family.

O'Connell, John and Cush Rosenburg used the newly discovered alien wisdom and science to expedite terra-forming of new worlds and to design and manufacture advancements in weaponry. They built secret manufacturing facilities to advance their new line of weapons on the Rosenburg Ranch. Soon, they were forced to move most of the factory production to other more discreet locations.

O'Connell was brought to Sikorsky's Planet by the invitation of the Glorious Leader and John Rosenburg to pose as a Professor at the famous Sikorsky's Academy. His real mission was to construct the most deadly weapons ever known to mankind. O'Connell, with the assistance of John Rosenburg, spent years designing many new items for warfare. Their discoveries and creations had been kept secret for the last decade. Now, by order of the Glorious Leader, O'Connell would unleash one of the most destructive fruits of his hard work.

O'Connell used a small transport ship to fly to the outer regions of Sikorsky's Planet to his secret underground weapons construction plants. His ship was flown by three robotic beings that resembled humans that O'Connell had created and built. The Professor did not like using slave labor as the Sikorsky family had been known for. Nor did the Professor use the Replicants, also known as clones that were also common for the Sikorsky's. O'Connell chose to use top scientists, engineers and metallic androids as his labor force. He also had recruited thousands of trained soldiers to act as his security forces. The majority of his forces were from the Military Intelligence branch. He had a battalion of Marines and another battalion of weapons experts that assisted and were ready and willing to repel any attack on the complex.

Vladimir Sikorsky had given John Rosenburg and Professor O'Connell over fifty square kilometers of land on Sikorsky's Planet to utilize for the development of new weapons. The area selected had been a munitions manufacturing concern for the indigenous alien race of Sikorsky's Planet. The Akarzdamedian's had been far more advanced than humanity. Their weapons were deadlier. O'Connell and Rosenburg explored the alien buildings and drew up plans on how to utilize what the alien race had left behind.

After the plans were completed, O'Connell and Rosenburg meticulously selected each and every engineer, metallurgist, computer programmer, military tactician and construction worker to make the plans a reality. The workers had to be able to maintain confidentiality and be completely loyal to their Glorious Leader. After the team had been selected the work began in earnest. They were on a mission to make history and to make mankind a force in the entire Universe. With the weapons they would create, no other species would ever dare to challenge the Glorious Leader. It had taken the engineers two years to build the facilities to match O'Connell's blueprints.

As his transport ship flew close to his concealed manufacturing buildings, O'Connell saw in the horizon twenty-four large red colored sky-scrapers. O'Connell had been the director of the construction of those structures. Any human flying over would believe they were looking upon tall, one hundred fifty floor high buildings.
But they were not buildings.

The tall red sky scrapers in disguise were actually weapons of mass destruction. They were able to wipe out the population of an entire planet, but leave the existing infrastructure intact. Professor Andrew Brey O'Connell had called them "Red Javelin" after the Celtic myths of his youth to signify a weapon that would destroy its' target no matter where the weapon was thrown from and no matter where the target lived.

O'Connell lamented the fact that John Rosenburg would not be by his side, to celebrate the launch of one of their world killers. Due to the events on the Blood Moon, Rosenburg had been forced to return to planet New Edinburgh to run the Rosenburg Corporation. John Rosenburg's brother had died on the moon orbiting planet Semiramis just a few months earlier, causing John Rosenburg, as the oldest living member of his family business, to return to the day to day management of the Rosenburg Corporation. It would have been a glorious event had John Rosenburg and O'Connell been able to launch the Red Javelin weapons together. O'Connell had purchased a three hundred year old bottle of expensive whiskey that they could toast to their success when the day arrived.

O'Connell lamented that he would open that bottle of spirits alone.

O'Connell reached his facility and was greeted by many of his loyal engineers and scientists. He informed them all that the day of reckoning had arrived. There was thunderous applause from his staff when he ordered that twelve of the twenty-four Red Javelin's be immediately launched. Eleven were to remain in orbit around Sikorsky's Planet for further use, if necessary. The twelfth was launched on an intercept course with the moon called Chronos.

There were many celebrations occurring on the Moon called Chronos. The successful humans used the end of the rebellion to begin a new form of democratically elected government. They wrote a constitution and it was quickly ratified. The people elected a twelve member committee to draft a new form of government, with free elections. They created their own flag, after publicly burning all of the flags of the United Nations of Earth. The leaders of the Chronos revolution explained to the news media that they rejected the two hundred year rule of the Glorious Leader. Thousands were dancing in the streets. Unknown to each of them was that the Glorious Leader they openly rejected had already sent his response to their disloyalty in the form of an instrument of doom. They had no advance warning of what was coming in their direction.

Their joy was as short lived as their lives.

A single large, red projectile, the length of over a one hundred fifty floor building, entered the atmosphere of Chronos. It was not detected by the military security stations and radar scans until it was too late. When it was detected, many of the Chronosians thought it to be an alien space ship. Others thought that it might be a new form of transport ship developed by the Allen or Fenster families. None of them had any idea that this new object was the last thing most of them would see.

The Red Javelin had flown many astronomical units to arrive at the destination of the moon named Chronos. It entered the atmosphere as the speed rapidly decelerated. When the weapon was a mere ten kilometers from the surface of the moon, the citizen leadership of Chronos launched a flight squadron of two dozen small space craft to intercept her.

As the twenty-four one man small Allen Corporation fighter type ships approached the bright red weapon, the pilots reported that the strange object was beginning to glow. The pilots advised that the temperature on the object was increasing rapidly. In a matter of seconds, the brave pilots lost control of their ships as their engines stopped working. They began to spiral to their deaths on the planet surface. Their ejection functions on their individualized ships were inoperable as well. The Red Javelin erupted, causing a brilliant flash of yellow, orange, red and white colors. The bright spectrum of colors spread over the entire surface of Chronos. As the powerful beams of radiated light filled the atmosphere and settled on the surface the human population encountered pain as they had never known. Their flesh began to boil and fall in chunks from their bodies. Children were not spared the agony of the weapon from Sikorsky's Planet. The screams of the dying were broadcast to all of the inhabitants of the seven conquered solar systems and the system of Old Earth. Humanity witnessed the over eight hundred thousand people die, their bodies boiling. Many were writhing on the streets in pain and screaming for mercy. Some of the people were seen pulling the burning flesh off of their faces in a futile attempt to end the pain.

But the only mercy shown to them was that the agony ended with their eventual deaths.

Enrique Ortiz died with his wife and three children as their bodies were ravaged by the effects of the Red Javelin weapon. Ortiz stood in the middle of one of the main streets in front of his bar and cursed Sikorsky as his flesh fell from his body in small pieces. He screamed in agony as his eyes began to burn and the heat seared him to the bone. He had sought freedom and justice and was killed for having the audacity to demand those principles. His wife and children died just as he had. Their flesh began to melt and fall from their bones. The pain they each experienced was immeasurable.

But that was the desired effect. The Glorious Leader wanted the rest of the eight solar systems to see the pain that the Red Javelin weapon would inflict upon human life.

In less than half a day, the population of eight hundred thousand seventeen humans on the terra-formed moon named Chronos were dead. As far as humanity was concerned, the moon had been hit by a single weapon of unknown origin. A wall of white and red heat engulfed the entire lunar surface. All of the bodies of the inhabitants were reduced to smoking ash.

Twenty-four hours following the mass murder of the entire human population on the moon called Chronos, the Glorious Leader, Vladimir Sikorsky, took full responsibility for the disaster. He warned the rest of humanity that he would not hesitate to strike any disloyal planet, moon or space station with the same swiftness. His words echoed over dozens of worlds.

"Insurrection and rebellion will be rewarded with certain death. Challenge me and you shall join the dead criminals of Chronos," Vladimir Sikorsky threatened the rest of humanity.

He would soon learn that his threats and the genocide he ordered on the citizens of Chronos would not have the effect he desired. Rebellions began to commence in other planetary systems, and each one produced numerous casualties.

A civil war was beginning.

It was a war that the Glorious Leader intended to win, even if it meant the death of every living man, woman and child that stood against him.

CHAPTER THREE

It had been a long flight from planet Athena to New Edinburgh. The Allen Corporation military transport named the Venerable was able to comfortably carry two hundred passengers through space and had a crew of six pilots, three engineers, one doctor, two nurses, a ship ranking officer of Lieutenant Commander, two chefs and two computer technicians. The passengers were mostly Marines and Military Intelligence enlisted women and men that were being sent to replace the deceased soldiers from the raids brought by Junior Ragnarsson.

Corporal Kiana "Miyu" Tamura of the MI branch was one of the passengers on the ship. She had kept close to her small group of friends, three other enlisted women that had served with her on Athena, and ignored the remainder of the crew. Her last assignment had led to many problems for her due to an ill-advised choice in a relationship. She had been pursued, seduced and bedded on numerous occasions by General Napoleon Sikorsky, the supreme commander of the planetary defense of Athena. Tamura had found the General to be handsome, charming, and smart and he was a man that would not take no for an answer. After a few weeks of wooing her, the General succeeded in getting Tamura to sleep with him.

The relationship did not end due to one of the General's wives finding out and throwing a jealous rant. They parted ways over Tamura's refusal to follow a direct order to assassinate an alien princess. Tamura had been a part of the team that had killed the king and queen of the White Mountain Babcottiatta. The General ordered the offspring to be killed as well. Tamura had the princess in her laser sighting scope of her sniper weapon and she refused to pull the trigger. The General signed an order transferring Tamura to planet New Edinburgh and refused to speak to her regarding the events.

Tamura spent time in the gymnasium to keep herself fit for duty. The day before the transport ship was to land, she worked out with her three friends, LeVega Farley, Zerena LeBosh and Jade Afzal. The four women had come to terms with the fact that after they landed, they may never see one another again. Each of them had received assignments to different areas of the planet. Tamura was to report to Clovis City and join an MI platoon that was a part of General Tan's Brigades.

"I wonder the ratio of men to women is the same here as it was on Athena," LeBosh stated out loud as the four women were walking for the showers.

"It can't be worse," Afzal responded as she began to pull off her two piece pink and black work out suit. "The worst thing about Athena was all those Harcourt's. They could read your mind and even make you do things against your will. It was always unsettling for me to be around them."

"Harcourt's are living in all corners of the eight solar systems," Farley laughed as she undressed. "I slept with one of them and he was a pretty good lover. I'd do it again."

Tamura pulled off her half shirt and moved her tight shorts off. She shrugged, "Well, had I not been involved with someone I would have gladly jumped a Harcourt. Many of them had handsome features."

"But you did not need to jump any of those white skinned abominations," LeBosh pointed her bar of blue soap in Tamura's direction. "You had the General by the balls. Literally. Speaking of which, I have been dying to know, what was the age difference between you two?"

Tamura stepped underneath one of the shower spouts and directed the hidden computer microchip to douse her with soapy water. She began to lather her body and faced the other three women to answer the question. "Napoleon was just over one hundred years old."

"And you are twenty?" Afzal asked her.

Tamura nodded, "Yes, you were all at my birthday party. Remember? Look, he may have had eighty years on me, but he was in great shape, he benefitted from numerous organ transplants and had several cosmetic operations. I really thought he was in his early thirties when I first met him."

"So you had everything with this guy. We all envied you, not in a bad way, mind you. But we all saw how you were spending your nights in that mansion behind the pearl gates and manicured yard with flowers and row after row of trees. Why did things end between the two of you?" LeBosh asked. "Was it because you refused to shoot that alien? Was it the age difference? What was it?"

Tamura lathered up her long dark hair and rinsed it off as she considered her response. The three girls were her only friends and accordingly she could trust them. "Okay, he transferred me off the planet precisely because I disobeyed his orders to kill the alien. He was really pissed off and I thought he would kill me."

"He wouldn't have done something that drastic," Farley blurted out.

"Yes he would have," Tamura told them with certainty. "He was a very cruel man. I wanted out of the relationship for several reasons. He was demanding that I get some cosmetic surgery myself."

Afzal laughed, "Why would you need surgery? You have to be one of the prettiest girls on this ship. Me? I could use a new nose."

"First of all, he had me get that laser treatment to remove all of the hair from my legs and pubic area. He then had me remove my MI tattoo that was on my right shoulder. After that, he demanded that I get breast enhancements. I always thought I had nice enough tits so I argued with him over that demand."

Farley walked up behind Tamura and cupped her breasts in her hands, "You have a little more than a handful which is good. Anything more would be a waste. If I were a man I would bend you over and give it to you every conceivable way possible."

"Thanks. Now let my tits go," Tamura laughed as Farley moved back under her own shower spout. "But the real reason I wanted to get away from him was his propensity for violence. I watched him do something that scared me. He strangled one of his young wives, right in front of me. I don't even know what she did to piss him off so much. I heard her beg for her life, her gasps for precious oxygen and her kicks as she struggled. He snapped her neck like a twig, with one hand. He just dropped her body on the palace floor like she was trash. I think I disobeyed him just to force him to transfer me. That poor girl was my age and I kept thinking that if I continued sleeping with him that he would kill me next. I am glad to be going to this new planet and away from him. I hope I never get involved with a Royal ever again."

"You never told us that story," LeBosh whispered as some other women walked into the showers. "No wonder you were willing to let all of those nice clothes and your posh quarters go. By the Stars, Miyu, why didn't you ever tell anyone that before?"

Tamura leaned toward her three friends and whispered, "Because he is a Royal, the grandson of the Glorious Leader. Speaking out against them is a crime. I knew if I refused his order he would oust me or kill me. Either way I would be free of him. Luckily he did not kill me."

"Your secret is safe with us," Afzal assured her. "So, enough of the past. How are we four single ladies going to land a man to plow our fields?"

The others laughed out loud.

LeBosh spoke up first, "When we land, I am being sent to the polar ice caps so I just hope that there will be some horny men up there to keep me warm during the fifty below nights. How about you?"

Afzal shrugged, "I am being sent to an outpost in the middle of the Northern Continent to guard scientists while they check seismology trends and drill for minerals and precious metals. I'll take on the first man that wants to bend me over."

"I think I might go lesbian and just start sleeping with women," Farley told them. "We girls are all competing for a small pool of men and the odds are against us. I am about ready to just give up."

Tamura spoke next, "Well, I intend to find me a common man. I hope that whoever he is that he will be handsome and have some smarts about him. But I will never get involved with a Royal again. I would just assume to shoot them dead than sleep with one again. That time of my life was a nightmare. I am just grateful to the Stars that I am getting a fresh start on Clovis City. I am really going to miss the three of you."

"We should promise to keep in touch," Afzal said. "I promise to send each of you a message at a minimum of once per week. We should always remain friends."

"Agreed," Farley hugged Afzal.

"Friends for life," LeBosh promised the others.

"Friends for life," Tamura repeated.

The four women embraced for a few seconds before splitting up, taking some bath towels and dried themselves off in silence.

The next morning, Tamura woke up on her small bed in the enlisted quarters. She heard the annoying computer warning that the ship was landing on Clovis City. Tamura leaped to her feet and found her one piece black uniform on top of her black duffle bag. She quickly pulled on some black lace panties and a sports bra before pushing her legs through the uniform. She pulled the sleeves over her arms and zipped the front of the uniform up. She could hear the commotion out in the hallway from other soldiers as they rushed down the metal floors toward the rear exit of the transport ship. Tamura's entire belongings were inside her duffle bag. She threw it over her shoulder and walked proudly out into the hall. She looked left and then right for her three friends before moving toward the rear of her ship. It was the beginning of a new life for her and she looked forward to that fresh start.

Tamura walked down the lowered exit ramp to the transparent metal landing field. She could see the purple sand underneath the metal flooring of the landing strip. She squinted her eyes due to the red orange hue of the skyline. Several of the soldiers that had been on the ship with her were being greeted by members of their new units. Tamura walked past the departing crew members and looked over her shoulder for Afzal, Farley or LeBosh. The three women were nowhere in sight. They had said their farewells the night before. Tamura recalled that her drill instructor at basic training warned her that the military life was difficult on relationships and friendships. She squinted her eyes due to the brightness of the light. She pursed her lips, turned away from the transport ship and began walking out into the middle of the long strip. All around her she saw rows of Allen Fighters that were parked in a perfect alignment, Raumschiffs and other space craft. The smell of the planet seemed drier to her. Athena had been a wet climate with morning dew, fog, intermittent showers throughout the day and more thunderstorms than she cared to remember. New Edinburgh seemed to be a planet more conducive to outdoor activity than planet Athena had been.

"Corporal Tamura?"

Tamura turned around and smiled at the two enlisted soldiers standing there. "Yes?"

The female reached out to shake her free hand, "I'm Sara Stewart. I will be your bunk mate at the platoon barracks. This is Corporal Robert Preston."

Preston smiled at Tamura and shook her hand, "Pleasure to meet you. Here, take these. They will help your eyes."

Tamura smiled back at them and took the pair of Fenster Corporation sunglasses that Preston was holding in his other hand for her. She put them on and found that the glare of the sunlight was eliminated and she no longer had to squint, "Believe me when I say that the pleasure is mine. How far is our unit from here?"

"A few kilometers," Preston said. He was still smiling at her. Tamura had seen the look he was giving her from men before. It was obvious that Preston was attracted to her.

"Well, on the way there, is there a nice place to eat breakfast?" Tamura smiled back at Preston.

Stewart nodded, "Follow us. I know the perfect place. Great poggie bacon, toast, eggs, waffles, coffee, juice and a large fruit bar. Once you get some chow down you we will report to platoon sergeant Lund. You'll love it here. Lund is a good NCO to serve with."

Tamura followed the two, "And our platoon leader?"

"KIA," Preston told her. "Here, let me carry your duffle bag for you. I am sure you are exhausted from you trip."

Tamura smiled and handed the man her bag, "Polite and handsome. I like a gentleman."

Preston seemed to blush as he lifted her bag over his right shoulder, "Thank you."

"So what happened to the platoon leader?" Tamura urged them.

"She was killed during a raid on the Rosenburg Ranch Territory," Preston told her. "Several of our platoon mates died with her."

"I'm sorry," Tamura noticed that Preston was still emotional about the loss of his co-workers. "What was her name?"

"Lieutenant Ling," Preston responded. "She was a good officer, by the book and fair."

Stewart sensed the sexual tension that was going between her old friend and the new arrival. Preston had been extremely selective with the women he choose to sleep with, so selective that Stewart never could get a read on what type of woman Preston found attractive. With the arrival of Tamura, Stewart learned the answer to that question. Preston liked the athletic looking Asian women.

Tamura carried on as if Stewart was not walking with them, "I was informed that the MI unit I was being transferred to had only women. How is it that you are a part of an all-female set of brigades?"

Preston laughed, "The units under the command of General Tan in Lynott's Land are made up of all women. In the other regions of the planet, Tan relaxed her restrictions against men so that the local populations would be more willing to allow Tan to deploy platoons and companies there. In this platoon, I am one of three men. All of the rest are women."

"That's good odds for you and the other two men."

"Potentially, yes it is."

"You have many lovers, Corporal Preston?"

"Call me Rob, and I am uninvolved at the moment."

"Really? Where I came from a handsome man like you would have had many women fighting for your affections."

Preston shrugged, "I haven't been moved to pursue any of the women here, until now. I would love to show you around so that we could get to know one another."

Tamura smiled at him, "I would really like that, Rob."

"So would I."

With that small exchange, Tamura and Preston began their relationship together. They shared breakfast before getting her checked into the barracks that were located a few miles from the large governmental buildings. Stewart realized that three was a crowd and made an excuse to part from the two. Preston took Tamura to the large United Nations building and then on the moving passenger sidewalks which went throughout the city. She was impressed by the massive Great Protective Wall around the city as well as the tall Rosenburg Building. They shared their first kiss while eating dinner at an Italian food restaurant named Angelo's.

Their kiss grew into more kisses, hand holding and laughing at each other's jokes, even if they were not humorous at all. Preston took her to the weapons supply building and they selected matching Rosenburg Corporation long range laser sniper rifles and spent several hours at the target range. Tamura proved to be a far better shot than Preston, although he was not a bad marksman himself.

He next took her to the location where the statues of the Glorious Leader and his offspring adorned the outer limits of the massive courtyard leading to the governmental buildings. With each experience, they would share kisses which heightened their mutual desire. Tamura wanted to make love to him and she did not care where it happened, just as long as it did and quickly. Preston shared her lust, finding the feel of her body against him to be very pleasing and the passion behind her kisses caused him to want more from her. He wanted to be with her more than he could ever recall wanting a woman.

After a day of showing her the city, Preston was rewarded by Tamura's sexual prowess. She seduced him with little effort and made love to him in the barracks showers and restrooms. He mounted her in one of the shower stalls and then on the red tiled floor. After they finished their love making, Preston asked her if she would be willing to start sleeping with him on a regular basis. Tamura was more than willing to agree to that arrangement. Preston cautioned her that the platoon sergeant did not allow the soldiers to sleep in the same bed together, so their sexual encounters would have to occur elsewhere.

After Preston fell asleep on his bed, Tamura crawled up to her bunk bed. Stewart was lying on the top bunk and looked down at Tamura, scowling at her.

Tamura whispered, "Did I do something wrong?"

"I hope not," Stewart whispered back. "Rob is one of my best friends. If you hurt him I will cut out your liver."

Tamura smiled, "I have no intention of hurting him. I really like him."

"That much is obvious," Stewart was glaring at her. "Most of us here in the barracks could hear how much you like him while you were having sex in the showers. He rarely dates anyone so he is not wise as to the evils of women. If you are just using him for a few nights of sex, please tell him so that he will not get hurt."

"I promise you that you have nothing to worry about with me. I really like him. The fact that he has a friend like you as loyal to him as you are tells me a lot about him. I am not just using him, by the way. I really like him."

"Good night then," Stewart whispered as she rolled over on her side to go to sleep.

Tamura slid onto her bed and laid her head down on the pillow. She pulled the dark red sheets and comforter over her and closed her eyes. As she slipped into deep sleep, she wondered whether or not Afzal, Farley or LeBosh had fared as well as she had. She could not wait to tell them of her new man.

CHAPTER FOUR

It had been at least four year earlier that he had last seen the man seated in the café. They had been rivals when attending the Academy together. Lester Brey Gillis hoped that the man failed to recognize him as he sat down at one of the corner tables of the forty small four seat tables in the quaint local café. He was certain that if the man at the other table took just more than a fleeting glance at him he would most certainly remember him.

Gillis had been one of the fortunate survivors of the Blood Moon Incident. But his participation in that highly viewed and publicized battle brought Gillis much unwanted attention. At first he shunned the fame. He despised the autograph seekers that would approach him each day. After much reflection, Gillis embraced his new status and began using it to his profitable advantage. He began endorsing products of all sorts. He was on the satellite feeds of all the Seven Conquered Solar Systems and those of the system of Old Earth. He smiled for underwear ads, toiletries, clothing, shoes, hair care products and space ship transportation companies. Gillis earned money with each ad and used it to buy nice things for himself and his lovely wife, Sophia.

Gillis was wearing his green turtle neck sweater, white cargo pants and brown boots which were his standard issue cadet uniform for the Doctoral Program in Military History at the Sikorsky Planet Academy. As a creature of habit, Gillis ate breakfast each morning at this specific café. He had learned that the establishment had the best coffee and French toast. It was also fairly expensive, but with the income Gillis had been earning as a spokesman he could easily afford the menu. His two normal breakfast companions, Siobhan Collins and Julia Steiner were late. Gillis determined that he had best place his order so that he could eat and leave quickly if the man at the other table recognized him. He looked at the keyboard that was part of the metal table top of the corner location he had selected and began typing his order for breakfast into it.

Gillis looked around at the rest of the customer base of the trendy restaurant. There were numerous officers from the Military Intelligence, Space Command, Marines and the Army enjoying breakfast and coffee. There were also several business men and women coming and going, most of them were ordering a coffee drink at the counter and taking their morning java to go. There were a few Akarzdamedians that were present that were sitting and enjoying a fresh cooked meal.

The Akarzdamedians all had their own sense of style. They wore one piece outfits, similar to ancient Japanese kimonos, which covered them from their neck to their ankles. The only difference between the Akarzdamedian clothing was the colors of each individual. Gillis wondered whether all of the native indigenous life forms to Sikorsky's Planet, the Akarzdamedians, had the same microchips embedded in their brains as the ones he had faced on the Blood Moon.

He recalled the one that called himself Cla Cuchulain that had been liberated from the microchip in his head. Gillis wondered what had become of that Akarzdamedian. He had learned that the majority of the twenty million Akarzdamedians living on Sikorsky's Planet had fully accepted the domination of the human occupation and no longer needed to be controlled by such means. A few of the Akarzdamedians were interacting with humans easily and Gillis detected no animosity between them. He had once read a history paper that claimed that before the humans invaded Akarzdamedia, their population was estimated at a trillion and a half.

Vladimir Sikorsky and his invasion almost wiped out the entire population on the home world and in the subsequent bombings of the other planets populated by them.

Gillis glanced over at the man at the other table and wondered if he should just go over and say hello to him. Gillis dismissed that thought quickly and his mind wandered back to the last time he saw the man.

Gillis recalled it had been during his freshman year as a student at the Clovis Academy located on planet New Edinburgh. Gillis had been lucky to be assigned as his Drayton Love-Easter as his dormitory roommate. In a short time, both Gillis and Love-Easter were invited to join a gang of fellow students that had been called Gorski's Gang. Through that association, Gillis made many friends and enemies. He also found love twice. The first love he met had been at the same time he first met the man at the other table.

Gillis allowed himself to reminisce of that time. His mind went back to time he stood at the base of the mountain range named Knox Peak at the southern border of Lynott's Land. He had attended a lovely wedding ceremony that day and in the evening he met Reynita Calderon. It was a whirlwind romance that ended almost as quickly as it had started. But it was also the night he met the man on the other side of the restaurant.

Gillis smiled to himself as he remembered Reynita. His large latte, water, French toast with scrambled eggs were delivered by a waiter in a black tuxedo. Gillis looked over at Azeem Nour who was the man sitting at the table across the room. Nour was wearing a long sleeved solid black one piece uniform that had a gold zipper that went from under his neck to his mid-section. Gillis knew that the black uniform meant Nour was in the Military Intelligence branch of the Space Command. Gillis looked over the rest of Nour's uniform and noticed that he had a silver bar on the left side of his collar which meant the man was a First Lieutenant. Since Nour had graduated from the Academy just a little over four years earlier, Gillis deduced that Nour had excelled as an officer. Nour had a patch on either shoulder that was gold with red lettering. The letters said simply "Javelin Brigade." Gillis had never seen that patch before, nor had he ever heard of the Javelin Brigade.

Nour no longer had his goatee and his long dark hair had been cut to military standards. The man seemed to be in excellent physical condition. Gillis observed that Nour was drinking a large coffee and was constantly checking his holo-com device. Nour seemed nervous about something. Gillis went about finishing his breakfast and tried to ignore Nour. That is until the Yutong brothers arrived.

Gillis took a long sip of his coffee cup as he watched Zou, Guo and Dong Yutong enter the café and shake Nour's hand. The three brothers sat down with Nour and they began talking in a low tone to avoid others from hearing their conversation. Gillis noted that the Yutong brothers were all wearing similar black uniforms with the "Javelin Brigade" patch on their shoulders. Zou Yutong was also a First Lieutenant. Gou and Dong were wearing gold bars signifying them as Second Lieutenants.

Gillis had kept track of the assignments that his closest friends received upon graduation. He had not been interested in the Bragg Gang members' whereabouts. Gillis never felt that they were worth his time. But here, on Sikorsky's Planet, were four of the older Bragg Gang members serving in the Military Intelligence branch. Gillis was a bit relieved that they had not yet recognized him. He was certain that the former friends of William Bragg would blame him for his death. Gillis decided he would be better off if he left the café quickly and avoid detection from the four former rivals.

Before Gillis could act on that thought the café doors slid open and Julia Steiner walked in with Siobhan Collins at her side. The two women were talking loudly and laughing as they entered into the establishment. Gillis groaned as they would certainly attract the attention of the four men with their loud and boisterous demeanor. Steiner would especially attract attention since she had been a big player in the Gorski Gang for three years and had also survived the Blood Moon ambush.

Siobhan Collins was dressed in her all white medical school uniform. Steiner was wearing civilian clothes as she was studying for her doctorate in terra-forming. Steiner had on a blue button down blouse and black slacks with flat shoes. Her hair was pulled back into a pony tail. She had on matching oval garnet earrings and necklace. The two women noticed Gillis and walked to his table and sat down in some of the empty seats.

"Sorry we were a little late," Collins leaned over and gave Gillis a hug. "Ginger is almost out of communication range and she contacted me right after I got out of the shower. I had to spend some time talking to her since she may be gone for a very long time."

Gillis nodded and smiled. Ginger Collins O'Grady had joined her husband Eamon on a mission that would take her outside of the eight solar systems run by humanity. The mission was so far out of range from the nearest broadcast satellite that any time Siobhan could spend speaking to her sister was time well spent.

"I understand completely. I just hope that she and Eamon return safe from their mission. I really miss both of them. And you, Julia?"

Steiner laughed, "One of my professors has been trying really hard to seduce me. He showed up at my dormitory room this morning with flowers and wanting to come in. I thought I would never get the man to leave."

"Professor Rooker again?" Gillis deduced.

"The one and the same," Steiner looked at Gillis' empty plate. "What did you have? Let me guess, French toast?"

"You know me well," Gillis answered.

"As do we," came a voice from across the room.

Steiner, Collins and Gillis all looked over to see that the Yutong brothers and Nour were approaching their table. Steiner immediately recognized the four men and she cursed under her breath. The Yutong brothers and Nour quickly surrounded the table in which the three were sitting.

"We know you all too well, Les Gillis," Nour snarled. "I heard from Lisa Bragg that you and your idiot friends got her little brother killed."

Gillis sighed. Nour was as predictable as the sun rising in the morning. He decided to make an attempt to diffuse the situation to avoid a physical confrontation. Getting into a brawl with four MI officers was a sure fire way to land up in the Tank. "You heard wrong. Bill was murdered by some assassins sent by the Rosenburg family. No one felt worse about what happened to him than me. Bill wasn't the only one that was killed by those pigs. How have you guys been? How long have you been stationed her on Sikorsky's Planet?"

Nour leaned into Gillis and glared at him. He glared at Steiner as well, turning his head back and forth between them.

"Don't act like we are old friends you piece of poggie shit. We all remember you Gillis and you too, Steiner. You two think that we would forget the shit you did to us? Because of you imbeciles, I got arrested by General Tan's troops. My father had to pay Tan over a hundred Lynott's Land dollars. Remember that?"

"Azeem, we were all young and just doing our thing,"

Steiner glared back at him. She remembered Nour and the Yutong brothers with clarity. Steiner had been in a few bar fights with the men and there was no love lost between them.

But, like Gillis, she realized that fighting the four men in black uniforms was not in their best interests.

"As far as I am concerned it is all in the past."

"Well, it certainly is not in the past to me," Nour glared at Steiner. "You little poggie dung outlanders caused my friends and I a lot of trouble."

Gillis shook his head. He had taken enough. "Azeem, you caused your own trouble. You got arrested by General Tan's soldiers because you marched in and disrupted a peaceful wedding party. The other brawls were started by your group, not us. All Julia and I ever did was defend ourselves against your aggressive actions. If anyone here should be angry then it should be Julia and me."

Zou grabbed hold of Gillis' left shoulder with his hand and squeezed. "You taunted us, you and your friends. Your friend Harrison deflowered my sister and got her pregnant. The Italian soccer players were fucking my other sisters. Your friends disrespected my family. Did you know that Harrison had never paid any child support to our sister? What kind of man abandons his child? You and your friends have no values. We had no choice but to engage you. Now, Azeem and I are officers and my two brothers are as well. You and Steiner better watch your backs. Any excuse we can find to lock you two up and we will. And look at you! You are attending the Academy here and you have your hair longer than regulations allow? I should blow your head off right here and now for your insubordination."

"Good to see you again, too, Zou." Gillis countered with a calm tone of voice, keeping his eyes locked on his.

"You mocking me?" Zou Yutong demanded.

"You better treat us with respect Irish," Second Lieutenant Dong Yutong warned as he punched his index finger into Gillis' chest. "We are in the MI branch now. You screw with my brothers or with me and things will go bad for you. We aren't as stupid as those Rosenburg fools you killed on the Blood Moon."

Gillis glared at Dong and recalled that in one of their brawls, Sophia DuBravac had knocked out one of his front teeth. Gillis smiled and thought that his attempts to make friends with the Yutong's were in vain. It seemed confrontation was a forgone conclusion with the clowns.

"So, Dong, you ever get your teeth fixed?" Gillis asked sarcastically.

Dong Yutong growled and lunged at Gillis. Before he could reach him, Nour held him back.

"Cool it, Dong! You are in uniform and there are too many witnesses here."

"Did you hear what he just said to me?" Dong snarled at Nour. "His bitch girlfriend busted out one of my teeth! Remember?"

Nour tightened his grip on the younger man,

"No, I had already graduated and knew nothing of it. If DuBravac busted your teeth then go after her. But she is not here now. So calm down before we all get into trouble. You do not need the negative write up in your file. It would be bad for your career."

"She's my wife now," Gillis said with laughter in his voice. "She really kicked your ass that day, Dong. You were crying like a baby that had just been spanked."

"Hey tone down the testosterone," Siobhan Collins said in an attempt to cut through the tension that was building up.

"New planet, new lives and new direction. Right? We have never met. My name is Siobhan. What are your names?"

Collins held out her hand in expectation that the four men in black uniforms would shake it and introduce themselves. She was wrong. Nour and the three Yutong brothers turned their attention to her.

"You are one of the daughters of that lawyer that is a traitor to the Glorious Leader," Nour said as he moved his head only a few inches from her face.

Collins winced and concluded that Nour had forgotten to brush his teeth that morning. "My father is a good man," she said defensively.

"Your father is a traitor and needs to die," Nour sneered. "I would love to be the one that gets the pleasure of skinning him alive with a spoon and then dip him in lemon juice. We are all waiting for the Glorious Leader to ask for us to go back to New Edinburgh and wipe out all of the traitors on that planet."

"You three watch yourselves," Guo Yutong warned them as he began walking for the door. "We will get you. It is only a matter of time."

Nour nodded, "Right. We will see you three around and when we do it won't go well for you. You know that Bill Bragg wanted to ratchet up the gang violence between us. Zerbe would never let him do what should have been done. We won't make that mistake now. Bill was right and Francois was wrong. We should have gutted the lot of you when we had the chance. Had we done so, you and the others would not have become such great heroes on that Blood Moon and Bill and Roy would still be alive.

I see you three around and I will stick my military service knife deep into your hearts."

Nour turned to the other two Yutong brothers.

"Let's go."

Steiner, Collins and Gillis watched the four bullies from their old Academy depart the café. They remained silent for a moment.

"What in the name of the asteroid belt did you two do to those Bragg Gang people? You guys really pissed off a lot of people when you hung out with my former boyfriend," Collins observed out loud.

Steiner laughed, "Siobhan, if you and Yuri had continued dating you know you would have become a member of the gang."

Collins thought about Steiner's assertion for a moment, "Yes, maybe. Maybe I would have. I suppose I would have been a Gorski Gang member if Yuri and I stayed together. But I would not have condoned his violence. I would have put Yuri on a tight leash unlike Jen and Mary."

Steiner laughed, "Nobody puts Yuri on a leash."

"Well, now that we know we have a minimum of four Bragg Gang members on this planet with us I propose we start a new gang," Gillis laughed.

"What would we be called?" Steiner laughed with him.

"We could be the Collins Champs or something like that," Gillis responded.

Siobhan Collins shook her head as she failed to see the humor in any of the events that had just occurred, "Why did they call my father a traitor?"

Gillis stopped laughing and took her hand in his,

"Don't worry about them. They were only trying to provoke you. That was how they always worked to pick a fight. Ignore it. Remember that the Nour's and Yutong's are very powerful and wealthy families on New Edinburgh. They need to have someone like your father maintaining the law enforcement of the planet so that the rich can stay rich. Nour knows that the last thing his family needs is for some uprising of the poor to storm their mansions and take from them what they wish. Your father is fine. "

"Okay. So what happens when we run into them again?" Collins wanted to know.

"We throw down," Gillis told her flatly. "Never back down to an abuser because it only encourages them. They want a fight I will give it to them."

CHAPTER FIVE

He had been locked in his ten by twenty foot black brick dungeon for almost five months. There were no windows that the prisoner could see out of. The door to his cell was solid black and made out of a metal alloy. There was little light in the room. In the far corner of the cell were a toilet and a sink.

His captors fed him three times a day like clockwork. His first meal was always at five a.m. and would consist of poggie bacon, plantana's, various juices, scrambled jumper eggs, bread slices and water. At noon he would receive his second meal which was always a plate of fruits and raw vegetables with water and juice. At six p.m. they fed him a slice of well-done meat, boiled potatoes, tomato slices, raw carrots, water, coffee and a slice of cake or pie. He was allowed access to a gymnasium once a day for an hour. Lately the captors began to offer him more liberties such as old printed books to read. They also allowed him to view the news.

The prisoner began to catch up on the past and current events. He focused in on reports dealing with the Blood Moon. His face never showed any emotion when he learned the identities of those that had lived and died in that conflict. The prisoner began to silently formulate plans for his escape. He had no idea the exact location in which he was being held. However he had used deductive reasoning to conclude that he was still on planet New Edinburgh. The poggie bacon was indigenous to his home world as was the reptilian Jumper and banana hybrid fruit called the plantana.

The prisoner thought of the last memories he had from almost a year earlier. He was at a bar and buying drinks for a beautiful Asian woman. He recalled losing his equilibrium at some point. He remembered falling to the floor and passing out. He was certain that the lovely woman that he hoped to share a night of romance with had drugged him. When he woke up, he was in his new surroundings, this drab cell.

The day finally arrived that his captors had decided to reveal themselves to him and state the reason for his imprisonment. The man did not know it yet, but he was about to become relevant once again.

Seven attractive women escorted the man from his cell to the gymnasium. All of the women were wearing the black uniforms of the Military Intelligence Branch of the United Nations. The prisoner observed that the women were in excellent physical condition. They each had good muscle tone, very low body fat, alert eyes and they were well armed. He looked over the ranks on the sleeves of the black uniforms. One of the women had three gold stripes which signified that she was a sergeant. The other six were sporting only one gold stripe and were therefore privates.

After his workout and breakfast, he was taken to an elevator lift that he had seen before in passing only. This would be the first time he would be taken into the large lift. He was pushed into the large elevator and watched in silence as the doors closed. The seven women were still with him, watching his every breath. One of the women in black handed the prisoner a pair of sunglasses. The prisoner accepted the gift and put them on. After a little under five minutes of ascension, the elevator doors slid open to reveal the bright red orange sunlight of New

Edinburgh. The prisoner closed his eyes due to the glare of the sunlight and smiled as he was pushed out of the elevator.

He took in a deep breath of the precious fresh air that had been denied him over the time of his incarceration. The air smelled divine. He slowly looked at the surroundings. There were several large, towering buildings to his left and right. Behind those buildings were several high rise structures that towered over the closer buildings. Before him was an open set of walkways and in the distance there was an airfield. The prisoner smiled when he saw over fifty solid black Raumschiff space craft.

He deduced that he was in Military Intelligence facility on planet New Edinburgh. That meant only one thing, which he was on Lynott's Land territory.

And that he was a prisoner of General Leta Tan.

The prisoner knew all about General Tan. She hired only women to serve in her fifteen thousand strong Military Intelligence unit. Her reputation was that she loved women and hated men. Tan was known to force many women under her command to perform sex acts for her in return for favorable annual reviews and recommendations for promotions or transfers to the most desirable assignments. The prisoner noted that he was surrounded by hundreds of women wearing the solid black uniforms.

He was led down the white steps from the elevator toward the transparent metal streets. Under his feet he could see the familiar purple sand of planet New Edinburgh. After walking about twenty feet the soldiers stopped him. An attractive Hispanic woman was approaching them from the west. The prisoner looked her over and noticed she had a gold bar on her uniform sleeves, just below her shoulder, which identified her as a Second Lieutenant. The seven women stood at attention and saluted the woman. She returned the salute.

The woman stood in front of the prisoner and smiled at him. "Sir, I have been ordered to deliver you to General Tan."

The prisoner looked at her name tag above her left breast. He studied her lovely facial features and the curves of her body. He estimated she was in her early twenties. He concluded that the woman was in excellent physical condition from the way she walked. She carried no weapons which indicated she was not afraid to face him alone. "Well then, Second Lieutenant Calderon, please lead the way."

Reynita Calderon had graduated from Clovis Academy the month prior. She received her commission as an officer and entered what was known by the military commanders as "the draft." The proper term for the "draft" was really called the Annual Vacancy Selection in the Sikorsky Code of Military Justice, which was the system that commanders selected graduating cadets to fill vacancies in their units. She waited patiently to receive the computerized notification of what unit and planet she would be assigned. She met her selection to serve under General Tan with mixed emotions. On one hand, she was elated because all of her sisters, brothers and parents lived in Clovis City, planet New Edinburgh. She would be close to her siblings. On the other hand, she knew of General Tan's reputation to use her women for sexual pleasure. Calderon had gone through that kind of pressure when she studied at the Academy. A female professor named Rand had once blackmailed Calderon to perform sex acts in return for a better grade.

Reynita had no desire to be used that way again. She had hoped to one day find a decent man to love and have children with. Her relationships were generally short lived. Her first serious boyfriend had been a senior at the Academy when she was a first year cadet. His name had been Francois Zerbe. He had been the founder of what came to be called the Bragg Gang.

Zerbe was handsome, tall and muscular and had a dynamic personality. He was also a master at hazing underclassmen and women. Reynita became Zerbe's bed partner for several months until he tossed her aside for another female cadet in his small group.

She then briefly found romance with a cadet named Les Gillis. He was perhaps the smartest man she had ever met. She had hoped that he would be a long term option for her. But she made a huge error one night. William Bragg, who would become the leader of the Bragg Gang after Francois Zerbe graduated, got her drunk and took her to his bed. Bragg refused to let her go after only one night and often demanded that she continue to sleep with him. Calderon could not decide between the two men and maintained the two romances as best she could. Bragg knew all about her sexual relationship with Gillis. Gillis did not know that she was seeing Bragg behind his back. When Gillis learned of her intimate relationship with Bragg, he did not get angry as she thought he might. Gillis simply wished her well and walked away from her. Over the following three years Gillis probably only said a handful of words to her. When they graduated, Gillis did not bother to say goodbye to her. Looking back at her short life, Reynita regarded her betrayal of Gillis as her greatest mistake.

Then came Professor Rand who tried to force a lesbian lifestyle on Reynita. As her Professor in several classes, Rand was able to wield her power and threaten her to begin a sexual relationship to avoid flunking her. Reynita attempted to avoid the blackmail by pointing out that she had good grades and was a capable student. But Rand would laugh and indicate that as her primary instructor, she could fail her and no one would question it. She capitulated and became Rand's sex toy. After a year passed, she mustered the courage to turn Rand in to the Academy Dean.

The Academy Police investigated the claim and Rand was placed on a partially probated suspension. Reynita was not granted permission to transfer her classes away from Rand. Reynita was disgusted by the lack of support she received from Dean Harvard during the incident.

Reynita would spend her last two years dating random men but love would always elude her. She stayed as an active member of the Bragg Gang almost to the day she graduated. That is until the time period of the Blood Moon Incident. She turned her back on the Bragg Gang forever when she heard their rude and inappropriate comments when some of their Clovis Academy classmates were being wounded and killed.

Accordingly, she graduated from the Academy with very few friends.

In her last year at the Academy, Reynita had been given a high rank in the cadet corps and was on Eamon O'Grady's executive staff. She was put in charge of the entire personnel management of the over fourteen thousand cadets. She handled her duties skillfully and upon graduation, O'Grady and his wife presented her with a nice plaque to thank her for being a great asset and loyal to the Academy. She had also been recognized by her instructors as one of the five best sharp shooters on campus.

And now she was living out her childhood goal which was to be an officer of Military Intelligence. General Tan assigned her to command a platoon of forty-five women. Reynita had spent her first month bonding with her platoon and working to make them the best soldiers in Tan's Brigades. She initiated early morning runs, personal training drills and strict adherence to military discipline. Most of her platoon seemed to enjoy the direction of her leadership. There was the occasional soldier that would complain or resist. Over the short time she had with her platoon, Reynita won them over one soldier at a time.

When General Tan contacted her to escort this special prisoner to her palace, Reynita was thrilled. It was the first time that the General seemed to notice her. She inspected the prisoner from several feet distance. He had long blonde hair that desperately needed to be washed. He was tall and slender. He had sad looking blue eyes. He had a beard that indicated he had not shaved in months. Reynita speculated that his demeanor and appearance was due to his many months in isolation. General Tan indicated that this man was extremely important. But Tan would not reveal the identity of the prisoner. She wondered who he was and why he was so important. She led the prisoner toward the high rise buildings in the distance for their rendezvous with General Tan.

General Leta Tan ordered her personnel officer, Colonel Tina Zenawi, to assemble the new members of her Brigades at 0800 hours sharp in the courtyard surrounding her Military Intelligence Towers. The Towers, or the palaces as Tan referred to them as, were five buildings that stood over one hundred thirty floors high and took the ground space equal to four square miles. Each building was white in color with white steps leading to the entrances that were adorned with white Doric columns.
Tan had recruited thirty new officers that had been commissioned as Second Lieutenants in the Military Intelligence Branch. She further received three platoons worth of new enlisted women that were finished with their basic military training. The assembly was a training method Tan used to keep the new additions on their toes. Tan could not tolerate complacency in her troops.

As Colonel Zenawi rushed to conduct the inspection on the new arrivals, Tan smiled when she saw Second Lieutenant Reynita Calderon walk into the large palace ball room with their prisoner.

Reynita had never been given the opportunity of seeing Tan's palace in person. The ceilings of the lower floor were forty feet high and covered with murals of naked women making love to one another. The walls were adorned with paintings from many famous contemporary artists of their time, most of them depicting orgies and executions of men. She was unsure if the paintings were copies or originals.

There was a thick beam that was embedded in the walls from east to west. She noticed that several men were dangling in the air, nooses around their necks and tied to that long beam. The hands of the hanging men bound behind their backs. The majority of the hanging victims were dead. There were three that were fighting, struggling, for each breath they took. Underneath one of the men was a small amount of urine and blood on the floor. Each of the men had been castrated; even their testicles had been cut off. Tan seemed to find pleasure in their suffering. Tan sat at the north side of the massive hall in a chair that was more like a King or Queen Seat of the monarchs from old Earth's history. The chair had plush leather, the actual seat was twice as wide as Tan's body and the back rest was two feet higher than Tan's head. The chair was up on a stage so that she could be looking down at anyone that entered her palace. The view from above made Tan feel like the monarchs of antiquity.

Tan was wearing her solid black Class A uniform. Her four silver stars were on her shoulder lapels to signify that she was a full General in Military Intelligence. Her left breast pocket had her name tag while her right side was covered in numerous medals that she had been awarded over the years. Around her neck was her Medal of Valor. She was eating a long item that looked like a chocolate bar on a stick.

Reynita saluted her general, "Ma'am, Lieutenant Calderon reporting as ordered."

Tan returned the salute and looked Calderon over. Tan noted that her new Lieutenant was beautiful. Tan decided that she wanted her in her bed, but pleasure would have to wait as more important business had to be conducted.

"At ease, Lieutenant," Tan instructed and the seven MI soldiers that stood beside her and each of them switched their position from attention to parade rest. Reynita had not noticed the stench of the male prisoner when she was outside in the fresh air. Now that she was in an enclosed room with the man, she concluded he was in desperate need of a bath. "Would you care for a chocolate covered penis on a stick?"

Reynita did her best to hide her disgust at the question. She watched as Tan took another bite out of the chocolate covered item. She would never have guessed that Tan was actually dining on a male sex organ. She heard the crunchy sound as Tan bit into the item, tearing off a piece of penis and dried chocolate. As Tan chewed on the item, Reynita shook her head in the negative, "No thank you, General."

"Perhaps some testicle soup?" Tan offered as she swallowed the mouthful of chocolate and manhood that she had been chewing on.

Reynita bit her lip, "No thank you ma'am. I already ate." The rumors of Tan's hatred of men were true. She had heard the stories from her father regarding Tan's sadistic treatment of men. Reynita hoped that she would have an opportunity to transfer out of the unit to serve under a saner commander at another base.

The prisoner glared at Tan with contempt, "Why didn't you just leave me where you found me? You should have killed me when you had the chance."

Tan laughed at his statement and pointed upward at the men that were hanging above her. "I could have you killed right now! You are only alive because it amuses me to see you suffer."

"You enjoy my suffering because I am a man? My family never did you wrong. We were always cooperative with you, in fact we sent you men so that you could torture and kill them. We turned the other cheek as you built up your freak show here on Lynott's Land."

Tan leaped to her feet and pointed her right index finger at the prisoner. "How dare you call what I have built here a freak show? Your family far worse than I could ever hope to be!"

Reynita and her seven MI soldiers remained silent during Tan's tirade. They had all heard the rumors regarding Tan's explosive temperament. Reynita wondered to herself who this man was and why Tan would have locked him up for all those months. What was it that this prisoner did to justify his long incarceration without a trial?

The prisoner did not flinch at Tan's emotional outburst. He smiled back at her, "You killed all of these men. I am certain they did nothing to deserve it."

"They outlived their usefulness," Tan said of the hanged men. Her tone of voice was flat and had no emotion at all. "My women got what they needed from them. Men only good for producing sperm. That all. Now they die badly and we all get to enjoy watching them die."

Reynita had heard from other women in the Military Intelligence section that Tan would find homeless men, or men that had broken the laws and would use them to satisfy the sexual urges of the women that were not lesbian. Other men were sent to the doctors to give semen samples so that the lesbian soldiers could be artificially inseminated. Once the men had been used for sexual acts they were tortured and then hung until dead. It was Tan's way of punishing men for having lust in their loins for the women in her Brigades. Reynita averted her gaze back to the white tiled floor when one of the men struggling to breath looked into her eyes. The man was near death but his eyes cried out for hope, for someone to pardon him or save him from his cruel fate. At that moment, she felt remorse that she was a part Tan's unit. This was not what she had signed up for.

The prisoner that Reynita had escorted laughed at Tan. "So then, General! You did not bring me to your Hall of Horrors to have small talk. Why am I still alive? And tell me why you have brought me before you on this specific day?"

Tan laughed with him, "Always to the point, Matthew?"

The prisoner snarled at her, "My family and friends get to call me Matthew. You can call me Doctor Rosenburg. Now please tell me why am I still alive?"

Reynita hid her emotions when the identity of the prisoner had finally been revealed. She had believed that all of the Rosenburg's were either dead, captured or on the run. She had seen the computerized posts for all of the most wanted in the solar system. Matthew Rosenburg had been in the top ten for the last several months. Sean Collins and Colonel Gorski thought they had rounded up all of the defendants living on the planet. Yet one of the most wanted Rosenburg's had been on planet New Edinburgh all along. The bigger question was what General Tan wanted with this specific Rosenburg. He should have been turned over to Collins for prosecution. Reynita wanted to hear the answer to Matthew Rosenburg's question.

Tan walked around Rosenburg, "You smell Matthew. You need shower. I will tell you why you alive. Sean Collins and Colonel Nikolai Gorski turned over a Super Raumschiff to me. It was called the Blitzkrieg. Mean anything to you?"

"Never heard of it," he remarked quickly. He was lying to the General as he was very familiar with all of the Rosenburg and Ragnarsson space craft. As Tan glared at him, Rosenburg wondered why the Lynott family, with all of their wealth and influence, would continue to allow Tan to operate her twisted designs on their land.

"It was owned by Dell Ragnarsson, Junior. He killed a lot of people using that ship," Tan told him. "He caused extensive damage to the space station. When the cadets at Clovis Academy brought that ship down they found something very odd in the lower storage room of the ship. When the ship and her contents were turned over to my investigators and I personally saw what was there, I realized that I kept you alive for a good purpose after all."
Matthew remained silent for a moment as he thought over his next words to Tan. "I rarely interacted with those social deviants named the Ragnarsson's. I am a medical doctor and a scientist. I have never killed or caused any person to be killed."

"But you caused people to be cloned, duplicated," Tan clapped her hands at two squads of Military Intelligence women that were standing on the Far East side of the large palace room.

The women departed through a side exit. There was silence in the room for about five minutes until the women returned through the same door they had left through. But when they returned they were pushing a large hospital bed that was on wheels into the room. There was a single figure lying on the bed. Reynita noticed that it was a male and that his skin pigmentation was a light green. His eyes were closed and he was breathing.

"Can you explain this thing?" Tan asked Rosenburg.

Matthew walked around the hospital bed and inspected the dormant figure. He looked up at Tan and smiled. "How many of these did you find?"

"What makes you think there were more than this one?" Tan shot back.

"Because I know things. There would not be only one. How many?"

"Fifty," Tan admitted.

"And none of the fifty were awakened?"

"None. They are all sleeping just like this one."

"And they are all here in your palace?"

"Yes."

Matthew nodded and began backing away from the green figure in the bed. "I would say that the shit will hit the fan very soon."

"Why you say that?" Tan demanded.

"This is a clone of Junior Ragnarsson," Matthew concluded that the assassin must have used the technology they had found on the alien space craft that was buried under the grounds of Rosenburg Ranch. It had been a rush job as the skin color was not correct. But the facial features and body structure was perfect.

"What you mean?" Tan demanded.

"A duplicate. A clone. Not a good job of it, but a clone nonetheless." Matthew looked into Tan's eyes. "Fifty super assassins under the same roof is not wise, dear General. This clone was made from the DNA of one of the most dangerous men I ever met. He could kill a man, or a woman, thousands of different ways. Or, rather, I should say he did kill thousands. You wake these clones up, there will be a war in which you and all of your officers will suffer in ways you cannot imagine. The host of these duplicates, I take it he is dead?"

"Yes."

"That explains some things," Matthew continued to walk around the green skinned clone. "You want my help? Here is the deal. I get my freedom, unconditional freedom. I want a Raumschiff fully stocked with supplies, food, water and the dunkle materie converter to be fully operational."

"Agreed," Tan said quickly.

"What happened to all of my wives and children?"

"They were arrested."

"Where are they?" He growled angrily as he believed that Tan most likely had everything to do with the disappearance of his family.

"In the prison on Clovis City."

"I get my wives and children back and then I give you what you want," Matthew told her softly.

"And what do I want?" Tan laughed at his insolence for assuming that he, as a man, could decide for her what she wanted.

"You want to have immortality, dear General. You also want to eliminate the need for the procreation with males. Once you learn the cloning process, you might believe that males will become obsolete, which I know you secretly desire. You get my family back to me and you shall have it."

He pointed at the green Replicant of Junior Ragnarsson, "There are only six people that know how to make the perfect duplication of a human. Two are now dead. My two sisters are missing. Uncle John will not help you, assuming that you could even locate him. That leaves just me. I am your one and only option. Only I will make certain that your skin color is perfect."

Tan glared at Rosenburg for about five minutes as she considered his offer and her options. No one else dared speak lest they might suffer the wrath of their unstable General. But then none of the others that tan had interacted with over her lifetime had the knowledge or connections as the man before her had. The silence made several of the onlookers to shift uncomfortably as they waited for Tan to issue her next orders.

Finally Tan pointed at the sleeping green colored clone. "I want you wake them all up. All fifty. I want see if they work properly before any deals are made. You show me they work and then I get you what you want."

Rosenburg nodded slowly and pointed at the prone green clone. "Dear General that would be highly ill advised. If those Replicants have the brain prints of Ragnarsson in their heads, and we activate them, we could be inviting wholesale slaughter to your palace. All of your Amazon soldiers standing around you would die badly in a matter of seconds. If Ragnarsson is dead as you claim he is, then these Replicants will want revenge against the killer."

"Against Yuri Gorski?" Reynita spoke up and regretted it when Tan shoot her a disapproving look.

Matthew laughed at the mention of Gorski. "The man that caused the death of my father? He killed Ragnarsson, too? No wonder he was such a difficult target on the Blood Moon. Too bad you only allow women in your brigades. That Gorski could have been a great addition to your numbers."

"Gorski just another brat cadet," Tan said with a dismissive tone in her voice. "He and his friends got lucky."

Matthew looked at Tan for a moment as his mind raced through his options. Clearly Tan was not as astute as he had been led to believe. There was more to young Gorski than Tan gave credit for.

"If you kill a Ragnarsson, then you are not lucky my dear General. Just one of these Ragnarsson clones could easily wipe out one of your platoons. If you wake up all fifty you would find yourselves in the middle of a war that you cannot win. Fifty Ragnarsson's working in concert, single minded in purpose, would take Lynott's Land in less than a day and you and your brigades would all die badly."

"You threaten me!" Tan's eyes were flashing with anger. Even though the man showed some insolence against her, she recalled that the man named Junior Ragnarsson had almost single handedly wiped out the defense forces of Space Station Cy-7.

"No, I only tell you that to protect you from doing something you would later regret. So, do we have a deal?"
Tan wondered if Rosenburg was lying to her about the danger of waking up the fifty Ragnarsson clones. The question was whether or not she could take the chance that he was right and that those fifty would cause mass slaughter of a large number of her troops.

Tan determined she could not take the risk and slowly nodded in Rosenburg's direction. "Deal. I find your wives and children."

"Who is your best contact in Clovis City?"

Tan shot an ugly glance in his direction, "You no trust me?"

"Of course I do. I trust you just as much as the rest of the people that kidnaped me and locked me in a jail cell without due process." Matthew was sarcastic in his response. "I want verified proof that my wives and children are alive. When I get that, you get to live forever. So, I ask again, who is your best informant in Clovis City?"

Tan walked over to her oversized red and gold throne chair and sat down. Her best operative in Clovis City had been a Lieutenant named May Ling, but she was killed during the raids on the Rosenburg Ranch a few months earlier. She had no other officers that she could fully trust stationed in that province. Tan looked over at Reynita Calderon and smiled.

"Lieutenant Calderon, you lived your whole life on Clovis City, yes?" Tan leaned forward to listen to her response.

"Ma'am, yes ma'am. I was born on a transport ship that took my parents, my aunt and uncle and grandparents to Clovis City. My family opened some business operations there. My whole family lives there still." Reynita answered.

Tan pointed at Calderon, "She my best operative in Clovis City."

Matthew looked over his shoulder at Reynita, "A little young isn't she? You don't have a more experienced officer to represent your interests with Gorski, Evart and Collins fucking things up for us?"

"She will do fine," Tan stood up and walked in the direction of Reynita. "She not close to the Gorski's or Evart's at all. She rarely interacted with Collins family. But they all know who she is. They will trust her as a fellow officer. She can get you what you desire."

Reynita hated to ask, but she did so anyway. "What exactly am I going to do over in Clovis City?"

"You will take command of third platoon from E Company," Tan instructed. "The position has been vacant a few months. You will have an experienced platoon sergeant in Sergeant First Class Mark Lund. Your platoon very well trained. You go now."

Matthew walked over to her and looked into her enchanting brown eyes. He sensed that she was uneasy about the assignment that had just landed in her lap.

"My dear Lieutenant. You will find proof that my family is alive and safe. You will then forward that evidence to me. Nothing illegal about that."

"And if Collins and Gorski ask me why I am snooping around?"

Reynita fidgeted where she stood as she was uncomfortable with being ordered to conduct this assignment. She had never been fond of Yuri Gorski and his confidants. As a member of the infamous Bragg Gang for her four years at the Academy, she had fought the Gorski Gang in several bar fights. She had no problem taking actions or omissions that might be counter to the interests of Yuri Gorski or Michel Darcel Evart. But Gorski's father and Evart's uncle were different altogether. They were officers and decent men. She held both men in high regard due to their accomplishments leading the military forces at Clovis City. To complicate matters more, her father and uncle had served under Colonel Gorski in the Dinosaur Wars. Although her uncle did not survive the experience, her father claimed it was Gorski's leadership that put his soldiers in the best position to survive.

"I kill them all," Tan waived her hands in the air. "No one get in my way. Gorski afraid of me. Collins only talk, he no fighter. Sigebert Evart is my oldest friend. I give him one of his wives and she give him daughters. Evart no fight me. You go now and bring me what Doctor wants."

Reynita stood at attention and saluted her General. She waited until Tan returned her salute and she left the large hall as fast as her legs would carry her. She was excited that she was going home and would be close to her family. She was apprehensive in that she did not like being asked to steal information from people she respected and admired. She did not know how this Doctor Matthew Rosenburg ended up in a dungeon on Lynott's Land, but she was determined to find out. The fact that she was leaving the place that Matthew Rosenburg referred to as a horror show was the best news she had received all week.

Reynita rushed to her one bedroom quarters located in one of the many high rise military buildings over a kilometer away from Tan's palace. She had to pack quickly and get over to Clovis City to begin her investigation into the mystery of Matthew's family and how he came to be incarcerated by Tan.

Reynita first stopped at a room several floors above hers. She knocked on the metal door, looking over her shoulders to make certain she had not been followed. The door slid open and Reynita rushed inside.

"What gives, sis?" Estrellita Calderon wondered, seeing the urgency in her eyes. She hugged Reynita in an effort to calm her.

"Something big, I think. You up for a little intrigue?"

Estrellita was wearing a pink lace bra and matching panties as she had just showered. She had a dark sweater dress hanging on the bathroom door and was brushing her long dark hair as she spoke.

"Really? I just got transferred over here to the civilian computer section and you want me to get involved in some intrigue? Is this the kind of stuff that could get me fired or arrested? Tan doesn't have a reputation for lenience. What do you want me to do and why?"

Reynita felt the fine material of the sweater dress hanging on the doorway. Estrellita was the same age as Reynita, part of a birth group of five. Although they were twins, they were not identical. Reynita had always considered Estrellita to be the sister with the most sex appeal.

"I want you to use your skills to get close to a man named Matthew Rosenburg. He is being held at Tan's palace. She has some clones of Junior Ragnarsson and is using Rosenburg to bring them back to life."

"Sounds quite dangerous," Estrellita smiled.

"This is no joke, Strella. There is something big going on over at Tan's Palace. You know what the Ragnarsson killers did to some of our friends. Lupita almost died because of them. I need you to use your computer skills to find out all you can about a Matthew Rosenburg and the clones of Junior Ragnarsson. If you can, use your other assets to get close to him, if you know what I mean."

"So you want me to spy on Rosenburg's and Ragnarsson's under the nose of Tan? Are you suffering from schizophrenia or something? You do remember what those people are capable of, don't you?"

"Quit being such a lloran," Reynita told her.

"I am not a cry baby. You and Yolanda were always the ass kickers in the family. Karlita and I were always the studious ones. How often did you and Manuel have to fight when some boy was making a pass at me?"

"Seven times."

"Eight times," Estrellita corrected her.

"The school boys really liked the way you looked."

"They liked my tits and curvy ass, Reynita."

"Well, I was including those assets in my comment."

"Just remember that I never got the specialized training that you did. I am just a techno student and can't even fire a laser pistol. Compared to you I am a little wimp."

"I am counting on you being discreet and careful. Look, sis. If you even sense that there is trouble, just walk away and stop everything. Do not get yourself into a situation where you are cornered. Be smart and you will be fine."

"Consider it done. What are you going to do?"
Reynita shrugged, "I'm going back to Clovis City. I was given orders to locate all of Matthew's family members and arrange for their transfer to Lynott's Land. Tan is making a bargain with this Matthew to get herself cloned."

"You saw these clones?"

Reynita nodded, "I sure did. They look bizarre. Green skin, faces distorted but the rest of the body looked normal. They were muscular and looked quite imposing. I never thought such a thing possible."

Estrellita smiled, "Sis, it has always been possible. It was just illegal to clone humans. People have been doing it with livestock and pets for centuries. It sounds like these Rosenburg's are into all kinds of illegal activity. Go on to Clovis City; give my love to our brothers, sisters, abuelita and mom and dad. I will cover your tiny ass over here."
"I knew I could count on you."

CHAPTER SIX

Vladimir Sikorsky finished his day as he did every other. He ate some meats and fruits with several of his wives. He had sex with some of them and demanded that the others perform sexual acts on each other while he watched. He needed to relax after the past month.

People had rebelled against him and he was forced to kill them all. He did not like having to give such an order even though it was necessary to maintain order in the Eight Solar Systems. Then, his son and Chief Justice of the United Nations Criminal Appeals Court, Madison Sikorsky, informed him that the lead prosecutor on planet New Edinburgh disobeyed a direct order to dismiss the indictments filed against several member of the Royal Family.

The Chief Justice had called on Sean Collins personally and demanded that the Rosenburg family members be released. Collins refused. Since a direct order did not work, Madison Sikorsky attempted to bribe Collins financially. The man refused money. He refused the promise of promotions. He even refused the offer of sex slaves in the sex and species of his choice.

When Madison Sikorsky informed his father of the rejections he received by Collins, the news put Vladimir Sikorsky in a dour mood. He needed to relax, and the best way to put his mind at ease was to bring in as many desirable men and women as his palace play room would hold for unbridled sex.

As the orgy commenced, Sikorsky ordered his palace security computers to play the audio of the live closing arguments in what had been called "The Trial of the Century." The captured and surviving defendants of the Blood Moon Incident were about to face judgment from a jury of their peers on planet New Edinburgh. The Glorious Leader had taken a personal interest in the litigation as many of the accused were either related to him or had been used by him in the past. Sikorsky had used the Ragnarsson assassins over the years, just as the Rosenburg's had done. Given the unstable political climate, the Glorious Leader was listening to every word, every witness and viewing every document. His goal was to make sure that there were no accusations made against him personally so that he could maintain his two century rule.

He relaxed as he listened to the defense lawyers plead for leniency for their clients. Their arguments went on for hours. Sikorsky did his best to stay awake. Lawyers are long-winded, he thought to himself.

Finally, Sean Collins announced ready to deliver his rebuttal to the defense. Sikorsky yelled at two of his younger wives to be quiet. He wanted to hear what the smooth talking lawyer had to say.

"Ladies and gentlemen of the jury. Your Honor and opposing counsel. You have heard the evidence that we offered to you over the prior month." Sikorsky recognized Collins' voice. "We presented many eyewitnesses, tapes, documents, computer print outs, photographs, physical evidence, DNA evidence and the portions of the Blood Moon Incident that were not blocked by the Jammer capability of the defendants and their co-conspirators.

"I ask each of you now to remember the victims as you deliberate on the fate of these defendants. Remember that these victims walked among us. They were our friends, our brothers and sisters to wonderful families. They were children to caring parents and some of them were either parents or expecting parents. They lived among us. They were all good citizens and these animals that stand accused took these good people from us. It is time that we send a message to the rest of Clovis City and the entire planet New Edinburgh. Let us send a message to the rest of the Conquered Solar Systems. Let us tell all of humanity that the lack of regard for human life will no longer be tolerated. Let us demonstrate that slavery is a cancer that should be forever removed from our culture. Let us show that we believe with every fiber of our being that the killing of innocents will be punished to the full extent of the law.

"That is correct. I speak of the penalty of death. Each of you viewed the events as we played them for you in this court room. You heard the evidence of how many of the victims died. Remember each of them for they were our fellow citizens. Remember that they each walked among us. Computer, display the three dimensional portraits of the victims for the jury.

"Remember Roy Starr and Tina Martinson. They were both Academy cadets that had a dream to serve all of us. They were in training to become officers in the Space Command because serving humanity was their hope. It was their aspiration. Remember how they heard that the Blitzkrieg was wreaking havoc on innocent cadets and Marines. Roy Starr and Tina Martinson did not hesitate to act and protect their fellow man. They ignored the potential danger to themselves and leaped into their space craft and flew into harm's way. They did it for all of us here. They wanted to help and protect each of us. Now, it is your turn, ladies and gentlemen. Protect and honor the memory of Roy Starr and Tina Martinson by convicting these defendants and send them to the death chambers. Honor Martinson and Starr as they deserve to be honored.

"Honor each of the brave soldiers that died on Space Station Cy-7. Recall the replay of Captain Traxler and his command staff as they were swept out into outer space for a cruel and painful death. Many of them were parents and their children are now orphaned. These defendants set in motion those events. They had no regard for all of those lives that were lost. You will have pictures of each of these victims to refer to in your deliberations. Look at each picture of the victims as you consider your final judgment. Do not forget these men and women.

"Honor the brave soldiers that died here in Clovis City at the hands of these defendants. Bill Hodges served with distinction and had been a good soldier. Lieutenant May Ling died attempting to serve warrants on wanted criminals. Lance Corporal Kendra Foster died as she attempted to assist cadets in distress at the graveyard ambush. These defendants were either directly responsible for those deaths or participated in the grand conspiracy that led to the untimely end of these brave men and women.

"Finally, remember the victims on the Blood Moon. The unarmed and innocent Judges that were massacred there. The Tyr Academy Cadets that were all brutally ambushed, killed, raped and left for dead. The numerous Newton Academy cadets that died on that moon. None of those victims were warned that these defendants intended to slaughter them. These defendants epitomize evil. Their actions were barbaric and they killed innocents without a second thought.

"And remember Pierre Zerbe and Porfirio Cardenas. They both walked among us. They were fellow citizens of Clovis City. These defendants put into motion the events that led to the murder of Pierre Zerbe. His girlfriend, Cara, sits in the pews to my left and your right. She has been her for every single day of this trial. Cara is pregnant with Zerbe's children. These unborn children will never know their father. These defendants are the reason for that. Honor Pierre Zerbe so that Cara can tell their children that while he died a hero, the community stood up as one and condemned his killers. Honor how Zerbe lived and loved as a man among us. Look at the evidence we have proven in this trial and find these defendants guilty of his murder.

"Recall the testimony of Ellen Benson and her statement during the Blood Moon Incident. She said that the most courageous thing she had ever witnessed in her life was when Porfirio Cardenas led his four small fighter space ships into battle against twenty-four. Four against twenty-four! Perhaps his faith in his God, his love for what he called his Lord and Savior, gave him the strength and the courage to fight against such overwhelming odds. Porfirio Cardenas did not hesitate to lead Marco Andolini, Mary Lincoln and Jurgen Doernitz into that battle. Cardenas knew that there were fellow cadets in danger. He knew that at that moment he had to face the enemy in defense of others. He did not flee. He did not run. He made a difficult decision to lead his friends into a battle that they might not survive. Cardenas rushed in to defend others. He did not know any of the Newton Academy cadets. He defended them anyway and he fought bravely. He lost his life in that battle. But that single moment was, without a doubt, a major turning point on that Moon. Cardenas gave his life so that others could live. Honor him and his sacrifice.

"And his widow has been here every day. She is sitting next to Cara. Freya and Cara have been here every day because they care. They want justice to be done. They want to hear that the men that they loved are not forgotten. Porfirio Cardenas had so much to lose. He will never see his son and daughter grow up. He will not be there for their weddings. He will not get to see his grandchildren. Porfirio Cardenas represented what is best in men. He was a loyal friend, loving husband, a wonderful father and he had a burning desire to protect others.

"Now his memory cries out for each of you to take the evidence and make the most important decision of your lives.

Do we allow such barbarians like the defendants that sit in judgment before you to live? No. We must make sure that the rest of the United Nations of Earth understand that when you attack one of us, you attack us all. Bill Hodges showed us that value by his example as did Roy Starr, Tina Martinson, Pierre Zerbe and Porfirio Cardenas. Show the rest of the planets that our community will stand together. Show the rest of the settlements around the Seven Conquered Solar Systems that we will protect our own. Show them these values through your verdict. Show everyone that the killing of innocents will not be tolerated on planet New Edinburgh. Show them that we do not care if you are politically connected or wealthy like the Rosenburg family. Show them that justice is not a silly word. Show them that justice is a word with meaning. Do not forget your home town victims. Do not forget that they walked among us. Do not forget that these defendants took them from us.

"I thank each of you for your service as jurors and I thank you for remembering all of the victims and their families. The decision is now yours."

Sikorsky growled when he heard a news reporter comment on how Collins maintained eye contact with the jury and that many jurors were in tears. Some jurors were glaring at the defendants as Collins spoke.

Sikorsky ordered his computer broadcast system to shut down. He was exhausted and wanted to sleep. He needed to eliminate the trouble maker Sean Collins and his team of lawyers that refused bribes. He resolved to take care of them later. It was time for his body to be at peace and relax.

He then retired to his huge sleeping chambers.

Sikorsky lived in the large and tall sky scraper Sikorsky Tower on Sikorsky's Planet. His tower was over one hundred thirty floors high. He lived near the top floor and governed the seven conquered solar systems from all of the floors above and below. For two hundred years he had been the ruler of all humanity. Under his dictatorship, Earth had flourished. They conquered worlds and enslaved the indigenous survivors. Humanity then occupied those other planets and spread its influence. Sikorsky considered himself the greatest conqueror in the vast history of mankind. Others military leaders took nations. Sikorsky was the first and the only human military leader to subjugate entire planets. Even Alexander the Great could not compare with Sikorsky's accomplishments.

Sikorsky's bed chamber was about the size of fifty yards by twenty five yards. His bed was a king size with furs of endangered species used as his bed covers. He had a huge walk in closet and several escape doors that were kept in secret in case he had to escape an assassination attempt.

Around the west and east wall were the stuffed bodies of his deceased wives. They were all leaning against multi-colored Doric columns, each of their bodies preserved with oils that kept the skin from rotting. If one did not know any better, they would believe the stuffed corpses were actually alive. Sikorsky would kiss each of the stuffed corpses on the lips before he went to bed. On some occasions he would take the body of one of the dead wives off the display stand that kept them standing upright and carry them to bed and pleasure himself with them. The laws against necrophilia did not apply to Sikorsky. He was the Glorious Leader. He was the law. If he wanted to make love to a corpse then he would do so. And he did so on a regular basis.

Sikorsky walked to each corpse and kissed them goodnight. The first wife, Ekaterina Sikorsky, was the one that he kissed first. She had been his first love. When she had been offered the opportunity to have immortality by taking the internal organs from younger girls, Ekaterina Sikorsky refused. She told her husband that such an act was obscene and an affront to God. She passed away from a heart attack at the age of fifty-seven.

The next corpse he kissed was that of Wanda Welker. She also refused the chance to live forever. Sikorsky recalled her to be a fantastic lover in his bed. He missed her greatly. He squeezed her breasts as he kissed her.

He kissed the other corpses, one by one. Lidia Urbanczyk, Gilda Rosenburg, Ana Murdock, Aliah Sowa, Pamela Goodman, Lia Ming, Natalia Feklisov, Helen Perdiccas, Elsa Janssen, Kia Tsukifuji and Margaretta Rendon. He had loved them all and missed them. His only regret was that he had not targeted New Edinburgh sooner in his career. He would have been able to duplicate his wives before they died. He could have had them forever.

Each of the wives bore many offspring for Sikorsky and each of them in turn refused the gift he offered so they could live forever. Fortunately the children chose wiser and took the internal organs of the innocent to live many more decades and, for many, centuries.

Many other wives took the ambrosia of immortality offered to them by Sikorsky. Each of them lived in the large towering building with their powerful husband.

Sikorsky settled into his bed and fell asleep. As the night passed, Sikorsky experienced what had become a reoccurring nightmare. He was regularly reliving the battle against the Akarzdamedians in his sleep. He would toss and turn and sometimes cry out. Many times he would wake up in a cold sweat because He would not go away. He was Robert Richard Andrews, the man that had commanded the science ship named the Calypso. He visited Sikorsky in his dreams which quickly became nightmares. Sikorsky would relive his fateful orders of over two hundred years ago to fire nuclear weapons on the Calypso. He gave the order due to the meddlesome Andrews making requests, no demands, that they cease the invasion of the alien planet Akarzdamedia and discuss a peace treaty with the Queen of the aliens named Danu.

Sikorsky and his other military commanders were not interested in peace. They were sent with one mandate and that was to take the planet over. His orders read: "To conquer the new world and kill as many as possible." They were to capture and enslave the survivors, if any. Andrews and his constant annoying pleas for peace was not a part of the plan. Sikorsky told his other commanders to fire upon the smaller science vessel. Sikorsky watched as Andrews tried to escape the heat seeking nuclear missiles by flying the Calypso toward the binary stars that planet Akarzdamedia orbited. Sikorsky did not ever confirm whether the Calypso was destroyed by the nuclear bombs or if she melted in the heat as she was pulled into one of the two stars. He never cared. The point was that he was forever rid of the man of peace Andrews. The world view, or the universal view of Sikorsky, did not include men and women like Andrews and they had no place in his long term goals.

His only goal was to take, conquer and kill.

And Sikorsky was the best ever at that game.

Sikorsky woke up again, screaming, from his nightmare of Robert Richard Andrews and his daughters all accusing him of murder. They would come to his dreams and accuse him of ending their lives. They would threaten that they would return to humanity and expose Sikorsky as a fraud. After waking up in a screaming fit, Sikorsky sat up in his bed, sobbing and holding his chest with his left hand.

"Why won't Andrews just go away?" Sikorsky yelled to the empty room.

"Because, my love, you killed him," Ekaterina Sikorsky's corpse answered him.

"He trusted you and you betrayed him," Margaretta Rendon's body added. Sikorsky blinked his eyes as he could swear he saw each of the mouths of the corpses moved as he heard them speak to him.

"He did not share your dream of a far reaching empire for humans," Lidia Urbanczyk told him as she did every night when he woke up screaming.

"You did what you had to do my husband. Andrews would not have allowed our children and grandchildren to use the body parts of young women to live forever." Gilda Rosenburg's voice soothed him.

"Look at all the good you have done over the last two hundred years," Ana Murdock's stuffed body smiled down at him.

"You kept humanity safe through strength," Aliah Sowa assured him.

"Remember what I taught you when I first met you. Weakness is provocative. We had to show all of the species in the universe that we meant business," Pamela Goodman whispered.

"The people of Earth are grateful that you killed the peace mongers like Andrews and his stupid daughters," Lia Ming laughed.

"You are a God, Vladimir. The people worship you because you did the right thing that day. Andrews had to die." Natalia Feklisov added in support of her deceased sister wives.

"All of the alien races you wiped out over the last two hundred years would have done the same to us had you not attacked first," Helen Perdiccas told him with her strong Greek accent.

"And because you were so decisive, our offspring have flourished." Elsa Janssen said with a grateful tone in her voice.

"Remember to trust no one but family, my love. Andrews was not family," Kia Tsukifuji warned him.

"Come, Vladimir. Come and embrace me as you did all those years ago. I miss your arms around me and the smell of your cologne," Wanda Welker beckoned him.

Sikorsky continued to sob as each of his deceased wives comforted him with their words. The Glorious Leader never once wondered how the dead women could speak to him. His untreated paranoid schizophrenia did not allow for him to understand that the nightly ritual of him conversing with the stuffed corpses was due to a brain disorder.

None of his offspring had the courage to tell him that he desperately needed psychiatric intervention. They were all terrified of how Sikorsky would react to that form of advice. They were afraid that they would end up dead like the Andrews family.

Vladimir Sikorsky stood from his bed and walked to the stuffed body of Wanda Welker. He lifted her into his arms and began kissing the corpse passionately. In his mind, she returned the kisses with just as much fervor. He carried the body to his bed and began removing her clothing, kissing her bare breasts and moving her legs apart to accept his throbbing erection. He made love to the corpse of Welker with the same ferocity that he did when she had been alive. In his mind, Sikorsky could hear her moans and her voice begging for him to continue.

CHAPTER SEVEN

"Guilty!"

The verdict of the jury was read loud and clear for all present. The word echoed over the hushed court of law. The defendants sat, mostly stone faced. One swallowed hard, worrying about the sentence the Judge would impose. One, a woman, covered her face and wept.

The courtroom had white walls and ceiling. The ceiling was fifty feet from the floor. The floors were tiled with black marble. The court room was one hundred yards long and sixty feet wide. At the head of the court room was a large black marble seating area about ten feet above the floor for the Judge to sit. To the right of the Judge was the court reporter. To the left was a section for the Clerk of the Court. Against the left wall were twelve seats for the jurors to sit. To the far right was a table and chair for the witnesses to offer testimony. Across from the Judge were two sets of black rectangular tables where the litigants would sit. In between the two rectangular tables was a podium for the lawyers to stand behind and question witnesses or offer arguments to the Court. Behind the tables for the litigants were several dozen rows of pews for audiences to observe the trials. There were several dozen white Doric columns that went from the floor to the ceiling.

Sean Collins and his three prosecutors were sitting at the rectangular table closest to the jury. The lawyers tried not to smile. They had prepared for weeks for the trials against the Rosenburg Conspirators. They went without sleep; they had anticipated every possible defense, every conceivable cross examination. They had read, re-read and read again each document that would be introduced into evidence.

Sean Collins left nothing to chance. He and his lawyers even practiced their reactions to the jury verdict. No celebration. They helped each other select their suits for each day of the long trial. They were professional lawyers, prosecutors. The champions of justice and they had won justice for many that had been murdered by the defendants.

Avery "Big Bad" Jackson, guilty of all counts on the indictment. He had no reaction as his numerous accusations were read out loud by the jury foreman and the pronouncement of guilty was given. Jackson looked over at his lawyer. He wanted to break his neck for losing the case. Jackson sat and watched his lawyer get his butt kicked all over the courtroom by Collins during the month long trial. He hoped his worthless lawyer would visit him in jail so he would have the chance to break his neck.

Cleon Alexander was equally stone faced as the verdicts were read as to his charges. He tried to not listen and to tune out the monotone voice of the jury foreman. He fantasized about one of the female lawyers on Sean Collins team, a striking brunette. Alexander thought about her and how much he would enjoy it if she were stripping her clothes off in front of him and performing a lap dance on him. Alexander knew full well that where he was going. Naked women would be something he would never see again. He silently regretted that he had allowed Caine Rosenburg to talk him into following him to the Blood Moon.

Burton Stapler heard his findings read against him. He silently cursed the day he ever met Caine or his damned family.

Although Stapler had enjoyed his experiences with Caine, he could not accept that his life would have gone in the direction it had if he had never met the man. Caine had been a serial rapist and murderer. Stapler had been a student at a military academy when the Rosenburg lad approached him and recruited him to join in on a life of deviance and brutality. Stapler had never raped a woman before he met Caine. But after the first rape, he found the brutal act enjoyable. He especially enjoyed it when the victims begged for mercy. Stapler wished he could have been lucky enough to have died on the Blood Moon with his friends Kai Chin and Keith Austin. Stapler knew from the stories he had heard from other prisoners around his jail cell that death would be better than imprisonment on planet Cootron.

Alfred Rosenburg, III, closed his eyes when heard the jury pronouncements against him. He had been a good and successful lawyer with a profitable law firm in which he had owned fifty percent ownership. Now, he was disgraced, disbarred and going to spend the rest of his life in prison. He was used to wearing the best suits and the most stylish outfits. He had dozens of women that had thrown themselves at him when he was a free man. He drank the finest whiskey and bourbon. He had wine bottles from the best vineyards in the Eight Solar Systems imported to him. The costs were of no consequence to him. He had obtained plenty of wealth over the years, but ever since his arrest, he had become a non-entity. Nobody came to visit him in jail. Most of his siblings were either dead or incarcerated. His wives had fled the planet and took all of his children with them. He stared at the white ceiling in disbelief. He had lost so much.

Ellis Ragnarsson bit his lower lip. He glared at his sister, Ella, who had given testimony against him. Ellis had been Rosenburg's law partner. He was similarly left without his license to practice and faced with a life time of incarceration. In the last several months he had lost his father, a brother and a sister and now he had lost his career. He thought he had been smarter than Collins. He had been wrong. Ellis's lawyer and occasional lover, Jada Ying, whispered to him that she would initiate an appeal first thing in the morning.

Ivar Ragnarsson received only three findings of guilt which was the least of all of the other defendants. Ivar was not a killer or a hardened criminal like the others. His father, Dell, had sent him to the Academy to study and become an officer in the Space Command. His father had chosen Ivar to be the one son that was not a member of the criminal activities. The main reason for the decision was that Ivar seemed to have a mind for the sciences. He had been more astute as a young boy than his siblings. His father saw potential in the lad and attempted to cultivate that and pushed Ivar to study. But Ivar had wanted to be involved in the family business, which was taking lives.

The young teen could not believe that his father would abandon him during his time of need. Ivar continuously looked over his shoulder during the trial, expecting that his missing father would show up and rescue him. But his father did not appear. He began crying when he had heard his name called by the jury foreman. He had only wanted to fit in with his family. That was all he had ever desired. Due to his involvement in the Sandstorm Incident, he had been expelled from the Academy. Soon he would be sent to prison for the rest of his life. He could not believe that his sister testified against him and against Ellis. He looked over at Ella Ragnarsson and saw her crying as well. He wondered if she felt any guilt for betraying her family.

Ella wept as her guilty findings were read. She had turned on her brothers and the others in exchange for a recommendation by Collins for a more lenient sentence. Ella looked at her brothers and they both glared at her. She hid her face in her hands out of the shame she felt. She did not have these feelings because she was sorry she had killed people. She was ashamed that she had betrayed her siblings and she feared reprisals from her father and her other numerous siblings that were still free in the various solar systems. Although Ella had given much information to Collins, she had not told the lawyer everything. Ella was cognizant that her other siblings would seek retribution. Many more people would soon die.

Nikko Xian was equally silent as he listened to his name read. The findings of guilt against him were not surprising. Nikko had been a willing murderer and paid assassin for over a decade. He was thankful he had not stood trial for all of the murders he had participated in over the years. It would have taken all day to read his indictment alone. Xian knew he was guilty and only nodded as if he agreed with the jury in finding him guilty.

Raul Quintana was the last of the defendants. He smiled at the jurors as they read his sentence. He wanted to tell them all that, if he ever escaped, he would track them all down and cut their throats. But, that sort of outburst would not go over very well with the Judge. Quintana remained silent as the jurors' verdict was read, finding him guilty on eighteen different felony counts, including the murders of several cadets and Military Intelligence agent Bill Hodges.

Each of the defendants had shackles on their legs and metal cuffs on their wrists. They were dressed in the Clovis City prison clothing. The dark blue pull over shirts and similar colored pants were loosely fit over each defendant, their white slippers for shoes exposed their toes and heels.

Seated behind the prosecutors was the courageous and lovely Dulce Maria Reynolds Hernandez Ragnarsson, the widow of Dell Ragnarsson, Junior. During the trial, she had testified against the defendants. She told the world of the hell she lived with after she had been kidnaped by the Rosenburg family and forced to marry her assassin husband. With the verdict in, she was now free to return back to Earth to find her mother and father. Her siblings and cousins were also somewhere in the vast eight solar system dominion of mankind. Each day she had waited to testify was torture to her. The time had finally arrived for her to go home.

Seated next to Dulce Maria Reynolds Hernandez Ragnarsson were Sergeant First Class Mark Lund, Staff Sergeant Benjamen Zhao and Corporal Frank Preston. They had also been witnesses for the prosecution.

Lund and Preston had been acting as undercover agents at the Academy and played key roles in the Sandstorm Incident in which Bill Hodges and many others had died. Zhao had joined Lund and Preston to replace Hodges. All three men were involved in the Blitzkrieg Incident that caused many more deaths.

Lund, Preston and Zhao were members of the United Nations Military Intelligence. They were wearing solid black Class A uniforms. Their uniform jackets had three gold buttons that fastened the jacket together at the center of the chest of each individual. Their rank was sewn onto their long sleeves. Lund had on his Medal of Valor attached just above the left breast pocket of his uniform. They seemed satisfied that the jury did the right thing. The verdict was justice for Bill Hodges, who had been killed by a flame dart which burned him alive, while fighting some of the defendants in the court room.

"This was for you Bill," Lund whispered to himself.

The parents and siblings of Tina Martinson were in the back row of the large court room, crying as the sentences were read. They had lost their daughter when her small fighter space craft was fired upon by the Raumschiff owned by Dell Ragnarsson, Jr. Tina Martinson died when her ship was blown out of the sky. Her only fault was that she had tried to redeem herself by helping others in danger.

Next to the Martinson family was Doctor Freya Doernitz Cardenas, whose husband had died because of the accused. Cadet Porfirio Cardenas had been killed on the Moon orbiting planet Semiramis. He died a hero, leading four cadet pilots against twenty-four enemy ships. His courage and leadership was critical in saving other lives. Freya fought back the urge to weep openly. She had loved her husband more than life. Now he was gone and she was a single mother of two children. All thanks to the actions of the defendants in the court room and their deceased co-conspirators.

Other victims and family members were present to hear justice be handed out.

Cara Perez Guerrero smiled and was nodding with each pronouncement of guilt. She was many months pregnant and her twin children that would be born without a father. Pierre Zerbe had been killed because of the actions of some of the people receiving their sentences today.

Cadet Bret Bragg was seated near the front. His older brother had been murdered at the attack on the local hospital during the Sandstorm Incident. Bragg glared at the backs of the defendants. Bragg hated them all. His older brother had been the closest person to him in his life. He silently hoped that the trial Judge would mete out justice by assessing the death penalty. Nothing less would satisfy Bragg. Several of the other Bragg family members were sitting next to him.

His older sisters Daniella and Lisa were wearing their dark blue Class A uniforms of the Space Command. The two women were pilots and had the rank of Lieutenant on their collars. They had been the two that had brought William Bragg into the gang life. Both Daniella and Lisa Bragg were serving as Space Command pilots on Dakota Province which was located near the massive Murdock Ocean to the far west of Clovis City. Dakota Province was the location of the majority of the New Edinburgh fighter pilots and had three companies of fighter squadrons under the command of Lieutenant Commander Lidia Rendon. The two Bragg women were in command of two flight groups of forty pilots each and a few dozen engineers and mechanics. The parents of the large Bragg family were silent as the verdicts were read and held hands. The patriarch, William Bragg, Senior had six wives and there were a total of twenty-six children from those unions.

Cadet Junior Jurgen Doernitz was present with his wife, Cadet Lila Zapata. Doernitz was the only cadet that had been able to offer testimony in person regarding the incidents on the Semiramis Moon.

With his broken leg completely healed, Doernitz told the jury his tale of how three of the accused took part in a plan to kill Doernitz and all of his friends. He also told the jurors of the Blitzkrieg attack which cost the lives of Roy Starr and Tina Martinson among many others. The other survivors of the Semiramis Moon plot had graduated and no longer lived on planet New Edinburgh. Doernitz was the only one of the Semiramis Moon attack to give live testimony. The others, Yuri Gorski, Les Gillis, Julia Steiner, Drew Harrison, Marco Andolini, Eamon O'Grady, Mary Johnson Lincoln, Sara Barnes, Alan Anderson, Hal Palmer, Laurence Thompson and Angelique LeClair testified by way of remote three dimensional broadcast.

Jurgen Doernitz had grown to despise the celebrity status he had achieved from his role in the Blood Moon Incident. Strangers would approach him to meet him, tell him how great he was. Others would want autographs from him on pre-printed color photos of the young man in action when he was fighting for survival. Doerntiz had learned some people were taking signed pictures of him and selling them on other outposts and planets for several hundred Empire Dollars. After he became aware that others were profiting off of his signature, and more importantly, from the deaths of his brother in law Porfirio and his friend Pierre, he began refusing to sign for any one.

Cadet junior Elektra Papanikolaou Frazier had testified regarding the attack at the Academy graveyard. She related to the jury the events that left her near death and with a severed arm. She further pointed out the men that had attempted to rape her on Space Station Cy-7. She spent an hour relating to how she was rescued by Cadet Drayton Love-Easter and that he had fought valiantly against some of the defendants on trial. The defense attorneys made her confess to killing Darryl Rosenburg. She wept as she recounted the events in which she impaled the man in the chest. The attack on her credibility in such a manner seemed to garner sympathy from the jury and they did not hold it against her during their deliberations.

Cadet junior Lupita Calderon testified as to her bravery chasing the Raumschiff named Blitzkrieg. She related how Roy Starr and Tina Martinson were blown out of the sky by the occupants of the Blitzkrieg and of her own harrowing struggle to survive when her vessel was also shot down. She received emotional support from her parents, grandmother and a large sibling group that were in attendance. Lupta had been petrified regarding her in court sworn testimony, especially with each of the defendants in court, staring her down, as she related to the jury her experiences. She overcame her fears and performed admirably. She smiled when she heard the verdict.

Second Lieutenant Reynita Calderon, Lupita's older sister, was working security at the trial. She smiled at her family members to reassure them all that everything was going to be fine. Reynita was dressed in her Class C solid black uniform signifying her as a member of Military Intelligence. She had an armor piercing laser rifle slung over her right shoulder and a laser pistol hung on a holster connected to her black web belt. Her long dark hair was tied back with a black elastic twist. She had graduated from Clovis Academy and was selected to serve under General Tan's Brigades of Military Intelligence soldiers. Assisting her with the security detail was a platoon of Tan's soldiers. Each of them was clad in solid black uniforms with laser shotguns slung over their shoulders with silver straps. The laser shotgun was a staple for the Tan's Brigades. They were shorter at the barrel than the laser rifle and would simultaneously unleash about twenty laser bursts from a canister shell full of laser energy. The blast would spread out wide to cover about a twenty foot radius in front of the person pulling the trigger. Any person in that area would most likely be hit by one of the laser slivers.

Sean Collins had produced over two hundred witnesses to prove his case against the defendants. Many were survivors from the attack on the space station. Others were men and women that lived through the attack during the Dust Storm. He had produced photographs, medical records, business records and security computer down loads to make sure there was no doubt that these defendants should be found guilty of the charges against them.

The trial Judge asked the defendants to all rise. They stood with their lawyers next to them. Some of the accused were fidgeting as they waited to hear their ultimate fate. Alfred Rosenburg was not concerned as he was related to the trial judge. He was certain he would receive a light sentence from his great uncle. While his co-defendants were staring at the floor and licked their dry lips, Rosenburg smiled.

Judge Carlton Sikorsky was in his nineties. He had grey hair and was wearing the ceremonial black robe that had been passed down over the centuries as the ceremonial dress for jurists. Judge Carlton Sikorsky was a grand-son of the Glorious Leader, Vladimir Sikorsky. Judge Carlton Sikorsky took the three hundred page indictment from one of the several armed guards in the court room. The extra security was ordered by the Judge for this particular trial since some of the accused had proven to be expert escape artists. Due to the publicity of the trial and the events surrounding them, the Judge concluded that he could not give his relatives a pass. He had no choice but to sentence them all harshly.

"I have been a Judge for a long time. A very long time." Judge Sikorsky began, his voice sounded tired. "I have heard some horrible cases right here in this very court room." He paused for dramatic effect, pointing to the ceiling as he said 'This very court room.' The news media was present, filming his every word, commenting on each expression he made. "This is the most violent and evil group of defendants to ever come to my court. You attacked a space station and killed over seventy people. You blew up a transport that was carrying innocent civilians. You killed a judge. You killed Academy Students. You killed Military Intelligence officers. You were a part of several murders at a local hospital. You killed doctors and nurses. You ambushed innocent cadets on a faraway moon. You caused many children to be left behind as orphans. Each of you are despicable."

The Judge stopped and drank from his glass of water on his desk. "I find no redeeming qualities in any of you. In accordance with the recommendation of the jury, I hereby sentence each of you to death, save two. Ella Ragnarsson and Ivar Ragnarsson, I sentence both of you to fifty years to be served on the Prison Planet Cootron. Mrs. Ragnarsson is being spared only because she cooperated with the authorities by offering sworn testimony against her co-conspirators. Ivar Ragnarsson is spared only in that he was remotely involved. Those that are to be executed, you will be transported to Cootron to await your execution. If there are any Gods out there, I hope they show your souls no mercy. I order that you be transported to Cootron on the next available prison shuttle cruiser. Mr. Collins, I congratulate you and your staff on presenting this case.

Your service in defense of the rule of law, the victims and the survivors should stand as an example to law students everywhere. May the Stars bless our Glorious Leader! Court is dismissed."

The Judge slammed his gavel on his large desk top and walked out of the court room. The observers began applauding the sentence. Collins and his legal team began hugging one another. Jurgen Doernitz hugged his sister, Freya.

Alfred Rosenburg was stunned. He had expected that he would receive a short stint on probation from his great uncle. But instead he had been given the death penalty. Rosenburg collapsed into his chair and put his head down into his hands. Never had a Sikorsky betrayed a Rosenburg. Never. He could not fathom why the judge made the ruling that he had. It went against the past two hundred years of practice between the family members. The Royal Family was to stick together, no matter what. He winced as he heard the loud applause behind him from some of the families of the victims.

There was not only celebration in the court room, but in the streets as well.

Many of the other cadets at the Clovis Academy in Clovis City celebrated by meeting at O'Malley's and began doing shots and sharing pitchers of ale and beer. Many of the sophomores, juniors and seniors at the Academy had known one or more of the victims to the massive crime spree committed by the villains that had just been convicted.

The defendants were led out of the court room by armed guards. Avery Jackson knew all too well what a death sentence meant under the Empire law. It was not as simple as a firing squad, or a hanging or lethal injection. Jackson and the others sentenced to death would be killed in a similar manner that they had murdered their victims. Jackson recalled the vivid account that was related from the testimony of Ella Ragnarsson of his part in the rape and torture of Alejandra Khartov. Jackson walked slowly from the court, contemplating his body being chopped into pieces while he was still fully conscious, as he and his friends had done to Khartov. He closed his eyes. He began to think of any way he could to die a quicker and less painful death.

Jackson had heard the term 'suicide by cop' which was a description of a person that forced a law enforcement officer to kill them. Jackson had determined that might be the least painful way for him to face his own demise.

As Sean Collins was shaking hands and receiving hugs from family members of the victims, he was approached by several of the defense lawyers. Collins did not want to converse with the opposing lawyers any longer. He was ready for some rest and a well-deserved vacation. Jada Ying, who was a member of the Ragnarsson defense team, was able to push her way through the crowds and get to Collins.

"We need to talk," Ying told Collins as he continued to shake hands.

"I have nothing more to say to any of you," Collins answered abruptly as he kept accepting the accolades and gratitude from the crowd. He hated how defense lawyers would typically want to negotiate only after things had gone badly for them in court. Collins no longer had any reason to bargain with the opposing lawyers since the jury found in his favor.

"Maybe you have nothing, but I do." Ying handed Collins a legal document that was about forty pages long. "We are appealing to the Superior Court. I expect Ellis will remain here pending the appeal."

Collins accepted the papers from Ying and nodded to her, "As per the law. I will make the necessary arrangements."

Ying knew that she could accept Collins at his word. He was not like some prosecutors that would lie to defense lawyers. He was a proven straight shooter and kept his promises. Ying turned and noticed that Ellis Ragnarsson had already been led out of the courtroom. Collins continued to shake hands as he tried in vain to go home.

The remaining cadets of the self-named "Gorski Gang" assembled at the bar named O'Malley's. Although the founders of the Gang had all graduated, the membership had grown from the previous year. The cadets needed the verdict. The victims needed the finality so that closure could be sought out from the losses suffered.

Sophia DuBravac, a cadet senior and Gorski Gang member learned of the verdict from the screams in the streets. She ran to O'Malley's, with a huge smile on her alluring face and pulled out her hand held computer/communication device. She asked her computer to connect her to her husband, who was currently living on another planet. The connection took several minutes as her request bounced off a few dozen satellites across two solar systems. The wait had been worth it. She heard the voice of her husband, Les Gillis.

"Amor!" Gillis said as he saw her image. "What happened?" He had been waiting to hear about the verdict. Gillis had been in the middle of several of the attacks from the criminals. He had survived each offensive and he had even killed a few conspirators in defense of himself or others. Gillis had been one of the heroes on the Semiramis Moon, also called the Blood Moon. Gillis had suffered several injuries, but he fought until the end by the side of Drew Harrison and Yuri Gorski. He had also lost a friend on that moon, a cadet named Pierre Zerbe.

"Honey, they were all found guilty," DuBravac said joyfully. "Two got a fifty year sentence. The rest the death penalty."

"Thank the Stars!" Gillis said with relief. He had been concerned that the remaining Rosenburg family members would find a way to bribe the jury or the judge or cause some other act of mayhem to thwart justice. He felt as if he and his friends were now, finally and forever, vindicated. "I love you babe."

"I love you too," she told him, looking up into the red-orange skyline of planet New Edinburgh. "I want to see you. I miss you."

"And I you. Just think, the December and New Year's break is just two months away. We can spend two weeks together."

"But most of the time will be spent with one of us flying to meet the other," DuBravac complained.

"Not so my love," Gillis told her. "I have secured for us reservations at a hotel on Space Station Cy-5 which is exactly half way between New Edinburgh and Sikorsky's Planet. That means we get more time together."

"I love you, Les Gillis."

"I love you more. I have to go babe. I will be on the three dimensional broadcast tonight after class. See you then?"

"You know it, honey!" DuBravac smiled.

Even though they spent considerable time in class and studying, they still made time for each other on the technology driven broadcast system. The separation was difficult for both, but the nightly talks helped them cope.

DuBravac ran toward O'Malley's and saw Rolf Rhinehard kissing a woman near the entrance of the establishment. DuBravac had always liked Rolf's older brother, Klaus, but she was cool to Rolf. Both Rhinehard brothers were cadet pilots and Gorski Gang members. Over the years that DuBravac had been a member of the Gorski Gang, Rolf had caused a few bar fights due to his womanizing. He had a nasty habit of pursuing married women and women with boyfriends. Due to his handsome face and muscular body, Rolf had no trouble picking up women. DuBravac could not understand what his infatuation with women in relationships was.

As she walked past Rolf, DuBravac noticed that he was kissing Mia Nguyen, another Academy student. DuBravac scowled at the sight. Nguyen was the girlfriend of Piotr Gorski, Yuri's younger brother. Rolf hit a new low by stealing a girl away from a fellow Gorski Gang member. DuBravac was saddened for Piotr as he had been enamored with Mia Nguyen for at least a year. No doubt Nguyen's betrayal of Piotr with Rolf would cause some friction within the Gang.

DuBravac resisted the urge to drop kick Rolf to the pavement. She walked into the sliding doors of O'Malley's and was greeted by the hostesses wearing uniforms in the colors of the old flag of old Ireland. They recognized her immediately and told her that the rest of the Gorski Gang was waiting on the fifth floor.

DuBravac climbed the several flights of spiral stairs to the level where her friends were waiting. When she arrived she could hear the O'Malley family playing old school music from Ireland on the main stage. Her friends were all sitting around a rectangular table, which was actually several table set together for the Gorski Gang. She smiled at the sight of Jack Harcourt, one of the cotton white skinned Children of Athena, who was flirting with one of the waitresses.

Klaus Rhinehard was there with his pregnant wife, April Mejia, sharing a bowl of fruit. Some of the new additions to the Gang were also present, sharing pitchers of beer. Daniel Choi, Norman Porter, Ye Yibing, Lucius Andolini, Venus Andolini, Giola Andolini, Paolo Andolini, Stella Andolini and Therese Fenster were laughing at some story Dirk Fenster had just finished telling them. They each waved at DuBravac when they noticed she was approaching them. Harumi Shigeta was the first to give DuBravac a hug. Although the Gang had grown in numbers, it was not the same.

Yuri Gorski, Drew Harrison and Dominic Andolini were off serving under Colonel Lincoln on the Cortez. Mary Lincoln had volunteered to join the mission to find the missing Battle Ship called the Bismark. Michel Evart was a pilot in Admiral Yamamoto's Fleet. Marco Andolini was serving as a pilot in Captain Bruce Allen's ship. Drayton Love-Easter and his wife, Yesenia Guevara, were stationed together on planet New Berlin.

Julia Steiner and Siobhan Collins were earning their doctorates on Sikorsky's Planet. And Sophia's husband was studying to earn his doctorate in military tactics at the War College at Sikorsky University. DuBravac missed all of her friends and would often reminisce of the early glory days of the Gorski Gang.

Around the bar there were tables filled with cadets from other gang factions. Near the west end of the bar was a set of three round tables occupied by members of the infamous Bragg Gang. Their leader, Bret Bragg, had a new female cadet in his lap kissing her neck and whispering in her ear. DuBravac noted that the girl was wearing dark shorts and a tube top, advertising her slim body to Bragg. He seemed to be oblivious to anyone else as his full attention was on the girl. Bragg came from a large sibling group that had moved to New Edinburgh fifteen years ago. One of his brothers, William, had been killed by the assassins employed by the Rosenburg family. Although the Bragg and Gorski groups clashed often, they had their mutual hatred of the Rosenburg's in common.

James Cobb would occasionally glare in the direction of the Gorski group. He was a cadet pilot that was also from one of the older families of New Edinburgh. He followed the footsteps of his older siblings to attend the Clovis Academy and become a staunch defender of the Bragg Gang. His former best friend had been expelled from the University for violating the safety rules over the Forbidden region. After that event, Cobb grew closer to Bragg and some of the other members of their group.

Some of the Calderon brothers, Juanito, Jose, Pepito, Manuel and Xavier, were relaxing in their seats taking shots of tequila and chasing them down with beer. They were the younger brothers of Reynita and, like James Cobb, followed their oldest sibling to the Clovis Academy and the Bragg Gang. DuBravac learned that the families that had been original settlers of New Edinburgh, such as the Bragg's, Cobb's and Calderon's, viewed the new families and students as foreigners that were arriving only to attempt to steal their opportunities from them. That level of animosity was the catalyst that sparked many of the bar room brawls that the Bragg's started.

Cadet pilot John Gauthier was arguing with fellow astronaut candidate Basil Varek about some new report that was released regarding The Lost Fleet. The two men were now in their last year at the Academy and would soon be assigned duty stations to begin their careers. Gauthier looked like the copy of one of the movie stars from the 1950's, tall, dark, handsome and even the razor thin mustache to go with his strong chin and cheek bones. Varek, on the other hand, was short and a bit pudgy in the middle. DuBravac had learned from experience that Varek's looks were deceiving. He was actually in very good shape and had a deadly right hook.

Derek Regehr and his younger sister, Elsa, were eating sandwiches, potato wedges and drinking juice. Elsa Regehr was in her first year at the Academy and had not declared a major although she seemed to enjoy working on weapons systems and computers. The Regehr family had arrived to Clovis City several years ago and began a business in manufacturing. DuBravac never grew close to them but had heard there were several younger siblings that would one day apply for acceptance at Clovis Academy and become Bragg Gang members. Regehr had been known as one of the pilots that had been able to fly the new under water Raumschiff space craft, code named Orka, along the ocean floor of planet New Edinburgh. Both of the Regehr siblings were blonde with light blue eyes. Elsa's eyes were lighter than Derek's. They were both white skinned with accents different from the average family of New Edinburgh in that their parents were from Iceland of Old Earth.

Bret Bragg had convinced his two younger sisters to apply for admission to the Academy and they were easily accepted. Bret Bragg immediately drafted them into membership with his gang. Their names were Zoe and Shanna Bragg. They were identical twins and each sported long, curly dark hair and were six feet one inch tall. The girls were not as militant against the other campus gangs as Bret, but they seemed to show little fear when a fight began. Zoe normally wore metal heeled boots and knew how to use them for maximum effectiveness in a fight. Shanna preferred to use her talents in martial arts to best her opponents. Like Elsa Regehr, Zoe and Shanna Bragg had not declared a major as they were still trying to determine where their career interests might lie.

The round table closest to the bar was occupied by the Collins brothers, Sean and Liam. Sean had a new girlfriend sitting next to him that DuBravac did not recognize as a student or a local. She speculated that the woman might be a visitor, tourist or a pilot passing through on the way to another distant star system. Liam was in a discussion with a female orange furred Kotek sitting to his right. Her pointy ears were up and her green cat's eyes wide open as she listened to the Collins lad. She had a bowl of milk before her and plate of grilled chicken strips. A few of the O'Malley family members were at the table as well, drinking and telling stories.

Cadet senior Jen Staszko entered the upper level floor of the bar and smiled at her friends at the Gorski tables. She had heard the news of the convictions at the female student dormitory. Staszko, who had been one of the cadets targeted for death by the individuals indicted, was certainly in the mood to celebrate the event. As normal, she was wearing a multi colored long skirt, a white top with several colors of thread woven in to the neckline and the end of the short sleeves. She had on a matching set of amethyst earrings and necklace. She was wearing green boots that made a clopping sound as she walked over the tiled floor. Her long hair was held back by a Sterling silver clip that had been given to her as a gift for her bravery in the Blitzkrieg attack. The first of the Gorski Gang to run to greet Staszko was Giola Andolini. She hugged her close.

"Aunt Jen!" Giola screamed as she embraced her. "I am so happy that you came!"

Staszko hugged the girl close, "Me too. This is a wonderful day. All of our lost friends got justice today."

Giola was wearing a long white dress that covered her from neck to ankle. She had on a string of black pearls around her neck and black high heeled shoes. Her long dark hair flowed gracefully behind her as she moved. She was attractive to a fault. Staszko could see the lust in several of the military and civilian customers at O'Malley's following Andolini as she moved. The Italian cadet did not seem to notice or care that her full breasts, slender waist and firm buttocks attracted so much attention. Her smile was perfect and revealed white teeth that gave her lovely face a radiance that would cause any man to swoon before her.

Over the three years and four months that she had been at the Academy, the Andolini family had welcomed Staszko and the other Gorski Gang members in as if they were family. Staszko had developed a close relationship with the Andolini girls and each of them referred to her as Aunt Jen. Giola was born with four other siblings. Her parents answered the call of the Glorious Leader to produce more offspring so that there would be more humans to populate the conquered worlds in the outer solar systems. The Glorious Leader requested that families submit to a drug regimen that increased fertility in men and greatly increased the egg count for women. The result was that women were having more twins, triplets and even larger amounts of children. The Glorious Leader ordered that each family that was compliant and participated in the program would be paid five thousand Empire Dollars for each child produced using the special drugs.

Giola's identical twin was Venus. Her other sister was Stella and she was as lovely as the Giola and Venus. The remaining two members of the five children were twin brothers, Paolo and Lucius. For some reason, the drugs that made such large birthing groups a reality also made the children devastatingly attractive and blessed with incredible athletic abilities. Paolo and Lucius Andolini were handsome beyond description. Both of them followed the footsteps of their older brothers and were stars in the Clovis City futbol, also known as soccer, team called the Rattlesnakes.

Paolo and Lucius had many women that followed them everywhere they went. Staszko noted that Paolo and Lucius both had about a dozen girls standing around them, each competing to get the attention of the young cadets. Giola, Venus and Stella were beautiful and each had taken modeling jobs to earn extra money as they studied at the Academy. They had appeared on many posters wearing slinky bikinis and other revealing outfits.

Venus had landed a temporary gig as a spokes model for a blue jeans corporation. Giola and Stella were constantly appearing in public in bikinis to promote summer time swim wear. The lovely Andolini girls were constantly approached by men that would try and bed them. All three of the girls had fantastic bodies with measurements that attracted attention to them even in conservative clothing and virtually no fat on them. Giola was a star competitor on the Academy swim team. Venus was one of the best students on the archery team and loved playing poker. Stella was planning on attending the elite Spetsnaz training during the summer break, citing Uncles Yuri and Dray as her role models.

The Andolini family was not alone in volunteering for the fertility drugs. Prominent families on New Edinburgh such as the Harvard's, Li's, Day's, Bragg's, Starr's, Calderon's. Glenn's, Cobb's, Goldsmith's and Evart's were regular participants in the program. The Andolini's had produced fifteen children in all.

Some of the other families produced far more offspring than that.

Staszko walked arm in arm with Giola toward the Gorski Gang tables. The other Andolini's rushed Aunt Jen and hugged her close. Many of the groupie women that were lusting after Paolo and Lucius gave Staszko dirty looks when they observed that Paolo paid her so much attention. Clearly the groupies did not like competition from other women. Staszko smiled pleasantly at the women that were competing for attention with Paolo and Lucius. She noticed that the twin brothers were sharing a large bowl of caramel gelato, which was their favorite dessert.

Piotr Gorski arrived with two pitchers of beer in his hands. He sat them on the table and was hugged by Lucius Andolini. Stella Andolini stood and hugged the younger Gorski and motioned for him to take the seat next to here. Staszko smiled when she saw Gorski and Stella Andolini sit down and she leaned her body into him and held his hand. Staszko had always hoped that the two would one day figure out what everyone else saw in them. Stella and Piotr were in love, but were too young to realize it. Staszko liked the match and was encouraged when she observed them holding hands.

Ye Yibing was one of the newest additions to the gang. She primarily spoke Mandarin Chinese, but could communicate in English with some difficulty. She would constantly ask others to speak slowly to her so that she could follow what was being said to her. Yibing had been born and raised on a freighter ship that was owned by her parents. Most of her life was spent helping her family transport goods from one planet to another for a fee. She wanted more for her own life so she applied to the Academy and was admitted. Her parents were not happy as they had hoped she would take over the family business one day. Due to her experiences with her family, Yibing was already a skilled pilot and an excellent computer programmer. She could write computer code and even mastered the art of hacking into secured networks. She was over six feet tall, slender, with long dark hair.

Yibing had been the object of lust of a military Lieutenant named Dante Friedmann. He was working on Space Station Cy-7 when he first noticed Yibing. Since their first encounter, Friedmann had been sending her flowers, gifts and using the universal network system to send her encrypted e-mails begging for a date. His unyielding pursuit was to the point of pathetic. Yibing constantly rebuffed his advances and yet he kept after her. On his days off, Friedmann would catch the first available transport from the space station to Clovis City so that he could find her in person.

Staszko was not surprised to see Friedmann there, at the table next to Yibing, attempting to charm her. Yibing gave Staszko a weak smile as their eyes met. One of the jokes among the gang was that Yibing would have to request that Sean Collins to file a restraining order against Friedman to get him to leave her alone. The man certainly could not take no for an answer.

Staszko sat down next to DuBravac and Harumi Shigeta and gladly accepted a beer from them. DuBravac brought Staszko up to date on the judgments from the trial and the three women began to discuss their mutual elation in that so many of the defendants received the death sentence. All three of the women had suffered emotionally from the Blood Moon Incident. Although they cared for each of the ten cadets from Clovis Academy that had been targets of the Rosenburg killers, they each had a special person that fought for survival.

"I think that the news of the convictions demand an O'Malley's toast," Staszko said to her two friends. "Les and Eamon used to give toasts all the time, remember?"

"A set of cheers would be suitable," Shigeta agreed.

DuBravac stood up, climbed onto the table top and began stomping her feet on the table. "May I have your attention? Quiet! Attention!"

The bar patrons began to hush as she was demanding. It had been a long standing O'Malley's tradition that toasts were appropriate, even encouraged and all of the patrons were expected to participate.

"I have some toasts to make!" DuBravac said as she walked in circles on the table top and looking into all of the faces of her fellow cadets. "Everyone take your drinks in your hand!"

Everyone in the bar complied by standing up and holding their drinks high.

"To Sean Collins!" DuBravac yelled as loud as she could.

The entire bar repeated her toast and everyone drank, even the Bragg Gang members joined in. DuBravac was happy to see that Shigeta, Staszko and Klaus had joined her on top of the table.

"To Pierre Zerbe!" Klaus yelled. The entire gathering in the bar repeated the toast and drank in honor of their deceased friend.

"To Tina Martinson!" Staszko yelled out. The bar patrons continued the repeating of the toast and drinking.

To the surprise of the Gorski group, Bret Bragg climbed up on his table and held a beer stein up high. "To Roy Starr!"

Everyone toasted to the memory of the dead cadet.

Shigeta shrugged and yelled out, "To William Bragg!"

The bar drank. Bret Bragg bowed in the direction of Shigeta in a way to thank her for honoring his brother.

"To Porfirio Cardenas!" Doernitz yelled out from the stairwell entrance. He did not have a drink in his hand. He had just arrived as the toasts began. Standing next to him was his wife, Lila.

A cadet pilot named Trey Glenn ran over to the couple and gave Doernitz and his wife drinks. The couple gratefully accepted the gift and drank the cold beer in honor of the fallen. Glenn had watched the entire Blood Moon event and had become a fan of Jurgen Doernitz based on his heroics.

The evening progressed with toasts to each and every cadet victim and the other eight Blood Moon Tournament Team survivors. And, for the first time in about four years, the Bragg Gang and Gorski Gang actually interacted amiably. The most grateful group in the bar was the O'Malley family since they didn't have to replace any broken tables or chairs.

In his office, retired Admiral Seward could hear his staff shouting with joy over the jury verdict and the sentences imposed. Seward was sitting in his chair, drinking his coffee. He, among all of the professors at Clovis Academy had reason to join in on the festivities. Seward had lost four students in his cadet pilot program over the previous year due to the Rosenburg co-conspirators. Seward sipped his cup of coffee and smiled.

"A new day is dawning," Seward said to himself. He felt in his heart that perhaps this year would go without incident. He hoped that the cadets and the Empire would have a well-deserved year of peace.

"Here is to a year of smooth sailing," Seward said to himself and drank from his coffee cup that had the logo of the orange and blue United Nations flag adorned on it.

Little did he know, his wishes for a peaceful year would go unanswered. Events were already in motion that would ensure the entire Earth Empire would be engulfed in the greatest crisis it had ever faced.

Seward stood and looked out of his office windows that overlooked the cadet parade ground, the cadet space ship hangars and in the far distance was the cadet graveyard. The events of the past year had caused several new head stones to be planted there.

Seward reflected on the cadet pilots lost in the previous year. Amir al-Nasser, Roy Starr, Tina Martinson, Pierre Zerbe and Porfirio Cardenas. Good kids with potential and amazing leadership qualities. Seward mourned them all. Each death had been unnecessary. He shook his head and turned back to his desk to begin drafting his lecture for the next morning class.

CHAPTER EIGHT

After the inner circle of the Glorious Leader had received a report from the Battle Cruiser Colorado regarding a mass assassination of all members of the Royal Family on that ship, a secret meeting was convened. Captain Carol Ruiz was not the only one that was concerned by the disturbing murders. Vladimir Sikorsky, the Secretary General of the United Nations of Earth, the Glorious Leader of the entire Earth Empire for the past two hundred years, was worried. Sikorsky had seen attempted insurrections against his rule before. Each of the small rebellions was easy to quash. Sikorsky had loyal family to kill and silence the dissenters. They had many professional assassins to do their dirty work for them.

But this time, it seemed different. Sikorsky had never seen his descendants targeted for assassination. Someone, or several individuals, were systematically killing his children and grandchildren. The murderers were even decapitating Sikorsky's issue further down the family tree and he was naturally concerned for himself.

But he was more livid in that any person would be so bold and insolent to target his family. Sikorsky summoned many of his family members and most trusted advisors to his Royal Palace. Admiral of the Fleet William Sikorsky was brought in to offer any tactical advice that might be helpful in the situation they found themselves in. His half-brother, Admiral of Scientific Exploration Wallace Welker, was also summoned to attend for his vast knowledge of the sciences and the sociological make up of all of the colonies on the conquered planets in the Eight Solar Systems.

John Rosenburg, the Chairman of the Rosenburg Corporation, attended the secret meeting. Rosenburg had promised the citizens of planet New Edinburgh that he would not be like his deceased brother. Rosenburg had lied. He was far more ruthless than his little brother had ever dreamed of being. Rosenburg had worked with Professor O'Connell for several years, assisting in developing many new deadly weapons for the Sikorsky family. Rosenburg's finest creations had never been revealed to humanity. He had put together plans to build the best Fleet of war ships that ever existed. Rosenburg had succeeded in his plans. The deadly fleet was finished, each of the space craft fit for travel and for combat. For a man in his early nineties, John Rosenburg looked as if he had just turned twenty. His body was indeed just twenty years old. But the brain inside the body had all of his memories, education and experience downloaded so that he was in the best condition of his life. His old body had been discarded long ago.

Pravda Sikorsky, a great grandchild of the Glorious Leader was there holding a crystal wine glass full of an expensive Merlot that she was sipping on. She had grown to be one of the best covert operatives for the family. She was beautiful, toned and always prepared to follow the bidding of her leader. She kept her youth by doing as Vladimir Sikorsky had done, harvest other young humans for their body parts and use them for herself.

Pravda Sikorsky had killed for her family many times. She was also a student of tactics and held a doctorate in psychiatry. Vladimir Sikorsky valued her advice and often included her in clandestine gatherings such as this. Pravda Sikorsky had been given the code name "Princess of Death" due to the many successful assassinations she had carried out for her family.

Ulla Ragnarsson was also invited to attend the meeting. She was one of the daughters of the assassin Dell Ragnarsson. The Ragnarsson woman was a trained killer, just as her siblings had been. She possessed no empathy or sympathy for her victims or any person that happened to be collateral damage in one of her hits. She had been married once to a wealthy computer programmer that she killed to inherit his fortune. Since her father had been missing after the incident on the Moon of Semiramis and many of her family were either dead or incarcerated, she had become the de facto leader of the Ragnarsson assassins group. Ulla was every bit as lovely and deadly as her sister Ella. Ulla and Ella had different mothers, both of whom had been absolutely lovely.

Ulla and Ella had grown up together and were quite close until their father killed all of the mothers of his children and separated many of the siblings so that they could be trained to be killers for hire. Ulla and Ella had worked together on several missions and enjoyed their collaboration. Ulla was very disappointed when she learned that her sister Ella had been the one that had betrayed the family. Had she done the right thing and taken her cyanide pill, then the trial and the subsequent convictions of all the defendants in Clovis City would never have happened. Ulla had vowed that she would never allow herself to be taken captive by the pigs in law enforcement. She would die before she allowed herself to suffer that fate.

Vladimir Sikorsky regarded the five trusted individuals for a few moments. He sighed and slapped the palms of his hands on his legs. They had much to accomplish if they hoped to maintain their power in the Eight Solar Systems.

"Thank you for being here," the Glorious Leader began. "I fear that we are being attacked by individuals that have insider knowledge of our family. The fact that four Science Cruisers were boarded and only Royal Family members killed leads me to conclude that we are being specifically targeted. We must find the persons behind this plot and eliminate them."

"Has the crew of the Colorado determined how these assassins gained access to the ship?" John Rosenburg asked as he poured himself a drink of bourbon into a crystal tall glass from one of Sikorsky's crystal decanters.

"No, John." Sikorsky shook his head when Rosenburg motioned to the decanter as an offer to pour him a drink as well.

"They are working on it, but I imagine these assailants covered their tracks quite well. They have scanned for DNA, fingerprints and the security logs to try and identify them. But as of this moment, we have no suspects."

Rosenburg sat down on one of the plush leather couches and smiled, "It would seem we are facing someone that is quite intelligent."

"I have teams prepared to investigate and track whoever is behind the murders," Pravda Sikorsky said softly. Her speech pattern was always calm, no matter what the stress level of the situation might be. "Give me the word, and I will find these conspirators and kill them all."

Vladimir Sikorsky smiled at her willingness to take lives for his benefit. "Thank you, Pravda. Naturally, I authorize for you to take any and all action necessary to bring me the corpses of these monsters that would attack my offspring. The rest of you need to help me end the rebellions on Earth. If Earth were to declare and win freedom from us, from my domain, then other planets would likely gain the boldness to follow."

"Father, we have been working on a plan that I think would work out to our advantage," Wallace Welker said. "We believe that since our laws against owning weapons have worked to keep weapons out of the hands of all citizens, humanity cannot beat our military. That is, unless, those that manufacture the weapons for us turn on us. William and I agree that we need to ensure that the Brackenridge, Allen, Fenster and Breckenridge families stay loyal to us. Since our laws against civilians possessing or owning weapons have been enforced for over one hundred years, the common man and woman are at our mercy. The average will not be able to rise up against us, which was our goal when we eliminated private weapon ownership. But the powerful and wealthy families can afford to ignore the weapons bans."

"And how do you propose to ensure that those families do not turn on us?" John Rosenburg interrupted after he swallowed some bourbon.

He was aware of how successful the weapon ban had been in preserving the two hundred year rule of Vladimir Sikorsky. They had taken the example of the communists, the Nazis and other anti-liberty despots and tyrants in Earth's history on how to control the masses. They had controlled the weapons, manipulated the news media and silenced the dissenters with certain death. Vladimir Sikorsky copied those tactics to preserve his own rule.

"Rich people love money," Welker continued. "But they love their children more. Their legacy is not so much their business interests. It is their descendants to carry on their name. So, William and I propose we use their young children, grandchildren and further down their family tree, to keep those families from supporting any rebellion."

"Keep talking," Vladimir Sikorsky encouraged his son.

"Ulla here devised a plan to kidnap several of the younger children of all four families." Welker motioned to Ragnarsson, "I think it is a good plan."

Ulla Ragnarsson nodded in agreement, "The Admiral is correct. I have teams ready to, shall we say, acquire, about two to three of the most favored children of the four families. We bring them here, to the vicinity of Sikorsky's Planet and blackmail their families to stay on our side. We hide the hostages on one of our Battle Cruisers so any private investigators hired by those wealthy families will never find their children. To keep their children alive, they will have no choice but to help us crush any rebellion."

"Do it," Vladimir Sikorsky ordered after considering the proposal for all of five seconds. "Now, John, how is my Ragnarok Fleet? Is it ready to go to war?"

"Yes, Glorious Leader." John Rosenburg assured him. The Ragnarok Fleet was the code name given to the secret set of war ships Rosenburg had designed with Professor O'Connell. The construction of the fleet had taken less than a decade to complete.

The entire compliment of the Ragnarok Fleet was hidden behind the dark side of the largest moon orbiting planet Semiramis.

"I need many of our family members with battle experience to be freed up to command the ships. We designed and constructed mechanical humans and Replicants to staff the ships with. But they are not leaders so we need some of our Captain's and Admiral's to be transferred to follow your directives. Professor O'Connell and I have installed the best weapons systems ever created by man or woman. No Battle Cruiser will be able to stand against the might and power of the new fleet. Any that try will perish. We also designed and built thousands of drone fighter ships and they are on the Ragnarok fleet ships. The specialized weaponry that Andrew and I created are all still in the testing stages. We are not ready to deploy them as of yet. We need time to test those weapons."

"Thank you," Vladimir Sikorsky smiled and looked to his son, William. "Warn all of our family that they are being targeted. Also let the family members that are currently assigned to Battle Cruisers or Space Stations know that they need to be prepared to use force to keep any rebellion from growing. Tell them that any act by the non-Royal Family members that indicate a lack of loyalty must be dealt with."

"It shall be done father," William Sikorsky promised.

"That brings us to the incorruptible leaders on my home planet," Rosenburg raised his left index finger in the air. "My nieces and nephews are being oppressed by the prosecutors for the Security Council. As we speak many of my family are languishing in prison due to the power grab by a few on New Edinburgh. We need to free them and make examples of those on that planet that would refuse to honor the Royal Family."

"I agree," Vladimir Sikorsky nodded. "I have followed the news there and on planet New Berlin. The local Assembly members on each planet have gone too far. Examples must be made."

"With that in mind, should I prepare a hit list for Princess Death here to begin working on?" Rosenburg walked over to the bar to pour himself another few shots of bourbon. "The prosecutors and their families must all die. The military leaders in Clovis City and their children need to be publically executed."

"Yes, prepare your hit list for Pravda and Ulla here. Also, I want one of the Ragnarok ships to be sent to planet New Berlin to crush the growing rebellious leaders there. The people have been unruly and disloyal on that planet for the last few months. Send in one ship so that the citizens of the other planets can witness the technology and weaponry of our new space craft."

"Yes father," William Sikorsky nodded.

"I know just the ship to send," John Rosenburg sipped the smooth bourbon. "We will send in the Alcibiades to New Berlin and the people that stood against us will shiver with fear as they watch their co-conspirators die."

"And I want to send in my personal Battle Cruiser to New Edinburgh," the Glorious Leader ordered. "The lawyer there, Collins, and all of his staff have committed treason and must die. I also want the military leaders in Clovis City replaced. Dead or alive, I do not care. But replace them. If we lose New Edinburgh it will only encourage those that are leaning toward regime change. We must crush them all as an example to the other billions of people out there."

"Yes father," William Sikorsky responded. "We will dispatch the ships as per your direction immediately and ensure that New Berlin and New Edinburgh will not be lost."

Vladimir Sikorsky clapped his hands together. Things worked so much better when all of his orders were followed without question. "Bravo. Bravo. Bring in the prisoner!"

The others watched in silence as a young nineteen year old woman was dragged into the chamber by eight wives of the Glorious Leader. The girl was nude and had a hole that had been drilled into the back of her skull with a special instrument created by some of the torturers in the palace. John Rosenburg turned his head away, knowing what was about to happen. He had seen it before. The Glorious Leader had his surgeons used a special instrument to drill a hole in the back of a person's skull, just wide enough for Sikorsky to thrust his erection inside. The drill also secreted an acid substance that weakened the membranes that surrounded the brain, which enabled an easy penetration for the Glorious Leader.

The others watched as Sikorsky removed his clothes and approached the woman from her backside. His wives held her arms and legs as she begged for mercy. Sikorsky grabbed her long dark hair and maneuvered his erect penis into the opening in her skull. He pushed his erection into her brain and she let out a blood curdling scream as he pulled his penis out and then pushed it back in, over and over again until he ejaculated into her skull. By the time he climaxed, the woman was already dead, her brain scrambled by his twisted sex act.

Sikorsky let the corpse fall to the floor and smiled as one of his wives knelt down before him. She began to lick the blood and brain matter off of his erection, swallowing it as she worked. She did her best to avoid gagging or coughing on the sick taste of the brains and blood. The last woman that gagged while cleaning off Sikorsky's penis was executed for not being sensitive to the needs of the Glorious Leader.

"That's it, clean it off. Clean it all off," Sikorsky whispered.

John Rosenburg walked out of the large chamber and out into the hallway of white and black granite floors and walls. He had seen the horror show before in which the Glorious Leader would "screw the brains out" of some innocent victim. He wanted to rid the Royal Family of the clearly psychotic Glorious Leader and have another member of their family take over as leader. The ultimate dilemma would be which one would be stable enough emotionally and mentally to rule. The choices were few. John Rosenburg departed the hallway and found himself in the lobby of the ninetieth floor. He kept walking and did not look back.

When he arrived at the gold and silver escalators, his personal pilot was waiting for him. She was leaning against one of the pink granite walls at the west end of the lobby, watching a three dimensional news report on the elimination of all life on the moon called Chronos. She was dressed in an olive green flight suit with black boots. Her long dark hair was bound up in a twist tie and pulled over to her left side. All around the lobby were Akarzdamedians that undoubtedly had mind control microchips in their heads, numerous Royal Family members dressed in either military uniforms or some of the finest civilian linens. There were ten three dimensional news broadcasts on so that the passersby could view the current events of all of the eight solar systems.

She smiled when she noticed that John Rosenburg was approaching her. "Well, was William still the yes man in the group?"

John Rosenburg took her left arm into his hand and whispered into her ear, "Mary, you should really learn to hide your contempt better. You are surrounded by my family members here and everything said in these lobbies are recorded by the MI. The answer to your question is yes, William is still kissing his father's ass every chance he gets. They are doing a great job of turning the people against us."

Mary Flynn nodded and whispered back, "Thanks for the reminder regarding the security systems. When we arrived the other night, I had dinner at a small pub at the edge of the city. I met a local Larianette trader and was able to put down some earnest money on six of those warhorses for you. We already loaded them aboard the ship and drugged them for cryo-sleep. While I was at the bar, I overheard several conversations from the patrons. Many of the local citizens are grumbling about the Blood Moon incident and how heavy-handed the Glorious Leader was to the Chronosians. I am really worried. There is talk of rebellion in several solar systems. All the people need is a leader to push them."

Rosenburg nodded and motioned for the busy escalator, "Thank you for getting those horses for me. The Larianette's are the strongest in the eight solar systems and are very useful for our work on Semiramis."

"Well they are the only horse-like creatures with six legs. The four eyes on their heads really creep me out."

"Let's get back to Semiramis. I cannot stand it here with that constant sound of chimes and the silver grass and dirt. I need for you to get ahold of your father. Do you know where he is hiding?"

"Barry? Oh, he's still on Old Earth at a hideaway because he thinks he will get arrested for what he did on the Blood Moon."

Rosenburg never allowed his children to refer to him as "John" as Barry Flynn seemed to allow his children to call him by his first name. The Flynns and the Rosenburgs had been friends and business associates for several decades. But even with a strong friendship between John Rosenburg and Barry Flynn, their ideas on parenting were vastly different. "Well, contact him and tell him that I need him to move some of my assets off of old Earth."

"Why do you need to do that?" Mary Flynn whispered.

"Because I have a feeling that the Glorious Leader will soon use one of those Red Javelins on Earth. I need my property off of the planet before that occurs."

"Consider it done, sir."

"Good. Let's get off of this planet immediately. We need to press our engineers to move up the scheduled launch of the Ragnarok Fleet. I believe that we will need all the firepower we can muster to repel whatever comes next."

CHAPTER NINE

Lieutenant Reynita Calderon had met her platoon on her first day following her transfer to Clovis City. She spoke with her platoon sergeant first and then her four squad leaders. She laid out her expectations for the platoon to them in clear and concise terms. She then ordered that her entire platoon assemble at the parade grounds that were located a kilometer south of the United Nations Building. She personally introduced herself to every man and woman under her command. She shook their hands and looked them in the eye and told them she was proud to have been chosen to lead them.

Sergeant First Class Mark Lund stood in the back of the formation watching his new platoon leader as she shook hands with each member. He found he could not take his eyes off of Reynita Calderon. She walked with confidence and poise. Her solid black uniform was perfect, not a wrinkle in sight. Her long dark hair was folded under her black beret. Her black boots were polished. Lund watched her smile at each of the platoon members as she spoke to them. She seemed to have a sincerity about her in a way that Lund had not observed in other officers he served under. It was as if she could understand and empathize with the average soldier.

When she was speaking to the third squad, she must have sensed that Lund was watching her. She glanced his direction and their eyes met. She smiled at him. Lund smiled back.

"Damn, she is hot," Lund said to himself. Lund had worked undercover for several months at the Clovis Academy as Yuri Gorski's shadow. He had met many of the students and even slept with one of the widows of a cadet that had died in the Forbidden Region. But Lund never recalled seeing Reynita around. He was certain he would have remembered her.

After the formation was excused, Reynita hoped to go to the local prison. Her squad leaders and platoon sergeant stayed behind to see if their new platoon leader needed any extra assistance.

Since that first meeting, her platoon had been asked to provide extra security at the trial of the century. Her unit provided that service and even assisted on securing the convicted prisoners at the holding cells until the transport ship arrived to take them to the United Nations Space Command ship Virginia. The Virginia would take the condemned to the prison planet Cootron for execution. Only Ella, Ivar and Ellis Ragnarsson escaped the death penalty for the time being. Ellis was still in danger of execution if his appeal did not reverse the sentence. The three Ragnarsson's were placed in holding cells by Reynita and her MI soldiers.

Reynita spent most of her spare time with her sisters Lupita, Jorge and her parents. When she was not with her sisters Reynita carried out her order and spent her time investigating the location of the family of Matthew Rosenburg. She spent hours at the massive sky scraper UN Command Headquarters researching confidential documents. She did not find Matthew Rosenburg's wives listed in those files, but she did locate some of his siblings. They were being held in cells at the Clovis City Prison-South.

Reynita transferred the information of each sibling to her holo-com device. She decided to pay them a visit.

She had not found her own housing as she elected to move in with her parents. With the savings from her salary, she purchased a used model Allen Corporation Mach Nine two wheel motorcycle from an auction computer store. She rode her motorcycle to the distant prison so that she could interview the Rosenburg prisoners for clues as to Matthew's family. She had on her solid black Class C uniform and left all of her offensive weapons behind at her office.

The prison covered approximately one square mile. It was surrounded by a brick wall that was forty feet high. There was only one entrance to the facility which was a metal door that slid open when ordered by the security guards in one of the twelve ninety foot high towers that were around the walls. Each tower had two Marines on duty at all times armed with laser rifles and a rapid fire laser gun mounted to the top of the tower and facing the interior of the prison.

The actual prison had seven levels that were underground and twenty-five levels above ground. The lower levels contained the prisoners and the cafeteria. The first floor was the administration room. The second floor held the cafeteria for the jail employees and some meeting rooms. The third floor had the sleeping quarters for the Marines and guards. The fourth floor was used for meetings, parole hearings, counseling sessions and some of the educational classes. The fifth floor was for security. Reynita had never been able to learn what the top twenty floors were used for. The subject was labeled as Top Secret in all of her computer searches.

There was a parking area outside the wall. She parked her motorcycle next to some small space craft and other transportation vehicles. She received some odd stares from the Marines in the towers. Some of them had never seen a motorcycle before. Reynita pulled off her helmet and laid it on the seat of her bike. She put on her black beret and began walking for the entrance. She was led by three female Marines into the security entrance and quickly cleared the mandatory computer background check.

She was led by one of the Marines toward the main prison building and taken inside. She was met by a civilian that had on a name tag with the jail logo inscribed in gold and his last name that read "Yueying."

"You are here to see the Rosenburg prisoners?" Yueying asked suspiciously. He had been instructed by a prosecutor named Goldsmith to not allow any visitors unless he approved them in advance. But he could not refuse the demands of an MI officer.

"Yes," Reynita noticed that the man was looking her over.

"You know we cannot vouch for your safety downstairs." Yueying was staring at her slender body. "A woman like you might get into trouble down there."

"A woman like me will kick some ass if I don't get to see the prisoners I have requested to see." Reynita glared at the man.

"No need to be confrontational," Yueying said meekly. "Security, open the doors and take this officer down to the lower levels. Good luck, Lieutenant."

Reynita followed three Marines down a long hall to an elevator. They waited for a few minutes until the doors to the elevator slid open. She noted that the floors and walls were all made of some form of concrete. Everything was grey and there were no pictures were on the walls.

She stepped into the elevator and only one of the Marines stepped in with her. The other two said nothing as the doors slid shut.

"Level U-three," the Marine said.

Reynita was surprised by how rapid the descent was. Within a few seconds, the elevator doors opened again and she was three floors underground. She observed ten by ten foot cells to the left and the right of the fifteen foot wide hallway. The cells were enclosed by unbreakable transparent metal. As Reynita followed the Marine down the hallway, she observed several prisoners staring at her from behind their transparent metal cells. Some would whistle at her, others would curse at her due to her black Military Intelligence uniform. Many of the prisoners had brands on their arms and numerous tattoos.

Many of the cells had posters of naked women or women in bikinis or risqué outfits. Reynita knew that such memorabilia was allowed so that the male and female prisoners would have sex and create children for the orphanage homes of the Glorious Leader. One of the men had posters of the three Andolini girls in bikinis. Reynita saw two men having sex in one of the prison cells as she walked past it. In another there was a male prisoner that was covered with multi-colored tattoos having sex with a female prisoner on the floor of their cell.

Reynita was led all the way to the end of the hall to a twenty foot by ten foot interview room. There was a single grey metal table in the center of the room that was bolted to the cement floor. There were only two metal chairs, one on the north side of the table and the second on the south. She sat down on the chair that was furthest from the door and then she waited.

After ten minutes the doors slid open and an attractive woman in a blue prison uniform and blue slippers was shoved inside. The doors slid shut behind her. She had the look of a scared, trapped animal. She looked suspiciously at Reynita.

"You are militzia," the woman said with her voice displaying fear. "Are you here to kill me?"

Reynita realized the woman was terrified of the Military Intelligence. She pointed to the empty chair. "Please have a seat."

The woman reluctantly sat down. Reynita speculated that the prisoner was in her early twenties. The prisoner crossed her arms and was looking around nervously.

"What does militzia want with me?"

"I am Lieutenant Reynita Calderon. MI does not want anything from you. I am here on a fact finding mission. I just want to interview you to hopefully help out one of your family members."

"All of my family is either dead or arrested."

"Not all of them," Reynita corrected her. "Can you tell me your name?"

"Juliana. Juliana Rosenburg."

"When is your trial date, Juliana?"

"My lawyer said that I face a jury trial in two months. They want to execute me."

Reynita nodded slowly, careful not to show any reaction. "I am sorry. Juliana, I need your help. And with your help I might be able to help some of your family."

Juliana began to cry. She covered her face and laid her head down on the table. "I don't want to die. I didn't know about all those things. Why are they going to kill me? Why? My father and Caine were the bad ones. We were forced to do things. If any of us dared turn on father he would have killed us. Please help me."

Reynita waited for a few moments as the woman continued to cry on the table. Her voice was desperate and full of fear. "Juliana, I cannot promise you that I can make a difference in your case. But if you help me, I will personally speak to Sean Collins about you. I will ask him to show you mercy."

Juliana looked up at Reynita with tears till flowing down her cheeks. "Do you know that a jail guard rapes me about once a week here? I told the warden, Mister Yueying, and he laughed in my face. This place is not safe."

"I am sorry that has been happening to you. Juliana, if you help me I will try and help you. Deal?"

Juliana stood up and wiped the tears from her cheeks. "My father used to have sex with my sister, Carla. All the time. I always thought it was sick. I avoided my father on purpose because I knew he wanted me, too. I always thought that one day I would meet a handsome man that would take me away from the Rosenburg Ranch. My hero never arrived. I thought he did once. He was so handsome. He was an officer, like you. He wore his uniform with such pride and dignity. I asked myself how I could get this man to take me away. I never saw him again."

Reynita watched as the distraught woman walked in circles around the room. Juliana finally stopped walking and sat back down in the chair. She leaned across the table.

"If I answer your questions, will you get a message out to him?"

"Of course I will," Reynita promised. "Who is he and what would you like me to tell him?"

Juliana stared off at the wall, "He was a Captain. His name was Tierney. Tell him that I wish I had been born into a different family. Tell him I wish I could have helped him. Tell him that I would have really liked to have gotten to know him better. Could you tell him that I really did like him? I wasn't just acting when I met him. I really, really did like him."

Reynita nodded to each of her requests, "Juliana, I happen to work with Captain Tierney. I can tell you that you read him correctly. He is a good and honorable man. I will tell him everything that you asked of me."

The Rosenburg woman nodded and smiled, "Thank you. I have one other request."

"What is it?"

"Keep our conversation private? My sisters Carla and Victoria are here in this prison. They will kill me if they find out I talked to anyone. So would my brothers Thomas and Peter. The one I fear most is Peter. He used to deal in the drug trade. He has killed before to advance his growing drug import and export business. He killed his own fiancé so I know he would not think twice about eliminating me. Carla, Victoria, Thomas and Peter are completely loyal to the family. If Rebecca is here, she is the worst offender. Tell her nothing. If she even thinks that you are her enemy, she will kill everyone close to you."

"Done. Our conversation will be just between us. I will never reveal where I obtained my information."

"Ask your questions."
"You have a brother, Matthew?"

"Yes."

"How many wives did he have?"

"Seven."

"Children?"

Juliana paused and was counting in her head. "They had twenty-four that I was aware of. They were all sweet kids. I used to babysit some of them. Smart, too."

"Do you know where his wives and children are?"

Juliana frowned at the question, "You should know that already. Most of the children were shipped off to the Clovis City orphanage. His oldest son was killed here, in this prison. It happened just last month. These caged animals in here beat him to death. The guards stood back and just laughed. I pleaded with them. We pleaded with them to save him. The guards just shoved us aside and kept laughing."

Juliana nervously wiped more tears from her face as she recalled watching the son of Matthew Rosenburg suffer such a horrible death. "His two oldest daughters are here. But they have been raped by the guards, just as I have been. All of the other kids were under the age of seventeen at the time of the arrests and sent to the orphan homes."

Reynita was silent for a moment. The fact that the oldest son had been murdered as the jailers cheered it on would not go over well with Matthew Rosenburg.

"What about his seven wives? Where are they?"

"They were shipped out to go to Cootron. They should be on the Virginia."

"All seven?"

"All seven," Juliana stared at Reynita in disbelief. "You militzia don't talk? You should know all these things. They were taken by men and women in black uniforms, just like yours. You really don't know this information?"

"You saw them? The people that took the wives?"

"Yes, I saw it."

"Did you see any name tags on the soldiers? Were there any patches on the sleeves of the uniforms?"

Juliana closed her eyes in thought. "I don't remember any patches. They had black uniforms. One of the men was the one that everyone thought was dead. The one that my brother Caine thought he had killed."

"Who are you referring to?" Reynita felt her heart sinking into her stomach.

"Drayton Love-Easter. He was with the ranking officer from the militzia that came and took Matthew's wives away."

Reynita felt her blood go cold. Love-Easter had been stationed on one of the moons orbiting planet New Berlin. He had not been on New Edinburgh for months.

"You are certain it was Love-Easter?"

"Yes, I am a news junkie. I followed the case closely, mainly because I learned at the Ranch that Caine was behind it. I remember his face well. It was him."

"When Colonel Gorski rounded up your family members, did he get them all? I mean, did he get the ones that had committed crimes?"

Juliana sighed and leaned forward on the table. She put her mouth close to Calderon's left ear and whispered into it.

"When you say family members, you forget that I have over one million cousins out there in this universe. We are related to the Glorious Leader. My grand-father was his son. My uncle John is someone you should be very afraid of. He is a genius and uses his intelligence to build things. Horrible things.

Never trust anyone with the last names of Murdock or Sowa. They are like my family; they will cut your throat without a second thought. The Rendon's are also evil. Watch your back, Lieutenant. The family will not take what Gorski and Collins did to us lightly. They will retaliate. Soon. You can bet on it."

"What would they do?"

Juliana looked at the ceiling and took in a deep breath.

"Remember the city in Poland that was reduced to nuclear waste? The Royal Family did that. They will send in elite forces and crack down on the leadership of this planet, Reynita Calderon. They will come I promise you and when they do, all those that assisted Colonel Gorski or the lawyer Collins will be hunted down and be raped or tortured and then murdered. They will make examples out of all of them."

"Why are you telling me this?"

She shrugged, "Because I like you. I don't want to see you be gang raped and killed. You need to decide what side you will chose. Because the day is coming when you won't have a choice."

Reynita nodded and decided she would warn the Colonel and Collins about the veiled threat given to her. She asked a few more questions of Juliana and then had her escorted back to her cell. She was taken back to the elevator and to the first floor security office. As she was greeted by the security officers she demanded to speak to Yueying before she left. One of the enlisted marines dutifully summoned the man back to the office. Reynita sat down in one of the metal chairs and waited patiently for Yueying to arrive.

The warden finally showed up after a fifteen minute wait.

"Lieutenant, they said you had an urgent message to deliver to me?" Yueying said as he walked into the security office.

Reynita stood up and slowly walked toward the man, grabbed him by the throat with her right hand and his crotch with her left and threw him to the ground. Yueying cried out in surprise. He landed hard on the floor and cried out in pain as she squeezed his testicles tight in her hand. Two female Marines made a move to draw their laser pistols.

"Holster those weapons, ladies!" Reynita ordered as she drove her knee into Yueying's groin. Yueying continued screaming in pain.

The two female marines were torn between following a direct order of an officer from MI and protecting their Warden.

"Mister Yueying!" Reynita snarled as she glared at him. "During my little investigation, I learned that your men are raping the female prisoners here. I also heard that they turn their backs and let other prisoner's rape and kill each other. If I come here again it will be because I learned that the rapes here are continuing. I will castrate you before I cut your heart out. You feeling me? No more rapes! Say it!"

"Okay, no more." Yueying cried out. "I will make sure of it. I swear it!"

She released the man and stood up and faced the female marines before her. "You know who I am and where to find me. If any of the other women prisoners are assaulted, then you contact me right away. That is an order."

"Yes ma'am," one of them said loudly.

Reynita glared at Yueying. "Warden, there are two female prisoners here that need to be released to the custody of General Tan. Do you have a problem with that?"

"No problem," Yueying said with a terrified sound in his voice. The mention of General Tan's name seemed to inflict fear in all circles of life on planet New Edinburgh.

"Good. Have them ready by tomorrow morning at six a.m. I wrote their names down on the legal pad on the desk over there." She walked toward the exit, paused and looked over her shoulder at Yueying. "And you better hope I don't have to come back here."

The two marines helped Yueying to his feet as Reynita walked quickly to the wall surrounding the jail. She pulled out her holo-com and requested a direct communication with General Tan. She found that the current state of the correctional community was in need of reform. The information that Drayton Love-Easter was back on New Edinburgh was news to her. He would have brought Calderon's old rival, Yesenia Guevara, with him. The entirety of the Gorski Gang would have been celebrating their return. Something was amiss.

Reynita stood next to her motorcycle and waited for Tan to respond. She finally received a beeping noise and then Tan's three dimensional and life sized view appeared before her. Tan was wearing a red silk bathrobe and her hair was wet.

"What you want?" Tan demanded. Her tone of voice indicated that she was irritated by the interruption of her daily lesbian orgy.

"I have news regarding the wives and children of Matthew Rosenburg," Reynita said quickly so that Tan could return to whatever it was that she had been doing before she contacted her. "The wives were transferred to the former Battle Cruiser Virginia for transport to Cootron. Two of Mister Rosenburg's daughters are incarcerated here in Clovis City at the main prison-south. I have arranged for the two to be released to you at six a.m. Rosenburg's oldest son was beaten to death in the same prison. The rest of his children were dumped into some orphan homes for adoption."

Tan listened intently to the information from her Lieutenant. A young looking blonde female with large breasts appeared on the holographic screen and began nibbling on Tan's neck. "Good work. I send ship tomorrow for the girls. You go back to work at the office. I want you find those other children. Yes?"

"Yes, General." Reynita answered as Tan's image faded away. She closed off her holo-com and placed her helmet back on. She got on to her motorcycle as pulled out her plastic swipe card to start the engine. She needed a drink.

General Leta Tan had been in the middle of an orgy in one of her large hot tubs when Reynita called her. There were over thirty naked women that were in the hot tub waiting for Tan to return. Tan's first instinct was to return to the tub and enjoy the company of the other women.

She had set up a makeshift laboratory in one of the lower level underground floors and had the fifty green skinned duplicates of Dell Ragnarsson transferred there. She set up Matthew Rosenburg in a suite next to the laboratory and gave him a staff of armed guards, computer technicians, geneticists, bio-chemists, surgeons and nurses to work on the dilemma of the malfunctions in the duplicates.

In addition, she had allowed Rosenburg to return to his home at the Rosenburg Ranch Territory to retrieve some of his medical machinery and equipment. Tan sent a squad of her best MI soldiers along as escorts to ensure that he did not escape. After they returned, Rosenburg had his laboratory in Tan's Palace set up and functioning within twenty-four hours of non-stop work. He had made another request to return to the Rosenburg Ranch Territory which Tan intended to grant if she observed some progress by the prisoner.

Tan excused herself for a moment, wrapped a light grey bathrobe around her nude body and took seven of her MI soldiers as escorts to the lower level. The news Calderon had reported was a mixture of good and devastating. It should be given to Rosenburg in person.

Jen Staszko and Sophia DuBravac arrived at O'Malley's after their sniper proficiency class had ended. Staszko was in her normal gypsy style dress and DuBravac was still in her cadet uniform. They met Harumi Shigeta who had arrived earlier and saved them a table. None of the other Gorski Gang were there. The three ladies enjoyed a few crème Brule martinis with a steak dinner, salad and green beans. As they finished their meal they noticed that several members of the Bragg Gang entered the bar and began to take over a set of tables next to them.

"And here we thought we would have a nice and quiet girl's night out," Staszko said to her two friends.

DuBravac grimaced when she saw Bret Bragg, James Cobb and Juanito Calderon approach a table of new cadets. She had seen that horror story before. The Bragg Gang were infamous for committing acts of hazing against other cadets, especially member of the freshmen class. She shook her head at Staszko and Shigeta.

"How many times do we have to kick their ass?" DuBravac asked the others as if she were bored.

"About every other week," Staszko sighed. "I thought that we had all decided to be friends. Let's see, there's Bragg, Cobb, five Calderon brothers and Gauthier. Eight against the three of us. Hardly seems fair."

Shigeta took a sip from her martini, "Let's wait and see what they do. Maybe they will be calm."

Staszko laughed, "What did they put in your martini, Harumi?"

Cobb grabbed a young lad at the table by his arm and flung him to the floor. He was wearing a cadet pilot uniform with the rank of Airman on his collar. The other cadets at the table were too afraid to move and help the cadet that had been singled out. The young cadet was trying to get back on his feet when Bragg pushed him back down by using his foot on his back.

"You need to learn when to stay down, punk," Bragg told the cadet.

The cadet was begging Bragg to leave him alone.

Pepito Calderon pulled out a plastic bag full of poggie dung from his pocket and handed it to Cobb. Cobb then opened the bag up and knelt down to the cadet.

"What's your name?"

The cadet was crying now since he did not understand why anyone would pick on him in such a manner.

"My name is Trey."

"Trey what?" Cobb demanded as he squeezed the cadet's shoulder.

"Trey Glenn. Please, can I go back to my friends?"

Manuel Calderon, sporting dread locks that were below his shoulder, laughed at the quivering cadet. "You can after you taste something we just cooked up."

The three Gorski Gang women raised their eyebrows at each other when they heard the name. There had been Glenn family members that had been members of the gang over the years.

"Do you think he is related to Aura Lynda and Frank Glenn?" DuBravac thought out loud.

The Glenn family consisted of numerous siblings, even more than the Andolini family, which caused DuBravac difficulty in remembering them all. The point was that two other Glenn's that had graduated, Aura Lynda and Frank, had been good friends to the Gorski's and Andolini's. Defending a Glenn was a responsibility of any and all that would join up with the Gorski Gang.

Staszko stood up and nodded,

"What are the odds? Time to kick ass."

Gauthier noticed that the three Gorski Gang women were standing up from their table.

"We don't want any trouble from you three."

"Then let the kid go," DuBravac said as she was walking toward them.

Cobb, who seemed oblivious to the threat of the three approaching women, was attempting to force the poggie dung contents of the plastic bag into Trey Glenn's face.

"Open your damn mouth and swallow it!"

Seeing that Cobb had refused to release the Glenn cadet, Shigeta began running and leaped into the air. She kicked Gauthier in the chest with her left foot. Her right leg was bent behind her back as she collided with him. The cadet pilot was knocked backwards and off his feet. Gauthier landed on his back and slid a few yards before coming to a stop. Shigeta wondered why Gauthier did not make any attempt to parry her kick. He was known to be well trained in self-defense and he had just stood there and allowed her to kick him to the floor.

Cobb heard the impact of his friend when he hit the floor. He released the terrified cadet, dropped the package of poggie dung to the floor and turned to face DuBravac. Cobb had his fists balled up and was holding them in front of his chest as DuBravac walked closer to him.

Bret Bragg was bracing himself to parry an attack from Staszko. The two were circling one another like boxers in a ring, sizing one another up for a weakness in their defense. Bragg was relieved that he was facing off against Staszko instead of DuBravac. The last time he had an altercation with DuBravac, he lost a front tooth.

"Enough!"

The loud voice echoed off the walls of the facility. The Bragg Gang members and the three Gorski women turned toward the voice and saw Lieutenant Reynita Calderon standing at the stairwell entrance. She slowly walked over toward her five brothers and began yelling at them in Spanish.

"What is she saying?" Shigeta asked.

"She is telling her brothers that they are a disgrace to the family," DuBravac was listening intently and then translated for her two friends. "She told them the next time she will arrest them."

"But, sis! You did this all the time with William and the others!" Pepito Calderon was protesting loudly.

"Just because I did it doesn't make it right," Reynita told them as she offered her right hand and helped lift cadet Trey Glenn to his feet. "Now go home and study. Mama and papa have high hopes that all of you will make the top ten percent. Do not disappoint them. Get out of here."

The five Calderon brothers shook their heads at their sister as they began to exit the bar. Gauthier, Bragg and Cobb glared at her with anger.

"You think that just because you wear a uniform you can push us around?" Bret Bragg demanded of her. "You were always with my brother doing this exact same thing. You think you are better than us now?"

Staszko helped Reynita with Glenn; each of them held one of his arms and lifted him upright. They both ignored Bragg's tirade. Reynita refused to respond to Bragg's ranting.

"Are you alright?"

"Yes thank you," Glenn responded with a soft voice.

"Go to the bathroom and clean off your face," Staszko told Glenn. "You are related to Frank and Aura Lynda aren't you?"

"They are some of my older siblings."

"Then that means you are a member of our gang," Staszko told him sternly. "Tomorrow morning you eat with us at the cafeteria. I will introduce you to Klaus and the others. I think we will make you the double for Quarter."

"What's a double?" Glenn wanted to know.

"A double is our term for the person you always hang out with. Quarter is one of our new members and he does not have a double. When you are not in class or with your family, you stay with Quarter at all times."

"Thank you," Glenn repeated to the four women as he ran for the men's restroom. He looked over his shoulder to make certain Bragg was not following him. Glenn had been informed by his siblings of the gangs on campus and recalled them telling him many stories of how they were in the Gorski faction. He decided that he would graciously accept the invitation to join up for his protection.

Cobb was livid and pointed his index finger at Calderon, "Reynita, you were one of us!"

"Go back to the dormitories and call it a night," the Lieutenant told him. "All three of you. You have class in the morning. Next time I will arrest you."

Bragg walked up to Reynita and Staszko, "You know, Reynita, my brother always said you were a great piece of ass. He never said you were a complete bitch."

Reynita did not respond and watched as the three stormed out of O'Malley's spewing threats that they would be back.

"We did have it all under control," DuBravac said after a few seconds of silence.

"I could tell that," Reynita nodded. "But your way would have left a lot of chairs and tables broken. I apologize for my brothers."

Reynita began to walk away from the three women when Staszko spoke up. "Wait, Reynita. Wait."

She stopped and faced Staszko, "What's on your mind?"

"You and I had a few fist fights in the past. You and Yesenia really had it out once that I remember. And I remember that black eye you gave Julia. You were a hell of a fighter."

Staszko held out her hand.

"Maybe, you know, we can let the past go. Maybe we could be friends."

Reynita paused for a moment and then took Staszko's offered hand and shook it. "I would like that, Jen. I would really like that."

"Then why don't you join us at our table?" Shigeta offered. "We just finished dinner, but we were drinking some of the martinis."

Reynita had been an original member of the Bragg Gang and had fought all three of the women before her on several occasions. But Staszko was correct; perhaps the past should remain in the past. She smiled at Shigeta, "I would really like that."

DuBravac put her arm around her, "Well come on then. We want to hear all about how your career is going."

"   Do you still have that death skull tattoo on your back?" Shigeta asked Reynita as the four women began to sit down.

Reynita laughed, "Yes it is just behind my left shoulder. I am surprised you remember that. I also have the scar on my lower back from the time Mary Lincoln kicked me into that bar table at the Blue Ribbon Bar."

Staszko began pouring beer into a glass for Calderon. "I remember that fight. You and Mary really went at it. Didn't you have to go to the hospital for that one?"

Reynita smiled and accepted the glass of beer. "Yes I did. Mary really flattened me that night. That was the same night that Les broke Bill's nose."

"And Yuri knocked that one guy down the stairs, what was his name?" DuBravac was thinking and snapping her fingers.

"Brock," Reynita told them while she was laughing out loud as if to some inside joke. "Carletto de Vida Brock. He graduated two years ago. Yuri kicked the shit out of him."

"Yes he did," Staszko agreed as she recalled the bar fight Calderon was referring to.

"No, I mean Yuri really did kick the shit out of him."

Reynita was still laughing and hit her palm on the table top.

"Brock shit his pants because he was so scared. You guys never knew that?"

The other three women began laughing at that.

"When we celebrated Brock's last birthday I bought him a pair of disposable diapers. After that he has barely said five words to me," Reynita recalled.

"Too bad you weren't one of us," Staszko told her.

"You would have fit in great with our group," Shigeta added. "Especially with my husband. You two were well known as the best snipers in your graduating class."

"Well, I did grow up with your husband. My father and uncle arrived on this planet with the Andolini's and Gorski's. All of my siblings and cousins were on the same ship. We were really close for a few years until the Bragg's and Lipinski's started splitting us up into groups. They got the Nour's. Starr's and Cobb's to join them and the Yutong family followed later. I can't even recall why I joined them. It was a stupid thing to do. I am really sorry about all the times I did bad things to you three," Reynita told them after she sipped from her glass. "I was a mess, letting Francois Zerbe and Bill Bragg lead me on the way they did. I am sorry that I did all those things to each of you and your friends."

"It is in the past," Staszko assured her. "Besides, I would rather have a biker girl like you fighting on my side than against me. You were the toughest of the Bragg Gang. You do know that, don't you?"

"You mean of all the girls in the Gang?"

"No," Staszko waived her index finger at her. "I mean all of them. When we got into the fights with you all, we all feared you. Even more than the guys. Hell, I beat down Angus McWilliams all by myself once. Sophia there knocked Bret Bragg and Cobb on their asses with one hit. But you? You kept coming at us. No matter what we did, you kept fighting back. And that death skull tattoo was pretty scary when we each first saw it on you. It said you meant business."

Reynita thought for a moment, "Well, I appreciate that you all think I was the toughest, but I know better. The toughest of all was Francois Zerbe. You three never saw him in action, but he used to take on Yuri, Les, Drew, Marco, Drayton and Dominic all the time. Francois was really a brawler and he could fight. One time we tangled with some rogue pilots in that bar called Two Red Jacks. Francois put one of them in the ER and two others left the planet with broken ribs."

"Pierre's older brother?" Shigeta asked.

"Yes. The one and the same."

Staszko looked into Reynita's eyes and smiled at her. "You were his lover at one time, weren't you?"

Reynita looked shocked at that, "Who told you that?"

"Your eyes did," Staszko answered. "I can tell things by the way people look, especially in their eyes. Did your relationship last long with Zerbe?"

She looked at the three women as an O'Malley girl approached. She ordered a steak and salad with a bowl of cabbage soup. The waitress departed after she confirmed the order. Reynita then nodded, "We were together just a few months. Francois was one of those men that wanted to have sex with all kinds of women. He tossed me aside pretty quickly after he hooked up with some other lady."

"But yet you stayed with the Bragg Gang after that?" Shigeta asked with a bit of disbelief in her voice. "If Dominic had done that to me I would have walked."

"Yes I did stay. But I did get rebellious with them a little." Reynita looked over to DuBravac.

"Before you were a student here, I was keeping Les warm at night."

DuBravac looked surprised, "You slept with my husband?"

"Several times. So many times that I lost count. He was a remarkable lover."

"He never told me that he had been involved with you."

"It was many months before you arrived on New Edinburgh," Reynita shrugged. "You are very lucky, Sophia. I should have held on to him. He was really good to me and I betrayed him. I regret what I did to him. I am really happy for you both that you found one another."

Sophia leaned in closer to Calderon, "So, later when it is just you and me, can you give me some advice on what to do to Les in bed that will really rock his world?"

Reynita laughed,

"I am sure you curl his toes quite well without my help. Hell, he married you. Les is a one woman man; he always was and always will be. After we broke up, he had several women throwing themselves at him. If he picked you out of all the other available options out there, then I am really sure you are doing all right in the bed. Besides, with your body, I bet he lusts for you every time he lays eyes on you."

DuBravac smiled, "Well, yes. He does. I was just wondering if there was anything special I could do to please him."

Reynita set her beer down on the table and tapped her fingers together for a moment as she thought about Sophia's question.

"Okay, he liked the fact that I had a motorcycle and he really liked it when I wore black leather biker clothes. Les loved that. So, if you want, I can go with you to the leather store on the south side of the city and help you pick out some things."

"Leather biker outfits?" Staszko cut in. "Les likes women that wear that stuff? I would never have known that about him."

"Oh, yes. Les really liked it and he liked riding on my motorcycle. If you want, Sophia, I will teach you how to ride. Maybe for his birthday you could surprise him with a bike. That would probably do more for him than anything".

"That really sounds like fun. Sure, it's a date!" DuBravac hugged Calderon.

As the evening progressed and a few more drinks were shared, Reynita mustered the courage to ask the question that was bothering her the most at that moment.

"Are Yesenia and Drayton back in Clovis City?" Staszko shook her head, "No, not that we are aware of. They were assigned to work with the military outpost on planet New Berlin. I later heard a rumor they were on some moon orbiting planet Athena but that was not confirmed. There was another rumor that he had been seen back here in Clovis City. It is almost like Dray has a bunch of people out there that look just like him. I am certain if they had left New Berlin, Yesenia would have given me the news of their transfer. I haven't heard from them in a while but I am sure they would have contacted us if they were in town."

"They certainly would have let me know," DuBravac nodded. "Dray and Les were best friends. No, they are not here. They are at their duty station on New Berlin."

"Why do you ask?" Shigeta was suspicious of the direction the conversation was going.

"I am working a case," Reynita answered. "Top secret stuff. But one of the collateral witnesses claimed that Love-Easter was here just about a week ago. I knew it had to be flawed information, but I had to follow up on it."

"Well they are most certainly not here," DuBravac laughed. "So, Reynita, I hear the men in the Marines are great lovers. Have you had any time to confirm the rumors about those men?"

The women all laughed.

Reynita Calderon was glad that she had agreed to join the three former rivals at their table. By the end of the night, she had gone from no friends to three.

CHAPTER TEN

Sean Collins had taken several well deserved days of leave from his demands as lead prosecutor for planet New Edinburgh. He ordered his legal team from the prosecutions of the Rosenburg and Ragnarsson families to take the week off. He spent his week off with his younger children and enjoyed the role of father to them. His two previous wives had died, leaving him four children by his first wife and five by his second. His two oldest were no longer on New Edinburgh. They were both off beginning their own lives as adults and making their own way. He hoped he instilled in them enough values and work ethic that they would become good citizens and live long, fruitful lives. His next two oldest were still studying at the Academy and lived at home as opposed to the Academy Dormitories.

His five youngest were ranging in age from five years to eleven years old. They were all girls. During the last few months of his trial preparation, Collins had relied on his two older sons, other Academy cadets and trained nurses to provide supervision of his younger offspring. Now that he was finished with work, Collins spent every moment with the girls that he could.

His house was a mansion in comparison with the other homes in his neighborhood. He had a two level basement and three floors from the ground level up. The first floor had no bedrooms. It was the kitchen, den, playroom and meeting room all separated by walls. The second and third floors each had twelve large bedrooms.

Now that Ginger and Siobhan had left home, two of the largest upstairs bedrooms were empty. The rest of his children occupied the majority of the upper level bedrooms. Other rooms were for guests, nurses, baby sitters and friends that were too tired or inebriated from a night of libations to safely return home. Collins had turned his lower basement floor into a wine and whiskey cellar. The upper basement level was his own private work area and required security codes for entry. He trusted no one, not even his children, with those codes. The upper level basement was made of metal alloys that would need high level explosives to crack open.

Collins had learned that Dulce Maria Reynolds Hernandez Ragnarsson had made contact with a great aunt back on old Earth via computer research. Collins had secretly and legally changed her name to Mary Sierra to protect her from potential retaliation from those that she had testified against. After he obtained the name change he had the entire legal file marked sensitive and confidential. Mary Sierra had been saddened to learn that the Rosenburg's had murdered her entire family after she and her siblings had been taken. Although she had planned on going home after the trial, she no longer had family to return to. Collins had been kind enough to offer her one of his spare rooms until she got back on her feet.

With the majority of the children attending school save five year old Bree Collins, Mary Sierra was essentially alone in the large home with Sean Collins during the majority of the day. In the evenings the children would all be home doing homework or eating at the large dinner table with their father. The children seemed to have accepted Mary Sierra into their home as they interacted with her easily. Sierra even had a seat at the kitchen table for each dinner, lunch and breakfast.

Mary Sierra waited one morning for the children to go to school and for Bree Collins to take her normal ten a.m. nap. The former assassin enjoyed her time with the Collins family as she no longer had to worry about pleasing her cruel husband or catering to his socially deviant family members. The Collins family seemed like nice people and treated her with the respect and dignity that the Ragnarsson's never did. After a quick shower, Sierra put on some jeans and a red t-shirt that displayed the Clovis City Rattlesnakes logo on the front. After a long bout of soul searching, she had many questions to ask Sean Collins and determined the best way to approach any sensitive subject matter was to bear gifts first.

Sierra walked down the winding staircase of the home to the lower level basement and retrieved a bottle of red wine. She brought the bottle up to the first floor of the home, opened the bottle and found two wine glasses. She carried the bottle in one hand and the glasses in the other to the study where Sean Collins was working.

Sierra had grown accustomed to seeing Collins in his black or dark blue business suits with red or blue neck ties and white dress shirts. But since he decided to take the week to relax, he was wearing sweats and tennis shoes as he spent time with his family.

Sierra knocked on the door, "Would you like to take a break, counselor?"

Collins was seated in front of an antique roll top desk made of cherry wood. On the desk top were a small computer type pad and a projection screen. He turned his head and saw that his house guest and former star witness had a bottle of his favorite wine in her hand.

"Yes, please have a seat." Collins smiled at her.

Sierra sat down in the black leather couch that was next to the roll top desk and poured the wine into the two glasses. She handed one glass to the outstretched hand of Collins. He took a small sip.

"So, Sean Collins, my hero," Sierra began as she set the bottle of wine on the desktop. "You know everything about me and my life, but I know nothing about you."

"You know plenty about me," Collins said before he drank from the glass. "You know of my nine children. You know I am a lawyer."

"And little else," Sierra cut in.

One thing that the Ragnarsson family had trained her to do was to read people. She was certain that Collins was more than a mild mannered lawyer. She had observed the way he walked with fluidity and grace which reminded her of the manner several men from her past. They were masters of some martial art. His eyes were sharp and seemed to see everything around him. His level of awareness was similar to the men she had associated with when she was being trained to be a killer by her husband.

"I think you are hiding things from me and everyone else."

"What would I be hiding?"

"I think there is more to you than just a mere prosecutor."

"Why would you think that?" Collins laughed at her observation.

Sierra leaned in to him and whispered.

"Because you just prosecuted several members of the Royal Family and you are still breathing. No man or woman would dare to take them on, all of them on, the way you did. It is almost as if you have no fear of death. You were the lead lawyer in the trial of the century. In addition, you prosecuted or indicted the remaining Rosenburg's. Some of them were convicted in separate trials and you have them all waiting for transportation to Cootron to serve their sentences. The rest are waiting for their day in court. Any other man or woman that had the cajones to do what you have done would be dead by now. The Sikorsky's or the other Rosenburg's would have wiped you from the face of the planet for what you have done. Why not you?"

Collins drank from his glass slowly and looked over the attractive former assassin. "It would seem that you have formed some theories about me. What exactly are you wanting to know?"

"Your two wives that died? They were not just normal house wives were they?"

Collins began to stand up but Sierra grabbed his wrist to stop him. He paused and looked at her thoughtfully. "I don't like talking about them to strangers."

"But I am not a stranger. You changed my life and you freed me from those horrible people. I told you about my whole life. I testified for you so that I could be a part of putting some really evil people in prison. You helped me with the courtroom dynamics so that I would be prepared for the defense cross examination. We have eaten dinner together many times and I am now a guest under your roof. That means we are friends in my book. Please sit down, Sean. I will not tell your children anything. Your first wife, who was she and how did she really die?"

Collins sat down and drank the rest of the wine in his glass. He had held secrets of his past in for the last two decades. He looked into the eyes of Sierra, formerly known as Dulce Maria Reynolds Hernandez Ragnarsson for several minutes. He could tell that she was a woman that could read others quite well. He sighed.

"What I tell you stays between us."

"Naturally," Sierra agreed.

"My first wife committed suicide. She was like you, Dulce. She had been a killer and she turned on her employers. I changed her name and protected her. During the stress of the trial and the secrecy of her location, we fell in love. Ginger was born first, then Siobhan. Sean and Liam came later. But then the unthinkable happened."

Sierra poured more wine into his glass, "They found her, didn't they?"

Collins nodded and had a sad look in his eyes, "Yes. Yes, they did. To save her children, she took a fast acting poison. She was dead in seconds. I never knew why she killed herself until I found her personal holo-com device. She left me an encrypted message to explain why she did it and to tell me good bye. She told me that the men she helped me send to jail had hired a killer to find her. The killer confronted her and my wife made a deal with the assassin, to let her children live in return for her taking her own life. My wife kept her side of the bargain."

Sierra nodded and took Collins' hand in hers, "You never told anyone about this?"

"Never."

"And your second wife?"

Collins sighed and looked up at his ceiling, "She was so beautiful. I loved them both, but my second wife was innocent. She had been a nurse. We met at a New Year's Celebration. It was a lightening romance. After we had our five daughters, I was prosecuting a powerful drug lord from Lynott's Land. He was a thug and ran illegal weapons across several solar system jurisdictions. The defendants had a hit team kill her to send me a message. She was one of the Dark October victims. I assumed, at first, that she was killed as collateral damage, since the majority of the dead on Dark October were top ranking officers. Later, I realized that my wife was also targeted. I was so angered by what they had done and I got them all for what they did."

"You prosecuted them anyway?"

"No," Collins now whispered. "I tracked them down, at least the ones I could identify, and killed them with my bare hands. They could not be allowed to live after what they took from me."

Sierra held his hand tight.

"A lawyer, an everyday average lawyer would not do such a thing, Sean Collins. I know that Felix Ragnarsson had been the brains behind the Dark October hit. He was found dead in Lynott's Land, strangled. Are you telling me that you killed him? So now I go back to my original question. Who are you really?"

Collins leaned closer to Sierra, "I have Royal Blood in me. My mother was a descendant of Sikorsky. That is why the Glorious Leader does not know what to do with me."

"Where is your mother now?"

"She is still with him, on Sikorsky's Planet. My mother is Shannon Collins. She descended from Diarmuid Collins and Keira Brey."

"The heroes of the war against Akarzdamedia?"

"The very ones and the same. Diarmuid and Keira followed Sikorsky and Huang Tan to conquer Akarzdamedia over two hundred years ago. They both played a part in the subjugation of the aliens and the original military style occupation of that planet. While they assisted Sikorsky on the alien world, they had three boys. One of those three boys was named Gavan and as an adult he was one of Sikorsky's most loyal soldiers.

Gavan Collins killed for the Glorious Leader and helped in the invasion of what was to be called planet Athena. Gavan Collins had several wives and many children. One of his sons, named Wallace, continued to serve the Glorious Leader as his father had. Wallace Collins married a woman named Brenda Welker, a granddaughter of Sikorsky. They had several children as well and they both accepted the gifts of immortality."

"You mean by taking the body parts of innocents to keep living?" Sierra cut in.

"Yes. They became as evil as Sikorsky. One of their children, Jonathan Collins, became a Marine Corps officer and helped in the invasion of another planet that would be later named New Vladivostok. John Collins never married but he had several women that he slept around with. One of his daughters was Shannon Collins, my mother."

"And your father?"

"My father, according to my mother, was Vladimir Sikorsky the Fourth."

Mary Sierra sat back into the leather couch and was silent for several minutes.

"So that is why they did not send a hit team to stop you from prosecuting the Rosenburg's?"

Collins stood up and looked out of his large window at his manicured yard and garden full of colorful flowers.

"Maybe. No, I do not know why. I thought that they did not send a team because of what I did to that drug lord several years ago. You see, the drug lord I tracked down and killed was no common criminal. He was a man named Ivar Ragnarsson."

Sierra looked at him and frowned.

"But you prosecuted Ivar. He was in court with the others. He was no drug lord, he was a scared boy."

"Not that Ivar, it was his grandfather. I killed the father of Dell Ragnarsson. Then I killed Felix and the whole family knew that it was me."

"How did they know?"

"I told them," Collins said simply. "Dell said he respected me for taking revenge and indicated that we were even."

"And how did a mere lawyer learn how to kill a pair of universal assassins?"

"My first wife trained me. She was worried that one day her past would find her. She ended up being right, of course. She was always right. She wanted me to learn to defend myself and our children. She had been an excellent teacher."

"So it would seem."

Collins stood up and extended his hand to her. She took it and stood next to him.

"Let me show you a secret so monumental that it could potentially shake the United Nations and the Glorious Leader to the ground."

"What are you referring to?"

"I am certain that you wondered why I have my first floor basement secured."

"Yes, that had crossed my mind."

Collins led her by the hand toward the stair well. "There is something in there that my family has kept safe for almost two hundred years. It was passed down from Keira Brey to Gavan and to his daughter Kaitlin and to her son Liam and from Liam to George. Eventually the duty of guarding the secret landed in my lap. My mother Shannon gave them to me for safe keeping."

Sierra followed Collins to the landing of the basement on the first floor. She watched as Collins placed his palm on a scanner on the wall. After a few seconds, a metal door to Sierra's left slid open. The door was two feet thick as were the walls. Sierra concluded that Collins was hiding something very important behind those massive metal walls. She wondered how long it took to construct the underground facility and what form of metal was used.

She followed him into the pitch black room. In the distance she could see small red, yellow, orange and blue lights that were blinking. Collins led her by the hand and stopped her.

"Computer, activate the ceiling lighting," Collins instructed.

Sierra watched the large room illuminate with light. She looked around and observed rows and rows of floor to ceiling computer banks. There were numerous old style monitors, seats and keyboards. In the center of the room she saw twenty cylinders that were made of metal and glass. Each of the cylinders was ten feet long and five feet wide. The top and bottom of the cylinders were flat while the rest was rounded. Each of the cylinders was lying on top of medical tables and had computerized devices attached to them.

"What are they?" Sierra whispered.

Collins walked over to the closest and placed his hand on it.

"This one has Keira Brey sleeping inside of it. These are the original cryogenic sleeping tubes found under the capital city of Akarzdamedia. These tubes were designed by the Akarzdamedians thousands of years ago, perhaps tens of thousands. Vladimir Sikorsky stole the technology from them after he conquered their home world. The one next to Keira's is her husband, Diarmuid. The other eighteen are the biggest secret of all. They contain non-humans."

"Who are the occupants of the other eighteen?"

"Queen Danu of the Akarzdamedians and some of her children and grandchildren. Two hundred years ago, Sikorsky believed he had killed them all. He did kill most of the leaders of the aliens, but these escaped and the others were either enslaved by humanity or they fled to some undisclosed location. Keira Brey realized that Sikorsky could never be fully trusted so she and Diarmuid found Queen Danu and developed a plan to help her escape certain death. They placed her and what remained of her family in these Cryogenic sleep tubes. My family has been their sentinel for almost two hundred years."

Sierra walked over to one of the tubes and looked at the protective glass casing. Inside she saw a black colored being that was similar to Anubis of ancient Egyptian lore. Sierra observed that the sleeping Queen seemed peaceful in her rest. Her eyes were closed and there seemed to be a smile on her face.

"By the Stars. Do your children know of this?"

Collins shook his head, "No. I was trying to determine which one would replace me when I passed on. I had thought Ginger would be the logical choice but she joined her husband on the Fleet that is being sent out to locate the missing Bismark. It is a dangerous mission into an area of space that is virtually unknown to us. Siobhan might be the one. She is finishing up her medical training and would be the most logical given her stated desires to return to New Edinburgh and work here."

"Did any of your ancestors ever wake them up, to talk with them?"

"Not that I am aware of."

"Will they ever be brought out of this state to live again?"

Collins nodded, "They are only in deep sleep. I was told by my grandfather that I should wake them all up when the time was right."

"What does that mean?"

"I don't know. My grandfather always said that I would know. He said it would be obvious that they needed to be revealed to the worlds. I have been waiting my whole life for an event that would warrant waking them. I have not seen it yet."

"Who else knows about them?"

"Just you, me, and Shannon. Everyone else that knew of them is deceased. But Shannon does not know where I hid them."

Collins motioned for her to follow him, "Come on, we should get back upstairs before the little one wakes up from her nap."

Sierra stood and stared at the long tubes for a moment longer. She knew that if the Glorious Leader ever learned that the Queen of Akarzdamedia and some of her offspring were still alive he would carpet bomb the entire planet in an effort to kill them.

Sierra was glad her instincts about Collins were correct. There was clearly more to him than just another lawyer. She followed him back upstairs to talk some more and wait for Bree to wake up from her nap.

Colonel Nikolai Gorski reported to work early that morning at his office in the United Nations Building located in Clovis City. He was wearing his Marine Corps Class C uniform. He was drinking a hot cup of coffee as he considered the paper on his desk. It had been sent via encoded e-mail to him from the Space Command and was signed by Admiral Sikorsky. It basically informed Gorski that he had been removed from the short list of names for promotion to General. It also stated clearly that he was going to be relieved of command of the military presence on Clovis City.

He met his second in command, Major Sigebert Evart, in the hallway leading to Gorski's office. Evart was also wearing his Class C uniform. Evart had a large twenty ounce cup of coffee in his hand when they met.

The two officers walked into the office without saying a word. They paused as Gorski's doors slid shut behind them to ensure they would have privacy from the rest of the United Nations employees that might walk by.

"You heard?" Nikolai Gorski asked in a low tone.

"Yes," Evart sat down in one of the seats. "I guess the Space Command disapproved of our work. I was really hoping that you would get that well deserved promotion to Brigadier General. I am so sorry they are passing you over, Nikolai."

Gorski smiled at his friend as he sat down behind his desk. For over a year he had managed the day to day military efforts in Clovis City and the rest of New Edinburgh. Only General Tan outranked Gorski and she never once stood in the way of the mission or the defense efforts. Tan pretty much wanted nothing to do with the daily routine as long as she was able to maintain her unit of Military Intelligence Brigades in

Lynott's Land. Gorski had hoped that he would be promoted to General as a reward for his hard work and dedication. Alas, that was not to be. The Space Command sent word that a Battle Cruiser was being sent from Sikorsky's Planet with a large number of high ranking soldiers to take over the military mission and replace Gorski. The news had been a blow to the Marine Colonel.

"Where do you think they will transfer us to?" Gorski wondered out loud.

"I hear there are rebellions popping up on some of the other settlements and lunar locations," Evart shrugged. "With our skill set, we might be sent off to one of them to quash the protestors on one of those faraway spots. I heard rumors from some transport pilots the other night that planet New Quebec erupted in a full scale civil war. They said that anyone with vacation plans to that area should cancel them. It is a hot spot right now. They told me that several thousand have died in the fighting. I saw an illegally obtained news broadcast from New South Africa that one of their main islands had been overrun by rebels."

"Amazing that the government controlled news media failed to get us that information." Gorski shook his head and picked up the picture on his desk of his deceased wife.

"What have we been doing all these years, Sigebert? Our leaders suppress information, lie to us and send us in to kill humans that only want basic freedoms. And how many times have we wiped out entire species on other worlds to expand our empire? I was loyal. I fought when I was told to do so. I killed when I was ordered to kill. I did it all for my sons. Not the government. For my sons. As a single father I had no real choice in the matter. I had to advance in rank to earn better pay and therefore provide better things for Yuri and Piotr. I had hoped to retire here, Sigebert. I wanted to see Piotr graduate and then submit my walking papers. I do not want to leave him behind. I got Yuri off and in his career. I wanted to do the same for Piotr."

Evart leaned back in his chair and thought for a few moments, "Nikolai, your son is a good kid. He will be fine here if you have to leave due to transfer. Most of my daughters are much younger and would have to leave behind their schools and their friends. Piotr is in his first year at the Academy and will graduate soon enough. He has many friends and a good study ethic. He will be fine. It is time to worry about yourself, my friend."

"Why do you say that?" Gorski frowned.

"We destroyed the majority of the Rosenburg control on this planet, at least we helped do it. Collins and his team of prosecutors had something of a hand in it. Some of the General Assembly representatives gave us their support. But the Rosenburg's were all Royal's. I think this approaching Battle Cruiser is a way of the Glorious Leader communicating to other commanders that we are not to arrest his family members. We are guilty of that."

"So, are they going to arrest us?" Gorski laughed.

"I hope not, my friend. I think my delicate skin could not handle a stint at Cootron."

Nikolai Gorski stood and looked out his windows. He admired the beauty of all of the large buildings around the United Nations Building. He reflected on all of his accomplishments. "Me too. We were both loyal to a fault. Hopefully you are reading too much into this."

"I hope that as well."

"You remember how they called me the Dinosaur Hunter?" Gorski thought back. "Before you arrived in New Edinburgh, most of Clovis City was a jungle. My platoon and I fought like Russian bears, they called my unit the Medved Platoon. We were on the front lines for months while we cleared out all of what you see here in the distance." Gorski waived his left arm out toward his windows.

"My sons Yuri and Piotr remained with the other children on the Battle Cruiser as the war waged here on the surface. Colonel Knox was a brilliant leader. We beat back the creatures and slowly took this land. The Protective Walls around Clovis City were built in three weeks by engineers and construction workers as my platoon held the Verburgt and the Dozal at bay. I was injured badly in the defense of some engineers. There were hundreds, no, thousands of different life forms here. We killed so many. After the wall was erected around what is now Clovis City, my platoon and I were assigned to take over the area now called Lynott's Land. We fought off so many of the indigenous creatures there."

"And you received the Medal of Valor," Evart reminded him.

Gorski nodded silently, "Yes. Among other awards for my work. When Colonel Knox was promoted to General and eventually transferred out, I made Captain. I had my own company at that point. I was always a soldier. I led my troops into the hostile territory that is now called Gellar's Province. From there we led the charge in the area now named Hope City. I had the lowest casualty rate of all the other company commanders. In the area known as Nuevo Santiago the Marines sent in an entire division which was wiped out.

My company was sent in to rescue the survivors. It was the bloodiest battle of my time in the service. I saw those creatures fighting back against our superior weaponry. As I killed the Dozal, the Jumpers and the Verburgt I began to feel sorry for them. This was their planet and we took almost the entire Northern Continent from them. I never cared about the politics of what I did. I followed orders. I led my troops into battle and put them all in the best position so that they had a chance to survive."

Gorski paused for a moment and turned to face Evart. "Once Clovis City was considered safe, Yuri and Piotr were transported to the planet surface with all of the other children of the colonists and soldiers. While I was out fighting, Yuri and Piotr stayed with the Andolini's. They were such a generous and kind family. When I made Major the Marines stationed me here in the United Nations Building. I spent all of my spare time as a father. I tried to raise my sons to be good men and make up for all the time I was away from them. I wanted them to become men that Melita would have been proud of."

"And I can assure you, both of your sons have grown into good men," Evart said. "If Yuri or Piotr were to fall in love with one of my daughters I would be the happiest man alive. You have been a fantastic father and your sons are destined for greatness. You instilled values in them of loyalty and hard work and they both are a lot like you. Yuri especially. He is a medved if I ever saw one."

Nikolai Gorski smiled at that comment and drank the last of his coffee. "Yes, yes he certainly is and I would also be very proud if he married one of your daughters. You have been a great father as well, my friend. If we get transferred off on separate planets I will certainly miss you."

"And I you. Come on, let's go to the cafeteria and get another cup of coffee. I have a feeling we will be needing it."

CHAPTER ELEVEN

Charles Bennington had been asleep for several hours in his small ten feet by fifteen feet quarters. He had abandoned his post as chief of the Criminal Investigation Division on Space Station Cy-7 to follow Penelope Rosenburg and her sisters in a wild attempt to bring down the Sikorsky family. Bennington had been a loyal officer in the Space Command before retiring and joining the civilian CID. Bennington had personally witnessed many atrocities during his service and never felt he had the ability to force changes in the way the government worked. He changed his perspective after Penelope Rosenburg explained her schemes to him.

Bennington personally watched as Penelope's half-sister, Doctor Nicolette Rosenburg, brought to life fifty more duplicate humans from long cloning tubes. Bennington was in awe when he saw fifty perfect copies of two men that had died, Frank Garrison and Drayton Love-Easter, were living again due to the alien technology of the Danaraja species.

Bennington left Space Station Cy-7 with Penelope Rosenburg, twenty-four duplicates of Love-Easter, twenty-five duplicates of Garrison, Doctor Nicolette Rosenburg and Doctor Kristen Rosenburg on board the Super Raumschiff named The Peacemaker. The crew of fifty-three first stopped for a visit with a Fleet Admiral named Cardenas on a Battle Cruiser named Cleopatra. Penelope used her vast knowledge of the security systems to board the warship Cleopatra without detection. She met Admiral Cardenas and discussed her plans with him. To

Bennington's surprise, she convinced the Admiral to join their cause.

Admiral Cardenas agreed to be a willing participant in the insurrection against the Glorious Leader.

Penelope had assisted the Admiral to eliminate the majority of the Sikorsky descendants that were posted on the five Battle Cruisers under his command.

Admiral Cardenas urged Penelope to leave his fleet to take on the fleet of science cruisers in the far western quadrant so that those ships would be without any Sikorsky influence. Cardenas gave two Raumschiff's to Rosenburg in return for many duplicate Love-Easter's and Garrison's. By the time the Peacemaker had arrived at the location of the Cleopatra, the two Rosenburg Doctor's had created another fifty duplicates of a female assassin named Ella Ragnarsson. But the Ella Ragnarsson replicas were created with a twist. Nicolette Rosenburg made them to have the body and physical abilities of the Ragnarsson woman but implanted the mind of Penelope Rosenburg inside the brains. Thus they were all named "Penelope Ragnarsson" also known as "Penella" to reflect that they all had the memories and knowledge of Penelope Rosenburg as opposed to Ella Ragnarsson.

Penelope turned over all fifty of the replicants of Penelope Ragnarsson to Admiral Cardenas. The treasonous minded conspirators agreed that the assassin body melded with the knowledge of Penelope would make formidable combatants against the forces of the Glorious Leader. Nicolette had another fifty clones of Ella Ragnarsson being created in her alien machinery.

Once the Peacemaker departed the Cleopatra, Bennington became the de facto pilot of the ship and guided her toward the science fleet as Cardenas recommended. Penelope Rosenburg took control of the Raumschiff named Antony 9 and Kristin Rosenburg was in charge of the Antony 11. They flew at best speed to begin the slaughter of the Sikorsky presence on the five science cruisers. As they traveled, Nicolette ant Kristin Rosenburg began to create more duplicate humans. They made another fifty Love-Easter clones and a similar number of additional Garrison's. They created an additional fifty Penella mixes. Nicolette and Kristin created clones of themselves, twenty-five each.

When approached about being copied or cloned, Bennington politely refused. After much thought and soul searching, Bennington did not want any copies of himself wandering around the galaxy. He felt uncomfortable with the thought of a perfect duplicate of himself out there living a life that was meant to begin with his natural birth and his eventual death. Although Bennington recognized that the duplication technology would virtually assure immortality, he did not desire that for himself.

Bennington felt that such science was against the values he had been raised with. He wondered if any other person would feel the same as he did about the issue. The replica would be him, but not really him. It was a Pandora's Box that he did not want to open for himself.

After the Peacemaker arrived in the area of deep space where the science cruisers were located, they realized that all five of the ships were not present. Four were there. The fifth, the one named the Wisconsin, was missing. Penelope decided that they would begin the work of cleansing the four ships that were present of all Royal Blood. Using the alien technology to conceal the Peacemaker, Antony 9 and Antony 11, they hit all four ships and eliminated all on board that were descendants of the Glorious Leader.

Bennington assisted completely in the executions of the Royal Family members. He had become a true believer in the mission as Penelope had explained to him. Once the heads of the dead had been collected, the three Raumschiff's began to split up on different missions.

Bennington was to take the Peacemaker to Sikorsky's Planet. He was given the real Doctor Nicolette Rosenburg, a few duplicates of Love-Easter and Garrison as well as ten of the Penelope Ragnarsson clones. Their mission was to locate the two hundred year old wreckage of the lost historical science vessel called the Calypso. Bennington was grateful that on the long flight through space that he would have the intellectual Nicolette Rosenburg to converse with.

Within three days Bennington and Doctor Rosenburg became lovers. Bennington had one major concern in that he did not want to make the mistake of attempting to sleep with one of her clones. Accordingly, he requested that the real Nicolette wear a red bow in her hair in perpetuity, so that he would be able to differentiate her from the others.

Penelope and Kristin took the Antony 9 and Antony 11 on a voyage to their most dangerous mission yet. They were headed toward the Second Fleet under the command of Admiral Khan. Their hope was to add the five Battle Cruisers of that fleet to their side and to turn his entire crew into fellow rebels and outlaws.

Penelope noticed a dynamic among the clones on her ship the Antony 9. They each seemed to have developed an enhanced instinct to breed. She had caught a Garrison duplicate making love to a Kristin clone. On another occasion she found one of the Penella clones being mounted by one of the Drayton Love-Easter duplicates.

The replicas seemed to create their own bonds of friendships and the sex partners were developing into monogamous partners. They were not only physical sex partners but growing to care and love as actual humans. Penelope observed the ones that had become sex partners demonstrate acts of kindness to each other, simple things such as fixing a meal for the other or pulling a chair out for the other to sit in. Penelope began to grow close to each of them as well. Even though they possessed the downloaded memories from the diskette scans of the original person, the replicas were each evolving into their own person. They were creating their own lives and direction. It was a fantastic evolution to observe and be a part of.

CHAPTER TWELVE

The Dean of the Clovis Academy, Golden Harvard, was a man that was respected and admired by his peers. He had received numerous awards in the educational field. His career in teaching began as a college professor. Over the years, he went into public administration and learned the business side of running a large University or Academy. His efforts were rewarded when he was named the first Dean of the Clovis Academy. Now, after many years at that position, Golden Harvard had been honored to receive the call from the Glorious Leader, Vladimir Sikorsky, to relocate to Sikorsky's Planet and become a member of the United Nations ruling cabinet as Secretary of Education for the entire Earth Empire.

Golden Harvard could not turn down a request from the Glorious Leader, or such a high level position. His new official title would be Secretary General of Education. Long time Professor Warren was asked to succeed Harvard as Dean of Clovis Academy. Harvard was instructed to report to Sikorsky's Planet by the end of December.

In honor of the departing Dean, several celebrations were thrown. Many were rallies at the soccer field. The last celebration was to be a private affair, a black tie dinner at a cost of one thousand Empire Dollars per person. The formal event would be held at the three hundred thousand square foot ballroom at the five star Clovis City Hotel. The hotel itself was fifty floors high and each floor had a hundred rooms.

Harvard notified his several living wives and children and grandchildren so that they could all participate. Harvard was close to his seventieth birthday. He had been married twelve times. Six of his spouses had died over the years. The other six still lived with him, their ages ranging from thirty to sixty-three years old. Harvard had fathered three dozen children and some of them had produced grandchildren. This was Harvard's proudest moment, to be selected to such a powerful position. Never in his wildest dreams had he ever thought he would be sitting in the Ruling Cabinet with the Glorious Leader.

As the news of Dean Harvard's final black tie dinner was being circulated, many dignitaries in Clovis City began reserving tables of ten seats. Colonel Nikolai Gorski paid for a seat as did Major Sigebert Evart. Evart also purchased seats for his four wives and two teen aged girls. Sean Collins paid for a table of ten for him, his children and some of his staff members. Lawyers, Doctors, business men and women all began to pay the cost to attend the event.

Many of the cadets at Clovis Academy had wanted to attend, but the cost was far too high for them to pay.

Cadet Dirk Fenster, who had been and was still a loyal Gorski Gang member, was studying to become a pilot. He was a handsome man and he had a large allowance that his family sent to him each month. One thing that really disturbed his parents was that he was very generous with the monthly disbursements he received. Dirk helped charities, orphanages, folks in need. He would occasionally help pay for a persons' surgery, even complete strangers. The money meant little to him. His friends and his siblings were his priority.

Dirk's younger sister, Therese, had joined him at the Academy as a freshman studying engineering design and manufacturing. Both siblings were to learn their craft well so that after they spent six years serving the military, they would be able to become members of the family business. Dirk had been introducing his little sister to all of his friends. She had become a welcome member of the Gorski Gang.

Even though the Gang membership suffered losses due to the graduations of Yuri Gorski, Les Gillis, Julia Steiner, Drew Harrison, Drayton Love-Easter, Yesenia Guevara-Easter, Marco Andolini, Dominic Andolini and Michel Darcel Evart, the new members made the Gang as formidable as ever.

Before he left Clovis Academy, Yuri Gorski selected Jen Staszko, Klaus Rhinehard and Jack Harcourt to be the leaders of the group. The first act of the three was to allow any and all siblings of former Gang members into the group. That was how Therese Fenster was allowed to become a member as well as Piotr Gorski and five Andolini siblings that were entering freshmen as well. Other entering students were invited to join the gang. Among those that had accepted the offer were Daniel Choi, Norman Porter, Ye Yibing, Boland 'Quarter' Miles, and twin sisters Nola and Lola Belzyt. Dirk had not had the opportunity to get to know the newer gang members although his sister had. She vouched for them all as trustworthy.

Dirk knew that some of the Gang members would want to attend the Black Tie affair, so he withdrew money from his account and paid for a table of ten. Ten thousand Empire Dollars was a small price to pay to treat some of his best friends to a night out on the town. He smiled, thinking how furious his father would be if and when he found out that his son had done such an outrageous act.

He decided to invite several of his friends to the celebration. Many of the Gorski Gang were going to be leaving for the three week holiday to meet Les Gillis at Space Station Cy-5. Gillis' wife, Sophia DuBravac, wanted to take several of old and new friends to surprise Gillis. Since so many of the gang would be gone, that narrowed the list of names for him to choose from.

After much reflection, Dirk determined his new roommate, Lu Wang, would not be invited. Wang was a freshman to the Clovis Academy and hoped to become an officer in military intelligence. Dirk barely tolerated his new roommate. Wang hardly ever bathed, never used deodorant, never washed his clothes, rarely flushed the toilet after using it, interrupted Dirk when he was attempting to study and the most annoying trait of all was that Wang was a chain smoker. Dirk despised the smell of cigarettes in his dormitory room. Not so much for himself, but his pet timber wolf, Theodora. He was certain that Theodora would eat Wang alive to get rid of the awful stench of cigarettes in the room. After learning who he was, Wang was always asking Dirk for loans of cash money. Although Dirk was very generous, he hated it when people would ask for him to give them money. He preferred to give when he thought it might help a friend in need. Wang wanted money to buy more cigarettes or designer clothes in his endless pursuit of co-ed girls for sex. He once advised him that a bar of soap and some breath mints would be more helpful in meeting girls than a ninety dollar shirt.

Dirk's best friend and former roommate was Arch Frazier, a student of Explorations and Geology. Frazier was married to the lovely Corinthian cadet Elektra Papanikolaou. They both readily accepted the invitation. Naturally, he wanted his sister Therese to attend. She had been dating Piotr Gorski, who had recently broken up with Mia Nguyen. Allegedly, the younger Gorski caught Nguyen with the known womanizer Rolf Rhinehard. Therese seemed to enjoy the company of Piotr Gorski, so he invited him as well. Dirk was mindful of those members that were alone, separated from their spouses or widowed, so that prompted him to invite Harumi Shigeta Andolini and Cara Perez Guerrero.

Perez Guerrero had been in a relationship with Pierre Zerbe many months ago. They fell in love and she was pregnant due to their lust. Tragically, Zerbe was one of the victims of the ambush on the Blood Moon. Recently, Perez Guerrero learned she was going to have twins.

After the Blood Moon Incident, Sean Collins recommended that Perez Guerrero sue the Rosenburg Corporation. He referred her to a lawyer that he knew that was experienced in cases involving loss of consortium. Perez Guerrero received a cash settlement for herself and her two unborn children. She used the money to purchase a home on the west side of Clovis City in the same subdivision that Sean Collins and his family lived. Freya Cardenas bought the home next door to Perez Guerrero with some of the money she received in the same lawsuit against the Rosenburg Corporation.

Harumi Shigeta was without her husband Dominic, so a night out at a formal gathering with friends would do her a world of good. She had confessed to several of her friends that she felt lonely without her husband.

Dirk invited one of his favorite married couples, Klaus and April Rhinehard. Both were cadet pilots and good and decent people. Klaus was blonde with blue eyes, tall and athletic. He spoke with a thick German accent and was one of the most talented cadet pilots on the Academy. He had been named one of the four cadet commanders of the pilot squadrons. He was a senior and had planned on entering the annual selection process after receiving his commission as an officer.

April Mejia was short with dark hair and dark eyes. She had a lovely smile and spoke with a deep accent due to her family originally hailing from Mexico City. She was several months pregnant and showing. She was also a pilot candidate at the Academy and was in her junior year. Her pattern of speech was to mix Spanish with English words mostly since she had not learned a word of English until she arrived as a student at Clovis Academy. She worked hard at learning the second language with the help of her friends Harumi and Elektra.

Dirk then contemplated who to take as his escort. He had many women that he was sexually active with. But the one that seemed to stand out in his mind was Lupita Calderon. They had started spending time together over the summer. Her large sibling group of brothers was always accusing Dirk of sleeping with their sister. So finally, on their third date, he did take her to his dormitory room. Since then, they developed a 'friends with benefits' relationship. He enjoyed having Lupita in his bed as she had proven to be a great lover and she had grown into a good friend.

Lupita readily accepted the invitation, but lamented the fact she did not own a formal gown to wear. Her family had humble beginnings and had little money for extra formal clothing. Her father had been an enlisted soldier in the Marines and was one of the first to be sent to fight in the famous Dinosaur Wars. After her father retired, he used his pension to open a repair shop of space craft and other mechanical vehicles. Business had been good, but not great. There were several months when the number of clientele was lower than average and the Calderon family struggled. Recognizing that Lupita was not able to purchase a nice dress on her own, Dirk took her shopping to some of the most expensive retail stores in Clovis City and bought her a lovely white dress with gold trim.

The night of the celebration was memorable. Lupita had shown her mother and father the dress that Dirk had purchased for her. Lupita's abuelita, or grandmother, had been a professional hair stylist. She cut, styled and arranged Lupita's hair in a classic look that would have made Hollywood starlets of the nineteen fifties jealous. Her grandmother was a sweet woman that was unable to get around without the assistance of a mechanical walker to support her shaky legs. She had been a survivor of a worm attack and miraculously survived. But the poisons from the worm's skin saliva caused Lupita's grandmother severe nerve and muscle damage that would stay with her until the day she died.

Lupita's large sibling group, mostly brothers, had been giving Dirk much grief about seeing their sister. But, as they watched Lupita get ready for her date, they realized that she was happy. They could see the look of joy in her eyes that Dirk chose her to be his date. She was excited, but yet cautious in her relationship with him. He was from money and her family was working class and she barely had two Empire Dollars to her name. She found that after getting to know him, money meant nothing to him. He never judged her or her family, as the Calderon clan had feared. On the contrary, Dirk had been respectful to Lupita's parents and siblings, even the siblings that were members of the Bragg Gang.

Dirk rented a flying limousine to transport each of his guests to the event. One by one, Dirk had his rented pilot fly him to pick up his guests. The Brackenrdige Type Nine Flying Limousine was manufactured as a planet bound form of transportation. Thus, the flying stretch car could only go a half mile up into the sky. It had enough seats in the back to accommodate at least twenty people with several coolers for drinks in the passenger section that was covered in white leather.

Therese Fenster and Piotr Gorski were the first two that joined Dirk on the solid black flying limousine. His sister, Therese, was dressed in a stunning, low cut, red gown. Therese had grown into a slender woman with curves in the right places and was desired by many. Her low cut formal outfit that night confirmed that Therese had ample, well rounded breasts, a flat stomach and curvaceous buttocks. Dirk thought that his sister was looking more and more like their beautiful mother.

Klaus Rhinehard and his wife, April, lived in the married cadet housing. Both were cadet pilot candidates and had been long term friends to Dirk. April Mejia was lovely in her white formal gown. Her stomach was showing the twins that she carried. Klaus had a black tuxedo on that fit him well. He had the look of a super-spy from the old movies. April was a spit fire for a personality. Klaus had fallen in love with her almost immediately, mostly because of her personality. After their relationship started, April became pregnant. Some members of the infamous Bragg Gang spread rumors that Klaus was tricked into marriage. The truth was that he loved her and had always wanted her in his life.

The last of the guests that Dirk had picked up was his date, Lupita Calderon. He met her at her door, gave her mother a dozen roses to thank her for giving birth to such a wonderful lady. The entire Calderon family watched in awe as Lupita was led, arm in arm, by Dirk Fenster, to the large flying limousine. The Calderon family had never been wealthy and struggled at times to pay their bills. They were a family that believed in working hard and sacrificing for the future. The fact that one of their daughters had become involved with such a handsome and wealthy young man was beyond their wildest dreams. They were all ecstatic for Lupita and hoped that this relationship would be the right one for her.

After a short trip in the transport ship, the ten cadets arrived and were shown by a hostess to their round table.

April Mejia looked around and noticed that the room was packed with dignitaries. She noticed that the restaurant moguls, the Li family, had occupied a far south table. There were several members of the Goldsmith family at another table that were talking softly to one another. The members of General Assembly Representative Wyclyffe occupied two tables and were enjoying several bottles of the best champagne that the restaurant had to offer. United Nations Secretary General Alexander Lyss was in attendance and had a much younger woman sitting next to him, flirting and laughing with him. At the table next to Lyss were some of the naval officers that were rumored to sail off in their Unter-See Boats, also known as submarines, in the next few days. One was Admiral Themis Zachariades and another was her oldest son Captain Drimios Zachariades.

April tapped Elektra Frazier on her shoulder, "Hey, that table over there. Isn't that your aunt and cousin?"

Elektra stared off in the direction that her friend was pointing. She smiled and took her husband by the hand. He could tell by the look in her eyes that she was excited.

"Arch, come with me. My aunt is here. She made it."

Arch Frazier followed his wife to the table with all of the naval officers. She was elated to be able to introduce her husband to some of her family. The Frazier's began to converse with the famous Admiral Themis Zachariades and her son Captain Drimios Zachariades. They explained that their submarines would be mapping the entire ocean floor of planet New Edinburgh. The process should take them about two years of complete. The mother and son team had relocated to New Edinburgh from Corinth of Old Earth. Themis Zachariades had four children, Drimios being the oldest. All of the children of Admiral Zachariades had reached the age of eighteen and left their mother to go off to college and start their careers. Drimios had taken three wives and had nine children, each of his children were still in school, the oldest was sixteen. Drimios had been one of Elektra's closest cousins when she was growing up in Greece. He had always brought her gifts and inspired her to apply for the academy.

At the table that Fenster had paid for, the cadets mostly spoke of the recent disaster on Chronos. The conversation also touched on the names of children.

"Cara, have you settled on names for your children yet?" Lupita Calderon inquired.

Perez Guerrero rubbed her abdomen gently, "I was told by Doctor Freya that I was having twins. I thought if there is a boy then I would name him after his father. For a girl, I just don't know. My mother was named Maria after my great grandmother. So I thought that would be a nice name to give my child. What about you, April?"

April looked at her husband and they both started laughing.

"What is so funny?" Therese wanted to know.

Klaus put his arm around his wife, "We have been arguing about the names for some time now. I want to call the children Kaiser and Elsa."

"You are not naming my son Kaiser," April blurted out.

"Kaiser sounds like a nice name," Lupita shrugged. "Kaiser Rhinehard. It has a good ring to it."

"No," April shook her head. "No, no, no. I want my son to be named after my uncle Manuel. Manuel Mejia Rhinehard."

"Sounds good, too." Lupita observed.

"And if you have another boy?" Shigeta asked.

"Kaiser," Klaus said.

"No Kaiser," his wife glared at him. "I am not going to go through giving birth to name my child after a bread."

"It is not a bread, it is a time honored name!" Klaus protested and turned his attention to the others to see that they were all laughing. "It is not brotchen, I mean bread. It is a good name. My uncle was named Kaiser. He was always good to me and my sisters and brothers."

"And for two girls?" Therese Fenster prompted.

April hit her husband in the chest. "Elsa? Okay, I might give in to Elsa. But I want to name our other child, if we have two girls, Mary after Mary Lincoln. She really took me in when I first moved here. I was scared and alone and Mary brought me protection. It's because of Mary that Klaus and I even met."

"Agreed on Mary," Klaus told her. "So Mary and Elsa for two girls and Kaiser and Manuel for two boys."

"Ah chinga!" April rolled her eyes at her husband. "Esta guey. Enough with the Kaiser!"

The others laughed.

At one point, April told their table she thought she recognized someone on the far side of the room. But she was not certain. The others looked around and did not see what she had been referring to.

Colonel Nikolai Gorski, the acting commander of all armed forces on planet New Edinburgh was present wearing his Marine Corps dark blue Class A uniform. The medals on his chest were as impressive as the rows of ribbons, each signifying recognition for some act during his career that warranted recognition. He was sharing a table with his acting second in command, Major Sigebert Evart, who was also wearing his best uniform. Evart was accompanied by his several wives and three teen-age daughters who were all dressed in some of the nicest white formal silk dresses in the ballroom. The remainder of his daughters were under the age of sixteen and back at their housing being watched over by one of the Andolini girls.

Attending the black tie affair, with disguises over their faces, was a team put together by assassin Ulla Ragnarsson. Each of her team was wearing a top secret product of the Rosenburg Corporation called the "Mask of Concealment." The product was a simple mask that was paper thin plastic that would alter the facial features of the person wearing it. It was not an item that had been sold wholesale, but was one of the better kept secrets of the Rosenburg family. The mask was necessary to avoid being recognized by some of the guests and to leave a false recording on the hotel security cameras when the investigation into the crime began. Ragnarsson wanted to leave nothing to chance. For a successful kidnaping, the escape had to be flawless which meant the team member identities had to be guarded jealously.

Ulla had brought in three men to assist her in her mission to deliver the children of the richest families to the Glorious Leader. The three helpers had been highly recommended by Barry Flynn, an old family friend of the Ragnarsson's.

Based on Flynn's advice, Ulla hired Jericho Griffin, Boris Ilyasova and Heinrich Jahn to eliminate the crowd and fly the kidnaped little brats off of New Edinburgh to Sikorsky's Planet. The three men had been pilots on the science vessel the Colorado. They had been disgraced and court martialed. After losing their officer's commissions, the three men became freelance pilots for the Rosenburg family.

Many flowery speeches were given in honor of the departing Dean. Harvard graciously accepted a plaque of gold inscription on black wood that thanked him for his years of service in building the Clovis Academy into the envy of all other military training colleges. The five course dinner of salad, soup, filet mignon, mixed grilled vegetables and crème Brule was delicious.

Lupita Calderon looked stunning in her gown. Dirk was proud to have such a striking woman at his side. And the company of dear friends made the evening even more special to Dirk. But he had no idea of the tragedy that awaited him and his friends that evening. The only drawback was that Piotr Gorski and Therese Fenster were behaving as two friends would. Dirk wondered what the reason was for the lack of romantic interaction between the two. He made a mental note to himself to discuss the issue with his younger sister.

After Golden Harvard received the large plaque thanking him for his years of service, the applause was interrupted by the sound of coughs and some of the people in the crowd were passing out. There was a foul smell in the air.

Arch Frazier began to cough and looked around the room at the other guests that were experiencing difficulty breathing.   He realized immediately what was happening. He looked to his friends with an alarmed expression. "Gas! We have to get out of here!"

Cara Perez Guerrero looked panic stricken as she smelled the odor. She did not want to lose her babies. She put her dinner napkin over her face as she stood up quickly as Elektra and Arch Frazier assisted her.

Klaus helped his pregnant wife, April, to her feet.

"The exits," Lupita pointed to the left with one hand and helped Rhinehard with his wife using her free arm.

Several of the crowd began to panic and run for the emergency exits. Some people fell on top of each other the gas began to create a grey smoke in the room, creating problems with visibility. Dirk saw that Piotr Gorski was holding Therese Fenster by the hand. Arch and Elektra Frazier were assisting Perez Guerrero toward the exit to the right. Klaus and his wife were right behind them. The unspoken priority between them was to get the two pregnant women out of the banquet hall and to fresh air.

Shigeta was also moving for that exit, holding hands with April. Klaus was next to his wife, protecting her from the panic stricken guests that were running this way and that. He knocked one man to the floor when he came to close to April.

Lupita latched onto Dirk's arm, "The exit to the right looks like it has less people."

Dirk noticed Calderon was covering her mouth and nose with her dinner napkin. There were several party guests unconscious, lying on the floor on face down on the table tops.

"Come on," Dirk urged and led Lupita, Piotr and Therese for the right wall exit.

Jericho Griffin had been fired from his job as an officer and a pilot on board the Science Cruiser Colorado. He and two other pilots had started a bar fight about a year earlier with the gang of cadets led by Yuri Gorski. Griffin and his friends had been tried in a court martial and disgraced. Griffin, following the lead of his friend, Boris Ilyasova, had accepted employment with the Rosenburg family. Since that fateful day, Griffin had transported illegal slaves and contraband weapons. He had gone from an officer and a gentleman to a well-paid criminal. With the fall of the majority of the Rosenburg family, Griffin and his friends were now employed by the new patriarch of the Rosenburg Corporation, John Rosenburg.

Griffin and his friends had been hired by John Rosenburg to attend the black tie affair, to stun several members of the crowd when the gas was released. Griffin stood and saw that Ilyasova, who had been seated on the opposite end of the banquet hall was also rising to his feet. Both Griffin and Ilyasova drew out their concealed hand held laser pistols and began firing.

That was when the real chaos began. The laser fire erupted. Several guests were seemingly randomly stunned. But Griffin and Ilyasova had specific targets in mind. Colonel Nikolai Gorski and Major Sigebert Evart were two of the first two in the large ball room to be hit. The military officers collapsed to the ground. The naval officers were likewise targeted.

The purpose was simple, eliminate the military presence in the ball room first. The civilian targets could wait as they would not be armed and ill equipped to resist. As the unconscious individuals were falling to the floor, Boris Ilyasova fired upon several of the fleeing invitees. Piotr Gorski was hit by a laser shot and he fell to the ground. Therese Fenster stopped to help him. She was hit in the back by a laser blast fired by Griffin. Dirk turned back to render aid to his friend and sister when he saw an old familiar face before him. The man was wearing a tuxedo, smiling and had a hand laser in his hand aimed right at Dirk's chest. The last time Dirk had seen the man was during a rumble at a bar called Tinkerbelle's on Space Station Cy-7.

"Ilyasova," Dirk said recognizing the rogue that had been fired from his position as a pilot on the Science Cruiser called the Colorado. He had been charged and pled guilty at a court martial that had been initiated by Captain Ruiz after he started the riot on Space Station Cy-7.

The disgraced former Lieutenant Commander, Boris Ilyasova, was standing next to a very attractive woman. She also had a laser pistol in hand and was wearing a formal white evening gown so that she could effectively blend in with the crowd. Dirk had never seen the woman before. She aimed her pistol at him and fired. Dirk felt as if he had been hit by a lightning bolt as the electrical energy from the stun gun enveloped him. He cried out and fell to the ground. He gasped for air as he lost consciousness.

Lupita Calderon watched helplessly as her friends and her date were hit with laser fire. She felt rage building up in her as she snarled and grabbed a steak knife off of one of the tables. Concluding that she was the only one in the ballroom able to defend Dirk, Therese and Piotr, she charged at the two perpetrators with the knife in her right fist, held over her head. Boris Ilyasova saw her coming out of the corner of his eye and blocked her knife thrust with his free left arm. Ilyasova then kicked Lupita to the ground and stepped on her abdomen. Lupita lost her grip on the steak knife from the impact on the tiled floor. He held her on the floor with his left floor planted on her.

She screamed as she struggled in vain to free herself. Ilyasova pressed his foot harder onto her torso to hold her in place.

The woman with Ilyasova picked up the dropped steak knife and knelt over Calderon.

"You," the woman said. "I know who you are. You were one of the cadets involved in shooting down my brother's ship."
"What are you talking about? I have never seen you before!" Lupita protested between coughs.

"My brother is dead thanks to you and your friends. Then you compounded your mistake when you gave testimony at the recent trial against my other brothers and sister. You must not have received the unwritten rule of humanity. You stay loyal to the Sikorsky family and never ever fuck with the Ragnarsson's." The woman growled as she spoke the words.

"Who are you?" Lupita demanded between coughs caused by the lingering effects of the gas. She wondered why the gas in the room had no effect on the strange woman.

"My name is Ulla. Ulla Ragnarsson. And you, my pretty young thing, picked the wrong party to attend."

The very mention of the name Ragnarsson sent chills up Lupita's spine. She had believed that Sean Collins had prosecuted all of the remaining Ragnarsson clan. Clearly, she had been mistaken. How many more were there, Lupita wondered.

Ulla smiled and showed the large steak knife to Lupita. She waived it in a menacing manner in Lupita's face. Ulla had read the profiles of all the cadets that had caused her family to suffer. She had vowed that she would kill each and every one of them.

Lupita screamed in terror as she realized the woman was going to stab her. She attempted to roll away, but Ulla trapped her arms with her knees. Lupita continued screaming for help as Ulla slashed her throat from ear to ear with the steak knife. Lupita felt her blood gushing out, she tried to scream again, but she could not.

Ulla stood over Calderon and watched with pleasure as the young girl bled to death on the floor. The beautiful formal gown that Dirk Fenster had purchased for her was soon drenched in her blood. Ulla's eyes showed no remorse for the act. She dropped the steak knife to the floor of the ball room as if it were a toy that had no further use.

"Was that even necessary?" Ilyasova asked, looking down at the bloody corpse of Lupita Calderon. He thought killing the girl was a waste of great looking woman. If it had been up to Ilyasova, he would have taken the Calderon girl as his personal hostage and sex slave.

"No witnesses," Ulla said softly. She had secretly planned on killing each and every person that had been involved in the death of her brother Dell and her sister Emma. It was a scheme she had not let Ilyasova in on. Killing Lupita Calderon was a good start.

Jericho Griffin was soon standing next to them with Therese Fenster in his arms. He was glaring at Ulla due to his disgust at killing the innocent girl. Griffin felt ashamed that he had not helped the girl. He looked down at her corpse and her brown eyes staring blankly at the ceiling. Griffin bit his lower lip and determined that he was finished working with the Ragnarsson family. They killed without reason and Griffin no longer wanted any part of their senseless vendettas. He would collect his pay for his role in the Fenster kidnaping and then leave the employment of the Rosenburg-Ragnarsson axis forever.

Using both hands, Ilyasova lifted up Dirk Fenster and threw him over his right shoulder. Griffin noted from his facial expression that his former commander cared little for the dead girl at their feet.

"We got what we came for," Ulla told the two men. "Now let's get out of here and deliver the two Fenster brats to their new home."

In the lobby of the Hotel, the majority of the guests congregated as several Marine Corps soldiers stormed into the ballroom. Shigeta was coughing due to the gas she had inadvertently inhaled as she had escaped the ambush. She searched for her friends, looking over the crowd. She saw that

Golden Harvard and his wives were out of harm's way. The Dean was receiving oxygen from a fast responding paramedic.

Several civilians were lying on the carpeted floor of the five star hotel, gasping for fresh air. Shigeta found Perez Guerrero first. She was sitting on a bench near the main exit to the hotel. The two women hugged briefly as they were breathing heavily. They were soon joined by the Frazier's and the Rhinehard's.

"Six of us," Klaus was able to state as he was also coughing. "Where are the others?"

"They might still be in the ball room," Frazier said and stood up.

"Where do you think you are going?" Elektra demanded of her husband.

"Back in there," Arch pointed to the ball room entrance. "Dirk is my best friend."

Klaus stood up with the intention to join Frazier. "You ladies wait here for us. We will be right back."

The two men pushed through the crowd to get back to the ball room entrance.

"I love my husband," April Mejia got out between breaths. "But sometimes he can be a macho cabron."

Perez Guerrero and Shigeta began laughing between coughs.

Frazier and Klaus worked their way through the crowd toward the entrance of the ball room. All of their efforts were for naught as they were turned away by Criminal Investigation Division detectives and Marines. Crime scene tape was being stretched across all of the entrances of the massive room. Sergeant First Class Mark Lund had arrived on the scene and was directing Marines to calm the crowd and pointing to other Criminal Investigation Division officers to secure the crime scene and interview all of the witnesses. Klaus overheard one of the Marines say that there were three casualties.

The reports of three dead caused the normally level headed Frazier to try and push his way through the Marines and MI soldiers back into the ballroom. Klaus had to assist the soldiers to restrain his friend, even though he also wanted to get back inside to check on the Fenster's, Gorski and Calderon. As the body of Lupita Calderon was being wheeled out on a stretcher, Frazier watched in silence as soldiers were holding his arms and chest.

"By Baelder," Klaus whispered to himself as he saw the lovely girl lying motionless on the wheeled medical bed. Her lovely dress was drenched in fresh blood and the gash on her throat was still open. Her pretty eyes were lifeless. "That's Lupita."

Two other corpses were soon to follow. One was a ninety-eight year old woman that had suffered a stroke during the commotion. The other was a nine year old girl that had been trampled to death by the panic stricken crowd. The parents of the child were wailing and crying when they saw their deceased child.

Frazier had been released by the soldiers after he stopped struggling with them. He frowned at Rhinehard. "Klaus, where are Dirk and Therese?"

Klaus was shaking his head as he watched the soldiers bringing out the unconscious soldiers that had been attending the event. He watched each of the wheeled stretchers being pushed by him, looking for their missing friends. He waited with Frazier for over thirty minutes until they received word that the last of the party guests that had been stunned or injured were already out of the room. One of them had been confirmed as Piotr Gorski.

But there was no sign of Dirk and Therese Fenster.

CHAPTER FOURTEEN

Sikorsky's Planet, the former home world of the alien race the Akarzdamedian's, was one of eight planets that were a part of a binary star system. The population on the planet was approximately one billion eighty million humans and twenty million Akarzdamedian's. At one time, over two hundred years ago, the planet had a population of five hundred million Akarzdamedian's. The war against Earth did not go well for the aliens. Humanity brought the war to their home planet and used weapons of mass destruction. The alien population was nearly wiped out. Those that survived became prisoners and slaves.

The Academy on Sikorsky's Planet was considered the best location for students seeking upper level collegiate degrees to attend. This was so for many reasons. First and foremost was that the Glorious Leader, Vladimir Sikorsky, demanded that the major Military Academy for the Earth Empire be located on the very planet from which he ruled. The Academy recruited the best Professors and paid them well. The research facilities were the most excellent in the Empire. The living quarters for the students were some of the most desirable as the dormitories were larger and more spacious than the other Academies. And, naturally, the academic demands for admission were draconian.

The medical school at the Academy on Sikorsky's Planet had been producing the best in the field for over two decades. Several of the graduates of Clovis Academy had applied to be accepted. Only three were admitted. Siobhan Collins was one of the graduates of Clovis Academy that had achieved high grade marks to compete for a position on the prestigious campus. She was the second oldest child of attorney Sean Collins. Her father had instilled in her the work ethic and the understanding that a top notch education was critical to advance in life. Siobhan was a lovely lady with long, curly red hair and green eyes. Her knowledge of bio-chemistry was vast and she had been proving herself to be one of the best medical students at the Academy.

Siobhan Collins was elated that two of her fellow cadets from Clovis Academy had joined her at the famous medical school. The other students attending medical school with her were Clark Blundell and Robert Windfohr. The two young men had set themselves up for admission by studying every day in their four years of undergraduate school while others spent their spare time carousing. Blundell and Windfohr were book worms, bright, friendly, and somewhat naive to the ways of the world and they were the type of men that were always willing to help others. They both genuinely wanted to become doctors to help others. Windfohr was a proper gentleman, with a strong English accent. Blundell had come from the city of Chicago in a country that had once been known as the United States.

Siobhan Collins enjoyed having the two men around as Sikorsky's Planet made her feel homesick. She missed her father, her older sister and her other siblings. But her home sickness was somewhat lowered due to the fact that Blundell and Windfohr were not the only other Clovis Academy cadets attending the Sikorsky Academy.

One of Siobhan's dearest friends, Julia Steiner, was also attending classes on Sikorsky's Planet, working on her doctorate in planetary terra-forming. Steiner had cherry-blonde hair and was athletic, smart and competitive. Steiner had been born and raised in Lauterbrunnen, Switzerland. She had attained fame due to her involvement as one of the Clovis Academy cadets that fought against all odds to survive on the Blood Moon. Steiner had used her scientific knowledge to save several lives of injured cadets and was awarded some prestigious medals for her actions. Steiner never spoke of her experience on the Moon of Semiramis.

She always attempted to change the subject whenever some random acquaintance would want to discuss the incident. Steiner had confided in only one person regarding the fight for survival she had been thrust in the middle of. Steiner lived each day as best she could. She had faced death in ways many never would. Steiner had killed a serial rapist-murderer named Caine Rosenburg. Steiner did not regret that she had killed the man. In her opinion, Caine needed to be removed from life, his death made the world a safer place for women everywhere.

Another friend of Siobhan Collins that was living on Sikorsky's Planet while studying for his upper level degree was Lester Brey Gillis. He had been one of the survivors of the Semiramis Moon incident along with Steiner. Gillis had been born and raised on Ireland and was sometimes a bit nationalistic in his thinking, which was common for those that were born on old Earth.

His mother had been in politics on the Emerald Isle and she had, at times, spoken of secession from the United Nations. Gillis was one of the smartest men Siobhan had ever met. Gillis was fluent in several languages, understood military tactics and was a historian. He was also a martial arts student and held a black belt. He had been accepted to the Sikorsky Academy to earn a doctorate in military tactics and history. Siobhan and many of the other girls back on New Edinburgh had attempted to become Gillis' girlfriend. He seemed to date often when he had started out as a freshman at Clovis Academy and then he met Sophia DuBravac. Siobhan recalled the look in the eyes of Gillis and DuBravac when they first met. It was love at first sight. Gillis and DuBravac had married in May.

Siobhan Collins had agreed to meet Gillis, Steiner, Windfohr and Blundell at a local restaurant named Sword and Scabbard. It was a popular destination for university students, professors and politicians. It was also infested with legal prostitution and the sale of drugs. Siobhan was dressed in a one piece sleeveless green dress that was form fitting and cut above her knees. As she walked from her dormitory room on campus to the restaurant, she had a few construction workers whistle at her and make offers of sex. She ignored the men and kept walking.

When Siobhan entered the Sword and Scabbard, she noted that business for the establishment was excellent. The place was packed with customers and employees. It was almost standing room only. She walked around, looking for her friends. She observed several Academy professors at the long cherry wood bar in the center of the restaurant, sipping on gin martinis and gossiping about the current events of the planet. They were surrounded by several female and male prostitutes that were looking for a client to service for the evening. There were about twenty officers in dark blue pilot's uniforms at the bar with beers in their hands and some were taking shots of some synthetic drinks.

There were several of the indigenous population, Akarzdamedians, which were in several locations around the bar. They were interacting with humans as if they were all old friends. Siobhan continued her walk around the large restaurant until she spied on her friends sitting at a large round table in the corner.

All four were present as were two other students at the Academy. One was a man named Laurence Thompson who Siobhan had previously met and was a self-proclaimed computer genius. The other was a lovely Canadian student named Angelique LeClair. Both Thompson and LeClair had been in the middle of the Semiramis Moon incident. Both had been injured and nursed back to health by Julia Steiner. Due to their mutual near death experiences, Steiner and Gillis had become close friends to Thompson and LeClair.

Siobhan observed that LeClair was wearing her usual revealing type of clothing. LeClair would dress up, even when she was going to class, in provocative outfits that were certain to get attention from men. Today was no different. She had on a blue and silver striped tube top, and there was very little to it, which showed off her cleavage and flat stomach. She had on a short black mini-skirt and black high heeled shoes. She had on a matching set of silver drop earrings and necklace. Siobhan thought that at least LeClair had the body to show off, many Academy women would dress provocatively and not have the curves to match the clothing.

As Siobhan made her way to the table, Steiner rose to give her a hug. There were a few pitchers of beer at the table and some empty plates that were stained with sauce residue, which suggested that the group had been there for some time. Siobhan saw that some of her friends had eaten some soup and already had their main course on the table top.

"How was class?" Steiner asked her.

"Fine. Doctor Carson kept us a little late, as he always does," Siobhan responded as she sat down. Gillis poured her a glass of beer from one of the pitchers.

"I am leaving tomorrow to meet Sophia for New Year's break," Gillis told the group. "Anyone want to tag along? The transport from here to Space Station Cy-5 is about six and a half days travel."

"I can't, Les. Too much home work." Blundell said.

"I am in the same predicament," Windfohr added. "Medical School is more demanding than undergrad was."

Both LeClair and Thompson shook their heads in the negative.

"I can't go either," Siobhan lamented. "I have the same busy schedule as Clark and Robert. The Professors have really been piling on the out of class work and laboratories."

"Julia?" Gillis asked the lone holdout.

Steiner had become withdrawn ever since the Blood Moon incident. She had saved lives and she had killed a man. She had found herself wanting to be alone for the most part. She had even broken up with her long distance boyfriend, Cormac Collins. She told him it was the distance between them, he being on planet New Edinburgh and she on Sikorsky's Planet. But the truth was that she did not want any emotional entanglements at the current point in her life. The three week New Year break, which was also the time of the birthday of the Glorious Leader, would be a wonderful time to go on vacation. But Steiner really did not feel like venturing out yet.

"I wish I could, Les." Steiner told him, "Give Sophia my best."

The group began discussing the planetacide of Chronos. Although Chronos was only given lunar status by the astronomers, the mass murder of the entire population there warranted the term "planetacide" which a new name was given to describe the complete demise of each and every person on a specific planet. All of them were disturbed that a tragedy of such magnitude had caused over eight hundred thousand deaths in just under two minutes.

Siobhan ordered a plate of corned beef and cabbage from the waitress as the sun light was fading and night set in. After an hour at the Sword and Scabbard, a few men approached the group. They began asking questions designed to see if Steiner, LeClair and Siobhan were involved with Gillis, Blundell, Windfohr or Thompson. Most of the men had their eyes fixated on LeClair's chest. The three women gave each other a frown to demonstrate no interest. So, Steiner told them, in a blunt manner, that they each already had boyfriends.

As the men departed, LeClair laughed. "Julia, you just lied to those guys. We don't have boyfriends. What if we see them again? They might ask questions."

"I did them a favor," Steiner was dismissive of the topic, waiving her hand. "We had no desire to get to know them. So why waste their time? Let them go off and find women that are amenable to their flirtation."

"I suppose that is one way of looking at it," Siobhan agreed with Steiner, but felt her friend could have been a little more diplomatic about the brush off of the men. She had observed a change in Steiner's personality ever since she returned from the Blood Moon incident. Siobhan secretly wondered whether there was more to the official story regarding Steiner's experiences in that tragedy.

Steiner's eyes widened as she watched two women walk in. "You got to be kidding me."

"What's wrong?" Siobhan asked.

"Les, over by the bar." Steiner said in a hushed voice. "It looks like another Bragg Gang member is here."

Gillis looked over at the bar area and saw that Steiner's eyesight was spot on. Renee Starr was laughing it up with a group of pilots. She had on the dark blue suit of a Space Command pilot and a gold patch on her shoulder that had black lettering saying "FIRST FLEET." She had the rank of Lieutenant Junior Grade on her collar. Starr was laughing and hugging a tall dark and handsome looking pilot with the same patch on his arm.

"First Nour, then the Yutong brothers now her," Gillis said to Steiner.

"Who is she?" Siobhan asked.

"Renee Starr. She was one of the original bad girls of the Bragg Gang. We fought her a few times back on New Edinburgh. She used to be a real brawler," Steiner told her.

"Like Calderon was?" Siobhan smiled as another round of drinks arrived.

"Yes and no, Reynita was the one that really could kick some ass. But Renee was not afraid to throw down," Steiner reminisced. "She made the First Fleet. I didn't know she had such a high grade average."

Everyone knew that selection into the First Fleet was a prestigious award. Only the best served there. It was the Fleet that guarded Sikorsky's Planet so the family of the Glorious Leader took extra care in selecting the individuals that would serve as their planetary security forces. They watched as Renee Starr accepted a shot glass of tequila and she downed it in one gulp.

Gillis suddenly smiled and jumped to his feet. "Uncle Andrew!" He called out and walked to a man in a nice black suit and pressed white dress shirt. The two men embraced.

Gillis turned to the table and put his arm around the distinguished man he had referred to as Uncle Andrew. "This is my uncle, Andrew Brey O'Connell. I am sure you all know him as one of the Professors in weaponry and metallurgy at the Academy."

Gillis introduced each of his friends to his uncle. LeClair found Gillis uncle to be very attractive so she stood up and leaned over the table to shake his hand, ensuring that O'Connell would get a good close up look at her cleavage. Professor Andrew Brey O'Connell was related to Gillis on the maternal side of the family. Gillis' mother was O'Connell's sister. Although Gillis had not seen much of his uncle over the last ten years, he had good memories of O'Connell from his childhood.

When Gillis introduced Siobhan to O'Connell, she stood and shook his hand. O'Connell smiled at her and she felt herself blush. She had always found older men more desirable than men her own age. O'Connell was handsome, dressed well, fit and looked about ten to twenty years younger than he actually was. Gillis offered his uncle one of the empty chairs at the table and

O'Connell accepted. He sat down next to Siobhan and smiled at her.

O'Connell had been one of the Professors that enjoyed the sexual companionship of female students. He pursued woman much younger than him. In O'Connell's mind the younger women had better bodies for his sexual pleasure and they were not very experienced, so he could generally mold the younger woman to do his bidding. His last undergraduate student had left the campus in June. O'Connell thought this Siobhan Collins would make a perfect replacement. She had sexy red hair and a slender body for him to enjoy. He made it his mission to pursue her and make her his next lover. He was happy to learn that she was single and available.

LeClair caught on quickly that O'Connell was more interested in Collins than in her. LeClair turned her attention to medical student Clark Blundell. He seemed to be a nice young man and he liked staring at her chest. LeClair moved closer to Blundell and began flirting with him.

As they conversed, Siobhan learned that O'Connell was an engineer, computer programmer, a master at working with metals and a weapons designer. She listened to him over the next two hours talk of his career. She was captivated by his eyes, the sound of his soft, baritone voice and his occasional complements as to her hair and dress.

As the evening moved on, Siobhan noticed that LeClair and Blundell had left the group, walking away arm in arm and laughing at some joke that the others did not hear. Laurence Thompson and Robert Windfohr were propositioned by two strikingly beautiful working girls.

The two men negotiated a price for the night with the ladies and then left with them. Steiner and Gillis observed that Siobahn and O'Connell were certainly hitting it off. Gillis made the excuse that he had to pack and leave early in the morning. He said good night and left. He was a bit speechless that his over fifty year old uncle would openly pursue a twenty-two year old medical student.

Steiner soon followed Gillis out the door. She figured that Siobhan was a big girl and could take care of herself.

After they were left alone, O'Connell asked Siobhan Collins the question he had found that each college girl he had asked said yes to: "So, would you like to see my engineering laboratory?"

"Where is it located?" Siobhan asked. She was flattered that the handsome man was paying so much attention to her. Siobhan was well aware that women out numbered men in the population at a ratio of eight point six women to every man. That made the competition for women to obtain a man that much fiercer. The laws allowing men to have multiple spouses helped cut down on the competition somewhat. But Siobhan had been without a serious boyfriend for two years and she yearned to make up for the lost time.

O'Connell moved closer to her and placed his hand on her leg and began sliding it up and down her upper leg. She did not attempt to stop him. He leaned forward and gently kissed her on the lips. Siobhan kissed him back.

O'Connell stopped kissing her for a moment and looked into her eyes, "Let's go."

She nodded and stood up next to him. "Are you not concerned that you are a Professor and I am a student? Doesn't the Academy have rules against this sort of thing?"

"Yes, there are rules and I think the rules are crap. And no, I actually have no concerns at all." O'Connell had his arm around her waist as they walked out of the Sword and Scabbard together.

Siobhan Collins swallowed as she felt his hand slide down her back to her rear and stayed there. "You realize your hand is on my ass. I am young enough to be your daughter."

O'Connell smiled. Her body was well toned. O'Connell liked the fact that she obviously took pride in keeping her body in shape.

"All I know is that you are a vibrant, intelligent and beautiful woman and I want to get to know all about you."

O'Connell led her to his waiting transport space ship about fifty yards from the restaurant. As they walked, he would stop and kiss her passionately and then keep walking. Siobhan felt her heart pounding each time he held her and kissed her. She let him lead her onto his Super Raumschiff. As the Back Bay doors began to close, she felt O'Connell behind her. He wrapped his arms around her and pulled her against him, her backside against his front. He began kissing her neck and shoulders. His hands roamed over her breasts.

Siobhan's heart was pounding with anticipation as his hands roamed over her body. She felt his manhood against her, hardening as his breathing grew faster and his kisses more urgent. She realized she could not say no. She wanted to be with O'Connell and her desires took over. She laughed as O'Connell lifted her in his arms and continued kissing her neck and shoulders. She allowed him to unzip her green dress. She watched his eyes as he pulled her dress off of her. She could see the pure animal lust in the way he looked at her. She loved how his hands on her body. She allowed him to take her for the first time on the floor of his ship. She moaned pleasurably as he kissed her breasts for several minutes before he thrust himself inside of her.

After they both climaxed, he carried her up to the pilot section, kissing her lips, neck and breasts as he took each step to the top of the space craft. O'Connell made love to her a second time on top of the metallic command dash.

As they cuddled together on the pilot's seat, naked and sweating from their lust, she hoped that her meeting Andrew Brey O'Connell was the beginning of something memorable. For her it had certainly started off that way. Unfortunately for Siobhan Collins, the man she was now involved with had been the principal perpetrator in the elimination of over eight hundred thousand men, women and children on the moon called Chronos.

Angelique Le Clair had come very close to death on the Blood Moon. The fact that she survived was a miracle. Le Clair had spent the last few months' soul searching and questioning her life and her decisions. She had always been attracted to the men that were the athletes, the most popular and most handsome on campus. But those relationships never seemed to work for her. After the sexual urges were satisfied, a couple had to be able to communicate and Le Clair found that she was far more intelligent than the average sports star. So she changed the profile in her mind of the type of man she wanted. She focused on finding a man that was smart and serious about his education. Blundell was all of those things and more.

As Le Clair walked down the streets of Sikorsky City next to the young future doctor, she reached out and took his hand in hers. They flirted and talked for hours as they walked across the main bridge over Andrews River. They leaned over the railing when they walked half the distance and looked out over the calm water. She realized that she was shivering due to the cold wind. Without her asking, Blundell put his dress coat over her shoulders. Le Clair smiled at him. He had lovely eyes and good muscle tone.

"I really like you," Blundell told her as he gazed into her eyes.

"I really like you, too," Le Clair responded quickly.

They moved together and began kissing. He pulled her into his arms and held her close. She felt this arms and chest against her. To her surprise, Blundell wasn't just smart but he was a man that took physical fitness seriously. His arms had muscle tone that was never evident from the baggy clothing he wore. Le Clair wondered if she had just hit the jackpot with Blundell. He had all the qualities a woman could want.

They continued kissing for several minutes until Blundell stopped and looked into her eyes. "Let's get out of here."

Le Clair nodded in agreement as he ran his fingers through her hair, "Where?"

"My place?" He suggested hopefully.

Le Clair smiled at him, "Let's go."

The next morning, Les Gillis boarded a crowded Fenster Corporation 7779 transport space ship which was capable of flying up to fifteen hundred passengers. The 7779 transport had been designed for private space lines, similar to the old airline businesses that were used on Earth many years earlier.

The only issues with such private transports was whether or not military vessels would be optioned to accompany them. Gillis had pre-paid for his tickets for the six a.m. flight that would be leaving for Space Station Sikorsky 3. There were five Sikorsky Space Stations in orbit around the home planet of the Glorious Leader. Each were used for various purposes. From the space station, Gillis would transfer to another transport that would take him to Space Station Cy-5 which was located at the furthest corner of the solar system. He looked forward to the seven days he would have to spend with his lovely wife Sophia and to see some of his old friends from New Edinburgh that were traveling with her.

His flight had families, single men and women galore. There were also some of the genetic spliced hybrid human-cats aboard. They were known as Kotek's, which was the Polish name for cat. The Kotek people were able to walk upright as any human, but could also convert to walk on all fours. They were covered with fur of varying colors and had eyes shaped like a cat. Their ears were shaped in a triangle, just as a domestic cat would have. They also had claws instead of finger nails and toe nails. They were known to have hyper mobility of their joints at the ankles, knees, shoulders, elbows and wrists. They each had long tails, unless they had elected to amputate them so that they could wear normal human clothing. The Kotek species had grown in population over the last twenty years as they were capable of two litters each year and they possessed a strong drive to reproduce.

There were also a few of the Children of Athena on the transport. Gillis had known about five of those individuals from his time at the Clovis Academy. They were human in every aspect except that their skin was as white as cotton. Their hair and eyes were dark. Then there were the powers they were born with. Each of the Children of Athena was able to project strong scents to lure sex partners to their bed. In addition, some of the second and third generation Children of Athena could read a person's mind. The stronger members could even project thoughts into a human's mind and force the human to do what they wished. It was mind control at a level that few of the Harcourt's dared to use out of fear of retribution from racist mobs or governmental legislation.

Very few instances were ever reported of a Child of Athena exerting such power over a human. Gillis always believed that if a Child of Athena had forced a human to commit an act by mind control, how would the human ever know that they had been used or manipulated? Gillis had good memories of his friend Jack Harcourt, who was a Child of Athena. There were others at the Clovis Academy that Gillis had not interacted much with while he was living there, Melissa Harcourt, Ann Harcourt, Brandon Harcourt and Donald Harcourt. Most of the members of the Children of Athena used the last name Harcourt. Some, and very few, would use a different surname.

Gillis observed some of the passengers were traveling with robot assistants, which generally would be machines that would walk in an upright position, shaped similar to a man with legs and arms and a head. The advances in robotic engineering had been positive for humanity. The advanced machinery made it easier to complete the most difficult of tasks. The robots could lift weights up to ten times that of a normal human. Some of the robots could expand their arms for up to thirty feet long. Others had multiple limbs so that they could complete several tasks at the same time.

Gillis sat in the bar of the transport and ordered a cup of coffee, an orange juice and some banana nut bread. He had dressed in work out sweats and had on a black leather jacket. Gillis hated being recognized since his role in the Semiramis Moon Incident. His face had been seen by almost every human in the Earth Empire due to a speech he delivered declaring that he and his friends would fight to the death. To avoid the notoriety, Gillis would turn up the collar of his leather jacket to cover half of his face. The flight to the space station would take about two hours. He faced one of the three dimensional broadcasts to watch an attractive man and woman deliver the news of the day. So far, so good. No one had acknowledged his identity yet.

Gillis sipped on his warm cup of coffee as he felt the transport ship begin to lift off. His thoughts reflected to the night before. His uncle, Andrew Brey O'Connell, had been estranged from the family. O'Connell left Ireland when Gillis was very young. His mother said some negative things about O'Connell over the many years. It was well known among the family that O'Connell preferred the companionship of women younger than he was. Gillis hoped that his uncle would not hurt Siobhan Collins.

She was a sweet girl and had been a good friend to Gillis. From what he could recall, Siobhan had not had a boyfriend of any significance in her life for almost two years. Gillis relaxed and enjoyed the flight to the space station. He watched through one of the observation windows as Sikorsky's

Planet began to fade, her silver blue surface looked beautiful from the sky.

Gillis enjoyed seeing the old castles and dwellings of the former indigenous population of Sikorsky's Planet. The Akarzdamedians had once been a vast empire. They had traveled to many planets that were void of any atmosphere or breathable oxygen.

They were essentially dead planets. The Akarzdamedians changed them into livable worlds by use of their technology and now they were each populated with billions of humans. The Akarzdamedians had claimed to have visited Earth thousands of years ago. The Akarzdamedian's even had names of Earth's ancient Gods such as Danu, Anubis, Shiva, Poseidon, Tyr, Hera and many others.

The Akarzdamedians looked similar to the jackal like statues of Anubis found in ancient Egypt. When the alien race returned to Earth and found that they were no longer the focus of worship, they were angered and attacked. The alien invasion had been named "The Racial Wars" by the historians, which Gillis felt the name should have been "Species War" instead. Most of Africa and the Middle-East was annihilated. But humanity rose to the challenge and fought back. After the victory of mankind over the Akarzdamedian's, Vladimir Sikorsky took power and seized the Akarzdamedian home planet and enslaved all of their survivors.

CHAPTER FIFTEEN

The private industry docking areas of Clovis City, planet New Edinburgh was always bustling with commerce. Shipments of goods were always arriving and departing. It was capitalism at its best. Each planet in the Eight Solar Systems would produce goods that might not be available on another location. So, the private transport business was a profitable enterprise in the economics of the future.

Giles Lancer had been one of the men that recognized that trend in the business world. Lancer had served the people of Earth bravely as a non-commissioned officer in the Marine Corps. When he neared the age of retirement, Lancer searched for a way to live out his years that would pay well. He had determined owning his own transport ship was the best way for him to maintain a better than average lifestyle. Lancer researched the space vessels for sale and found that he liked the Fenster Corporation Raumschiff's.

Lancer cashed in all of his retirement money to purchase a brand new space ship from the Fenster Corporation. Lancer had to teach himself how to fly and operate the newly acquired space faring craft. He took hours and hours of lessons. Soon, he was ready to start his own private transport business.

Giles Lancer named his ship the Blues City. At first, he was hired to take weaponry and livestock from one solar system to another. In time, he began to obtain loyal customers that would hire him to take them to other places. For the cadets attending Clovis Academy, Lancer had become the unofficial pilot for the students. He primarily flew his ship for the ones that called themselves Gorski's Gang. He charged the kids less money than his boring and stuffy corporate clients, mainly because Lancer really liked the kids. They were all interesting and had a zest for life that Lancer found refreshing.

When Sophia DuBravac approached Lancer for a price quote to take her and some of her friends for a week on Space Station Cy-5, Lancer was happy to assist. He quoted a very competitive price and the beautiful woman readily accepted and paid the fee. Lancer could remember when DuBravac was a freshman at the Academy. She had been a passenger on her ship several times. Now she was a senior, just seven months away from graduating. Lancer recalled the first time he transported her with Les Gillis. They were inseparable. He knew by the way DuBravac and Gillis interacted that they would always be together. Lancer was in his late fifties and had seen many planets full of people of different backgrounds and cultures. Over time, his one main acquired talent was to recognize true love when he saw it.

Early in the morning, Sophia DuBravac woke up and walked quickly from her dormitory room to the large Clovis City landing strip. She arrived at the Blues City with a large suitcase in her left hand and a blue back pack slung over her right shoulder. She was dressed in khaki shorts, slippers and a light blue pull over blouse. She had on a pair of sunglasses and her hair was pulled back in a twisty.

Walking next to her were Jurgen and Lila Doernitz. Lancer had never met the two young cadets in person. But he had seen the events in live three dimensional broadcasts from the Semiramis Moon. Jurgen Doernitz had been one of the many heroes from that incident. His skills as a fighter pilot were extraordinary. Doernitz walked without effort, suggesting his broken leg had fully healed. Lancer personally welcomed the couple on board his ship, shaking their hands.

Jack Harcourt and Rolf Rhinehard led a small group of newer cadets that Lancer had not met before. Lancer remembered Harcourt, the Child of Athena, with fondness. He had been loyal to Gorski and the gang and generally was the quietest member. Harcourt had special abilities that most humans only dreamed of obtaining. Lancer wondered why Harcourt never used his special powers to his advantage. Most of the Children of Athena would not hesitate to use their pheromones to lure a potential sex partner to bed, or read the mind of someone to gain an advantage over them or even use some of the rumored mind control powers that they possessed. Jack Harcourt seemed to very different in his personality from the rest of the Children of Athena in that he refused to take advantage of others using those abilities.

Rolf was the younger brother of Klaus Rhinehard. Both had been passengers on the Blues City in the past and were normally respectable young men. Klaus never gave Lancer any problems. But Lancer found that the younger Rhinehard had a bit of a devious streak in him. On two occasions, Lancer had witnessed Rolf attempting to steal another man's girlfriend away. Over a year ago, Lancer had caught Rolf having sex with a married woman in Lancer's gymnasium while the husband of the woman was asleep in his quarters. Rolf had big cajones, Lancer thought to himself. Lancer speculated that Rolf had little trouble in getting women. The young man was tall, muscular, and handsome and seemed to know how to say the right things to a woman when he wanted to. Rolf walked with an air of superiority about him. He grinned at Lancer as he boarded the Raumschiff.

There were several new cadets that Lancer had never met that accompanied the group. Lancer deduced that some of them were from the Andolini family. Their dark hair and olive skin and loud voices fit in with what Lancer remembered of Dominic and Marco Andolini. Lancer smiled, he could spend the six and a half day flight getting to know all of the new cadets that DuBravac and Jack Harcourt were bringing along for the vacation. The Andolini kids introduced themselves to Lancer as they boarded. They were Lucius, Venus and Giola Andolini. Lucius looked similar to his older brothers Dominic and Marco. Venus and Giola were lovely young ladies. Lancer watched the two Andolini girls as they walked by him, their curvaceous bodies and pretty faces that made him wish he was a younger man. The other cadets with them were Norman Porter, a pilot student and Daniel Choi, who was studying weaponry. Choi had a smile on his face that seemed to be perpetual.

Lancer thought to himself that his chosen second career was never dull. He was a lover of people. He enjoyed making new friends and learning about their lives. In many ways, Lancer lived vicariously through hearing the stories of others.

Lancer had taken on a few other passengers that were already on board his space craft. The other occupants were civilians from various careers and backgrounds. Lancer was certain the civilian passengers would have no difficulty interacting with the cadets. Two of the civilians were married with a child. The others were seeking passage to Space Station Cy-5 to connect with other flights to different destinations. One of Lancer's favorite passengers was an overweight man that was in his late forties named Joseph Bolt. Lancer liked Bolt because he always paid in cash and left a generous tip at the end of a successful trip. Bolt had eight wives, all in their early twenties and from varying nationalities. Lancer mused that Bolt had his own harem of women, each of his spouses were absolutely gorgeous. Lancer did not have any opinions one way or the other on those that had multiple spouses. Live and let live, Lancer thought to himself.

What Lancer did not know about Joseph Bolt was that the passenger had urgent business with the Royal Family at Space Station Cy-5. Bolt was an owner of several computer sales, repair and programming companies. The commander of Space Station Cy-5 was a Sikorsky that had privately contacted Bolt to give a quote on re-programming all of the security monitors and tracking devices for the entire station. Bolt informed the Sikorsky commander that his company could complete the requested task for a million and a half Empire Dollars. The bid was accepted, so Bolt rounded up his eight wives and his one year old son to make the trip to Cy-5 for his big payday. Most of Bolt's luggage consisted of state of the art security systems and monitors.

DuBravac felt terrible about leaving with the Fenster's missing and Lupita dead. The Andolini's all felt the same. Jack Harcourt felt the worst and had to be convinced by the others to not to cancel his travel plans. They all had to hope that the investigators would do their jobs and find their missing friends. Besides, Dirk would have urged them to go and enjoy themselves since there was little they could do that the military could not do better.

As the Academy cadets boarded his ship and stored their luggage in the numerous empty passenger quarters, Lancer began preparing his ship for lift off. He made his final checks in the engine room, ensuring there would not be any mid-space mechanical breakdowns. Lancer then walked to the bottom level of his vessel and made certain the weapons he had purchased were under lock and key. Lancer could not afford having any of the passengers stumble onto the stash of new items he was to deliver to a contact on Space Station Cy-5. If the cadets or civilians learned of the items Lancer had in his possession, their lives could be in danger.

Lancer, to make a good profit, sometimes dealt with some unscrupulous folks and the weapons he had in his cargo hold were for some individuals that claimed to run an illegal drug distribution.

The search for the missing cadets Dirk and Therese Fenster caused a slight delay in the departure of the Blues City as the Criminal Investigation Division of Clovis City had to conduct a sweep of all of the passengers. The entire city had been placed on top alert to locate the cadets. Lancer allowed the CID to sweep his craft with life sign scanners and to question each of the passengers prior to boarding the ship. Each craft departing the planet was subject to similar scrutiny by the civilian and military authorities. But the authorities were not the only ones searching for the Fenster's. Arch and Elektra Frazier had rallied several of the Gorski Gang members to contact friends, military contacts and access computer records of all documented space craft that had arrived a few days before their disappearance and recently departed.

Arch Frazier had confided in his wife that Dirk Fenster had related to him many instances of attempts to blackmail the family with kidnaping. Elektra Frazier made a request to her cousin, naval Captain Drimios Zachariades, to monitor the communication chatter between the Navy bases around the other planets for any clues as to the possible location of the Fenster's. Arch Frazier attempted to obtain the assistance of Dirk Fenster's roommate to help out in the search. But cadet Lu Wang refused to help and requested only that someone come to the dormitory room to get the scary wolf, Theodora, out of the room. Frazier obliged by contacting a cadet that worked in a local veterinarian office named Daniella Day to watch Theodora until Dirk returned.

What Wang did not tell Frazier was that he had told a man named Ilyasova where the Fenster siblings would be on the night of the kidnaping. Wang had been paid three hundred Empire Dollars by the Ilyasova stranger for the information.

Wang lied to the CID investigators as to whether or not he had any information as to Dirk's whereabouts.

April Mejia and her husband Klaus Rhinehard were going to classes to learn how to be good parents to their soon to be born twins. Mejia, seeing that her husband was disturbed by the lack of progress in locating the Fenster's, ordered him to join the unofficial search being led by Arch and Elektra. Klaus used his rank at the Academy to use several training Raumschiff's to transport them to locations that the evidence seemed to point toward. They first investigated the main landing port on Clovis City, since it was the most obvious location that a potential kidnaper would land and leave. It was the closest location for ship landings to the ballroom.

Jen Staszko organized some of the other gang members to interview the guests at the party that had been thrown in honor of Golden Harvard. She sent Boland 'Quarter' Miles, and twin sisters Nola and Lola Belzyt to obtain a list of all of the attendees and then to speak with them one on one. The military men and women refused to speak to the cadets. The civilians were mixed in their willingness to cooperate. Lola Belzyt located one of the party members that claimed that she saw Dirk and Therese Fenster being carried off by two rough looking men that were being led by a beautiful woman in an expensive nightgown. Belzyt got the witness to give her detailed descriptions of the men and the woman. Staszko thanked the cadet and gave the descriptions over to Shigeta and Elektra so that they could run it through the computer network to see if anyone would match them.

Elektra recruited Ann Harcourt, Brandon Harcourt, Donald Harcourt, Ye Yibing, Stella Andolini, Paolo Andolini, Piotr Gorski, Flora Evart, Mia Nguyen and Supreet Patel to interview everyone they could find at that landing area. They spent three days interviewing over seven hundred pilots, twelve hundred mechanics, numerous passengers and air traffic safety officers. Arch Frazier was able to board Dirk's private Raumschiff that was sitting unoccupied on the main landing strip in Clovis City. Arch checked the internal computer manifest and found that there were no pre-programmed flights planned by his missing friend. The cadets uncovered no clues as to the whereabouts of Dirk and Therese Fenster.

One of the pilots that was interviewed was Jericho Griffin. He was stopped by cadet Ye Yibing who politely asked him if he had seen anything out of the ordinary at the landing strip. Griffin was impressed by the level of loyalty demonstrated by the group of cadets toward the Fenster kids. Griffin found himself wanting to confess all he knew to the sincere eighteen year old Ye Yibing. But he held back and denied having any useful information.

As Yibing left him to speak with another pilot, Griffin felt more guilt swelling in him from his role in the whole affair. Griffin could not reveal his role in the deaths of the three innocent people and the kidnaping of the two popular cadets without betraying his friends Ilyasova and Jahn. In the distance, about two hundred feet away, Griffin observed two Harcourt's assisting with the questions. He wondered why they did not use their powers and read the minds of others to obtain the information that they needed.

After exhausting themselves for three days, the cadets boarded the training Raumschiff to return back to the Clovis Academy dormitories. Klaus flew the ship without making any comments to the others. He was certain that whoever had committed the criminal act was a well-financed group and that they were motivated to cover their tracks. He surmised that there would have been several people involved in the conspiracy which would include pilots and financiers. Bribes would have most certainly been paid to others in the form of cash. The problem with cash pay outs is that it was almost impossible to trace.

Klaus had no reason to suspect Dirk Fenster's roommate, Lu Wang. Nor would he have believed that two officers serving on Space Station Cy-7 also accepted money to help cover up the departing ship that carried Dirk and Therese Fenster from the solar system. Lieutenant Darby O'Neal was paid ten thousand dollars to falsify travel plans for the Super Raumschiff that belonged to Ulla Ragnarsson. Lieutenant Dante Friedmann took a similar pay off to wipe out the space station computer memory of the ship processing, purchases of supplies, food and solar energy batteries and refueling purchases.

Klaus returned to his university housing where his pregnant wife was waiting for him. April did all she could to ease his mind due to the lack of progress in locating their friends. They cuddled in their bed together with their retractable roof open so that they could watch the stars above them.

"Dirk and Therese could be anywhere," Klaus said as he held April close to him. "They were well prepared and knew exactly what to do and when to do it. I think they must have had inside information."

Mejia was lying on her side, facing him with a pillow behind her head and another long pillow between her legs to support her large stomach. She smiled as her husband rubbed her belly affectionately. "Klaus, stop beating yourself up over it. I know that you and Arch did all that you could. Hopefully it is a simple kidnaping. Money will exchange hands and then they will release Dirk and Therese. Try to get some sleep. We are going to be parents soon and our kids will need their father to be well rested."

Klaus kissed her on the lips, "I love you."

She kissed him back, "I love you, too. I can't wait to give birth so you can make love to me again and make more children."

"You want more?" Klaus kissed her on the cheek.
"Not really. I just like having sex with you."

Klaus kissed her again. He felt as if he was the most fortunate man alive to have such a wonderful wife to share his life with.

"Klaus, if something happens to me, like what happened to Lupita, I want you to get on with your life without me."

Klaus looked into Mejia's eyes and could see that she had a serious look in them. "April, nothing will happen to you. I am here to protect you."

She took his hand in hers, "Like Dirk wanted to protect Lupita? No, Klaus. No. This universe is not safe, just like Yuri always warned us. I love you so much, Klaus. But if I die, I want to know that you will live your life. I want you to find love again. You are a good man and you deserve that. Please do not let your life slip by without someone to love you."

Klaus squeezed her hand, "I promise that I will try and get on with my life without you. I want the same for you, April. If something happens to me, find someone to love you as I do. You are a wonderful person and I am so proud that you are my wife."

"I wish I could make love to you right now," Mejia smiled at him.

"Me, too. But we have to wait until after the babies are born. The doctor ordered."

Mejia sighed, "Damn doctor's and their rules."

Arch Frazier returned to his housing with Elektra. The couple poured themselves some glasses of Mavrodaphne wine from one of the bottles that Dirk Fenster had given them as a wedding gift. Even after several months of trying to deplete the supply of wine Fenster bought them, they still had three cases left. They ordered the housing computer to retract the roof so that they could cuddle on the dark shag carpeted floor and get drunk.

"I can't believe that none of those people we spoke with saw anything," Arch said as Elektra sat down next to him.

She drank from her glass of wine and smiled at him. "Lola was able to get a description of two men and a woman. Harumi spent several hours trying to find a match on the main frame computer at the Academy lab. Last I spoke to her she found over a thousand possible matches for each of the three people. That alone may be impossible to track down. We tried my dear. Try to get it out of your mind for tonight. Let's drink, make love and tomorrow we can check with MI and CID to see if they have any other leads. Jen and Harumi are going with Ye and Supreet and will be checking the space station and moon base landing and departing logs as we speak. Maybe they will come up with something."

Frazier wrapped his arms around her and kissed her passionately, finding that the pleasant closeness of her body was able to make him forget about his missing friend for a moment.

"Yeah, maybe."

In between gulps of wine, the Frazier's undressed each other. They made love on the rug underneath the star filled sky. For the duration of their passion, they were able to put out of their minds the fact that two of their closest friends were missing. But in the morning, they would be back at their tiresome efforts to find any evidence of who had been behind the kidnaping.

CHAPTER SIXTEEN

Lieutenant Reynita Calderon had maintained contact with her commanding General, Leta Tan, on a daily basis. After the murder of her younger sister, General Tan refused Calderon's request for some time off to grieve with her family. Tan's justification was Calderon's utter failure to locate the remaining children of Doctor Matthew Rosenburg. Reynita felt stunned that the draconian General would not even award her with a day or two to assist her family with the funeral arrangements.

Reynita considered resigning, but dismissed that thought when she remembered that the laws of the United Nations Space Command would either force her into the military service as a Private or send her to Cootron to serve a death sentence for desertion.

She had settled in to her new post in Clovis City which was a three floor building that housed her platoon of Military Intelligence Branch soldiers and a few dozen civilian Criminal Investigation Detectives. As the ranking officer, she was in charge of the day to day personnel issues, scheduling duty rosters and directing the course of any investigations. Her building was approximately five kilometers west of the massive United Nations Building. Since arriving, she had been drawn into the prosecutions of the Ragnarsson and Rosenburg defendants and now the kidnaping of the Fenster siblings and the murder of her younger sister.

Her office was twenty square feet wide and was separated from the main room on the second floor by brick walls.

She had one door facing the main room which was used for the MI soldiers to write reports on the computer desks that were there, five rows of fifteen desks. More than enough for her platoon of forty-five soldiers. In the basement of the building was a small gymnasium, storage lockers and a community shower. The second floor was used to store files and evidence. The third floor was for the local Precinct CID civilians.

Alone, Reynita sat at her chair and wept for a few moments over the loss of her sister. She had always believed that Lupita had been the best of all the Calderon kids. Lupita had the best grades, the most positive outlook on life and was the friendliest of all. Lupita also shunned the Bragg Gang from the beginning; even though some of her other sisters and brothers were major players in that faction. Lupita wanted to avoid the skirmishes on campus between the groups. Reynita wiped the tears from her cheeks and composed herself.

Reynita wanted to go out and beat down anyone that looked at her the wrong way. But that would not be conduct that would be acceptable from an officer. She decided that it would be better to take in a light workout in the basement gymnasium. She closed her door and changed out of her uniform into a half shirt and shorts. She slipped on a pair of tennis shoes and walked out of her office.

She passed several of her platoon members without making eye contact as she walked toward the staircase. Sergeant First Class Mark Lund and Corporal Frank Preston watched as their new platoon leader walked toward the staircase.

"You know, Frank? Our new platoon leader is pretty hot," Lund observed in a low voice.

Preston nodded and waited until their Lieutenant was out of ear shot. "She has quite a body on her, I will give you that. She is a brick house."

"Far prettier than our last platoon leader," Lund said.

Preston shook his head, "I don't know. Lieutenant Ling was an attractive lady. I really liked her. I think I liked Ling better."

Sara Stewart turned around from her desk and shook her head at them, "You two are ridiculous. She is our commanding officer. You should show her some respect."

"With a set of legs like that, I respect her plenty," Preston told Stewart.

"And she had really nice rear view," Lund added. "But Sara is right. We should not be in lust for our CO."

Stewart hit Lund with a piece of printing paper that she had balled up in her hands. "And you are her platoon sergeant, Sergeant First Class Lund. If the rest of the platoon saw that you are drooling over her, they are gonna start talking. And you, Frank? What if Tamura heard you?"

Preston had been dating one of the other platoon members named Miyu Tamura for the past week. Their relationship seemed to grow closer with each passing day.

"We are just playing around, Sara. You know that General Tan refused her leave request?" Preston asked them. "Our Lieutenant wanted to go help with the funeral plans for her sister and Tan told her no."

Lund looked down at the computer screen that was built into his desk top. "General Tan is a witch. I did not know that she did that to our leader. Look, we got along without an officer for a few months after Ling was killed. I think a few days won't hurt if the Lieutenant goes AWOL. We can handle things here."

Stewart leaned into the group and whispered: "What are you suggesting, Mark?"

Lund stood up and leaned over between Preston and Stewart, "I am going to tell her to go home to her family and we can run things for a few days without her. She probably does not know us well enough to ask us to do it for her, so I will suggest it."

"Good idea," Preston agreed.

Lund left the two enlisted soldiers and he found his way to the stairs and walked down. He found the gymnasium and saw that Calderon was the only person there. She was lifting weights to work on her shoulder strength. She had her back to Lund and did not hear him walk in. Lund approached her as she continued lifting weights.

Lund cleared his throat to get her attention, "Lieutenant, it's late. You should go home and get some rest."

Reynita turned her head in his direction to see who was behind her. Lund saw the tears running down her cheeks. She sat the weights down on the floor and wiped the tears away. She could not get the image of her dead sister from her mind.

Lund went to her, took her hands in his and knelt down in front of her. "Lieutenant, you need to go home to your family. I can run things here. Go home. Please."

Reynita nodded and stood up, "Thank you Sergeant. I, I just have some things to finish. I need to finish..."

Lund stood up and put his hands on her shoulders, "I got it. Go home, be with your family. If Tan contacts us I will inform her you are in the field. Go home."

She paused for a moment and then suddenly gave Lund a hug.

"Thank you."

Lund wrapped his arms around her. He was amazed at how nice it felt to have her body against him.

"You are welcome. Now go home."

She stepped away from Lund and walked toward the stairs.

"If anything comes up, you will contact me on my holo-com?"

"Yes, ma'am. You will be the first one I will call," Lund promised.

Reynita forced a smile and walked up the stairs.

Lund sat down on the work out bench closest to him. He shook his head as he reflected on how she felt in his arms. Lund realized he had a crush on his commanding officer.

"Damn she is really hot."

Cadets Ye Yibing and Supreet Patel had both volunteered to hack into the space station and lunar base computers in the effort to find Dirk and Therese Fenster. They were both imminently qualified to do so based on their knowledge of computer programming. But they also had been courted in the past by officers on each station.

Harumi Shigeta and Jen Staszko gave Yibing and Patel drugs to incapacitate their targets and get the security codes from them. Shigeta had attempted to shame Melissa Harcourt into helping them out in the endeavor to find the Fensters. She told Shigeta to go to hell.

Yibing and Staszko took a transport to the space station while Patel and Shigeta made their way to the lunar base by way of a charter ship. Their marks were surprised that the women made the effort to travel such a distance to find them.

Yibing had met a computer expert that served on the space station when she was arriving to the Academy. His name was Dante Friedmann. He had made numerous attempts to charm his way into her panties. But she had rejected his advances. He made several other efforts to bed her over the following months.

Staszko spent a few hours coaching Yibing how to seduce the man and then how to properly administer the drugs to knock him out. Although Yibing was new to the group, she was willing to sleep with the officer if there was any chance it would help Therese Fenster.

She had been the one to get Yibing into the protection of Gorski's Gang. Accordingly, Yibing owed the Fenster girl. So,

Yibing went with Friedmann under the auspices that a night of passion with her was imminent. She endured his hands running all over her body as he became aroused by the foreplay. He constantly told her how much he loved her and wanted to marry her. She humored him by smiling and pretending that she did not understand his English. Then, as he began to unzip her uniform, Yibing injected him in the neck with the drugs Staszko had provided her.

Friedmann fell face first to the floor with a thud. Staszko told her that the man would be out for twelve hours. As he slept, she stole the codes from his personal computer after hacking it. She left the man sleeping in his bed as she left to catch the first transport ship back to New Edinburgh. During the flight, she made a curious discovery when she began to inspect the data she had obtained.

"General Tan was contacted before the kidnaping by a woman named Ulla,"

Yibing read the print on her small hand held computer. She made a mental note to take the data to Harumi Shigeta and Elektra Frazier. They would know whether or not what she had found meant anything at all.

Patel slept with a Lieutenant Commander that was in charge of several squadrons on the lunar base command. She was able to get the codes from her after drugging her drink with truth serum given to her by Jen Staszko. Patel then met Shigeta at a civilian run bar on the lunar base and the two spent several hours sneaking past security and computer technicians on the moon base to download all of the information regarding arriving and departing space craft over the last several days. She found that all of the craft in the security memories of the base matched the information that Brandon Harcourt had procured from the CID data. Nothing helpful came from their efforts.

Patel felt terrible. She had committed several felonies in stealing Space Command confidential information and the woman she slept with to obtain the clearances to enable her to commit the crimes was a lousy lover. Patel wanted to get back to the Academy and shower. She felt dirty. More than anything, she missed her confidant and occasional sex partner Rolf Rhinehard. He had not shared her bed in quite some time and she longed to feel his arms around her. He had seemingly replaced her with Mia Nguyen which made Patel feel sick to her stomach. She had never loved a man before and her strong feelings for Rolf were growing into a deep depression without him in her life.

CHAPTER NINETEEN

The sight of the damages on the grounds below was humbling to Matthew Rosenburg. He had been successful in convincing General Tan to allow him to return to his homeland to recover some of his cloning equipment that would assist him in unraveling the mystery of the defective Junior Ragnarsson clones.

Matthew had been given a black Super Raumschiff with pink trim so that he could collect the machines. In addition, Tan assigned a pilot to fly the ship and a squad of MI soldiers to protect him. Matthew saw right through Tan's true intentions. The pilot was assigned to make sure that Matthew returned to Lynott's Land and the squad of MI soldiers was to ensure he did not attempt to flee.

The pilot, Lieutenant Maria Ishii, was talented and had several hundred hours of logged flight time. She had once served on one of the Planetary Defense squadrons that patrolled the solar system with regularity. Matthew found Ishii to be a woman of few words, only speaking when spoken to.

The squad leader was Sergeant Ann Vu, a real boisterous sort and a woman that loved weapons. Matthew noted that Vu had her utility belt that was over her shoulders and waist filled with laser pistols, knives and other types of darts. The other ten members of Vu's squad were dressed in a similar manner.

Since the death of Alfred Rosenburg, the majority of the Rosenburg Ranch Territory had been transformed into a military run province. Approximately thirty percent of the two hundred kilometers of land remained in the hands of civilians and was managed by John Rosenburg from his location on Sikorsky's Planet.

Matthew had been given everything he asked for from General Tan. She treated him to a warm bath in one of her ten yard long and five yard wide hot tubs, ordering some of her most desirable women to join him and give him whatever he wished. He made love to several of the women in the hot tub and was able to relax as they washed his body with nice smelling soaps. He received a professional haircut from Tan's personal stylist and was given his own room and a vast wardrobe of expensive clothing. When he asked Tan to allow him to make several flights back to the Rosenburg Ranch to retrieve some of his machinery to assist with the green skinned clones, Tan agreed without hesitation.

Matthew tapped his manicured fingernails on the metal wall behind him as he gazed out of one of the transparent metal observation windows while the ship sailed over the location of his old mansion. It had been reduced to rubble by Tan's troops many earlier. Matthew had been in the basement of his mansion when the attack occurred. He had been crushed under the tons of falling brick and mortar. But that had been a secret he had been keeping to himself. He died that day. It had not been a quick death, but a long lingering death, full of agony as he struggled to breath for the hour before he expired. His body had been rendered useless, his legs crushed, his ribs broken and his spine shattered. When death had come to Matthew Rosenburg, he welcomed it.

But when he died, he rose from the dead. His brain patterns, all of his knowledge and experience, were uploaded to the planetary satellite system by the microchip in his brain. All that he was had been sent electronically from satellite to satellite to a secret location where there had been numerous clones of his body waiting. One of those clones received the brain imprints and patterns and he woke up with a second chance at life. Matthew Rosenburg had attempted to begin plans to bring his family back to greatness just before some of Tan's undercover agents captured him. They had no clue that the person that they had apprehended was a duplicate.

"Where do we land?" Ishii asked over the communication speaker system of the space craft.

"The five floor light blue mansion with the gold trim," Matthew instructed. "The one that is three buildings to the east of my demolished mansion."

"You sound bitter," Vu observed.

Bitter was not the word for it. Matthew was livid, but he hid his feelings from the others. Tan, Collins, Gorski and the other powers in charge were to blame for his lovely mansion being destroyed. He planned on having his vengeance on each one of them. He sat in his seat near the observation window, watching as the ship descended to the grassy surface of the Rosenburg Ranch Territory, his home. He waited patiently for the ship to come to a stop. The sounds of the wailing engines were growing softer as Ishii shut down the booster rockets and then the rear thrusters. Matthew smiled as he watched Vu order her ten MI enlisted women to get to their feet. They had no idea what horrors were waiting for them inside the building that he would be leading them into.

Matthew walked with a fast gait down the narrow hallway from the computer section to the slightly inclined ramp that opened into the rear receiving and storage area at the rear of the ship. He heard the sound of several military issued boots behind him, clanging on the metal ramp. Vu and her squad had been given strict orders to watch him at all times. Matthew did not wait for permission before he slammed the palm of his right hand on the red button on the right side of the wall that was seven feet from the floor. The rear doors began to open upwards and a ramp that was under the space craft began to lower to the grassy surface. The ramp made an annoying creaking sound as it moved, leading Matthew to conclude that Tan's engineers had been slacking off on their maintenance duties.

"Leave the rear ramp down," Matthew ordered Vu as he glanced over his shoulder in her direction. "We will not be in the mansion for very long."

"You heard the man," Vu yelled at her squad. "Move it!"

Matthew walked down the ramp and stepped foot onto the manicured lawn that was so familiar to him. He did not wait for Vu and her squad as he walked in the direction of the large mansion with his chin up and shoulders back. The building had belonged to his deceased brother, Cush, and his wives and children. After Cush was tortured to death by his own father, his widows and children fled the territory and left the mansion behind.

The security protocols that Cush had installed were practically impregnable and only Matthew could obtain entrance. Cush had programmed his security system to admit Matthew and any person that Matthew vouched for.

As Matthew walked, he was cognizant of the floating, invisible computer monitors that were filming his every move and downloading the scans to a central computer located in the basement of the mansion to collate the images and determine the identities of those approaching.

Matthew was cleared instantly once the master computers recognized his face and retinal scans. Matthew spoke out loud to the invisible scanners that he knew were present, "Computer, clear the squad of female soldiers that are behind me for entrance. They are with me. Prepare for Contingency Number 44. Have the necessary hardware available for immediate implementation."

Vu and her squad did not hear him speaking and accordingly had no reason to be concerned. Vu admired the mansion that seemed to have an outer shell of metals, granite and stone walls. The large steps leading to the front entrance were an off white and Matthew ascended them with ease. For a man that had been imprisoned for as long as he had been, he certainly had a spring to his step. The gold double sliding doors opened as Matthew approached them. He walked into the foyer and continued walking rapidly. Vu and her squad picked up the pace to catch up to him.

When Vu entered the foyer she noted that there was a fully furnished study to her right and a wide hallway to her left. The floors were covered with black tile with streaks of grey and white. She walked down the hall and soon found herself standing in a vast room with high ceilings, metal floors, computers and other large machinery adorned the walls. Matthew was standing in the middle of the room, surrounded by hundreds of what appeared to be cryo-sleep tubes lying on top of multileveled racks. Vu noticed that Matthew had several small metallic balls that were floating around his head and shoulders.

"What in the name of the Stars is all this?" Vu asked him.

Matthew smiled at her, "This my lovely lady is one of the finest cloning hospitals ever created. It is all stolen technology from the Danaraja and the Akarzdamedians with the exception of a few improvements courtesy of my family."

"What are those small metal balls that are floating around you?" Private Lexi Fong asked.

Matthew pointed at the dozen balls that seemed to be in an orbiting pattern around his head, "You mean these? They are a creation of my uncle, John. We call them insurance. Loyalty insurance. You see, we found that anyone not related to us was a potential liability and could not be fully trusted. So John created these small devices to guarantee those we need to control would be forced to yield their free will to our needs. They are useful toys."

"How do they work?" Vu asked.

Matthew smiled and faced the eleven enlisted women, "Shall I give you ladies a demonstration?"

Vu recognized that his smile and tone of voice were not friendly. She began to draw her laser pistol from the pouch that was on her web belt. Matthew snapped his fingers and Vu was immediately paralyzed. She could move her eyes and breathe, but her arms and legs felt as if they were being held by some invisible force. Private Fong and the others found themselves unable to move. Their eyes were wide with fear.

Matthew calmly approached Vu, his strange metal balls followed, maintaining their circular rotation around him. He took hold of Vu's laser pistol and removed it from her. He showed the weapon to each of the eleven women, "These would not have done you any good. The moment you walked into this mansion, all of your laser weapons were neutralized by the security protocols."

The women watched as Matthew placed the barrel of the laser pistol to his head and pull the trigger. The women were horrified that the man would do something so reckless. But, as Matthew had stated, the laser pistol failed and did not discharge any energy blast as would normally be expected. Matthew dropped the laser pistol to the metal floor.

"What are you doing to us?" Vu demanded.

Matthew laughed as he responded, "I am going to give meaning to each of your wasted lives. I was able to scan each of your files on the flight over here. All eleven of you were raised in orphan homes, born to bitches that didn't have a pot to piss in. So, when you somehow miraculously survived the orphan life, you are impressed into military service and here you are. Most of you have no real goals in life other than to follow the orders of that lunatic Tan. \A few of you are pretty enough that you might convince a man of means like me to bed you and produce offspring. I know that Private Fong is taking computer lectures so that she can one day become a teacher. I saw your marks and they are quite good. You very well may have a bright future. The rest of you will die on some pointless battle that will change nothing. But I will now liberate all eleven of you and save you from that future of doom and despair. You will now serve me."

"You scanned us?" Vu tried her best to break the invisible force that held her.

"You didn't even get near a computer to scan us!" Private Jawalla Tiller growled as she tried in vain to move her limbs.

"I do not need a computer because I have all kinds of software in my brain. I can store thousands of terabytes of information in my brain. I am able to mentally access any computer system with a mere thought simply due to the fact that my body was constructed to be better than any other man. Now, you will each serve me and my mission."

Matthew flicked his fingers toward the eleven women and the rotating metal balls flew in their direction.

As the devices soared in the air, they each transformed into liquid. The women all screamed as the liquefied metal hit them in the face. The liquid entered into their mouths and noses and rapidly traveled down their throats. The women cried out, not from pain but from fear. The liquid metal split up inside their bodies and released dozens of microscopic micro-chips that flowed through their bodies, attaching to hearts, lungs, and kidneys and on their brains.

Matthew looked closely at their eyes and smiled as he observed their pupils enlarge which was his signal that the nanotechnology that he had developed with his brother Cush had taken hold of them. Vu and her squad were now under his complete control. He snapped his fingers and the invisible force field that had held the women still released them.

"Now you are all mine to control," Matthew said.

Vu knelt down and retrieved her laser pistol, "Sir, Lieutenant Ishii is still on the Raumschiff. She might be a problem. Should we eliminate her?"

"I already took care of her," Matthew pointed to some of the large machinery on the walls. "I sent one of my mind control metal balls to take control of her as we were entering the mansion. She is one of us now."

"Why us?" Fong asked as she moved to assist her squad members to begin loading the machinery that Matthew required to the Raumschiff.

"Why not you?" Matthew responded. "You are a well-trained unit of MI soldiers and your individual skill sets are potentially useful to me. Plus, I am surrounded by thousands of women that are loyal to Tan. I needed some soldiers that will work for my goals and best interests. I needed you because I already know what Tan intends to do with me and my children once I teach her medical staff how to clone. She will kill me and my daughters. She has no intention of allowing me to live. Now I have a squad of soldiers and a pilot under my control. If things get violent, and I have no doubt that they will, then I will be relying on you to assist me in protecting my children."

As he spoke, the soldiers removed the machinery that was lighter in weight than one would expect based on their size. Matthew, using the newly implanted micro-chips in their heads, informed them that the alien metals were much lighter than the metals of old Earth.

Fong felt compelled to educate her new master and spoke up. "Tan will most likely feed you and your children to her pets that are hidden under the main palace floors. She has several Jumpers that were captured a few years ago and she will feed them humans. I saw it once when she fed some protestors to those creatures. I can remember their screams and the sounds of their bones being crushed in those powerful jaws gave me nightmares."

"If Tan learns what you have done to us, she will kill you." Vu warned him verbally as she grimaced from a sharp pain due to her brain attempting to accept the non-verbal telepathic communications from Matthew.

"I will worry about Tan, you all worry about getting the machinery on board the ship. When we get back to Lynott's Land, act normally and do as you normally do. When I need you to back my play, I will inform you. And don't try to disobey my mental commands. If you try, the micro-chips in your bodies will explode. If they do an autopsy on your body, it will look like you suffered an aneurism. There will be no evidence of my implants in your bodies. If I have to kill any of you, keep in mind this is an exercise in self-preservation for me. I must protect my children at all costs. What I do now and the things I will be doing in the future are not personal."

The eleven women nodded as they worked. Upon completion of their task of loading the machinery on board the Raumschiff, Matthew took blood samples of the eleven MI soldiers and the pilot named Ishii.

Matthew did not tell them the reason he drew the blood from them and they were all too far under his control to dare and ask. He excused himself for a few moments to return to the mansion. Matthew put the blood of the twelve women in his data base and verbally ordered his computers to begin the process of cloning the women. If all went as planned, Matthew Rosenburg would have a few dozen of each of the women within a few weeks. His difficulty would be in sneaking his clones into Tan's Palace at the right time. He would need some inside help to do so. He would need a few computer experts and many more pilots to complete his goal.

"Why are you taking our blood samples?" Vu asked him.

"You will see," Matthew told her, smiling as if he had a big secret to tell. "You will see."

CHAPTER TWENTY

After being reunified with two of his daughters, Doctor Matthew Rosenburg was in a better frame of mind. He was angry that his oldest son had been murdered and that the rest of his children were taken to different orphanages. Since the social workers for the United Nations were not required to keep records as to where children were placed, it was nearly impossible to find them all. Matthew provided General Tan and Lieutenant Calderon with photographs and foot and finger prints of all of his missing children in an effort to make locating them all easier.

General Tan assured Rosenburg that his seven wives would soon be reunited with him. His daughters, Jamie and Maggie, were helping their father with the investigation into what went wrong with the fifty clones of Dell Ragnarsson, Junior.

Matthew Rosenburg took several days off from his work to reconnect with his daughters. They had been separated for about one year and had much to discuss. He learned that they had been forced to perform sex acts with the jail guards in the prison that they had been held in.

He was furious when General Tan informed him of the mistreatment. He toned down his anger so that he could take a more therapeutic approach with his daughters. Jamie was twenty-one years old and Maggie was twenty. The two girls had different mothers but had been raised together with their sibling group. He had wanted the best for all of his children. But due to the lunacy of his family, his children were arrested and now his son was dead.

Also in the laboratory with the three Rosenburg's were a dozen technicians, two geneticists, three nurses and three doctors. Among the technicians were LeVega Farley and Estrellita Calderon. All of the technicians monitored every second of the autopsy of the gutted clone from their numerous computer monitors and worked diligently to compile data that might prove useful to General Tan. Each of the techs, as they were referred to, were dressed in long sleeve one piece red jump suits so that they could be differentiated from the MI soldiers dressed in solid black.

Matthew used his position of trust within Tan's Palace to find several sex partners to satisfy his libido. His body was a clone that had ten times the strength and vitality of the average man and ten times the sex drive as well. He had slept with several of the woman from Vu's squad which was easy to accomplish given the implants in their heads that gave him complete control over their actions. He also seduced one of his computer technicians and made love to her in the bathroom. Although he missed the mothers of his children, he found that he was hoping that it took a long time before they were located.

"I just got laid," Farley whispered to Estrellita.

"You what?" Estrellita responded, hoping that her tech colleague would keep the conversation short so that she could continue eavesdropping on the Rosenburg's.

"Yeah, I got laid. Doc Matthew is one horny bastard. He caught me alone near the bath and shower rooms at the far end of the west wing. He grabbed me and started kissing me like he was crazy for me. I hadn't been laid in so long that I let him move me into the men's room and he took me on the floor."

"   I hope you enjoyed yourself. If Tan finds out you had sex in her palace with a man, she might have you killed."

Farley frowned, "They would kill me for that?"

"She's done worse."

"Shit," Farley sounded nervous as she spoke. "I hope no one saw us in the hallway. The bath room was empty so there were no witnesses. Say, you aren't going to rat me out are you?"

Estrellita shook her head side to side, "No, I think that we tech girls should all stick together."

"Me, too. I owe you one."

"No, you don't."

Estrellita listened intently to the conversations of Matthew and his daughters as she worked. When she was certain that no one was watching her, Estrellita placed small quarter inch radius disks on the other computers that were mini-computers. The disks were able to scan the hard drive of each computer and then send all of the information via the satellite system to Estrellita's home computer. She hoped that the information that she obtained would assist Reynita in her search for the other Rosenburg family members. Estrellita did not notice that the eyes of one of the green skinned clones of Junior Ragnarsson were watching her and following her every movement.

One of the computer technicians that was assisting with the research uncovered that the duplicates of Ragnarsson had received a wireless command to awaken. For some reason all fifty did not rise as commanded. There had to be some form of malfunction present.

During the investigation, Matthew Rosenburg determined that they needed to complete an autopsy on one of the fifty to see if there were any other defects. He was joined by some medical doctors that General Tan had supplied to him. They cut open one of the replicas and inspected every major organ in its body. They spent most of their time inspecting the brain.

Matthew removed a micro-chip from the brain of the Ragnarsson duplicate. He held the chip in a pair of clamps and noticed something that was odd. The chip looked like it had short circuited at some point. The micro-chip had burn marks on it.

"Jamie, what do you make of it?" Her father asked her as he passed the clamps to her. Jamie was the computer expert of the family. She took the burned micro-chip to a scanner and began work on what caused the malfunction and when it occurred.

Maggie had been in pre-medical classes just before her arrest. Maggie was a changed person due to her experience in prison. She seemed to have lost her sense of humor that she had. She was also short with others during conversations with them. She helped her father dissect the corpse of the clone Ragnarsson. It was a long process to try and uncover the secret of the failure. After weeks of running programs and scans, Jamie Rosenburg came to a conclusion. The micro-chip in the brain burned out because one person had downloaded their brain prints at one point. Then at another time, another person attempted to download another brain print to the chip. That caused the flame out, as Jamie called it.

They brought in General Tan to explain to her the problem.

"So, one person had all of their knowledge, personality, experiences, education and everything else that was in their brain downloaded to the micro-chip." Matthew explained to Tan. "So the chip was to transfer all of that information into the brain. Which it did not, for some unknown reason. Then at a later date, some other person attempted to download another brain pattern to the same chips. That caused the chips to flame out. The chip could not determine which personality to favor and therefore the cloned brains were fried from the overload. That is why they did not wake up when ordered. They were essentially brain dead."

"So who was the second person to download their, how did you say, their brain print?" Tan was skeptical.

"Correct, the brain print is my term," Matthew said. "We have finger prints. I believe that our transferred knowledge from our brain to another leaves our original brain print in the micro-chip. When a second person attempts to use the same micro-chip it created a conflict. The chip could not handle the two different competing personalities and that caused the flame out."

"So they are all brain dead?" Tan asked of the clones.

"Yes and no," Matthew answered quickly. "If we remove the chips we may be able to save some of the other forty-nine. But we need to wipe the memory from all of the chips. It would be very risky."

"Can you activate any of them?" Tan wanted to know.

"I would not risk it. They would be mindless, like zombies. They would only have the basic instincts with no guiding principles. It could be dangerous if any of the remaining forty-nine were awakened. I recommend that we terminate them all now before someone finds out they are here and attempts to use them for themselves."

"No, we will not terminate them. Not yet. What about the skin color?"

"Whoever created these did not know all the steps. They took short cuts in the creation process and that caused the skin color to mutate to green. This was not done by Cush or my father. Nicolette would not have made this mistake. Frankly, I am at a loss as to who the creator of these clones was. It was not any member of my family that I can assure you."

"Can the skin color be fixed?" Tan demanded to know.

Matthew stopped what he was doing and faced Tan. "General, I can fix anything. You want your knowledge, experience and everything about you programmed into the brain of one of these creations? I can do that. You want me to change the skin; I can do that as well. But to change the skin you need to find me about four young women that are expendable and won't be missed."

"Why you need four women?" Tan asked.

"Because I am going to strip their skin from their bodies and use it to replace the green skin on one of these replicants. There is only one question, General. Do you like to listen to the screams like my father and the Glorious Leader? They loved for us to keep the donors awake while we cut them open. Do you?"

Tan grunted, "I find four women for you. No, I want no screams. Kill them nicely, no suffering for women."

"As you wish, General."

"Let me know when we can download my brain into one of them," Tan instructed them. "I want to do it soon."

She stormed out of the laboratory.

"Did she even listen to anything you told her, daddy?" Maggie Rosenburg asked.

"I doubt that she did," Matthew looked over the nearest green skinned Ragnarsson duplicate.

"Let's prepare this one. We will remove the existing microchip and replace it with a blank one and then we will copy Tan's brain patterns for downloading. I hope we don't end up regretting this."

The two women began getting ready for the transfer procedure. As they did so, Matthew began working on the other forty-eight replicants and removed their computer chips from their brains. The operations took him almost a day to complete. The Doctor had plans for the remaining forty-eight that he did not share with General Tan. He was certain Tan would never allow him or his family to leave her palace alive. They would have to fight to escape. Forty-eight super assassins under his direct control would make a formidable opponent against a few brigades of MI soldiers.

Lieutenant Reynita Calderon had spent a few days with her mother and father making the necessary arrangements for her the funeral services. Her brothers and other sisters also gave valuable time and participated in the effort. When she was satisfied all was ready, she returned to her office out of fear that

General Tan would check in with her regarding her progress with the location of Matthew Rosenburg's wives. Reynita left the home of her mother and father and took the aerial bus system to her headquarters.

When she arrived it was almost two in the morning. Calderon used her security swipe card to gain entry into the building. She was wearing a matching set of black sweats with a white stripe running down the outside of the long sleeves and legs. Her black tennis shoes had similar white stripes on their sides. She carried a duffle bag that had her laser pistol and weapons inside. She walked past the rows of empty desks and opened her office door. She gasped when she noticed that someone was sitting in her chair waiting for her.

"Who the hell are you?" Reynita demanded.

The chair slowly swiveled toward her. Sitting in the chair was a man she had never seen before. He was lean but not skinny. He was handsome and tall, wearing a black sweater and black slacks with black boots.

She noticed the man was not armed. She wished she had not packed all of her weapons in her duffle bag. She quickly sized the man up and determined if he made any overt movements toward her she would go for his throat first.

"I apologize for startling you," the man told her. "I am Jericho Griffin. I had to meet you and give you some information."

"I have never heard of you," Reynita watched the man closely.

She was painfully aware that she was alone in the facility with this stranger who seemed to at the very least, have the ability to gain access to secure buildings. That talent alone made the man a threat.

"What information do you have for me?"

Griffin stood up and sensed that the woman was wary of him. He did not blame her for feeling that way toward him. He had silenced the building computer security system to gain entry and surprised her. He spoke quickly in an effort to ease her fears.

"I used to be a pilot in the Space Command. I was convicted in a court martial and kicked out. I deserved what happened to me. I really was not a good officer. I began working as a pilot for the Rosenburg family. I recently helped them with something that really has been sticking in my conscience. I saw who killed your little sister."

"What?" Reynita leaned against the wall and dropped her duffle bag to the floor. She was taken aback by the strange man before her. "Who?"

"Ulla Ragnarsson killed her," Jericho Griffin said softly. "And she is a real mean bitch. I have a description of her that I can give you. I am sorry that I have no photographs of her. She is a universal assassin and very secretive of her identity. But, you need to know something. Ulla was sent by Vladimir Sikorsky to kidnap the Fenster's. Your sister was in the wrong place at the wrong time. I am very sorry for what happened."

"You saw it?" Reynita was fighting back the tears. She watched Griffin place a piece of paper on her desk.

"I did. I have been having nightmares about it ever since." Griffin moved toward the door. "The paper I am leaving has a detailed description of Ulla. I checked out you and your family. You are nice people. Sikorsky, the Rosenburg's, all of them are evil. I can't work for them anymore. I have done some bad things in my life. Really bad things. But I can't keep working for people that kill sweet kids like your sister. I am so sorry for your loss. I wish I had been strong enough to stop it from happening."

Reynita shook her head as tears left her red eyes, "So do I."

Griffin began to walk out of her office.

"Wait. How did you get in here and bypass the security?"

"I am pretty resourceful," Griffin responded. "I hope you find Ulla and kill her. She is certainly a heartless woman and the eight solar systems would be better off without her. Good luck to you, ma'am. Don't try and find me, you won't be successful."

Griffin walked as quickly as possible to get out of the building before any of the other soldiers arrived.

She sat down at her desk and noticed that she had three dozen e-mails from General Tan. All of them were demands for information about Matthew Rosenburg and his wives. She began the tedious task of responding to each and every request for information. It was going to be a long night. She began scanning the photographs of Matthew's missing children into her data base and instructed her computer to find a match at the orphan homes.

Her first thought was to contact her sister Estrellita and get her working on information that would lead them to the whereabouts of the killer Ulla Ragnarsson. Like clockwork, Reynita heard the chime of her personal hand sized communication device that indicated Estrellita was contacting her.

Reynita placed the silver and black colored device on her desktop and ordered it to answer. A life-sized, three dimensional image of Estrellita appeared before her. Estrellita was dressed in a pink halter top and dark panties, her hair was wrapped up in a white towel,

"Hey sis!" Estrellita greeted her. "I just got out of the shower. I am in good with Tan and I am having some success in my efforts with Doctor Rosenburg. What's the matter? You look sad."

Reynita nodded, "I was just given a reliable tip on Lupita's killer. In all the news coverage over the past year, did you ever see the name Ulla Ragnarsson mentioned?"

Estrellita sat down on her bed and shook her head, "No. not Ulla. Why? Was Lupita killed by a Ragnarsson?"

"That is what we need to confirm, 'Strella. Be discreet. These people are dangerous."

Estrellita laughed, "Careful? You have me working under the watchful eyes of General Tan and a Rosenburg creep and you think I am not being careful? Okay, let's go on the theory that a Ragnarsson killed our Lupita. Let me see. Computer? Activate some extra three dimensional screens for me.

On screen one, download all immigration satellite feeds for any Ragnarsson that has entered the check points at Clovis City in the past month.

Screen two, download and save all information regarding an Ulla Ragnarsson.

Screen three; download any and all images of Ulla Ragnarsson.

Screen four; download any and all pending investigations in which Ulla Ragnarsson was a suspect.

Screen five; download any and all criminal charges pending against Ulla Ragnarsson.

Screen six; download the names of any and all associates of Ulla Ragnarsson."

Reynita listened and watched with interest as Estrellita was walking back and forth, using her index fingers to move information from one screen to another as she collated some of the information that appeared. Reynita saw ten floating screens around Estrellita.

"Anything useful?" Reynita finally asked her.

Estrellita continued walking from screen to screen, moving objects from one screen to another blank screen. "I got her picture, several of them in fact. Either she is a chameleon or there are a lot of women with the same name. No evidence of her ever living on planet New Edinburgh, no evidence of her ever checking in with customs in any of the main cities and no evidence of her ever visiting the space station."

"Which is no surprise since Mr. Collins found that there was no evidence in the city logs for the other Ragnarsson's either and they were all living here. What else?"

"She is wanted in the Martian Colonies for murder and was prosecuted in absentia on planet Athena for multiple homicides. In both of those crime scenes, her method of killing was a knife."

"Just like with Lupita," Reynita finished the thought. "How about any leads to her present whereabouts?"

"Nothing. It is as if she ceased to exist two years ago. Nothing." Estrellita frowned and then faced the holographic image of her sister. "I will scan the pics of this woman and send them to you. According to the planet Athena MI investigation, this Ulla killed an entire family. She might want to come and try to get the rest of us. We should warn mama and papa."

"Good point," Reynita nodded. "But what did our family ever do to the Ragnarsson's that would put us on their hit list?"

Estrellita shrugged, "Maybe Lupita just got in the way. Maybe this Ulla was afraid Lupita got a good look at her face at the ballroom when the Fenster kids were taken. You know Lupita would not stand idly by if others were in danger."

"I know."

"I miss her so much."

Reynita fought back the tears she felt coming, "Me too. She was the best of us. I have been such a crappy person my whole life. She was so sweet and decent. I wish that it had been me. She deserved to be the one that had a long and happy life."

Estrellita wiped the tears from her cheeks, "I would give anything to bring her killer to justice. Anything."

"So would I."

Estrellita moved over toward her bed and pulled on a pair of dark blue jeans. "I sent you all the pics of the Ulla woman. I have to report to work. Don't do anything without letting me know, deal? I want to be involved in getting revenge for Lupita."

"Right now it is just the two of us that know of Ulla and we might want to keep it that way. I will be in touch."

"Love ya sis," Estrellita told her as her image faded away.

Reynita wiped her eyes and looked at the pictures of Ulla Ragnarsson sent to her by Estrellita. She observed what she meant by Ulla being a chameleon. Each picture had the woman with different colors and styles of hair. In many of the pictures, her eyes were different colors. Reynita stretched her arms over her head and decided to turn her mind back to her work.

As she worked, her mind wandered for a while and she walked around the office to clear her mind. She took a change of clothes from her overnight duffle bag and walked downstairs to the showers. A cold shower would wake her up and keep her mind sharp.

Reynita undressed and stepped into one of the shower stalls and ordered the computer to begin the water. She let the cold water go over her body for a moment and then she used the soap dispenser on the shower stall wall to lather herself. She rinsed off and then turned off the water. She stepped out of the shower stall to retrieve a towel and saw that Mark Lund was standing before her. He was wearing skin tight red gym sweats that she presumed meant he was going to work out. She looked over his muscular body. She realized that Lund was staring at her bare breasts as their eyes met.

Lund was a bit surprised that his platoon leader was standing naked before him. He stared at her slender, toned body and looked into her eyes.

Reynita made no effort to cover herself. It had been so long since she had a man and she did not care if she outranked him. He was handsome, muscular and by the way he was looking at her, he wanted her. She moved into his arms and began kissing

Lund passionately. He did the same as they ran their hands over each other's bodies. She allowed Lund to pick her up and lay her down on one of the work out mats. She moaned pleasurably as he kissed her neck and shoulders. She placed her hands behind his head as he began sucking on her hardened nipples. She encouraged him by leaning up and pushing her breasts further into his face.

Lund quickly pulled off his sweats. He kept kissing her body and smiled when he looked into her eyes. She opened her legs and let him take her. She moaned as she felt him enter her. As they made love on the floor, they never lost eye contact until they both climaxed. They remained on the floor for a few moments in silence, breathing heavily and not caring if any of the other platoon members walked in and caught them together.

After a few minutes passed, she finally spoke up. "We can't tell anyone about this."

Lund nodded in agreement, "I know. I am sorry I lost control. I just had to have you. You are so beautiful and you are an amazing lover."

"No I should be the one apologizing," Reynita said as she closed her eyes and rubbed her forehead with her right hand. "I am an officer. I should know better, I just lost my head. You are irresistible and very handsome. I can't believe we just did this. You aren't married or anything? I don't have to worry about a jealous wife stalking me?"

Lund slowly sat up and pulled her into his lap. "No, I am very single. I won't say a word about this to anyone. I can't say I won't try and have sex with you again. So if I come on to you some time, please do not hold it against me. I know I am going to want you again."

She kissed him softly. "I would be offended if you didn't come on to me again. Just, be discreet. I would like to be with you again sometime. But we can never get caught. General Tan would court martial me for sure."

"Okay, we will be discreet. But I want to have sex with you again. Soon?"

She laughed. "Yes, real soon. We better get dressed. If anyone sees us like this..."

Lund stood up and walked toward the showers. "See you soon, Reynita Calderon."

Reynita sat up and found a towel to wipe herself off. She secured her clothes and dressed quickly. When she had returned to Clovis City she had no friends and no boyfriend. Now she had three friends in Jen Staszko, Harumi Shigeta and Sophia DuBravac. And now she added a secret lover. She wondered what would happen to her next.

CHAPTER TWENTY-ONE

Reynita Calderon arrived at her office building before dawn on her old fashioned motorcycle. She walked to the security entrance and used her plastic scan card to open the sliding metal doors. She told the computer to turn off all alarm functions. After walking around the offices she determined that she was alone in the structure. Over her right shoulder, she held a large gymnasium bag that she had brought with her from her parents' home. She walked through the dark hallways to her main office and then to her smaller personal office. She tossed her large bag on one of the spare chairs and looked at the mirror on one of the walls.

She took time to make sure her long straight hair was not tangled. She unzipped her black leather jacket and removed it. She walked to the large chair behind her desk and placed her jacket on the book case behind her. She was wearing a pair of jeans, black boots and a red short sleeved blouse. She took the gym bag and pulled out her Class A uniform, dress shoes, dress shirt and a satin slip and placed them on her desk. She undressed down to her bra and panties and then put on the slip. She pursed her lips in thought as today was the day she would attend the funeral for her little sister.

She started to reach for her dress shirt when she heard someone behind her clearing his throat. She turned and saw

Mark Lund standing in her doorway. He was already dressed in his black Class A uniform.

Without a word he walked into her office and closed her door behind him. Reynita took in a deep breath as Lund quickly swept her up into his arms and began kissing her lips. She kissed him back and put her arms around his back. She felt his hands moving underneath her slip and he lifted her up onto the desk top. She raised her arms in the air as Lund pulled her slip off of her. She smiled and reached behind her back and unfastened her bra. Lund pulled her panties off and began kissing her neck and shoulders.

"Did you lock the door?" Reynita asked.

"No," Lund said as he buried his face into her breasts. Reynita leaned back on her desk as Lund began removing his uniform.

"Computer," Reynita said as her heart began to race and Lund ran his hands over her body. She smiled up at Lund as he climbed on top of her and kissed her neck and shoulders.

"Yes, Lieutenant?" The computerized voice responded.

Lund thrust his erection inside of her.

"Aaaaaahhhh!" Reynita moaned pleasurably as she felt him enter her.

"Do you require medical assistance?" The computer asked.

"No," she said as Lund continued to make love to her. "Lock the doors."

"Doors locked," the computer responded.

After their passion had been spent they were lying on top of her desk, kissing each other. His hands were still on her bare breasts, softly fondling them.

"I am such a bad girl," Reynita told him as she closed her eyes.

"I like it when you are bad," Lund told her.

"No, I really mean I am a bad girl. I have done some horrible things. I am not the woman you want to take home to meet your mother."

Lund laughed as he continued to enjoy feeling her body.

"I think my family would really like you."

"Not if they learned about the things I did in my past," she lamented. "I used a nice man once. I think I hurt him really bad. I would help other guys I knew haze new cadets. I used to get into some really bad bar fights and now I am breaking the Code of Military Justice by having sex with my platoon sergeant."

Lund kissed her breasts some more and then looked at her face and her eyes. "I don't care what you did or did not do. I really like you and I want to keep seeing you. Understand?"

She smiled and kissed him. "Never say that I did not warn you."

"Duly noted," Lund whispered in her ear. "But I am bad as well."

"How so?"

"I am clearly robbing the cradle. How old are you, Reynita?"

"Twenty-two."

Lund laughed, "And you don't mind having a man older than you for a boyfriend?"

"How old are you?"

"I have almost six years on you."

She laughed at that, "Oh that is really robbing the cradle, Mark. Actually, I am glad you are older than me. You are more mature than the men I dated in the past. You are calmer than young guys. You are a better lover, for sure."

Lund kissed her gently and continued to caress her breasts. "Thank you. You are quite remarkable yourself."

"I need to tell you something. It is really important."

Lund kissed her and then smiled at her, "Tell me what?"

"It is about why I am here."

"You mean here letting me have sex with you?"

"No, I mean why General Tan sent me here. You must promise to tell nobody. It cannot get out of what Tan asked me to do here."

Lund looked into her eyes with concern, "Did she send you here to kill people?"

She shook her head from side to side, "If only it had been that simple. No. I was sent to find all of the family members of Doctor Matthew Rosenburg."

"You mean one of the fugitives that has multiple indictments pending against him?"

"The one and the same."

Lund sat on her desk next to her, "I take it Tan knows where he is hiding?"

"More than that, Mark. She was holding him in a cell for months." Reynita held his hand and sat upright. "That was why you all did not find him when you raided the Rosenburg Ranch. He was on Lynott's Land all along."

Lund sighed, "So Tan sent you back here to find his family?"

She nodded, "His children and wives. I found some of them, but not all. Most of his younger children were sent to the orphan homes to be adopted or experimented on."

"You know I should take this information to Sean Collins."

"I would not blame you if you did," she said softly. "If you and I hadn't started our office romance, I would have continued with my secret mission. But I just really like you. I don't want to keep anything from you."

"I feel the same for you," Lund told her as he looked into her eyes. "Why would Tan care about Matthew Rosenburg and his family?"

"Those green skinned humans that were on the Blitzkrieg. Tan wants to use them for herself. She is using Rosenburg to activate those things for the love of God. I think it is an abomination. Tan is crazy, Mark. She thinks those things will help her live forever. What should I do?"

Lund thought for a few moments. He had personally witnessed one of tan's rampages where she shot seven people in the back of the head and had no justification for doing so. "Tan is certainly crazy. You cannot disobey her. If she turned on you there would be no place on this planet that you could hide. You have to complete what she sent you here to do."

"And what about Collins and the warrants for Rosenburg's arrest?"

"The pending warrant for Matthew Rosenburg will soon be a moot point. When Tan gets what she wants, Matthew Rosenburg will be a dead man. She hates men. She will use him, get what she wants and then find some sick twisted manner to kill him. I have heard that Tan has some of those Jumpers under her palace floors that she feeds prisoners to. That is, after she castrates them and has their penises dipped in hot chocolate. You know that. You just need to demonstrate to Tan that you are her loyal officer. Get her to trust you so that her crazy train radar never gets aimed in your direction. You understand me?"

She nodded and then cuddled up into his arms. "Thank you for not judging me harshly on that."

Lund held her close. "Thank you for being here. I have connections in some of the orphan facilities. I can help you locate the missing kids. It will be our secret."

Being a part of the covert attempts to locate the Fenster cadets gave Cadet Ye Yibing a sense of excitement that she had never felt in her short life. She had returned to her dormitory room with several diskettes of illegally downloaded classified information from Space Station Cy-7. Never in in her wildest dreams did she think that she was capable of stealing classified information. But yet she had done so and it seemed so easy, so natural to her. She was grateful that Jen Staszko was with her on the return flight for moral support. Yibing hated allowing Dante Friedmann to feel her out. Since he was suspected of being involved in the kidnappings, she did not feel any remorse from her part that included injecting him with the drugs. That part of her role had been unavoidable if she were to successfully gain access to his personal computer. The scheme had worked. Yibing hacked Friedmann's system and stole the information.

And what she found was disturbing. Someone with access to the space station security system had been able to delete information of a certain Raumschiff that had landed on the station the day before the Fenster siblings were kidnaped. Yibing was certain that the CID officers would not have caught the computer tampering because they would not have been looking for it. But she was looking, for any clue, no matter how little. And she found that there had been a ship that arrived and left and that someone on that station covered it up.

Yibing and Staszko took the data containing the information to the Frazier's, Patel and Shigeta. The group analyzed the data and found that Yibing was correct. The main frame computer memory of Space Station Cy-7 had been altered. Fortunately Yibing was astute enough to see the shadow of data left behind by the deletion.

"You see, when someone deletes information from a main frame computer, there is always a backup in the hard drive that stores the deleted information," Yibing explained to the others how she was able to complete her task. She had a three dimensional view of the deleted information in glowing green print that clearly proved her findings for all to see, in the middle of the room. "Many hackers don't think of trying to dig that deep into the computer main frame because the passwords are different on most of the newer computer models to get to the backed up memory data. I did get those passwords and went the extra step. And this is what I found."

"The question now is, what do we do with this evidence?" Staszko asked the small group.

"And who do we trust?" Shigeta added. "Only a high clearance officer would be able to do this. That would suggest either bribery or a conspiracy or both. We turn this over to the wrong person and then we put ourselves at risk and this evidence will vanish."

Arch Frazier pursed his lips and looked at Elektra. "Honey, remember what happened when the Rosenburg's attacked you? That was a clear cover up. One thing is for certain, these people can buy off anyone. Anyone working on that station is a suspect. They were able to hide the attack on you and Dray with little effort."

"Including the man I stole this data from," Yibing added.

"Especially him," Elektra agreed. "He has the top level clearances. He is a computer genius. Yes, I would say that Dante Friedmann deserves a second look."

Yibing frowned as Elektra spoke, doing her best to follow her words. "So what do you want me to do next?"

"Play it cool when he contacts you, Ye." Staszko pat her on the shoulder. "And he will contact you. Play along as if you want to see him again, but don't do it too quick. Let us think up a plan. We need to trap him. If you are dating anyone here on campus, we might have to tell them that this is going on so he won't think you are cheating on him."

Yibing nodded, "Just tell me what to do. And, there is a student, his name is Dempster Harang. He likes me. I have gone out on two dates with him and he seems really nice. How do I keep this from him?"

Arch Frazier smiled at that, "I know him. He seems like a good kid. He is in some of my advanced science classes. I will keep him occupied if we need to have you meet with Friedmann again. You know what, Ye? Yuri and the other founders of this gang would be proud to know that you are one of us."

Yibing was aware of the legacy left behind by Yuri Gorski and the others. She smiled with pride at Frazier's compliment. "You really think so?"

Staszko gave her a hug, "Absolutely, Ye. You are a natural."

CHAPTER TWENTY-TWO

The Battle Cruiser Lysander entered orbit around planet New Edinburgh without fanfare or celebration. The Lysander was larger than the normal Battle Cruiser. It had nine decks as opposed to the specifications for five or six levels. The extra three levels of the Lysander were for additional crew, Raumschiff's and transport ships. Her outer hull was painted black with red trim. The weapons area occupied the entire second level and was stocked full of armor piercing nuclear warheads, rockets, laser batteries and titanium rods. The Lysander had been constructed with one goal in mind and that was to make her so powerful she could wage a small war on a planet on her own.

The crew was sent on a mission that few envied. They were to replace the current military leadership below and arrest any that resisted. The Glorious Leader was not pleased with the recent trial that concluded with convictions of many Ragnarsson and Rosenburg family members. Vladimir Sikorsky determined that fundamental change was needed for the current leadership of planet New Edinburgh. He ordered several of his children and grandchildren to take one of his personal Battle Cruisers to travel to New Edinburgh and take the planet in a new direction.

The orders were to replace Colonel Nikolai Gorski and relieve him of his post. Arrest warrants were prepared on Sikorsky's Planet for Gorski, Major Sigebert Evart, Captain Tierney, Captain Vanetta Hsu, Lieutenant Simms, Lieutenant

Price, chief prosecutor Sean Collins, assistant prosecutor Nia Li, assistant prosecutor Nathaniel Goldsmith and the traitorous General Assembly Representatives Soto, Wyclyffe, al-Nasser, Stroessner, Rice, Ward and Clement. Additional warrants were issued for all of the family members of those listed. The Glorious Leader wanted to leave nothing to chance. He demanded that his offspring take complete control of the day to day operations of the planet and those that had betrayed his family would be tried and executed for treason.

But the warrants for arrest gave the crew of the Lysander autonomy on how to serve the warrants. The language from the Glorious Leader required that the criminals be brought to justice either dead or alive.

Captain Vanetta Hsu was the first to fall. She had been the commander of the lunar base on the farthest moon from new Edinburgh. She had been a loyal member of the Space Command for about nineteen years and commander of the lunar base for the last three. She was married and had seven children. Her husband and two younger children resided on the moon base with them. The other five children had all gone off to various military academies to study and begin their own careers. Hsu had spent her first few years of service in the Space Command as a pilot and then spent several short tours as a section commander on one science cruiser. She applied for the opening to command the lunar base and was promoted into the position. Hsu had been a part of a large sibling group from planet Athena.

Her moon base was approximately twelve square kilometers of metallic buildings with underground chambers and rails systems. There was very little military value to the base except for the launching pads for one hundred Raumschiff space ships and one thousand small Allen Type Fighter craft. The moon was larger than the one that orbited Old Earth. The underground caverns that had been created by the inhabitants of the base were for the purpose of exploiting the vast minerals and metals that the moon had to offer. Hsu commanded a crew of just under six thousand men and women that were primarily scientists, miners and pilots.

Hsu was obviously receptive to the requests made by Military Intelligence General Kimberly Sikorsky to send in a surprise inspection team. Hsu felt honored that the Glorious Leader would send one of his own Royal family members to come and inspect her moon base. She ordered her security officers to make certain that the inspection team would be given full access to the entire base. Hsu and her top officers were impressed by what they observed when the Battle Cruiser Lysander arrived. The ship was much larger than the average Battle Cruisers. Hsu had never seen one of the personal ships of the Glorious Leader so close.

Captain Hsu asked that her husband, geologist Professor Ezekiel Hsu, join her and the base executive officer, astronaut Commander Joseph Kokinda, to greet the dignitaries from the Lysander.

Kimberly Sikorsky ordered that her granddaughter, Military Intelligence Major Katherine Sikorsky, lead the so-called inspection team. Taking five Raumschiffs full of MI soldiers, Major Katherine Sikorsky landed on the lunar base without incident. She was greeted by Captain Hsu, her husband Professor Hsu and the executive officer of the base. Hsu and her husband were immediately arrested and bound by the soldiers that accompanied Sikorsky. The executive officer of the base, Joseph Kokinda, protested which led to his head being blown off by a laser blast fired by Sikorsky. The soldiers under the command of Katherine Sikorsky rounded up the two infant children of the Hsu family and they were all taken to the nearest airlock.

Captain Vanetta Hsu protested her loyalty as she watched helplessly when her husband was forced into the airlock. Katherine Sikorsky coldly ordered the computer to open the outer doors. Hsu and her two children cried and screamed as the man was sucked out into space. Major Sikorsky then repeated the same act with one of the Hsu's children, a six year old daughter. They young girl cried with fear as the soldiers forced her into the airlock. Her cries ended when she was swept out into space to suffer the same death as her father had. Her four year old sister shortly joined her in death.

Captain Vanetta Hsu begged and cried as her husband and two children were cruelly murdered before her eyes. She was on her knees sobbing and crying hysterically. She had never betrayed her Glorious Leader and could not fathom why this was being done to her and especially to her innocent children. She hoped that her other five older children would not be executed for whatever crimes the Royal family accused her of.

Captain Hsu did not struggle when Major Sikorsky ordered that the enlisted soldiers throw her into the airlock. Hsu did not beg as she welcomed death. She could not live in a world so cruel and barbaric that innocent men, women and children would be murdered in such a harsh manner. Her only prayer was that the Royal family would not be able to find her remaining five children. As the airlock opened she felt the oxygen supply being forcefully drawn out into space and she with it. She struggled for breath and felt the skin on her body begin to shrivel up from the lack of an atmosphere and oxygen. Captain Vanetta Hsu died without knowing what her crimes had been.

Major Katherine Sikorsky reported to her grandmother that she was now in control of the lunar base. General Kimberly Sikorsky thanked her grandchild and then turned her attention to the command station staff aboard the Lysander.

"Our first order of business has been completed," she told her crew. "Now we need to take Clovis City. We can come back later and investigate whether any of the command staff on Space Station Cy-7 need to be removed. Prepare the Super

Raumschiff's and the transports for invasion. Once we land on Clovis City we need to free the political prisoners from their cells and then take control of the United Nations Building. Any questions?"

Kimberly Sikorsky walked around the lower level of the Command Station and heard no responses. "Good. Prepare my ship, I will lead the landing myself. For the Glorious Leader!" The crew repeated the phrase and began to follow her orders. Soon all of the individuals that had warrants would be apprehended.

Over one hundred transport ships and Raumschiff's were already fully loaded and boarded. The transport ships had a full complement of alien slaves to do the bidding of General Kimberly Sikorsky. There were one thousand Saharakaree with microchips in their brains to control their actions. To fight their sensitivity to sunlight, the Saharakaree were fitted with dark goggles over their large eyes. They waited on transports, their razor sharp pointed tails moving back and forth as they anticipated the battle that they would take part in.

There were two thousand slave Akarzdamedians that were sitting in the pilots seats of an equal number of Allen Type Fighter space craft. Their free will was also deadened by the microchips in their brains. They were programmed to fly over the northern continent of New Edinburgh and provide aerial cover for the ground forces. If any person or group were to resist the landing, the slave Akarzdamedians would take them out with lasers and rockets.

An alien race that called themselves Babcottiatta that were from the conquered planet Athena, were forced to take their places on the transport ships as well. The Babcottiatta were all nine to ten feet tall and had six muscular multi-jointed arms. Their hands had eight fingers and were known to possess enough raw strength to crush a human skull with little effort. Their legs had three knees that allowed them freedom of movement and they could turn completely in circles with little effort. Their massive feet had eight toes and the middle toe had a spike that extended two feet out and could impale flesh as easy as a knife cuts butter. Their shoulders were massive and the back muscles were large enough to handle their upper body muscle tone. The Babcottiatta were all light blue skinned and wore orange one piece outfits that were sleeveless to allow their massive arms freedom of movement. Their heads were huge with large mouths and sharp teeth. They had eight orange eyes that circled around their square shaped skulls.

On the top of each of their skulls were eight sharp spikes that the Babcottiatta used in battle to impale their opponents. Each of the giant aliens weighed at least five hundred pounds. Some were known to weigh in excess of a thousand pounds. There were over a thousand of these aliens, each with a microchip in their brains to control their movements. They had but one instruction and that was to kill any that resisted.

The Raumschiffs launched first, followed by the Allen Fighter ships and then the transports. They began landing on several locations throughout planet New Edinburgh. Many of the citizens of the northern continent were pointing to the sky as the ships descended. It had been quite rare for such a large military aerial presence to be seen. Ever since the majority of the northern continent had been taken and settled, military maneuvers had slowed to the occasional fly overs. But this display of strength was certainly grabbing the attention of the people.

The prison located in the southern portion of Clovis City was taken over first. Several Raumschiff landed along with two transports. Warden Yueying and the jail guards were stunned to see fifty Saharakaree and thirty Babcottiatta approaching the walls followed by one hundred Marines. The warden received orders from a Lieutenant Colonel Clea Sowa to stand down and turn over the prison to her control. The warden did not argue with the demand and ordered his guards to open the gates.

Sowa was about thirty years old and striking in her appearance. She stood six feet five inches tall and had long dark curly hair with dark eyes. She wore her solid black MI uniform with pride. She was followed by a dozen soldiers on either side of her that had their laser rifles cradled in their arms for use against anyone that stood in their way. She marched into the jail administrative offices and demanded to speak to the person in charge.

Warden Yueying was still emotional from his run in with Reynita Cardenas. He looked at Sowa with suspicious eyes.

"Good morning, Colonel. What can I do for you today?"

Sowa glared at the warden. He was overweight and smelled. Sowa despised any man or woman that failed to take pride in their personal appearance or grooming. She forcefully handed Yueying a printed white paper that was a list of seventy-seven names.

"I want all of those prisoners released to me in ten minutes," Sowa barked.

The warden looked over the names.

"It may take longer than ten minutes. This is a lot of prisoners. I need to make some calls to clear this."

Sowa pulled out her laser pistol from her web belt and blasted a hole through the warden's chest. Yueying fell to the floor without a scream. His chest had a small amount of black and white smoke rising from it. Some of the prison staff technicians covered their faces from the smell of the roasted flesh and internal organs. Sowa could not determine what smelled worse, the warden's body odor or his burned flesh. She turned to one of the jail guards.

"Yes, Colonel, ten minutes."

The guard stuttered and took the list from her. Her hands were shaking with fear and she immediately began barking orders for the release of each of the prisoners.

Sowa was pleased that fifty-one of the prisoners on the list were housed at the facility. She smiled when she saw the familiar faces of her distant cousins.

Peter Rosenburg was perhaps the tallest of the sons of Alfred Rosenburg. Standing at seven feet tall he towered over the others. He had been arrested by Colonel Gorski and his meddlesome Marines at the Rosenburg Ranch. Peter smiled as the sunlight hit his face for the first time in months. He had been charged with several crimes by the prosecutor Collins for which her was about to stand trial.

Among the charges were intent to smuggle illegal slaves, conspiracy to sell humans as slaves, multiple counts of kidnaping, several counts of murder, several counts of conspiracy to commit murder, several counts of human rights violations, several counts of torture and jaywalking. He had pled not guilty to all counts but told his lawyers that he was guilty of all the crimes that he was charged with and then some. He had raped slave girls, tortured them, strangled and stabbed others. Watching young girls die was a hobby to him. Now that he was free, he looked forward to finding his next victim. It had been too long since he spilled some blood. Peter was in his early thirties and had thick black hair and eyebrows. His deep blue eyes seemed sunken and his thin lips hid his perfect teeth.

"About time someone sprang us!"

Carla Rosenburg said as she hugged Sowa. She looked down on the floor and saw the corpse of the warden. "Glad someone killed that pig. He raped me and some of the others. Looks like you killed him too quickly."

Juliana Rosenburg was silent as she was led by a MI soldier toward one of the military transports. She hoped that this new found freedom would not be short lived. She wondered if her release had anything to do with the visit by Lieutenant Calderon. If so, Juliana shuddered at the thought that any of her private conversation with the woman would be revealed to her family.

She walked with her head down as she saw multiple siblings of hers cheering and hugging one another to celebrate their release. Juliana wanted little or nothing to do with her family. She wanted to keep walking and never speak to any of them again. She quickly wiped that notion from her mind out of fear that walking away may appear suspicious, especially to her psychotic sister, Carla.

Rebecca Rosenburg hugged her sisters and brother as she was delivered to the lobby of the prison. She held onto Sowa for several seconds, weeping on her shoulders and praising her for saving them.

"Does this mean I get my old job back?" Rebecca Rosenburg asked Sowa.

"Yes, you will return with me to the United Nations Administrative Building." Sowa told her. "Once we are there you will help your elders determine who needs to be arrested and given a quick trial before execution. Think you can handle that?"

She laughed, "I can tell you right now! Sigebert Evart, Nikolai Gorski, Sean Collins, Nia Li, Nathaniel Goldsmith and about three dozen General Assembly Representatives should be shot on sight. When we get to the building I can point out the others that need to go. And what about Lyss? He stood by and did nothing when they arrested me!"

Sowa nodded to each of the suggestions by the Rosenburg woman.

"All of those you named will be dealt with. Some are being removed as we speak. Get on board the transport and we will go take care of business."

"Gladly," Rebecca said.

She had used her slender body and lovely face to entice men and women alike to get information for her family. She had slept with Security Council Secretary General Alexander Lyss several times to spy on him. She hated sleeping with him as he was not really handsome and his hands on her body made her cringe. But it was for the family. She wanted Evart, Gorski and Collins dead since they had the audacity to reject her sexual overtures and then later arrest her along with her siblings. She wanted them to suffer for what they did to her and not just them. She wanted to get their children and make them feel pain like they never had.

Alfred Rosenburg and his law partner Ellis Ragnarsson were among the liberated. The attorneys were squinting their eyes due to the sunlight that had been denied them during their many months of captivity. Alfred took in a deep breath of the fresh New Edinburgh air and quietly rejoiced that he was free once again.

His first thoughts were to return to his law office building and attempt to put his life back together. Ellis had similar feelings of working in the legal field once more. The only issue that both men shared was that the licensing arm of the legal community had terminated their ability to practice. They would have to appeal that decision and reverse the findings before they could renew their chosen profession.

"My siblings, Ella and Ivar, they're not here." Ellis observed as he looked over the many prisoners that were being led out toward the waiting transport ships.

Alfred Rosenburg nodded as he looked around him. "Nor are the other assassins. Most of the people being released are my family members."

Ellis continued to look over the crowd, "The kids that were captured on the Blood Moon are not here either. They must have put them all on the transport to Cootron."

Alfred motioned with his head to Ellis, "Come on. We should get back to my high rise office building and start to work on getting our licenses back. I imagine that the Glorious Leader will send us both pardons and open the door for us to work again."

Ellis slowly gazed up into the sky with his eyes squinted.

"If your brother Caine was not dead I would have killed him myself for all the trouble he brought down on us. Now that we are free again, we can try and do everything right this time."

Alfred looked over his family members as they were being brought outside of the prison gates.

"I bet the majority of them will go back to the old ways. I propose that you and I avoid my family and make a new beginning for ourselves. We had a profitable practice before and we can do so again. Let's leave these others behind."

"Agreed," Ellis followed his former business partner out toward the prison gates. The two men refused to acknowledge some of the other prisoners that called out to them. They refused to look back as they walked past the gates. The two men refused the soldiers offer to take them in one of the transport ships to any destination they desired. They walked and walked for several kilometers to clear their heads and take in the smell of the fresh air.

Thomas Rosenburg was the last of the prisoners to be released. He was Peter's younger brother and had his facial features but was several inches shorter. Thomas had endured rape at the hands of several hardened criminals in the prison and a few beatings from the jail guards. He blamed Sean Collins and Nikolai Gorski for each incident her suffered while incarcerated. He was a Rosenburg and a member of the Royal Family. He felt it was his birthright to commit the crimes he had. Thomas had been arrested along with Carla, Peter, Juliana, Victoria, Joseph, Joshua, Jacob, William and many others. He saw them all walking toward the waiting transport ships to return them all to their former glory.

Thomas had never felt guilty regarding his part in the many rapes of children he had committed. The Rosenburg Ranch had thousands of human slaves that were there for his personal pleasure. He enjoyed taking young boys, especially under the age of ten, and molesting them. He would force the young boys to perform all manners of sex acts for him. If any of the boys failed to please him, Thomas would have them fed to the creatures held in the large Arena before the screaming crowds. He longed for those days to return. He also wanted revenge for the deaths of his full siblings Caine and David. Caine had been the one that first taught Thomas the joys of forcing young boys and girls to do everything he desired from them and then watching them die.

Attorney Nathaniel Goldsmith had been a major contributor to the prosecution of the Rosenburg-Ragnarsson faction. He helped prosecute Carla Rosenburg and was the lead attorney prosecuting Rebecca Rosenburg. Goldsmith had been successful in obtaining a forty year sentence against Rebecca for her role in the conspiracy to kill the cadets during both the Sandstorm Incident and the Blitzkrieg Incident. While he was the second chair prosecutor against Carla, Sean Collins allowed Goldsmith the honor of delivering the closing argument. The jury sentenced Carla for fifty years for her role in the many deaths.

Goldsmith was originally from the Martian Colonies and a member of a modest sibling group. He joined the Marines at the age of eighteen and spent six years fighting battles on other planets. After his six years of adventure, he went to college and studied to become a lawyer. He married five times and each of his wives produced many children for him. Some of his offspring had decided to pursue a career in law, others joined the military and some were still too young to determine which career path they wished to work on.

Goldsmith moved to New Edinburgh eight years ago to start a new law practice there. He had heard that there was a shortage of attorneys and the work was there for one that was willing to travel. He loaded up his family and found a home in Clovis City and they settled down. After a few years he befriended Sean Collins and he was recruited to join the United Nations legal team. Goldsmith had worked there ever since.

One of his daughters, Lynn, liked Clovis City so much that she enrolled in the Clovis Academy and had graduated with a degree in bio-chemistry with honors. Lynn was by far the smartest of his children and was currently working on her medical degree at the same Academy.

Goldsmith was in his early fifties. He had a full head of silver hair, blue eyes and a slender build. He was just a little over six feet tall and had a smooth baritone voice that captivated judges and juries. He was a natural.

His home in Clovis City was in one of the northeast controlled access subdivisions. It had five floors, thirty-two large bedrooms, numerous walk-in closets and bathrooms. The kitchen and living areas were spacious enough to house his large family comfortably. Goldsmith had resisted many offers of support from community members for him to seek appointment as a Judge or to run for election to the United Nations General Assembly. He detested politics and had no desire to become involved in the constant bickering and debates over silly issues he felt beneath him. He chose instead to spend as much time with his wives and children as possible.

Goldsmith never once uttered a word of sedition against the Glorious Leader or the Royal Family. So he was understandably shocked when a Raumschiff with black and red colors landed in the large cul de sac of his housing area and several Marines, Babcottiatta and Saharakaree began surrounding his home. Four of his wives were home with him as well as twelve of his pre-teen children. Goldsmith heard the loud demands from a soldier that identified herself as Captain Susannah Murdock that he and his family exit the premises with their hands up. Goldsmith thought the demands odd and he was deeply concerned that his home was being targeted.

He attempted to contact his friend, Sean Collins, to see if the events that were transpiring were some joke or prank. Goldsmith found that his hand held communication device was being blocked by some form of jamming technology.

Goldsmith directed that his family members that were present do as instructed and exit the home with their hands held high. Several of his younger children were crying as they were terrified by the scene before them. The soldiers were on their knees aiming laser rifles at the home. The Babcottiatta were wielding ten foot long glowing spears that were sparking with blue electrical energy at the tips. The Saharakaree were bobbing their heads up and down, their deadly tails wagging back and forth.

Goldsmith exited the front door of his home first with his hands up.

"Captain, I am coming out and I am unarmed."

He led his family outside onto his manicured yard full of colorful flowers and plants. He walked slowly toward the soldiers and aliens. His heart was pounding hard in his chest. He could hear the footsteps of his wives behind him and the sobs of his children.

He was ordered to stop by a female voice. Goldsmith complied and froze in place. He could hear the cool breeze around him as he looked over the soldiers that had him at gunpoint.

A woman in a solid black uniform approached him. She was attractive and walked with a purpose. She held a laser pistol in her right hand and stopped a few feet from Goldsmith.

"I am Captain Murdock. I want to thank you for cooperating with us."

"You're welcome, Captain. May I ask what this is about?"

"I have a warrant for your arrest and for the arrest of all of your wives and children," Murdock told him flatly. "I notice that the majority of your children are not here. Once we have all of you safely into custody we will need for you to provide us locating information as to your other children."

Murdock had little regard for other humans. She had already experienced young teenage girls being cut open as surgeons would remove their vital organs for Royal Family use. Murdock heard the high pitched screams as the scalpels cut the flesh of those young girls and their pleas for mercy. Murdock found she enjoyed the body organ harvests of her family and she was angry that she was sent here, to planet New Edinburgh, to arrest these disloyal humans and miss the next set of butcher sessions of young girls. She wanted to return home to Sikorsky's Planet soon so that she could celebrate with her family as lesser humans were carved up before their eyes.

"Warrants for arrest? For us?" Goldsmith was stunned. "But we have done nothing wrong. What are we being accused of?"

"Treason against the Glorious Leader is the charge against you counselor," Murdock answered him. "You have been a co-conspirator in the effort to arrest, indict, try and persecute members of the Royal Family. Your behavior cannot be tolerated by the Glorious Leader. Now, I need you to get on your knees and place your hands on your head so we can shackle you. We need to do the same with your wives and children."

"My children are terrified, Captain. Can't we do this some other way?" Goldsmith was shaking with rage.

Although it was true that the Rosenburg defendants were members of the Royal Family, they had committed violations of the law and the majority of the criminal acts were serious. Murder. Rape. Kidnaping. Slavery. Goldsmith understood now why his boss, Sean Collins, was so closed in his opinions. The Royal family considered themselves above the law. Everyone else was subject to the rule of law, but not the Sikorsky family. Since Goldsmith had been one of the many prosecutors involved these soldiers were sent to send other lawyers a message. And that message was to turn a blind eye to the horrors committed by the Royal Family.

"No. Tell them all to get on their knees," Murdock instructed.

Goldsmith turned his head toward his family members behind him. He was worried about his twelve year old daughter, Ariel, who was shaking with fear.

"Everyone kneel down and put your hands on your heads. We are going to be placed under arrest and taken in for questioning. If you all cooperate we will be okay."

The family members all slowly complied. Some of the children were cajoled by their mothers to keep still and keep their hands over their heads. Once the Goldsmith clan were all on their knees, Murdock motioned for the several slave Babcottiatta to shackle the prisoners.

Ariel Goldsmith screamed in terror when she saw the Babcottiatta approaching them. Perhaps it was the size of the aliens; perhaps the stress of the situation overwhelmed the twelve year old. Perhaps it was a combination of both that caused her to leap to her feet and run for the safety of her home. Her biological mother screamed for her to stop and she stood to give chase.

That was when the shooting started.

Ariel Goldsmith was sliced in half at her mid-section by several laser blasts from the soldiers. Her mother's head was obliterated by a direct hit. Nathaniel Goldsmith screamed for his other children to stay calm, but they all began to panic and run in different directions. He watched helplessly as one by one his children were cut down by laser fire. He screamed for the soldiers to cease firing. His wives instinctively ran to their children and suffered the same fate. Nathaniel Goldsmith remained on his knees with tears of anguish running down his cheeks.

Captain Susannah Murdock shook her head as she viewed the chunks of body parts that littered the Goldsmith lawn. Only Nathaniel Goldsmith remained. Murdock realized that a smooth talking lawyer that would be all too willing to relate the massacre to any reporter or news agency was a loose end that had to be silenced. She nodded at one of the Babcottiatta.

Goldsmith shook with fear as one of the giant aliens leaped into the air and landed next to him. The ground subsided a few inches from the impact of the six hundred pound alien landing on it. Before the silver tongued lawyer could say anything, the Babcottiatta grabbed him with four of its arms, lifted him into the skyline and began ripping his arms and legs from his body.

Goldsmith screamed in agony as each of his limbs was torn from his torso. His cries stopped when the Babcottiatta crushed his skull with one of his massive hands. His brains oozed in between the fingers of the giant alien. The alien dropped the remainder of the carcass of Nathaniel Goldsmith to the grass.

"Clean up the mess and search the mansion. Make sure there isn't anyone else hiding inside." Murdock ordered her soldiers.

She cared little that they had killed all of the children and the adult Goldsmith's that had been present. It saved space in the jails and avoided any nasty interference from any pesky news media hounds that would seek to exploit the story for their own career advancement.

CHAPTER TWENTY-THREE

The funeral for Lupita Calderon had started out as a peaceful gathering.

The services began at Saint Mark's Catholic Church which was where the Calderon family had worshiped every Sunday. Saint Mark's was able to hold just a little over three thousand guests. The citizens of Clovis City showed up for Lupita Calderon in numbers that had never been seen at the church. Mourners from the Academy that had appreciated her friendship and gentle nature attended to say good bye. It was standing room only.

The Priest, Father Kendall, had been a close friend to the Calderon family and had performed the baptisms of all of their children. Kendall recalled Lupita Calderon as one of the kindest parishioners he had ever had the honor of meeting. He related a story about Lupita when she was eleven years old and her search for her missing pet golden retriever. He told the congregation of the devotion that the young girl demonstrated for her pet and the lengths she went through to find her. He tied in the story to inform the mourners that Lupita had been a person that never abandoned those that she loved.

Her mother and father openly wept as the priest said the Lord's Prayer. Her sisters and brothers were also unable to hold back their emotions, tears flowing openly for all to see.

Lieutenant Reynita Calderon was dressed in her formal, button down, Class A Military Intelligence uniform. She had been the first from her family to learn of her little sister's murder. She had the unenviable duty to inform the rest of the family that one of their own would never come home again. She had stood over her body and swore to find who had been the perpetrator. But there were no clues, no evidence to tie the killer to the act. Reynita had one witness to provide leads to find the person that had done this to her sister, and to her family. And that person was gone. Jericho Griffin had made himself scarce.

Reynita's paternal grandmother had been so distraught by Lupita's death that she had to be admitted at the local hospital Emergency Room for stroke like conditions. Two others had died in the chaos of that night, one was trampled by the panic stricken crowd and the other suffered a stroke. Only Lupita had been intentionally killed.

Reynita hugged her brother, Cadet Juanito Calderon, and they cried on each other's shoulders. Lupita had been loved by them all.

Several students from the Academy were present to pay their respects. Virtually all of the cadet pilots were in attendance. Cadet Admiral Blossom Li was there with her brigade of cadet pilots. She had ordered that all of them wear their Class A uniforms to show their respect and admiration of the deceased girl.

Cadet Admiral Klaus Rhinehard had given a similar order for his brigade. He was holding hands with his wife, Cadet Captain April Mejia. She was crying as she saw the pain in the faces of the Calderon family. Arch and Elektra Frazier were standing behind the Rhinehard couple, their faces showing no emotion at all.

Medical student Lynn Goldsmith was standing with a group of cadets that had gathered to pay their respects. She was with Harumi Shigeta and several of the Andolini family members. Goldsmith had never been a Gorski Gang member as she had elected to keep to herself. She found that sometimes it was much safer to avoid attracting attention to oneself.

Cadet Colonel Jen Staszko was there as well. She had seen her share of tragedy over the last year and felt terribly for the Calderon family. Staszko felt the need to pay her respects since Lupita had once risked her life to help Yuri Gorski and Michel Evart. For that, Staszko would be forever grateful to the young lady. Staszko had sent word to Gorski and Evart of the tragedy.

Although everyone was mourning the loss, Staszko could not help but ponder the fate of Dirk and Therese Fenster. Who had done this, Staszko asked herself.

Bret Bragg had his entire Gang there to pay their respects. Although Lupita had never joined the gang, the majority of her siblings were members. Bragg had been demanding that the members of his faction stick together through any and all situations and required all of the members attend the funeral out of respect for a relative of the other gang members. Even Zoe and Shanna Bragg, both of whom had never known Lupita, were present to show solidarity with the Calderon siblings.

Sean Collins had brought his sons Liam and Sean, Jr., to the viewing the day before. The three Collins men had spent some time with the bereaved wishing them the best and expressing their sorrow for their loss. The majority of Collins team of trial lawyers and legal assistants that had worked on the Rosenburg prosecutions were also there at the viewing. Collins was made aware that the political situation for his family might become untenable. So, he instructed his sons to avoid the actual funeral services as a precautionary manner. He had given similar instructions to the Goldsmith and Li families.

Retired Admiral Seward had previously given his condolences to the family and departed. He had lost yet another cadet pilot. The number of deceased cadets at the graveyard at Clovis Academy seemed to have grown larger than he would have ever wanted. Each death weighed heavily in his heart. He did not have the stomach to sit through dozens of Hail Mary's and prayer offerings. Such ritualistic behavior was pointless to Seward and he had been exposed to it one time too many. He left after embracing each of the Calderon family members, telling them all that he was deeply sorry for their loss.

The large attendance for the services was not lost on the Calderon family. The grieving family members had always known that Lupita was special. That thought had been proven by the numbers that came to say good bye to her. She had been the most caring of the Calderon siblings and was missed by them all. Colonel Nikolai Gorski attended with Major Sigebert Evart at his side.

The two men had attended the event and were among the first to be fired upon by the individuals that probably murdered poor Lupita. Gorski felt responsible that he had not been able to protect her. Gorski had felt relieved that his son, Piotr, had not been harmed in the attack. With his son Yuri gone, Colonel Gorski only had his son Piotr to dote over.

But Colonel Nikolai Gorski had other issues on his mind. He had learned that the Space Command had sent in a new team of officers, mostly Generals from the Military Intelligence Branch, to take command of planet New Edinburgh. Effective immediately, Colonel Gorski had been removed as the commander of the military forces on the planet. Gorski had aspirations that the Space Command would reward his hard work with a promotion to Brigadier General and give him permanent command of the Marines, at a minimum, and perhaps even the rest of the forces.

But it was not to be. When the funeral was scheduled to end, Gorski was ordered to return to the United Nations building in Clovis City to meet his new superior officers. Gorski was mindful that he still had a few years to serve before he would be eligible for full retirement.

As the Catholic Priest began the services several space craft could be seen in the distance. Some were designs that the attendees at the funeral had never seen. They were larger than a Super Raumschiff and a bit wider. There were also several dozen Raumschiff's that flew overhead in the direction of the private landing strips. The strange wide bodied craft were flying in the direction of the massive court yard of the United Nations Building.

Each of the space ships was escorted by two Allen Corporation Fighter Type CC76A3 space craft. Colonel Gorski had speculated that the space craft carried the new officers to New Edinburgh.

Klaus and April Rhinehard stared into the sky, watching the space craft, trying to determine what design the new ships were. They had never seen such a craft, even in their studies at the Academy there had been no instruction as to this novel style of space vessel.

"What are those other ships?" Elektra Frazier whispered to her husband.

"Never seen that type of design before," Arch Frazier answered his wife quietly.

Gorski heard the sobs of the mourners as the priest spoke. With all of the space ship transports flying overhead, Gorski deduced that the Lysander had entered the orbit around New Edinburgh and the new commanders were arriving. Although he dreaded the changing of the command and what it would mean to his career, Gorski was ready to meet the new command. He also could not stand listening to any priest trying to tell him the meaning of life and death. Gorski found such sermons insulting as he learned the hard way and had his own theories regarding the subjects of life and death. No religious leader could do that for him. Gorski only knew that his wife was taken from him far too soon. If there were a deity out there for him to meet in the next life, Gorski intended to spit in the face of that being for taking his wife from him. Gorski nodded to Evart that it was time to depart. The two officers stood and slipped away to face their new commanders and learn their fates.

Evart and Gorski had grown into close friends over the last two years. They had accomplished many amazing milestones together. They had been in on restoring Space Station Cy-7, arresting the Rosenburg co-conspirators, restoring faith in the military for the civilian population and seeing off a good crop of graduates from the Academy. Evart had watched as three of his daughters had graduated from high school and left the planet to study at the Academy in Paris, France.

Gorski and Evart were met by Captain Tierney at the entrance to the massive United Nations Building. It housed the military top officers and their support staff, the United Nations lawyers and their support staff, the Secretary General and his staff, the elected Ambassadors from the other Territories of planet New Edinburgh and their support staff. All in all, there were about ten thousand employees that worked in the Clovis City U.N. building.

Tierney saluted the two men and they returned the respect and saluted him back.

"Colonel, our replacements are here," Tierney said with gloom in his voice. "And, they are all Royal's."

Gorski and Evart exchanged glances at that. Up until that moment, the Royal Family had played hands off on the operations of New Edinburgh, other than the Rosenburg's.

"How many?" Evart asked quickly.

"Two Generals, one Admiral, about a dozen Colonels and over twenty Majors." Tierney began informing them of what little he had been able to learn.

"And, sirs, John Rosenburg was with them. And so were several of the Rosenburg family members that were arrested were in the group. I saw Rebecca, Carla and Juliana Rosenburg entering the building. They were with the two Generals and the Admiral."

"How the hell did they get out of jail?" Gorski was vexed by the news. He had led the expedition into the Rosenburg Ranch Territory to serve the arrest warrants on several dozen Rosenburg's. Gorski prayed to the Stars that this was not the precursor of something sinister.

"No one would talk with me, sir." Tierney responded. "They walked past me and the men here like we were nothing."

"Let's go see how we can assist them in the transition. And see if they will give us an explanation as to why they have indicted criminals with them." Gorski told the men and led them into the building.

As men that had a duty to maintain themselves in the best physical conditioning, they took the stairs and walked rapidly up fifteen flights to the floor reserved to the military chiefs and their staff. Gorski walked into the hallway first, followed by Tierney and Evart. At the end of the long, winding hallway were the offices that Gorski and Evart had been working out of for the past year.

In Gorski's office they saw United Nations Secretary General and director of the Security Council of New Edinburgh, Alexander Lyss, standing near the windows conversing with about seven women. Gorski recognized some of the women immediately. They were some of the Rosenburg women he had arrested for Sean Collins. Gorski was confused in that the women were supposedly incarcerated and awaiting trial. He quickly concluded that they had been released without authorization from prosecutor Sean Collins. If they had been, Collins would have informed Gorski immediately.

The other three women were wearing military uniforms. One was in the camouflaged uniform of a Marine, another the dark blue of the Space Command and the third a solid black uniform from Military Intelligence. Gorski recognized the woman in the Marine Corps uniform as Elizabeth Murdock. She was a great great granddaughter of the Glorious Leader and a cold witch.

About four years earlier, she attempted to seduce Gorski at a temporary duty training camp on planet New Vladivostok. Gorski had been a Major at the time. Gorski refused the woman's romantic advances which caused her to throw a fit. He had heard that Murdock once shot a Lance Corporal in the head when he failed to prepare her morning coffee as to her specifications.

Based on her behavior, Gorski was certain that Murdock suffered from Bi-Polar Disorder at a minimum and she was in serious need of medication.

"Ah, Yuri, Sigebert!" Lyss smiled and waved to them as he noticed the men coming. "Come on in. There are some people here that you need to meet."

The three officers nodded and walked into the room.

"Um, Captain Tierney, you can wait outside. This meeting does not concern you." Lyss said softly.

"Yes sir." Tierney turned around and walked out of the office and did not react when the thick door was slammed shut behind him.

Lyss shook Evart's hand and motioned to the seven women. "You all remember Rebecca, Carla, Juliana and Nydia Rosenburg do you not?"

"Of course we remember them," Gorski nodded to the four young looking and attractive Rosenburg women. Gorski recalled that Rebecca had been the former personal assistant to Lyss before she was arrested for her part in the conspiracy to commit murder. She had been a thorn in Gorski's side for over a year with all of her snooping around and using her natural beauty in attempts to seduce others for information.

"I recall that all four of you should be in a jail cell. Care to enlighten me as to how you were released?"

"Enough of that!"

One of the other women in the black uniform barked, pointing her index finger in Gorski's direction in an accusatory manner.

"They were released by my order as they were being held illegally by you and Collins. I am Major General Kimberly Sikorsky from military Intelligence. I have brought with me as a part of my staff Marine Corps Brigadier General Elizabeth Murdock and Space Command Admiral Zara Sowa."

The other two women nodded to Gorski and Evart as they were introduced.

Kimberly Sikorsky was a great granddaughter of the Glorious Leader. She was about five feet six inches tall with dark hair and brown eyes. She was one hundred forty years old, but looked about thirty years of age. She, like the rest of her family members, kept herself young with metallic bones and skin and internal organs from unwilling female donors. Kimberly Sikorsky had gone through two different heart transplants, three kidney exchanges and many other replacement operations to keep her alive. Alas, the donors all died shortly after their body organs were forcefully extracted.

Zara Sowa was a great granddaughter of Vladimir Sikorsky. She was about one hundred ten years old. She also had kept herself young by the same immoral theft of body parts from innocent women. The Sowa line were all descended from Vladimir Sikorsky and an African wife he took two centuries earlier. Although the original Sowa woman had long since passed on, many of her children and their descendants lived on.

"Pleasure to meet each of you," Gorski said.

Elizabeth Murdock sneered at Gorski. By the look in her eyes, it was clear she remembered Gorski and his rejection of her sexual advances years earlier. Murdock was not a woman that took rejection lightly.

"Colonel, I was ordered to leave a comfortable position on Sikorsky's Planet to come here and fix your mess. The lack of discipline, the un-solved murders and the rampant disregard for the rule of law is appalling. You and Major Evart should know that we are bringing in a new crew of lawyers to replace Collins. His illegal convictions will all be overturned. And we will file indictments against you and Major Evart immediately."

"What the hell are you talking about?" Evart was always far more emotional the Gorski. "We protected the people of this planet to the best of our ability!"

"What about the assassination of Admiral Casados?" Sowa chimed in. "Please tell me why his murderers have not been apprehended and the other flag officers that were killed here in this city? Have you made any arrests? Have there been any convictions on those cases?"

"Well, no." Gorski admitted.

He had always felt terrible bout the fact that the Darktober killings had gone unresolved.

"But we have several Criminal Investigation Division detectives working those cases. Those Generals and the Admiral were friends of ours, they were my colleagues. Major Evart and I want the perpetrators brought to justice more than you can know. We believe that the assassinations were perpetrated by the Ragnarsson family. We just haven't gathered enough evidence to close those cold cases. And as for the Rosenburg women, they were involved in a vast conspiracy that resulted in the deaths of hundreds of men and women. You cannot release them. They are a danger to the civilian population."

"No, Colonel Gorski. No."

Kimberly Sikorsky walked up to him and stared into his eyes.

"It was you and your friend Evart here, you two killed the General's and Casados. You two had too much to gain by their deaths. You and Evart hoped you would both receive promotions to General so that you would get the pay increases and the extra benefits. You tried to frame the only law abiding family here, the Rosenburg's, with lies and innuendos."

"I protest, General! I have served the Space Command with loyalty and distinction!" Gorski raised his voice. "These four Rosenburg women conspired with their father to kill cadets on the moon of planet Semiramis, they assisted in two separate attacks on innocent cadets here at the hospital and the Academy which resulted in hundreds dead. And then there was the attack at Space Station Cy-7 that they helped with. The evidence is there!"

Kimberly Sikorsky ignored Gorski's objections and nodded to Lyss who responded by opening the door. Ten women and two men entered the office, all dressed in Class C solid black uniforms of the MI Branch. The highest rank that Gorski observed was a Sergeant, the rest were Corporal's and Private's. Each of the twelve must have arrived in one of the space craft they had observed from the funeral as none of them looked familiar to Gorski or Evart.

"As of now, you are both under arrest for treason against the Glorious Leader, the murders of Admiral Casados and the General officers of New Edinburgh." General Kimberly Sikorsky announced. "Sergeant, take Gorski and Evart into custody."

Evart looked to Lyss as he was being handcuffed by two of the MI soldiers. "Alex! Please tell them that we are loyal to the Glorious Leader! This is a mistake! We have done nothing wrong!"

Lyss, who had always been a paid conspirator with the Rosenburg's, only shook his head. He had always liked Evart and tolerated Gorski. He even attended several of the Evart family cookouts and New Year's Eve celebrations. But the Royal

Family were the powerful ones in the universe and they paid well. The Sigebert Evart's and the Nikolai Gorski's of the world would come and go. But the Sikorsky family would be the eternal rulers of humanity. Lyss made the decision to help in the purge of the Collins-Gorski-Evart triangle so that the Royal Family could take control of planet New Edinburgh once and for all.

Gorski said nothing as he was being shackled by the MI soldiers. He felt them removing his laser pistol and knives as he stared into the unblinking eyes of Kimberly Sikorsky. Out of the corner of his eye, Gorski could see Rebecca Rosenburg smiling at him as if his arrest was a personal victory for her.

Marine Corps General Elizabeth Murdock picked up a picture frame that was on Gorski's desk and looked it over. It was an eight by ten color photograph of Melita Gorski. Murdock walked over to Gorski, looking him over.

"We all know that you are a sad man. How many years have gone by that you have not had a woman? And for her? A corpse? Or were you a homosexual all along? No person stays alone for this long. Look at her picture, Gorski!"

Murdock thrust the framed photograph into his face. "She isn't even all that pretty. You wasted your life, Colonel Nikolai Gorski." She then threw the frame to the floor, the glass shattered on impact.

Gorski wanted to curse Murdock and the other women present. He wanted to break Alexander Lyss' skinny neck. For some reason, he sensed that Murdock was attempting to provoke him to do something stupid. He decided to take the high road and say only a few words to the group of snakes before him.

"You know, General Murdock, you may have contempt for me because I was fortunate enough in this life to find true love. It does exist, true love. Melita, she was everything to me. Her smile was enchanting. Her voice was full of joy and laughter. When she died, I was a lost soul. But at least I had loved and was loved back in return. So, yes, I was alone for all these years only because no other woman could match Melita in my heart."

Elizabeth Murdock spit in Gorski's face. "Get him out of here!"

"After you secure the prisoners, go and arrest all of their family members. If any of them even blink, shoot them dead. In fact, just kill Piotr Gorski and all of Major Evart's children on sight. Don't even give them a chance to surrender. No, wait. Take Evart's daughters and wives prisoner so we can all be entertained by watching them be raped by some of our sex starved Babcottiatta," General Kimberly Sikorsky added.

The mention of harming Evart's family went too far for the Frenchman. Evart was a man that would take insults personally and turn the other cheek. But threaten his children, was crossing the line with Sigebert Evart.

Evart growled at the Royal Family women and tried to jump at Sikorsky. Evart was able to get his hands around Kimberly Sikorsky's throat and squeeze before the Military Intelligence soldiers tackled the Major and began kicking him. Gorski attempted to help his friend, but with his hands shackled there was little he could do. Gorski was shoved to the floor by one of the soldiers. Gorski watched helplessly as Admiral Zara Sowa opened one of the large office windows and the soldiers lifted up the beaten Major Sigebert Evart.

"He assaulted a commanding General and a Royal! Touching a member of the Royal family is a death penalty felony offense! Throw him out." Sowa ordered.

"No!" Gorski bellowed, realizing why the three women were trying so hard to provoke Gorski and Evart. They wanted an excuse to kill them both. By killing them now under some real or imagined provocation they would avoid the publicity of a trial. Evart just gave them the reason to execute him that they had been searching for.

The soldiers obeyed the Admiral and carried Major Sigebert Evart to the open window. Evart screamed in fear, kicking his legs and struggling to free himself as the soldiers tossed him out the window. His screams could be heard by the civilians on the streets as he rapidly descended down the two hundred fifty foot fall. Evart's ribs, left shoulder and neck were shattered on the impact of the cement court yard below. His skull cracked open and his brain matter was scattered in several directions.

Witnesses in the courtyard screamed in horror at the death. Some of them recognized him as one of the Marines that had protected them over the years. One of the witnesses, Doctor Freya Doernitz Cardenas ran to the twisted body of Sigebert Evart and could tell that there was nothing she could do for the man. His body was splattered and blood was all over the transparent metal walkways that surrounded the governmental buildings.

Freya Cardenas had been on her way to work when she heard the screams from above. She noticed that hands of the corpse were cuffed. She pulled out her hand held communication device from her hand bag and activated it.

"This is Doctor Cardenas to the ER. I need a coroner to the United Nations Building. We have a fatality."

She looked around the courtyard at all of the strange space ships that had landed. She observed hundreds of Saharakaree leaping from the exit ramps that had been lowered to the concrete grounds, followed by dozens upon dozens of women and men wearing the black Military Intelligence uniforms.

The Saharakaree were waiving their deadly pointed tails menacingly as they leaped to the ground and began to form up with the several platoons of soldiers. Freya made a quick count of several hundred Saharakaree. She saw the larger Babcottiatta behind the Saharakaree. They were holding some glowing spears in their hands and watching the crowd of onlookers with menace in their eyes. She gazed up at the United Nations building and knew that something horrible was coming. Feelings of dread filled her mind and Freya was grateful her little brother, Jurgen, had left New Edinburgh for a vacation. He would be safe from whatever was about to happen.

Colonel Nikolai Gorski was silent, mourning the death of his closest friend. His mind was focused on how to stay alive and to formulate a plan for escape. The soldiers forced Gorski into the large meeting room that was just down the hall from his office. Gorski saw that Captain Tierney was sitting in the room already, his hands cuffed. The two men heard the doors to the meeting room slam shut and the automatic locks activated. Gorski put his head on the large conference table and closed his eyes.

"What is going on, Colonel?" Tierney was distraught. He had been arrested without explanation by the new soldiers occupying the United Nations Building. Tierney did not understand what was happening.

"They murdered Sigebert," Gorski told him softly. "It's only a matter of time before they kill us, too."

"The Major is dead?" Tierney's jaw was hanging open in shock. "But why?"

"Because there is a war going on out there and the three of us have been labeled as traitors. They will try to provoke you to attack them. Don't fall for it. No matter what, keep calm." Gorski answered the junior officer, seeing a look of despair in his eyes.

Nikolai Gorski hoped that someone with intelligence would see the body of Sigebert Evart and begin to deduce that all was not right. He was most worried for the life of his son, Piotr, and the children of Major Evart.

"I am so sorry. And the worst is about to come."

Piotr Gorski was among the crowd placing flowers on the coffin of Lupita Calderon before her casket was lowered into the ground. Even in death, the young cadet pilot was beautiful. The slash in her neck had been covered by a scarf, her hands folded under her breasts. Her eyes closed and her hair was fixed up nicely. Piotr Gorski shook his head as he walked past her in the procession. She had been his friend and he missed her.

For the first time in his life Piotr Gorski understood why his older brother Yuri always admonished that the universe was not a safe place. He noticed that Jen Staszko was standing next to a Military Intelligence enlisted woman and they were deep in conversation. Piotr recognized the uniformed woman as Sara Stewart, a person that had helped his brother in the past. The younger Gorski began to walk over to the two women.

A small transport ship landed about fifty feet from the funeral grounds. About a dozen Military Intelligence soldiers, clad in their Class C uniforms, jumped out of the side of the craft as it slowly opened its' walking ramp. They were each armed with laser rifles. They ran in formation, six by six with a female Captain in the lead. The cadets and community members at the funeral paused and watched the soldiers out of curiosity. They were coming to the funeral with their weapons ready.

Father Kendall smiled at the twelve soldiers and their Captain.

"Welcome my brothers and sisters. Have you come to pay your respects to sister Lupita?"

The Captain glared at the priest, "I am Captain Adellina Murdock from Military Intelligence. Our forces have taken possession of the United Nations Building and the Military Headquarters. We had no choice but to seize control due to the traitorous actions of Colonel Gorski, Major Evart and attorney Collins. They and all of their family are traitors to the Glorious Leader, Vladimir Sikorsky. I have in my possession arrest warrants for the entire families of Sigebert Evart, Sean Collins and Nikolai Gorski. Inform their spouses and children to step forward and surrender. Do it now, Priest, or we start making examples of some of the attendees here and create more funerals than necessary. Understand me?"

"Now, Captain Murdock, there is no reason for hostilities. This is a House of God and we are all here to pay our respects for a fallen loved one. I am certain we can work out this situation amicably," Kendall said in a calm voice.

Supreet Patel was sitting next to Flora Evart and grabbed her arm and whispered into her ear, "Don't move. Something bad is going to happen."

Flora Evart swallowed and took the advice of Patel. She wondered why these soldiers would want her aunts and cousins. Several of Flora Evart's cousins were sitting next to her in the pews, each wide eyed with fear for they all knew that a charge of treason carried the death penalty as punishment.

Captain Murdock snarled at Kendall and aimed her laser rifle at him. "Produce those that are wanted by the Glorious Leader for treason or you die with them."

Mark Lund, Sara Stewart, Benjamen Zhao, Miyu Tamura, Frank Preston and the rest of the platoon were watching the events unfold before them. All of the soldiers, as if reading each other's thoughts, slowly drew their hand lasers and hid them at their sides so that Captain Murdock and her soldiers would not see them.

Lund slowly nodded to the other four to be ready. Lund had always suspected that the Glorious Leader had more knowledge of the Rosenburg-Ragnarsson alliance than had been publicized. This act of aggression, to arrest the families of those involved in defeating the Rosenburg's was proof to Lund that his fears were confirmed.

"They are not traitors, I assure you good Captain." Kendall had his arms open, his palms facing the ceiling as a way to show Captain Murdock that she had nothing to fear from him.

The Captain responded by raising her laser rifle and fired into the torso of Kendall. The crowd shrieked in panic and fear as the priest's body was blown into chunks of meat and bone. The crowd began running in various directions. Some fell under the force of others shoving them and pushing and were then stepped on as the crowd tried to escape the enclosed church.

The Captain achieved what she had wanted, mass panic. Now they could kill the Gorski kid and the Evart family members easily.

Or so Murdock thought.

Lieutenant Reynita Calderon, having just witnessed the brutal murder of Father Kendall, the man who had baptized her and each of her siblings, pulled her hand laser from her web belt and fired upon Captain Murdock. Her aim was true and the murderous Captain cried out when Reynita's laser blast severed her left arm from her body and burned a hole in her left side. Murdock's body was thrown about three feet into the air from the impact of the laser shot and fell to the floor of the church with a thud.

To Reynita's relief, she saw that Lund, Preston, Stewart, Tamura and others in her platoon were backing her up. They were firing upon the squad of attackers. Zhao ran and tackled one of the women soldiers and pinned her to the ground. Tamura fired her laser pistol and took the head off of an MI sergeant. Preston fired at a Corporal and his laser beam entered her upper chest and blew a fist sized hole out her back. Stewart and Lund also fired their laser pistols, eliminating members of Captain Murdock's crew.

Jen Staszko joined in, pulling two razor sharp knives from her boots and threw them at the military intelligence attackers. One of her blades sank into the neck of a female Private who fell to the ground, clutching the hilt of the blade, her blood spraying from her severed jugular.

The fight was over quickly. The squad under the dead Captain Murdock was defeated. The crowd at the church were all silent and slowly looked to Reynita Calderon, Mark Lund and the other Military Intelligence soldiers in their platoon. Reynita realized she was the highest ranking military presence on the funeral grounds. Many of the congregation were looking to her, their eyes wide with fear.

Her family members were stunned that Kendall had been killed. Her father, a retired Marine Corps enlisted man looked upon his daughter with pride in his eyes. Others looked upon her in awe, as if they never believed their older sister had it in her, to kill so decisively.

"Lieutenant!" Lund barked, trying to get Reynita to concentrate on the events before them. They had all just committed treason in front of thousands of witnesses. Their only hope of survival was quick and bold action. Lund needed for his Lieutenant to understand the severity of their actions. He ran through the crowd and stood next to her. "What are your orders?"

Reynita shook her head and turned to her platoon, all of whom were looking at her with respect in their eyes. The enlisted men and women under her command had doubted her when she first became their new platoon leader. She was a graduate of the Academy but had never seen action. Now she had fired the second shot that would probably start a planetary war. "We take back the command headquarters."

"There's only forty of us!" Stewart protested.

"No, we are thousands." Reynita said, raising her voice for all to hear as she turned to Jen Staszko, Blossom Li and Klaus Rhinehard. "Aren't we?"

"Let's go kick their Damn hides to hell!" Jen Staskzo screamed to the assembled cadets.

The rest of the cadets began shouting their willingness to join the fight.

No one was allowed to disgrace the Academy Graveyard or a place of worship. And no one was going to walk away after threatening a fellow cadet.

Not even a Sikorsky.

Lund smiled at the show of bravery. He looked over at the distant United Nations buildings and military installations. Many were about to die and the majority would be under the age of twenty. He whispered to his young Lieutenant.

"We need weapons and an air force first."

Reynita swallowed hard. The implications of the past seconds were just sinking in to her. She had committed treason against the Empire and the Royal Family. She could not believe that these events were swirling around her; it was all happening so quickly. "Where do we get them?"

"Come on, I will show you," Lund said. "Round up Admiral Seward and the top ranking cadets. We need to organize for a lightning fast attack. Those Sikorsky forces will realize soon that Captain Murdock is not coming back. We need to hit them now and hit them hard."

Reynita looked back at the cadets, "Rhinehard, Li, Staszko, Regher, Black, Bragg, Frazier, Frazier and Shigeta... I mean Andolini, you are all with me."

"What about the rest of us?" Cadet James Cobb inquired.

Reynita saw that many of the cadet pilots were staring in her direction with a burning desire to be led. They wanted orders. Calderon nodded at Cobb and some of the other cadets she recognized. John Guathier was leaning against the west wall of the church with his arms crossed across his chest. Reynita pointed at them, "James, John and Tara, I need you three to get to Admiral Seward and warn him of what has happened. The rest of you that are pilots, get the Allen fighter ships ready for battle. Move it!"

"Sis, what can we do?" Manuel Calderon asked her. He was standing behind their wheel chair bound grandmother and was surrounded by several brothers and sisters. His father and mother were looking on in silence, still stunned and proud at the same time, due to the quick actions taken by Reynita.

Reynita pursed her lips and pointed to the door of the church, "Get abuelita and everyone else out of here. Once you get home and are certain everyone is safe, get the motorcycles ready. Manuel, I will need you and Pepito to back up Cobb and Varek at the flight school just in case there is trouble. Get the bikes and haul ass as fast as possible to that location."

Manuel nodded and motioned for the remainder of the Calderon clan to follow him, "Let's go. You heard her."

Cadet sophomore Tara Haddad followed Cobb and Gauthier as directed to seek out and locate Admiral Seward.

Cadet pilot Dino Black moved up with the others and followed Arch Frazier in line as Reynita led them, the highest ranking cadets at the Academy out of the church to plan an a war.

Many of the other cadets that were in the sciences and engineering sections were left behind with only questions in their minds as to what had transpired. Geology student Dempster Harang, also called 'Demps,' beckoned for them all to return to their dormitories until further notice. The students responded to his direction and began to walk quickly back to their rooms. Harang, who was in the same section of classes as Arch Frazier, wanted to find out how he could lend any assistance and he followed his friend, jogging to catch up to him.

CHAPTER TWENTY-FOUR

Army Weapons Supply First Lieutenant Carl Price was walking to work when Major Evart was thrown to his death. Price saw the body falling and heard the screams of horror from the civilians that observed the grisly event. Price was a good fifty feet away from the building and heard the crunch of bone when Evart's body impacted on the concrete ground.

Price surveyed the scene of all of the new soldiers and aliens surrounding the building. He knew that something was wrong and slowly changed the direction that he was walking in to avoid confronting the wall of alien slaves ahead. Price was certain that he was observing the start of a new regime. Normally a change of command would be done peacefully between officers. This was something completely out of the ordinary.

Price was twenty-six years old and had dark skin with dark hair and eyes. His handsome features complimented his lean frame. He had graduated from Newton Academy as a weapons major and was drafted to serve in the Supply Battalion on Clovis City. He was promoted to First Lieutenant a year earlier and put in charge of B Company. Price was single as he preferred dating several women and avoiding any form of commitment.

During his four and a half years serving as an officer in Clovis City he had grown to respect Colonel Gorski and Major Evart. They were good commanders to serve under. They had been fair and never asked their soldiers to do anything that they were not willing to do themselves.

Price noticed that Marine Corps Lieutenant Priata Shen was standing still in the middle of the large concrete courtyard watching the scene before her. Price walked quickly in her direction and stopped next to her. Shen was a woman of Asian descent; Price was not certain of the specific nationality as he never spent any time socializing with her. She was single and had graduated from Tyr Academy. She was a good officer, prompt, prepared and knew her regulations. Her uniforms were always neatly pressed, her boots shined, her rank insignias were always shiny and smudge free.

"Shen?"

"Yes?"

"I am Carl Price. You serve under Gorski and Evart?"

Shen looked at Price with concern in her eyes.

"Yes I do. Captain Tierney is my Company Commander. What is happening here? I have heard people in the crowd talking about a change in command. I searched my pocket computer to try and locate any new orders from the Space Command about the change and found nothing. Do you know anything about any new orders?"

Price looked into her eyes. "I don't know. But I will find out. If you are loyal to Colonel Gorski you should come with me."

"What are those blue giants?"

"They are called Babcottiatta. You don't want to mess with them. They are strong enough to rip your arms and legs out with little effort. They also like sex with human females, but their idea of sex involves tearing the legs off of the woman after the act is completed. I have seen downloads from the news about it. I assure you that it is quite gruesome. You need to come with me, Shen. We need to warn people."

Shen finally tore her eyes away from the sight of the aliens and looked at Price. "Warn people? Warn who? And what are we warning them about?"

"I think I know some people we can ask. I have a friend that is one of the Marines, named Salvatorre "the Pick" Simms. He is a Lieutenant under Captain Tierney. You should know him."

Shen laughed, "Of course I know him. He is one of the other platoon leaders under Captain Tierney. He's on duty patrolling the south sector of the Great Protective Wall."

"Then let's move out."

Shen shrugged and followed Price. She did not want to admit to him that she was looking for any excuse to avoid entering the United Nations Administrative Building at that moment. The giant aliens and the presence of so many Saharakaree terrified her.

The two officers found that a huge crowd of civilians were gathering to see why so many transport ships were landing around the Administrative Building. They watched as the other surrounding buildings were entered by the force of aliens led by the Marines and Military Intelligence soldiers.

Price and Shen found it difficult to push through the crowd but eventually found their way to a clearing on the southeast end of the paved plaza. Price led Shen to the ten foot wide moving sidewalks and they both jumped on. They walked as fast as they could and after thirty minutes they could see the Marine Corps barracks in the distance. During their entire walk, Shen and Price said nothing as they were afraid that the listening devices that were in the moving sidewalk would catch their conversation and alert the security systems at the Administrative Building.

They jumped off of the fast moving sidewalk and ran to the barracks. When they entered they saw that the Marines were all in uniform and had weapons ready. The men and women in uniform stood at attention for Price and Shen.

"At ease," Price told them as he kept moving toward the back of the building where there were offices for the administrative staff and the platoon leader.

Price and Shen ignored the two female civilian administrators that warned them that Lieutenant Simms was busy. Price walked past the two women in the office and toward the closed door that had a name plate for Lieutenant Simms on the upper part of the one way mirror door.

Price walked in with Shen on his heels. They both saw the entire office of Simms alive with numerous three dimensional broadcasts running simultaneously. They noticed that there were news reports coming from Space Station Cy-7, the moon base, the main Administrative Building, a reporter was speaking in front of the Clovis City prison-south, and there were reports coming in from civilians in front of private residences. Some of the private homes looked like they had been hit by laser and rocket fire.

Simms had spent all of his disposable income from his pay as an officer in the Marines on the newest and greatest technology available. He had computer systems developed and manufactured by the Breckenridge and Milos Corporations. Most of his systems had in excess of fifty terabyte of memory space which allowed his computers to work rapidly and without any glitches. He had the best three dimensional projection units and speakers that money could buy. His need to keep up to date was almost like an obsession. He loved knowing more than the next person. Simms told all of his friends that knowledge was power and that his constant surfing of many broadcast locations would one day come in handy.

"Good!" Salvatore Simms yelled out over the cacophony of news reports coming in. He had a toothpick in his mouth which always seemed to be there. That was why his friends affectionately referred to Simms as "the Pick."

"I was wondering when you would show up! How are things outside, Carl?"

Simms and Price shook hands, "Not good my friend. There are thousands of aliens and space craft in the plaza of the administrative complex. I decided to come here and see what you know."

Simms was a man that kept in good physical condition. He had his brown hair cut short and was a good officer by keeping things by the book. He was also a news and computer aficionado and would spend his free time monitoring news reports from New Edinburgh and beyond. He also had a knack for being able to tap into confidential sources and learn the back story of current events. Simms had developed his computer and hacking skills as a cadet at the Sikorsky Planet Academy. His interest in computer systems and hacking began when he was a young boy but his skills in that area took off when one of his professors recognized his potential and took Simms in as his cadet assistant. After four years under his professor, Simms found there were few computer systems he could not hack into.

"As you can see I am watching everything," Simms said as he hugged Shen. Unknown to Price, Shen and Simms had been maintaining a secret arrangement for casual sexual meetings. They had kept their clandestine meetings secret as they were concerned the straight laced Captain Tierney would not approve of two of his platoon leaders sharing the same bed.

"That was what I was hoping for," Price smiled at his friend. He and Simms had been friends for several years and respected one another. Price was always impressed by Simms aptitude with computer programming.

"They issued a warrant for my arrest," Simms reported. "And you, Carl. They already landed on the moon base and took it over."

"Who is they?" Shen cut in.

"The Royal Family. The Glorious Leader sent in some of his highest ranking offspring to clean us out here. They murdered Captain Hsu on the moon base and her executive officer. Threw them out of an airlock."

Simms pointed at the screen on his left wall that was showing the current events on the moon base. "They killed most of the Goldsmith family and are seeking out the rest of them for extermination. And, they killed our Major Evart."

Shen looked as if she were going to vomit. Her face lost all color. Evart had been like a father figure to her and showed her kindness when she was homesick. Evart had invited her to numerous family cook outs and functions. Shen had, over the short time she served in the Marines, grown close to all of Evart's wives and children.

"Why would they kill him? He was loyal to the Space Command."
"Not loyal enough," Price said under his breath. He had respected Hsu and Evart. They had been good officers.

Simms pointed to another screen, "They went to arrest Nia Li, one of the lawyers here. But the Li family put up a fight and killed about fifty aliens and soldiers. I don't think the commanders on the Lysander know that yet. We should help the Li family find a place to hide out. They will want to kill them all for revenge."

"Who else has warrants?" Price asked.

"Sean Collins and his family. Several of the United Nations General Assembly Representatives are slated to be arrested. They will come for me and you soon."

Price paced around and studied each of the screens before him. Simms was brilliant in his ability to tap into so much information.

"What should we do?" Shen finally asked to break the silence.

"We warn everyone to run and hide," Price concluded. "The reps are not soldiers so they would be wiped out like the Goldsmith family. Collins needs to be warned quickly. We already lost major Evart and losing Collins would be a devastating blow for this community. Can both of your platoons be trusted to help out? We will need all the warm bodies we can get."

"My platoon has no Royals and little love for them," Shen reported. "We can count on them when the time comes."

Simms nodded, "I can lead my platoon. They will follow me. What do you have in mind?"

"We need allies if we are going to save the Reps and Collins. And save ourselves at the same time." Price observed. "We need to warn these other people immediately. Wait a minute. I am getting a call."

Simms and Shen waited patiently as Price activated his hand held communication device. It was Sergeant First Class Mark Lund. His light red glowing image appeared before them.

"We need help, sir." Lund said quickly.

Price nodded, "As do we, sergeant. We should meet. Soon."

"Yes sir," Lund agreed. "How about at your weapons storage facility?"

"Excellent idea, Sergeant Lund. I am on my way." Price closed his holo-com and faced Simms and Shen. "It seems we are not the only ones that know something is wrong. You two start warning everyone to seek refuge somewhere. I will warn Collins and meet with Lund. We need to move on this."

"We're on it," Shen assured him.

Rebecca Rosenburg was elated by the events of the last two days. She had been released from prison, returned to power at the United Nations Security Council in a higher position she previously held and all of her former rivals were falling one by one. She received the holo-com call from Clea Sowa that another of her enemies had been apprehended. The General Assembly Representative from the south-west district of Clovis City had been Nelson Wyclyffe. He had been the man to draft, propose and push the authorization bill to fire her after Sean Collins had her arrested. Rebecca despised Wyclyffe for his role in her ouster.

And now he would pay.

Sowa informed her that Wyclyffe, his three wives, twelve children, one son-in-law and three grandchildren were being held in the top secret basement interrogation room of the United Nations building.

Upon receiving the report, Rebecca skipped down the hallway to the elevator that required a palm print identification before it would operate, placed her left hand on the scanner and tapped her right foot as the elevator descended. She cursed the elevator music and vowed to change it to something more raw and loud, such as twentieth century heavy metal music.

The elevator finally came to a stop and the doors slid open for her. She skipped out of the entrance, acting as if she were a third grader going to recess. She cared little that some of the MI soldiers gave her odd stares as she passed by them through the long, winding, sound proof, metal hallway. She finally made it to the thick light blue doors with red letters on the facade that stated "INTERROGATION ROOM 3." She placed her left palm on the security scanner and walked in as the doors slid open.

She smiled as she surveyed the large room. The entire Wyclyffe family was there. All of the adults and teenagers were chained with their hands over their heads and about a foot off the ground. She could see that their toes desperately were trying to touch the ground to relieve the stress on the arms, shoulders and underarms from the extended time they had spent in that position. They were all stripped naked. The children were tied to metal chairs with the exception of the three grandchildren who were nearing their first birthday. The adults had been whipped and burned with metal branding irons. The MI soldiers that were present had been torturing them to gain information as to the whereabouts of Sean Collins, Nia Li, and the other traitorous United Nations Representatives named Soto, al-Nasser, Stroessner, Rice, Ward and Clement.

From the looks of things the Wyclyffe family were either not cooperating or they had no useful information to share. Rosenburg said hello to the soldiers in the black uniforms. Some of them had blood spots from their prisoners on their otherwise pristine outfits. Lieutenant Colonel Clea Sowa was there and speaking in a calm voice to Nelson Wyclyffe. Rebecca could not make out what was being said as Sowa was whispering at the man, standing mere inches away from him.

Sowa recognized the Rosenburg woman and stepped back from Wyclyffe. "Welcome to the party, Madam Secretary General. I assume you are acquainted with Representative Wyclyffe?"

Rebecca sneered in his direction, "Yes, I know him well. And he knows me, shall we say, intimately. Isn't that right, Nelson?"

Wyclyffe had a large bruise over his left eye, his lower lip was busted and he had several cuts and slashes over his legs and torso. "You. How did you escape prison?"

Rebecca laughed at how his voice sounded muffled due to the busted lip.

"You know, Nelson, we had a deal. I let you fuck me in return for you killing Collins demands that I be fired by the Council. You were the chairman of the committee that handled all personnel matters. Not only did you not kill the bill, you wrote it and pushed it through committee and presented it to the General Assembly for a vote. And you did it after I let you fuck me in your office. Remember?"

Wyclyffe made a muffled sound from his throat. He could not deny her accusations. She was a devastating looking woman and he took advantage of her offer for sex. He thoroughly enjoyed the sexual moment with Rebecca and had hoped for more. But then when Collins later approached him for help and presented the evidence against the Rosenburg family, Wyclyffe felt he had to do his duty for the people. Deal or no deal. Now she was back in power and he was helpless.

He followed Rebecca with his eyes as she paced back and forth in front of him. She began shrieking loudly, "You humiliated me! No man does that and gets away with it! No man! You see, when I allow a man to pleasure himself with me, he owes me. You owed me after I let you stick your penis inside of me. I kept my side of the bargain and by the look of your overweight wives here, I was the best piece of ass you ever had. Now you will pay!"

Rebecca was pacing in front of the metal table covered with various instruments of torture. She found a foot long curved knife and picked it up in her right hand. "You are going to pay now!"

Wyclyffe watched as Rebecca walked quickly over to his three grandchildren. She grabbed one of them by the leg and held her upside down. The young child began crying hysterically. The adults were all begging for Rebeca to leave the child alone. The screams for mercy created a loud cacophony of noise in the torture room as Rebecca was haphazardly swinging the eleven month old child back and forth.

"Please. This is between you and me! Leave my family out of this!" Wyclyffe begged. The child was screaming as Rebecca cackled with glee at the plight of the entire family. As the begging and pleading was reaching higher volumes, Rebecca held the child still and thrust the curved knife into her abdomen. The child cried out in pain as the blade cut into her flesh and internal organs. The adults were screaming at her for being a cold hearted bitch. Rebeca pulled the knife free of the dying child and let the blood flow freely onto the floor. She tossed the carcass of the child at the ground just below Nelson Wyclyffe's toes.

"How does it feel, Nelson?" Rebecca was taunting him now. "All of you will die just like that little shit did. But you won't get as quick as she did. Each of you will be decapitated in front of the citizens of Clovis City in the courtyard of the United Nations Building. But you, Nelson, will be missing a part of your anatomy."

"No! Please!" Wyclyffe begged as Rebeca approached him with a look of evil in her eyes.

She laughed as he struggled in vain. She grabbed his penis and testicles in her left hand and placed the curved blade against the top of his sex organ. His begging and crying turned to screams of agony when she castrated him, moving the knife back and forth as if she were using a saw.

He was twisting in circles as howls of unspeakable pain escaped his throat.

Rebecca held his penis and testicles up for all to see. She saw a female MI sergeant watching the events and tossed the body part to her. The sergeant caught it. "A souvenir. Make sure you cauterize the wound so he doesn't bleed out. I want his head on a pike for all to see."

Sowa had no expression on her face as she observed the events unfold before her. She had been warned that many of the Rosenburg offspring were emotionally unstable. "Yes ma'am. If you will excuse me, they are hailing me on my holo-com from command. We will notify you, madam Secretary General, when the decapitations will begin."

As Sowa spoke, Rebecca was licking her fingers, cleaning the blood off. She said nothing as she departed the torture chamber. She had real work to do.

CHAPTER TWENTY-FIVE

Cadet James Cobb ran as fast as his feet would carry him to the main flight observation tower where Admiral Seward's office was located. John Gauthier and Tara Haddad were right on his heels, breathing heavily as they sprinted the two miles. Cobb knew that time was of the essence. If any defense was to be successful, they would need all of the Allen Fighter ships and Fenster Corporation Raumschiff's to fight for control of the skies.

The old adage of death from above was a truth that had to be respected in any combat situation. Admiral Seward was uniquely qualified to lead any aerial assault of space fighter ship confrontation. They needed the retired Admiral to join their desperate attempt to protect their way of life as they knew it.

The large manicured lawn surrounding the courtyard had rows of white, red and yellow rose bushes in full bloom. The paved area had many civilians and cadets walking quickly to their personal destinations. Gauthier, Cobb and Haddad cursed under their breath almost simultaneously when they saw the two platoons of MI soldiers standing in formation at parade rest. Haddad saw a captain, first lieutenant, two second lieutenants and about ninety to one hundred men and women. There were ten of the ominous looking Babcottiatta around the company commander and her executive officer in the front of the formation. The tall aliens were brandishing their seven foot long laser spears in one of their several large hands, their eyes scanning the crowds of passing humans.

Gauthier hoped that their fast pace would not attract the attention of the MI soldiers and the alien Babcottiatta. He followed Cobb into the sky scraper building with bold letters on the facade over the large thirty foot wide and twenty foot tall glass sliding door entrance stating: "SCHOOL OF ASTRAL NAVIGATION."

Cobb ran into a female Academy employee as he ran through the entrance, causing her to drop the files of paperwork in her hands. Gauthier spun by the woman with Haddad right on his heels. There were several students walking around the lobby as well as a few instructors. There was an information desk with computer screens for visitors to type in requests for the room number and floor of certain professors or lecture halls.

Basil Varek had been the commanding cadet on duty at the building. He had been contacted by Pepito Calderon via Holo-com, alerting him to the events at the church and to watch for Cobb and the others to arrive. Varek was wearing his Class C uniform and had organized five other cadet pilots to join them in the attempt to find Admiral Seward. He sent them to check all of the lecture halls and flight simulator rooms in the building due to Seward's reputation for popping in unannounced to check on the progress of his students.

"Where to?" Varek greeted his friends when he saw them running for the escalators.

"The faculty offices," Cobb was breathing heavily and pointed at the fifteen feet wide silver colored escalators. Sprinting was not one of his strong suits.

Varek took the lead and was running ahead of them.

One of the students, a new cadet pilot named Winter Truang, saw the three upper class men running for the escalator. She had spent a few nights of passion with the handsome and dashing looking Gauthier only to have him dump her with little more than a holo-com message he left for her. She soon learned that she was not the only female cadet to fall for Gauthier's advances. As she watched Gauthier running up the escalator behind Cadet Captain Varek, she thought their behavior strange and followed them. Her roommate, LaTania Serpas, knew of Truang's history with Guathier, and rolled her eyes when she saw him. Serpas motioned for some of the other cadets that were in the lobby to join the group. Something was going on and she wanted to be a part of it. Some of the other curious cadets followed the small group.

Varek ascended the escalator, running past civilians and cadets as he led the others the dozens of flights up to the flight instructor's offices. Varek did not look back to see how many cadets had joined them. He could hear that the footsteps were keeping up with him. Only Cobb had fallen behind as he tried to catch his breath. Cobb swore to himself that he would avoid the ales and beers in favor of spending more time running track. Varek finally made it to the level referred to as the Executive Suites where Admiral Seward and his flight instructors had their plush offices located. What Varek saw made him stop in his tracks.

There were scorch marks on the walls and the floors from laser fire. Several corpses of the retired officers that had been talented astronauts and teachers were lying all over the black and white tiled floor. Many of the civilian assistants to the teachers were dead as well. Some of the deceased had been dismembered. Varek covered his mouth and nose with his hand from the smell of burnt flesh. There was blood everywhere. Varek's eyes widened when he saw that a Babcottiatta was standing at the end of the bloody hallway, pointing a metal spear that was sparkling with red and yellow energy, staring him down.

"Ah, shit." Varek muttered as the Babcottiatta began charging at him, pointing the tip of the ominous spear in his direction. Each foot fall of the giant alien made a loud thud on the tiled floor as it quickly closed the distance on Varek. Varek was frozen with fear, unable to move his feet to try and avoid the imminent death blow.

Seconds before the giant alien's spear would have impaled him, Varek was tackled from behind by Haddad and shoved face first into a pool of fresh blood.

The Babcottiatta screamed in rage as it's' spear missed the intended target.   Gauthier grabbed the spear with both of his hands as the giant tried to turn around and attempt another pass at Varek. The Babcottiatta swatted Gauthier aside with one of its' other giant arms, sending the cadet flying into the air and slamming into the laser damaged wall. Gauthier cried out as he slid to the floor. Varek and Haddad were back on their feet and facing the alien. It had quickly forgotten about Gauthier and was focused back on his original target, Varek.

"Move!" Haddad urged Varek as the Babcottiatta charged at them again with the energy tipped spear aimed in their direction.

Both Varek and Haddad dodged the spear tip as it hit the bloody wall and made a loud sound of laser energy as it blasted a hole into the brick. The Babcottiatta made a large roar of anger in that it had missed Varek again. It jerked the spear free from the wall and screamed once again when several cadets grabbed it by it's' arms and legs. Gauthier wrapped both arms around the arm of the Babcottiatta that held the spear. Serpas and Truang grabbed an arm each. A cadet named Vezpucci wrapped up one of the large muscular legs with both of his arms. The alien began to throw them off like rag dolls, using his superior strength.

The Babcottiatta finally kicked Vezpucci over fifteen feet across the hall and roared as it focused in on Varek once more. It began to run at him and held the spear over its head. The cadets heard a loud blast from behind and watched as the Babcottiatta dropped the spear and began to stagger to the left and then to the right. It hit the wall and slid to the ground. A whimpering sound was emanating from its mouth as it coughed up orange colored liquid.

"Gotcha," James Cobb said as he watched the Babcottiatta slowly die. Cobb had found a laser double pump shotgun lying on the floor and used it against the alien. He shot it in the back as it attempted to charge Varek again.

Gauthier grabbed the spear and yanked it out of the hand of the dying Babcottiatta. The alien looked like it had an orange tear welling in one of its eyes. Cobb pumped the laser shotgun and placed the barrel against the skull of the alien. He pulled the trigger and the skull of the Babcottiatta split open from the multiple laser slivers that ripped into it from the shotgun.

"I never would have taken you for someone that would show mercy," Haddad said to Cobb. "What the hell happened here? Did this lone Babcottiatta kill all of our flight instructors? I think we walked into the wrong hallway."

Varek, Vezpucci, Serpas, Truang, Gauthier and three other cadet pilots began turning over the bodies and looking at their name tags. They were searching for Seward as they moved quickly down toward the end of the hallway where the last office was located. Gauthier jealously held the spear in his hand as he moved, just in case another of the giant aliens jumped out at them.

Cobb found two dead MI soldiers on the floor and quickly removed their laser pistols from their web belts. He tossed the first pistol to Varek and the second to Haddad. He found in their pouches several thermite grenades and knives. He pulled off the web belts and put one over his own shoulders and fastened it tight. The second he handed to Truang. Serpas found a laser rifle under one of the bodies and took it for herself as she checked the laser charge level on the side of the barrel.

Varek was the first to arrive at the closed door to Admiral Seward's office. There was a body of a flight instructor, lying face first on the floor with a hole in her back from a laser rifle blast. Varek moved her body aside with his right foot so that he could pull open the door to Seward's office.

The cadets heard a voice from inside the room call out to them. "I have a laser shotgun trained on the door! Try and come in and I will blast you to hell!"

"That's Admiral Seward's voice," Serpas hissed.

Varek nodded in agreement and raised his voice toward the door. "Admiral, it's me, cadet Varek! There are several of us here to help you!"

Inside the large office, Seward was sitting in his large black leather chair that he had bought for himself only two weeks prior. His right shoulder was bleeding from a laser pistol wound he suffered from one of the four dead MI soldiers that were laying on the floor of his office. When he had returned to his office from the funeral he was approached by a Major Feklisov from the MI. She had demanded his loyalty to the Royal Family and Seward swore he would always be loyal. Although Seward did not know what had happened at the church, he had concluded something went terribly wrong when Feklisov returned with several dozen MI soldiers and three Babcottiatta and attacked their offices.

The flight instructors put up a valiant fight against the better armed and equipped aggressors. Seward was able to get to his office in time to draw his own weapons and fight back. He killed all four of the MI soldiers that were bleeding on his personal office floor. During the battle, Seward was hit in the shoulder. One of the four dead was Feklisov. He breathed a sigh of relief when he heard Varek's voice.

"Come in cadet. I warn you that it is messy in here."

Varek slowly walked in with the laser pistol pointing downward at the floor. He counted the dead and smiled. He always pictured Seward as a bad ass for an old man. He saw that Seward was sitting in the chair with his weapon trained on the door.

"By the Stars, Admiral! You're bleeding!"

Varek rushed into the room and checked the wound in his shoulder. Haddad was next into the room and immediately ran to the aid of Seward. She ripped open his Class A uniform jacket and began inspecting the wound.

"The bleeding has stopped."

"I cauterized the wounds myself," Seward told them dryly. He placed his left hand on his large desk to push himself upright in his chair as Haddad was using his jacket to make a sling to support his arm.

"You did that to yourself? How?" Cadet Kazembe wanted to know.

Seward looked at the young pilot candidate and blinked a few times. "I used my hand laser on low setting and stopped the bleeding. It was quite painful, I can assure you."

"Looks like the four MI soldiers here didn't know who they were messing with," Cobb commented as he searched the bodies for more weapons. He found several laser pistols and some explosive packs on the fallen. He passed them out to the others.

"What is the situation outside?" Seward pressed the cadets.

"Major Evart is dead," Gauthier reported. "Most of the cadet corps is ready to fight the occupation but we have no real leaders. Reynita told us to come here and get you so that at least our aerial attack would have an experienced tactician. From the looks of what happened up here, you are the only one left. They killed everyone, sir."

"Colonel Gorski and Sean Collins?"

Seward nodded at Haddad as she finished the sling on his injured arm.

"No news, sir." Varek responded. "The invaders have put out death warrants on all of the Evart, Gorski, Goldsmith, Wycliffe and Li families. They are after others, too. I just cannot recall all of the names, sir."

Seward stood up with some difficulty. He had lost some blood and was still in pain from his injury. "Basil, remember what I said about coming into a briefing room with incomplete information?"

Varek looked at the ground with a look of shame. "That incomplete information can get a soldier killed. Yes sir. I apologize."

Cobb was standing by the large one way windows of Seward's quarters. He had pulled out his holo-com device and was barking orders into it. His elevated voice indicated that he was stressed and reaching a level of panic over the situation.

"Problem there Cadet Cobb?" Seward asked as he walked over toward his black metal wall closet and opened it.

Cobb looked over his shoulder at Seward, "I am trying to raise Reynita and some of the others. The only people I could reach for back up were the Calderon brothers and some of the Bragg girls. I was able to raise one of the Lipinski sisters but she does not want to get involved. We cannot rely on them, I am afraid."

"So we are on our own to face that company of MI soldiers down below?" Haddad's voice sounded like she was terrified of their untenable situation.

Seward pulled out several black back packs and handed them out to Vezpucci, Serpas, Truang, Kazembe and Gauthier.

"These are laser satchel charges. They have rip cords on the side. Once you pull the cord, you will twenty seconds to throw it. It has an explosive radius of thirty feet and will vaporize anything within it. So, make sure you are long gone before it goes off. The dead soldiers and aliens in the hallway were all armed, so search them all on the way out and take everything that they have. Before this is over, you will need every knife, therite weapon and laser pistol you can get your hands on."

"So we survive by becoming scavengers?" Gauthier grunted. "They never taught us that one in class."

The cadets were looking the packs over as Seward continued pulling out illegal weaponry from his closet. He started passing out pump laser shotguns, extra laser scatter shells for the shotguns, laser pistols, laser rifles and thermite grenades.

"Had you taken some of the advanced military tactics courses, you would have learned that using the weapons of your enemy is often times your best option. Now, if we are to get past those MI soldiers in the courtyard, we need our three best shooters to stay up here. We will synchronize our efforts and move at the same time. The three that remain up here will throw laser satchel charges into the middle of their formation. Wait until the charges explode and then you start picking them off."

"And the rest of us will be on the lower level and hit them head on?" Cobb asked.

"Exactly." Seward looked over the cadets. He could recall the majority of their names. Some of them that had been in the corps for more than two years, Seward had learned more about them. He knew that Basil Varek was a dual major and had been one of the most accurate cadet shooters with the laser weapons. He also was fairly talented at hand to hand combat.

"Varek, you were also a marksman in addition to an astronaut candidate?"

"Yes, Admiral." Varek affirmed.

"Good. You take the furthest north position on the roof of the building. Who else scored high marks on their long distance weaponry marks?"

"I grew up hunting live game on my home world." Kazembe spoke up. "I can handle it."

"I had good marks, Admiral." Vezpucci volunteered.

Seward pointed upward. "Okay, the three of you get on the roof and take north, east and west positions. Drop your charges in exactly ten minutes. Gauthier, Haddad, Cobb, Truang, Serpas, Shore and the rest of us will start firing after the charges detonate."

"And what about the Calderon brothers? They are on the way," Cobb reminded everyone. "They will be coming in from the north on old style motorcycles. There will be six of them. They won't be armed with anything but I bet their old school gasoline propelled bikes will rattle those soldiers out there."

Seward passed out fully charged laser cartridges to the cadets so that they could reload during battle.

"Then we wait for them. Varek, when you see them coming, you, Kazembe and Vezpucci drop your charges. The enemy will be focused on the roar of those machines and will be taken by surprise. Let's move out."

The three cadets assigned to the roof moved to the escalators going upward. The rest ran downward. Seward was moving slower due to the wounds he had suffered. Haddad helped him by holding his injured arm. The descent to the lobby took only a few minutes. When they arrived, they noticed that it seemed to business as usual. Seward knew that the upper floors were sound proof due to the loud noise the flight simulators could create.   Accordingly, it made sense that the people below did not hear a sound from the laser battle that had occurred in the Executive Suites.

Seward saw that there were several dozen other cadets in the lobby that had inquisitive looks on their faces. Cobb and Gauthier were motioning for the five cadets Varek had sent off to find Seward to join them. The quickly did so without question. Seward counted the number of his army. He had fourteen cadet pilots in the lobby and three above. Not much of an army to fight a war with. But they all seem filled with determination and bravery.

The retired Admiral hated involving his students in the sordid affair. The Royal Family was going through extra ordinary steps to eliminate all of the existing leadership in Clovis City. Seward had lived a long life, had children and seen many worlds. He was prepared to die. But the cadets were only starting out in life. The shroud of evil had descended on the lovely planet and no one was safe unless the people were able to take back what was theirs.

Seward watched Gauthier take up a position on the west side of the lobby entrance behind a large metal drum that had a rare tree inside of it. Cobb had done the same on the other side of the entrance. Haddad was shooing the civilians in the lobby to get up the escalator and out of the line of fire. Shore, Truang, Serpas, Wackowiak and the other cadets were standing behind the Doric columns in the lobby, aiming their weapons at the company of MI soldiers out in the courtyard. Seward could hear the sound of motorcycle engines in the distance. The Calderon brothers were true to their word. They were riding in on their home made two wheeled vehicles at speeds in excess of seventy miles per hour. Seward could not see them, but the engine noise was unmistakable.

On the roof, Basil Varek saw his fellow Bragg Gang members approaching from the north. He counted six motorcycles. He loved the Calderon family due to the fact that they had made him feel welcome during his time living in Clovis City. For Varek, joining the Bragg Gang had been one of his best moves since attending the Academy.

Varek nodded to Vezpucci and Kazembe that the time had come. All three of them simultaneously pulled the rip cords on their satchel charges and threw them downward toward the unsuspecting Babcottiatta and the company of MI soldiers below.

The charges fell rapidly toward their targets. As Seward had predicted, the soldiers were all distracted by the sounds of the approaching motorcycles. The satchel charge thrown by Varek landed next to one of the platoons full of soldiers. Vezpucci's charge landed just a few feet behind the company commander and her executive officer. Kazembe's landed on the head of one of the platoon squad leaders of the second platoon. The squad leader looked down at the satchel charge as it bounced on the paved area of the courtyard. She recognized it immediately and screamed.

The charges exploded in unison. The flash was bright and caused anyone that was looking directly at it to need several seconds to regain their vision. The company commander and the executive officer were vaporized. Nothing was left of them. The majority of the platoon that Varek had aimed for suffered the same fate. Only a few of them were outside the blast radius and survived. The second platoon had begun to scatter in different directions before the last charge erupted. The majority of that platoon escaped death for that moment.

But then the cadets on the lower level began firing. The soldiers were out in the open and had little natural or manmade structures to get behind for cover. Seward and his small army of heroes fired their lasers at will, dropping the soldiers one by one. But the MI soldiers were not the main concern. The ten Babcottiatta reacted with rage and began leaping high into the air toward the lobby entrance, brandishing their deadly laser spears in their hands. Killing a Babcottiatta was no easy feat. They could take several laser blasts and shake it off as a human might a mosquito bite.

Three of the Babcottiatta crashed through the front entrance and charged the cadets. Cadet Shore died first when one of the Babcottiatta impaled her in the chest with the spear. Shore's screams were high pitched as the weapon melted her flesh from her body. Wackowiak was next when one of the large

Babcottiatta grabbed her arms, one leg and her neck in its' massive hands. It ripped her body into five pieces with little effort. One of the other cadet pilots died when he attempted to stand and fight the third Babcottiatta. The creature raised two closed fists over its' head and slammed them down on the head of the doomed cadet, crushing his skull like an egg.

Seward fired his pump laser shotgun over and over again at the Babcottiatta that had killed cadet Shore. After several shots hit the Babcottiatta in the chest, the large alien slumped to the tiled floor. Cobb and Gauthier followed Seward's example and began firing at the monstrous aliens until they stopped moving.   Haddad was also firing her laser rifle at another Babcottiatta that had leaped into the lobby. She concentrated her fire on that one target until it fell lifeless to the floor.

The few surviving MI soldiers in the courtyard were firing back. Some were directing their laser fire at the roof where Varek, Vezpucci and Kazembe were leaning over the ledge and taking careful aim to finish them off. The remainder of the soldiers were moving quickly behind their Babcottiatta slaves, firing through the large entrance at the cadets that were fighting alongside Admiral Seward. Two more cadet pilots fell to the accurate MI laser fire.

Manuel Calderon led his siblings into the thick of the melee. He rounded up his brothers after being contacted by James Cobb. Using his holo-com, Manuel urged brothers Pepito, Juanito, Xavier, Jose and fifteen year old Jorge to mount their hand made replica motorcycles, modeled after a circa 1970 Yamaha brand, and rush into harm's way to assist their friends. Each of them were wearing leather jackets of varying colors, black leather pants, black biker boots and had goggles to protect their eyes. Juanito had put metal studs all over his own bright yellow jacket and painted a death skull on the back. Their oil and gasoline based machines reached speeds in excess of seventy miles per hour as Manuel gunned his accelerator, urging his motorcycle to move faster. Learning to design, build and operate a motorcycle was a talent passed on to all of the Calderon children by their father.

His hobby of welding metal and rebuilding old engines from browning and brittle repair manuals had become a way for the entire family to bond.

For Manuel, he loved to ride. Nothing compared to the thrill of the wind in his hair and the looks he received from lovely ladies when he sped past them. If anything, having an item to ride around on that no one else did was an excellent way to meet women. But this trip was not about meeting women. This was an errand to rescue his friends Varek, Cobb and Gauthier. They were in danger and the Bragg Gang never abandoned their own.

In the distance the Calderon brothers saw the explosions from the laser satchel charges. Pepito had to slow down as he made the mistake of looking right into the explosions. He was temporarily blinded by the brightness. After blinking his eyes several times he was ready to rejoin his brothers.

The mission as Cobb had explained it was to rescue Admiral Seward and get him safely to the cadet launching pads where there were over three thousand Allen Type single fighter ships and three hundred Raumschiffs waiting to be utilized. The hope was that Seward would be able to lead the cadet pilots into battle and oust the soldiers that had wreaked so much havoc on the good people of Clovis City.

The MI soldiers had turned their backs on the six approaching riders on their motorcycles to charge into the direction of the ambush. It was a textbook reaction. Whenever ambushed do not run away or scatter, return fire and attack the position of the opposition.

Manuel was the fastest rider and was the first to arrive to the blood stained courtyard. He skid to a stop nearby a dead MI soldier. He spied on the several weapons scattered about from the departed soldiers. He leaned over his seat and with his right hand grabbed the nearest laser rifle lying on the transparent concrete courtyard. Manuel checked the charge on the weapon and noted that it was full. That meant he would have about five hundred shots of deadly laser energy. He smiled as he watched his brothers mimic his example, each one coming to a stop to collect weapons that had belonged to the departed soldiers.

"Now what?" Jorge asked of his brothers.

"Now we take out those giant creatures and get the Admiral out of here!" Manuel yelled over the screams and sounds of the battle.

He throttled his motorcycle and turned his front wheel in the direction of the sky scraper building where the shootout was occurring. As he steered with his left hand, Manuel Calderon fired his newly acquired laser rifle into the back of a Babcottiatta. The creature roared with rage when it felt the laser burst rip a small cut in his skin. Before the Babcottiatta could turn and face Manuel, it was hit by five more bursts fired by the young cadet. The alien staggered backwards under the onslaught of laser fire. Manuel was guiding his motorcycle in circles around the alien as he kept firing the laser at it. The Babcottiatta finally rolled over onto the courtyard and gasped a last breath. The body of the giant alien was riddled with holes from the laser attack.

The other Calderon brothers were firing into the remaining MI soldiers and Babcottiatta. Gauthier and Cobb cheered for their friends on the motorcycles.

Seward was elated but did not celebrate. He had been through too many battles and knew from experience that anything could happen. Haddad had a Babcottiatta laser spear in one hand and a laser pistol in the other. She had some blood on her right side that came from a gash she suffered when nicked by a laser fired by one of the dead MI soldiers. Truang and Serpas were still alive. The rest of the cadet pilots that had joined the fight on the lower level were dead.

"Cobb! Contact Varek to abandon the building and make best speed to the landing strips!" Seward ordered and looked to Gauthier. "Can those machines hold more than one person riding them?"

"Yes sir!" Gauthier nodded.

Cobb was following Seward's orders and contacted Varek to get off the roof and out of the building.

"Now what, Admiral?" Haddad asked as she walked across the lobby. Just about thirty minutes earlier, the tile and the walls were pristine. The desk tops and computers were clean and presentable. Now there were dead bodies all around and blood everywhere. She grimaced at the sight of the thick orange blood of one of the dead Babcottiatta as she walked past it. It looked thicker than human blood, like a river of molten metal.

"Now we get the other cadet pilots organized for war." Seward told her. "Cobb, Truang, Serpas, Haddad and Guathier, get on the back of those motorcycles and let's take the airfield. Varek and the others will have to meet us there late."

The Calderon brothers were waiting near the entrance for the survivors. They smiled when they saw Seward emerge alive from the tall building. Seward climbed on the back of Manuel's motorcycle.

"That was some damn fine shooting, son," Seward complimented him.

"Same to you, sir." Manuel responded as he throttled the accelerator. "Hold on tight. I drive fast."

The six motorcycles departed quickly, each with two people on them. Basil Varek and the two brave cadets that fought by his side descended to see the destruction in the lobby. Some of the civilians and cadets that had run as opposed to fighting were starting to come out from their hiding places. One of the female computer technicians came out from behind the information desk. She was shaking from fear.

"Is it over?" She asked.

Varek looked at her and the others that were showing themselves. "No. It is just beginning. We just struck the first victory for the people of Clovis City."

"What do we do?" The technician asked him.

"Either join the fight or go home," Varek shrugged at her. "The invading forces will retaliate. Best thing to do right now is get the hell out of this building. They will arrive soon."

"We did it!" Kazembe said to him.

Varek was still looking at the bodies that were scattered throughout the lobby. He shook his head as he saw the remains of cadet Shore. He had liked that cadet. "All we did was start a war."

"We will win, right?" She asked.

Varek picked up some of the weapons that had belonged to the deceased and handed a laser rifle to her.

"You better pray to whatever deity you believe in. This war has the potential to last a very long time."

CHAPTER TWENTY-SIX

Estrellita Calderon was livid due to General Tan rejecting her request to attend Lupita's funeral services. In denying the simple humanitarian request, Tan want on a tirade of four letter expletives that included some words in a foreign language that Estrellita did not understand. Estrellita had contacted her family and expressed her regrets after her father talked her out of quitting her job. She had wanted to be there to say good-bye to Lupita with her family and friends. Given the current events, she was partially glad that she did not go.

But what she did not expect was that her personal dilemma was about to become as danger filled as the events at the funeral. Estrellita reported to work at the large laboratory that was being used by Matthew Rosenburg and his daughters to find the solution to what had gone wrong with the fifty clones of Junior Ragnarsson. For some reason unknown to her, Matthew kept the lab and the adjoining chambers warm. Accordingly, Estrellita had learned to dress to keep herself cool. She had on a red and yellow striped tube top, matching baggy shorts and a pair of red tennis shoes on. She had her long dark hair pulled back with a clip. She ignored the women that stared at her body as she walked past them in the halls of Tan's palace. All she could think of was that she wanted to finish her ten hour shift, go home and shower and then take the first civilian transport back to

Clovis City so that she could spend the evening with her family. She noticed that one of the MI soldiers, named Vu, had been sitting in the seat reserved to her in the main lab. Estrellita glared at Vu and stood silently behind her, watching her as she was checking the memory database of the computer.

"Can I help you with anything?" Estrellita asked Vu from behind her.

Vu stood up and smiled as she looked Estrellita over, "My, aren't we dressed down today?"

"The doctor authorized us to dress comfortably. May I ask what you are doing on my computer station?"

"Your computer station? No. It is Matthew's computer station. Everything here is his as long as the General authorizes it. You are merely here because you are a better than average computer programmer. I was simply checking your data for security breaches."

Estrellita kept calm even though her heart rate began to increase. She wondered if they were on to her sending information to Reynita via encrypted codes. "You mean somebody broke in to the lab?"

Vu shook her head, "No, I am checking to find out if anyone is stealing the information from Matthew. He has ordered that if anyone tries to send out his work that they be killed. He might allow you to live if you are the one doing it. He's always looking at you with lust. Play our cards right and use your nice body to advance yourself."

"I prefer to advance on my own merit."

Vu laughed, "Sure you do. That's why you are walking around almost naked. I do not blame you. If I had your body, I would do the same. Now get to work. Matthew will be ready soon to attempt a download of General Tan's mind into one of the clones. It should prove to be an interesting day."

Estrellita sat down in her pink swivel chair and waited until Vu left her alone. She immediately checked for any spy programs that Vu might have downloaded onto her unit. She found none. She also checked to make certain that her small computer scanners that she had placed on the base of some of the units were still in place. To her relief, they were all attached to the computers, exactly where she had placed them. She forced herself to avoid letting out a sigh of relief. She began reading the schematics that has been emailed to her that outlined what she needed to do during the transfer process.

"Two General Tan's," she whispered to herself. "This doctor is a guey if I ever knew one."

As she worked, Estrellita had a feeling of uneasiness settling in. She felt as if she were being watched every second that she was in the vast chamber provided to Matthew Rosenburg. She occasionally looked over her shoulder and observed that the majority of her shift, she was alone. At times, another one of the computer programmers would show up, work for a few hours, then leave. The only presence that was consistently in the chamber with her were the numerous green skinned Junior Ragnarsson beings, sleeping in their cloning tubes that were affixed upright on the far wall. After four hours of typing in narratives on her three dimensional type pad, Estrellita stood and stretched her arms over her head. She walked over to the closest cloning tube and looked at the man inside. He looked so peaceful and content. She admired his muscular chest, shoulders and arms as she looked over the nude body. She placed her hand on the tube near his face as she looked down at his penis.

"Wow," she said out loud as she noted that he was much longer than her two boyfriends in her life.

She turned her back on the clone and did not see his eyes open wide. Unbeknownst to her, he had been awake for hours and had been watching her every move. Matthew Rosenburg had told none of his workers the truth behind what he had done. He had brought the clones back to life without informing Tan or her top ranking officers of his duplicitous actions. While Tan was under the impression that Matthew would implant her memories into each clone, Matthew had only abided by Tan's demands with one of the clones. The other forty-eight clones had been given the memories, education, experiences and personality of Matthew Rosenburg. But that was not all that the forty-eight had received. Matthew and his daughters implanted knowledge of martial arts, weaponry and combat skills into the minds of the forty-eight clones.

What Matthew had not anticipated was that one of the clones would wake before activated. The one that was completely cognizant of his surroundings studied the backside of Estrellita Calderon. He marveled over the curves of her buttocks and her toned legs. The clone began to become aroused as he stared at her. Estrellita continued her work and multi-tasked as she made plans to take the last flight out from Lynott's Land to Clovis City.

While her back was to him, the clone pushed open the tube hatch and silently crawled out. His feet softly impacted the cold metal floor. His skin immediately changed color from green to grey, black and white, matching the surroundings of the laboratory perfectly. Seeing that he would be invisible to the naked eye, the clone walked slowly in the direction of Estrellita. He stood over her and looked over her shoulders and admired her cleavage. He wanted to touch her and make love to her, forcefully if need be. His one thought was that he had to have her.

As if she sensed something was behind her, Estrellita turned her head around in a rapid movement. Since the clone was that same color of the walls behind it, Estrellita could not see him. She shrugged and turned her attention back to her work.

In an adjacent office, the clone spied upon a grey short sleeved shirt and some matching sweat pants. He walked in that direction, looking over his shoulder to ensure that the desirable computer technician did not turn in his direction. His long penis was fully erect, which made it difficult for him to slide the sweat pants on. He pulled the shirt over his head and kept his eyes on the woman. He crept past her and made his way to the hallway outside the chamber. Since he had all of the knowledge of Matthew Rosenburg, he knew where the computer technician lived. He decided that he would wait until she finished work and then he would follow her home before taking her.

Estrellita left work several hours later. She had recorded the data that Matthew Rosenburg had demanded during the transfer of Tan's memories into one of the green skinned clones. As she walked from Tan's Palace to her high rise apartment complex, she began to feel uneasy, as if she were being followed by someone. She stopped and looked over her shoulder and saw only the normal bustle of the crowds of civilian and military women, hurrying to home or work. The transparent metal and concrete streets seemed as normal as any other day. Yet Estrellita still had that aching feeling that someone was watching her. She walked faster, pushing through crowds of women as she did so while looking over her shoulder. Her breathing quickened as she grew more apprehensive by the moment. She finally arrived without incident at the entrance of her high rise apartment complex. The security scans at the front entrance verified her retina, DNA and voice patterns before the doors could slide open for her. She quickly darted through the sliding doors and looked behind herself to make certain that the doors slammed shut.

After arriving back at her apartment, Estrellita quickly locked the door behind her. She felt safer since the high rise apartment building was one of the most secure living areas in the area. Without a security codes, it would be impossible to gain access unless some idiot allowed in whoever it was that she was certain was following her. She threw in several pairs of underwear, bras, shorts and tops into her open luggage that was lying on her carpeted floor. She pulled off her tube top, revealing her full breasts and kicked off her tennis shoes. She walked over to her closet and found a one-piece, thermal, white jump suit that she could wear on the flight to Clovis City. She tossed the outfit toward her bed in the far side of the room.

She screamed out loud when a green hand reached out and caught her white outfit in mid-air. She stumbled backwards and looked at the man holding her clothes. It was one of the tall clones of Junior Ragnarsson. Estrellita landed on her buttocks and attempted to crawl backwards toward her apartment entrance. Her heart was pounding in her chest as she watched the clone drop her white outfit to the floor. He began walking toward her with long steps. He was wearing a charcoal grey outfit that she had never seen on any of the clones before.

"How did you get in here?" She managed to demand of him as he walked closer to her.

"I can bypass any security system by little lovely computer programmer," the clone told her in a mocking tone. "It was obvious to me that you knew that I was following you. How did you know?"

"I felt as if someone was watching me," she said. Her voice was trembling and her body was shaking from fear. She screamed as he leaned forward and grabbed her upper arms in his hands and lifted her up in one swift motion, seemingly without any effort.

He laughed as he held her in the air. She continued to scream as the green skinned clone looked her over. She kicked her legs in hopes that she would strike him and that it would cause him to release her. But she never connected due to the long arm span. Her arms were trapped in his grip.

"Stop struggling," he whispered. "Your screams are doing you no good at all. Each of these apartments is sound proof and nobody can hear you."

Estrellita had a tear running down her left cheek, terrified of the fact that she was about to die. "Please, let me go."

The Junior Ragnarsson clone leaned his head back and laughed out loud. After a few moments he looked into Estrellita's eyes and looked over her body. He smiled, "You have remarkable breasts. Your legs are much more toned than I would have thought for a computer girl and your face is beautiful. I should keep you alive and breed with you. You would create amazing offspring for me."

Estrellita tried in vain to shake free of his grip once more. "I would never willingly let you have me! You killed Tina, Roy and countless others. I would never bring a child into this world for you!"

He laughed again and tossed Estrellita over his head. She flew in the air for several feet and landed harmlessly on top of her bed. She got onto her hands and knees and prepared herself to fight back as he moved toward her again.

"I killed no one my lovely," he told her. "I may be in the body of Junior Ragnarsson, but I am not him."

"Then you are General Tan?"

"Not even a close guess."

"Then who are you?"

"I am Matthew Rosenburg," the clone told her.

"How can that be?"

"How? I am the greatest doctor on the planet. I can do anything. I was able to scan all of my memories, training and education into this cloned body after I deduced what had gone wrong. It was an easy fix, for me anyway. Any average medical professional may never have unlocked this mystery. But I did."

"I do not understand."

"I am a master surgeon, but I am the most brilliant scientist in the eight solar systems when it comes to the art of creating life. I can create millions of clones with small samples of DNA and then place in those clones the intellect of any person or thing I chose. With my talents, I can create armies of aliens like the dozal, babcottiatta or saharakaree and unleash them upon any population that I see fit. I can step in and do as my father failed to do."

As the clone was ranting, Estrellita's eyes were darting back and forth, looking for any item that she could use as a weapon to aid her in an attempt at escape. She saw that there was nothing useful which left her with a feeling of hopelessness. This clone of Junior Ragnarsson would soon kill her and she was powerless to save herself. She decided that the only way she might survive was to outsmart the brilliant mind inside of the muscular body before her.

"Well if you are so powerful, then why are you here? You are obviously afraid of me for some reason?"

The clone roared with anger and leaped in her direction. He landed just inches from the bed and in one swift movement; he locked his right hand around Estrellita's throat and lifted her into the air. She kicked and struggled as she felt his grip tighten around her neck, cutting of the flow of oxygen. She grabbed his wrist lower arm, digging her fingernails into his green skin, desperately hoping he would release her.
He did not.

"I am so saddened to have to kill you," he said. "You are beautiful, sexy and desirable. I would have loved to have made children with you. With your body, I know you would have created magnificent offspring for me."

"Put me down," Estrellita managed to tell him in between her desperate gasps for air.

"Why would I do such a foolish thing?"
"I have an offer to make you," she told him after he loosened his grip around her throat.

Intrigued by her, the clone set her down onto her feet and released her neck. She fell to her knees, gasping for the precious oxygen that he had been depriving her of. After a few moments, she stood up and faced him.

"You said you have an offer for me?"

Estrellita nodded and made certain that she stood up straight so that the clone could get a good close up look at her breasts. "Yes. I want to make a deal."

"In return for my not killing you?"

"No. No. Kill me if you wish. I am offering that I will gladly let you have me. I will give birth to as many children for you as you wish. In return I only want one thing."

The clone smiled broadly and reached out and took her breasts into both of his hands. He softly squeezed them and enjoyed how firm they were.

"What do you want in return?"

She made no move to stop him from feeling her body. She continued to look directly into his eyes.

"You Rosenburgs were very close to the Ragnarsson assassins?"

"Yes we were," the clone responded as he walked behind her and cupped her breasts in his hands. He began kissing her neck and shoulders, pressing his body up against her. She felt his erection growing up against her as he did so.

"Good," Estrellita swallowed. "This is my offer. I let you fuck me day and night and any time you want. You can get me pregnant a dozen times over. Whenever you decide you are tired of me, just kill me. But I want in return for giving you children the head of Ulla Ragnarsson."

The clone walked around her until he was facing her. She extended her left hand out and began to run it up and down his erection.

"Ah, you are a women that is in it to please her man? That is good. Why? Why do you want Ulla Ragnarsson dead?"

"Because she killed my little sister," Estrellita told him. "I want to avenge Lupita's death. Will you kill her for me?"

"If I do as you ask, you will never betray me? You will never try and run from me?"

Estrellita was impressed that his erection was the longest and widest she had ever gotten her hands on. She continued to run her hand up and down his manhood, looking into his eyes as she did so.

"I promise to do everything you ask of me as long as you bring me that bitch dead."

"Deal," the clone told her and lifted her into his arms. He began kissing her lips, cheeks and neck with an uncontrolled passion as he carried her to the bed. In between the kisses he asked her: "What color do you prefer your men?"

"I don't understand your question," she told him as she lay back on the bed.

The clone pulled her shorts and panties off of her in one quick movement. He looked over her naked body and observed that she had virtually no body fat on her stomach and thighs. He leaned over her and began to kiss her nipples and spoke in choppy half-sentences as he enjoyed her breasts.

"I was able to determine why the skin is green on all of the clones. There is an undersea creature called the Britva. You know of it?"

Estrellita moaned pleasurably as he softly sucked her nipples in between his teeth. Despite the fact that she hated herself for giving the man or clone or whatever he was the pleasure of having sex with her, she found that she was enjoying herself.

"Yes, I know of the Britva. Ah, that feels really good. Yes, the Britva are big and dangerous."

"They are also chameleon like in that they can change colors to blend into their surroundings," the clone told her as he pulled off his grey short sleeved shirt.

Estrellita reached up with her hands and began to feel his firm muscular chest and shoulders. He pulled his grey pants down to his knees. He climbed on top of her and she opened her legs to him. He continued kissing her breasts and neck as he continued speaking to her.

"The clones were green, but that is because whoever created the fifty clones mixed in Britva DNA into the process. That addition gives me the power of stealth. I can change into any color you wish to please you."

She shook her head from side to side, "No. Make love to me as you are. I don't care what color you are. I want to feel you inside of me."

The clone smiled and did as she requested. He thrust his erection into her. She let out a loud moan of pleasure as she felt the length of his shaft sliding inside of her. His thrusts were slow and methodical at first. As their love making continued, he soon became more controlled by his animal instinct, ramming himself inside of her with a lust that his clone body had never experienced. With each thrust inside of her, his skin color changed to red, black, orange, white, blue, back to green and sometimes a mixture of each.

She had her slender legs wrapped around his waist, moaning and begging for more. When he ejaculated inside of her, he was breathing heavily and covered with beads of sweat. She let out a loud moan as she also climaxed. Her breathing was as if she had just run sprints.

After she caught her breath she looked into his eyes. She noticed that he was smiling at her. "What do I call you? Matthew? What name do you want to be known by?"

"Call me Adam," the clone told her. "I was the first one to wake so that name is appropriate."

"It is a good name," she told him.

"I am glad that you approve. Now that we have exchanged bodily fluids through our instinct to breed, I have a question."

"Ask me anything," Estrellita said.

"Why were you spying on us?"

She swallowed hard, "Because I despise General Tan and I wanted to know what she was up to."

"That the only reason?"

"No, I was also doing it for my sister Reynita. She was sent by Tan to save your children, or I should say Doctor Rosenburg's children. I wanted to learn all I could to help her if she needed it."

The clone kissed her lips and began to slowly move his erection in and out of her again. She stretched her arms over her head and moaned again.

"You are in luck," Adam Ragnarsson told her as he continued his thrusts inside of her.

"We all hate Tan as well. Perhaps we all have something in common after all."

"Stop talking," she whispered to him. "Just keep doing what you are doing. It feels wonderful."

After his lust for the woman was spent, Adam Ragnarsson rolled off of Estrellita and lay next to her. He spent a few moments gazing into her eyes, admiring the simple beauty behind them. He was confident that he had made the correct decision in not killing the woman. His attitude in that area was not solely based on how much he enjoyed having sex with her, but for more pragmatic reasons. First off, she was the sister of the woman that was locating all of Matthew Rosenburg's children. Secondly, the Calderon sisters seemed to share his dislike of General Tan. Third, Estrellita had proven to be quite resourceful in her ability to spy and obtain information in a covert manner. Fourth, she was quite intelligent.

Adam was able to use his enhanced mind to access Estrellita's grades from her university and found that she was one of the top students in the computer technician school. She was also a reliable person in that she was fiercely loyal to her family. That quality alone made her a person that Adam felt he could trust. As long as his interests did not threaten the Calderon family, Estrellita would never feel compelled to betray him.

Angus McWilliams was a man that had lost all of his dreams. He had wanted to be a pilot in the Space Command. As a young boy, he longed for the days that he would be old enough to fly a small one man fighter or a massive Battle Cruiser. To chase his dreams, the young McWilliams followed the advice of his foster parents and studied every night while in grade school, middle school and later high school. He made decent grades, especially in mathematics and the sciences. When he turned sixteen, he took a chance and applied to several of the military academies on different planets. After receiving three acceptance letters, he was faced with the decision others would envy. Which academy would he go to? He chose Clovis Academy on planet New Edinburgh due to the stellar reputation of the flight school instructors under the famous Admiral Seward.

McWilliams arrived as a loner. He was an eighteen year old on a new planet, living in the dormitory rooms in a new city and surrounded by strangers. He did his absolute best to avoid the hazing that was common for the entering class of students. As luck would have it, McWilliams roommate at the dormitory was a kid that had lived most of his life on planet New Edinburgh. His name was James Cobb. Cobb and some of his siblings had been a member of a local gang and soon invited McWilliams to join the group. He readily accepted the offer and became a fiercely loyal Bragg Gang member. He grew to enjoy the bar fights and found that hazing other students was much better than being the victim.

McWilliams became one of the student body bad boys and he relished the way other students would avoid him. He would daily bully cadets that were skinnier than him. Along with Cobb and some of the other Bragg Gang alumni, McWilliams would force cadets to eat poggie dung when they weren't hanging other cadets on flag poles by their underwear.

Yes, life was good for Angus McWilliams. He was learning to be an astronaut while he was a member of one of the most feared factions on campus. He dreamed of the day he would graduate and receive his commission with the Space Command.

But that day never arrived for him.

On one fateful day, McWilliams and Cobb did something stupid together while on a training flight over the Forbidden Region. Cobb chickened out at the last second. McWilliams was determined to violate the express orders of Admiral Seward and shoot a giant man eating lizard called a Verburgt. He wanted to prove he was the best pilot candidate and so he went after the biggest target.

Unfortunately for McWilliams, his wing woman panicked and crashed in a partially clear area of the Forbidden Region. She had been surrounded by all forms of flesh eating creatures. McWilliams abandoned her to die. Several other cadets attempted to rescue her which resulted in the death of cadet that Admiral Seward favored, named Al-Nasser. Several other cadets became the heroes that day. One was a rival of McWilliams named Marco Andolini.

While McWilliams fled, Marco landed his ship and fought off deadly tree spiders, a large worm and avoided a confrontation with a pack of Dozal. Marco rescued the girl and sealed a position for himself on the annual tournament team.

For his disregard of direct orders and endangering other cadets, McWilliams was expelled from the Academy by Admiral Seward.

Pursuant to his contractual obligations that were agreed to as a condition of his acceptance to the military academy, McWilliams was forced into the enlisted ranks. He found himself being assigned to the army corps light infantry. He was sent to basic training at the army base on Murdock's Province. While there, McWilliams excelled as a shooter and was assigned to the elite army corps of snipers. He was sent for specialized sniper training at the small training base located on Rosenburg's Ranch. He completed that course with the highest accuracy marks from his group.

McWilliams was promoted to Corporal and assigned to the third platoon of E Company and was living in the army enlisted apartments located in the Ferro Province. His primary duty over the past year had been to guard miners of minerals and iron ore from the occasional Cawler that might fly in for a meal of human flesh. He had to kill several of those flying aliens to protect the men and women that worked in those mines to recover the precious minerals and metals for the wealthy Nour family. McWilliams never lost a miner on his watch.

His record must have caught the attention of the Sikorsky family as he was immediately requested by General Kimberly Sikorsky to join the troops in the ouster of Colonel Gorski and his co-conspirators. McWilliams was more than happy to do so. His Bragg Gang friends had ceased all contact with him after his expulsion from the Academy. McWilliams wanted revenge against Seward and his former best friend, James Cobb. He hated Seward the most for expelling him.

McWilliams had been assigned by the Sikorsky commanders from the Lysander to join the sniper teams on the roof tops of some of the tallest buildings in Clovis City. He had mounted his sniper rifles on the safety ledges on the north, south, east and west of the Engineering School roof. He was alone with his four laser sniper rifles and his holo-com. He was dressed in his green, brown and black Class C uniform with black boots, a web belt filled with a laser pistol, several knives, and pouches filled with extra laser cartridges and grenades and a canteen full of mineral water. He would occasionally relieve his boredom by spying on people in the buildings nearby and the pedestrians below. Through his eastern sniper scope, he witnessed from his vantage point the battle at the flight academy building. He smiled to himself when he saw that his old friend Basil Varek was on the roof of the building. McWilliams whispered to himself how easy it would have been to kill his old friend. Just one pull of the trigger.

But he had not been ordered to engage. So McWilliams waited for such an order. He watched through his scope as the majority of the MI soldiers were blown up. He looked expectantly at his Holo-com device for the order to come. But it did not.

He was laughing to himself when he observed his old friends from the Calderon family ride to the rescue on their motorcycles. Part of him wished he was down there with his former pals, kicking ass like the old days.

Finally the call came. He heard his holo-com beeping and leaned over to pick it up. He flipped it open and watched as a life sized glowing red image of a female Lieutenant Colonel appeared before him.

"Corporal McWilliams," he spoke into the device.

"This is Lieutenant Colonel Clea Sowa. We have intelligence that the chief flight instructor named Seward is attempting to avoid arrest. You are ordered to take him out."

McWilliams smiled at the poetic justice in that order. He was going to kill the man that threw him out of the Clovis Academy.

"Order received."

"Do it now," Sowa's voice responded. "Sowa out."

McWilliams settled behind his sniper rifle and put his cheek against the barrel as he spied on the activity below. He watched as Seward leaped onto the back of the motorcycle driven by Manuel Calderon. McWilliams had no desire to harm the Calderon's as they had always been good to him. He patiently waited for a shot angle that would ensure that Manuel would not be hit. He slowed his breathing, slowly placed his finger on the trigger and then he squeezed the trigger.

Manuel Calderon did not hear the distant discharge of the laser weapon as he was driving his motorcycle in excess of seventy mile per hour. In the distance was the safety of the cadet landing strip and all of the space ships. He was only a few minutes away from the nearest Raumschiff when he heard his passenger cry out in pain. Seward felt the laser burst rip into his back, lacerate his kidney and exit through his side. He slumped forward into Calderon's back and struggled to hold on. Calderon looked over his shoulder to see if he could see who was firing at them. Seeing no shooters nearby, he quickly concluded that the enemy had posted snipers on the surrounding rooftops. He sped up with the hope the increased speed would make them a more difficult target to hit.

The other Calderon brothers were unaware that the man they had risked their lives to rescue had been shot. Even their passengers that were on the back of their motorcycles did not see that Seward was having difficulty holding on. Manuel gunned his motorcycle in the direction of the cadet training Raumschiff called Clovis 21 and prayed that they would make it. He was surprised that no other laser shots came in their direction. He saw that several cadets in the engineering and computer sections were watching them as they approached. One of them was mechanical engineering student Leeanne David, a cadet senior and well respected on campus. She was wearing her cadet issued one piece orange mechanic uniform. She had grease and oil stains all over the fabric and some on her face. She was scowling to see what kind of machines were coming in her direction.

Manuel Calderon got close enough to Clovis 21 and spun his motorcycle around the large space craft so that the snipers from behind would not have any further open shots. David was running to them and instinctively assisted the injured Seward off the back of the motorcycle. The other Calderon brothers were arriving and bringing their machines to a complete stop on the other side of the ship as Manuel had done.

Gauthier was the first to realize that Seward was in trouble. He leaped off the back of the motorcycle driven by Juanito Calderon and ran to the Admiral's side.

Seward was laid down on his back by Manuel and Leeanne David. He was coughing and grimacing in pain. Gauthier slid down next to him and grasped his hand in his. "Admiral! What happened?"

"Sniper got him," Manuel answered for the injured Seward.

"Cobb! Haddad! Get this Raumschiff ready for liftoff! We need to get the Admiral to a hospital!" Gauthier barked as he felt Seward's grip on his hand weakening.

"No, John. No." Seward told him softly. "I would never make it. You all need to get out of harm's way. They will be coming soon, with ships and more soldiers. Go."

"Admiral, we came to save you." Gauthier was shaking his head as he spoke. "We need you. We don't know what to do in a war. We need to get you medical attention."

Seward used what little energy he had left in him to force himself up on his right elbow. He was grimacing in pain.

"John, I am dying. They knew exactly where to shoot me. Each of you was well trained by me and my flight instructors. Those soldiers came with the intention of killing all of us. Looks like they succeeded. Haddad, you were one of the tops in you class for Fighter Squadron Tactics 1001. Gauthier, you have consistently been one of my best cadets. You are a very talented pilot. You both know what you need to do."

He groaned and fell back on his back.

Haddad was covering her mouth and weeping. She was in her third year as a cadet. In that short time she had grown to look up to Seward as a father figure. Seeing him die in front of her in such a painful way was tearing her heart open.

"My career was full of military victories," Seward coughed. "I sent two of my sons to become astronauts and lost them both. I was loyal to the United Nations of the Sikorsky regime and they sent soldiers to kill me. You all know what to do. You were trained to do what is right. You have to fight just to survive. They will be coming for each of you."

"What do we do, sir?" Cobb asked him.

"Get away from Clovis City," Seward coughed out some dark colored blood. He rolled over on his side and groaned. "Training you kids was my greatest honor. Thank you for trying to save me. May the Gods watch over each of you. Now go. Take this Raumschiff and go. Don't look back."

Gauthier gritted his teeth and then leaned over and kissed Seward on his forehead. "We all love you, sir. We will fight and make you proud. Manuel! Load your motorcycles on the Raumschiff. Everyone that is with us better board her now. Let's take the Admiral with us."

Cobb and Haddad were attempting to move Seward only to hear him scream in agony.

"Leave me," Seward pleaded. "Let me die in peace. Go. Get to safety while you can."

Gauthier nodded to Cobb and Haddad to honor Seward's request. They gently laid him back on the landing strip. Truang was scanning the news broadcasts on her hand held computer. One of the reports she found was about them, a group of traitors that were congregating at the cadet pilot landing strips. She listened to the news reporter as she reported that the new General in charge of the planet had dispatched ships to seek and kill the traitors.

"Hey!" Truang yelled. "There are two MI Raumschiffs coming in from the east!"

"Let's move!" Cobb screamed and helped Pepito Calderon push his motorcycle up the back entrance ramp of the large space craft.

The others were also rushing on board the ship. Some of the cadet engineering and computer majors were boarding as well. Cobb and Gauthier said their good byes to Seward as they rushed on board. The two men ran to the upper level of Clovis 21 and took the pilot and co-pilot seats respectively. Cobb began turning on the engines as Gauthier did a quick safety check.

Haddad climbed up the ladder to the pilot section and yelled at the backs of their heads. "The rear entrance is sealed! Get us airborne!"

Cobb obliged her as he took the half-moon steering column in his hands and maneuvered the Clovis 21 up into the sky. He was cognizant that two military Raumschiffs were closing in on them. He hated leaving Seward to die alone on the cold transparent concrete landing strip. He loved the man as much as any other cadet. He had meant so much too so many cadets. He deserved a better death than that.

Admiral Seward was breathing with great difficulty as he watched the cadets speed off into the sky on the Raumschiff. He felt himself going. He sighed as he took his last breath and died. His last thoughts were of his students and faculty.

Haddad took Truang, Serpas, the Calderon brothers, David and several of the other cadets and placed some of them in the weapons room, three in the computer room and sent David with three other engineering students to the lower level to work the engine room. Haddad counted eighteen of them on the ship but was certain that there were probably more cadets than that in the lower levels. She sat down in one of the weapons management seats and smiled at the Calderon brothers.

"All we have is pulsar blasts and non-lethal laser weapons." Xavier Calderon lamented as he was reading the ship inventory off a holographic screen he had called up. "We can't fight back if those other ships attack us."

Haddad turned toward Truang, "Get up in the pilot section and take the tactical seat. Tell Cobb and Gauthier that we have to outrun them."

Truang ran out of the weapons room and climbed up the ladder to the pilot section. She sat down next to Gauthier and smiled nervously at him.

"Haddad said we have no offensive weaponry," Truang reported. "Our only choice is to outrun the enemy."

Cobb nodded to them when Gauthier pointed in the direction of the Great Protective Wall that surrounded Clovis City.

Gauthier stated the obvious, "We need to get out over the Forbidden Region and try to get to one of the neutral territories. We will have to get this baby up to five hundred thousand kilometers an hour and outrun them. It's our only chance."

Cobb urged the ship forward by pushing the acceleration lever on the control panel forward. Gauthier raised his eyebrows at the move as it would eventually have the ship traveling at a speed close to seven hundred thousand kilometers an hour.

Gauthier pressed a red button on the control panel that was on the ceiling above him which initiated the Raumschiff internal communication system.

"Folks, you all need to strap in. We are going to be reaching maximum speed in about fifteen minutes. If the enemy fires on us while we are flying at that rate of speed it could go badly for us."

All of the cadets immediately took Gauthier's advice without making any comments. The Calderon brothers were thankful they secured their motorcycles in the lower level storage area with the metal safety cables before ascending to the other floors of the ship. All of them sat down in leather chairs and pulled the shoulder harnesses over them and secured the safety belts around their waists.

David checked on the other three engineering students before she secured herself into a seat. Fara Kiesbye gave David a thumbs up and a smile that seemed forced. The fear in her eyes betrayed the severity of their situation. Kiesbye had been one of the cadets that had garnered some fame around campus when she had joined Dirk Fenster on his rescue mission of the tournament team that was on the Blood Moon.

To the chagrin of the cadets on Clovis 21 they never made it to the top speeds. As Cobb flew the ship past the Great Wall, the on board computer sounded warning alarms to indicate that there were incoming missiles closing in on their rear. The ship was just reaching a speed of two thousand kilometers an hour which was not sufficient enough speed to outmaneuver any rockets.

"Shit!"Truang yelled as she looked over the tactical display on the control panel before her. The green and red grid screen revealed that there were two R-5 armor piercing missiles closing on them fast.

"Two missiles closing on us from the rear!"

Her voice could be heard over the ship intercom. Haddad was in the weapons section on the second level and began searching for anything that was there to assist in avoiding the instant death that would take them when those missiles hit. She found that the Raumschiff had a full complement of counter measures, which were metal slivers that could be ejected from the top rear of the craft and attract missiles that were primarily honed in with magnetic sensors. She typed out the necessary commands to deploy a canister full of the counter measures and announced for all to hear that she had done so.

The metal pieces flew out of the rear of Clovis 21 and created a small cloud of grey and light blue colors from the iron, tin and lead. The two missiles were taken in by the move and impacted the pieces of metal as opposed to following the Clovis 21 when Cobb turned the ship hard left. The explosion in the sky was bright and it created a concussion wave around it. Pieces of metal shards from the two spent missiles were thrown violently in all directions. The Clovis 21 was hit on the right rear propulsion area. The impact caused an explosion on the ship as the rear caught on fire and pieces of the metal hull were blown off.

The right rear propulsion mechanism was destroyed. Despite the efforts of Cobb, the Clovis 21 began to spin out of control. Truang could see the strain on Cobb's face as he fought to straighten out the space craft. She noticed that the two Raumschiffs that had been in pursuit had broken off and were returning back to Clovis City. She speculated that there was no reason to waste more missiles as the crew of Clovis 21 was as good as dead if they crashed into the Forbidden Region which was full of thousands of flesh eating reptiles, mammals and insects.

"Prepare for impact!"

Gauthier yelled out loud as he observed the large virgin forest below. He was filled with dread. If the crash landing did not kill them, the creatures below would find their way through the open holes and dine on each of them.

"Over there! At three o'clock!" Truang screamed to them as she pointed at the transparent metal observation window in front of them.

Gauthier and Cobb looked and saw that she was calling to their attention. It was a clearing of tall purple vegetation void of the normal tall tree clusters. Cobb was excited by the find as it would give them a chance to crash with minimal hull damages or breaches. He fought with the controls using the central and left rear propulsion to angle the ship in the direction of the open area below. He pulled back on the acceleration control to bring the ship to a complete stop as it angled in the direction of the purple vegetation. His aim was true as the Clovis 21 slammed sideways into the clearing and began to roll over and over for two miles before coming to a full stop. There was black and grey smoke billowing from the rear of the ship where the propulsion section had been damaged by the missile explosion.

Seventeen of the passengers were unconscious. Haddad was one of the few that was awake. She shook her head as she moved her hands over her body, inspecting herself to make certain that she was not wounded. She determined she had not suffered any broken bones. She removed her over the shoulder harness and seat belt, stood up, drew her laser pistol and set out to inspect the hull of the space craft for any breaches. She could wake up the others later. Her biggest fear was that a pack of hungry Dozal with their sharp fangs and claws would creep into the ship and kill them all. Or worse some sand spiders that would fill them full of poison and use their bodies to plant their eggs to create more of those creatures.

The lights of the ship flickered on and off. The red emergency lights were on, giving the interior of the ship an eerie feel. She asked the computer to identify any splits or tears in the hull. To her relief, the computer indicated that the hull was intact with the exception of minor damage in the lower level. She sighed and leaned against the wall and noticed that a female cadet in a purple uniform was lying on the floor, her head twisted in a manner that indicated that her neck was broken. Her eyes were facing the grey metallic walls to the east. Haddad knelt down next to the deceased cadet and closed her eyes. The nametag that was sewn in over her left breast read: Chan. Haddad walked past several toppled chairs and some metal sheets that were hanging loos from the ceiling over to where Manuel Calderon was lying on the metal floor and checked him for injuries. Once she was certain that he was fine, she woke him up.

"   What? What happened?" Manuel asked as his eyes flickered open. He looked confused as he regarded Haddad.

"We were hit by some shrapnel and crash landed," Haddad informed him. "We are in the middle of the jungle in the Forbidden Region. We need to wake the others quickly before those creatures outside come over to inspect our ship and start trying to find a way inside."

He kept looking into her eyes as he released his shoulder harness and then the seat belt. He stood up and sat back down again as he was dizzy. "Yeah. Let me get my wits about me. Any hull damage?"

"Nothing serious. We were fortunate," Haddad said as she walked over to Pepito Calderon to wake him up. "We need to get out of here, quickly. If any Verburgt descend on us, we are dead."

Manuel slowly stood up again and balanced himself with his arms on the metal rows of computer memory banks on the wall behind him. "You don't say. Any one hurt on board?"

"I found a tech student dead over there," Haddad told him as she moved toward Xavier Calderon.

Pepito started to move around, indicating that he would come to his senses soon. "What happened to us?"

Haddad leaned over another dead cadet that had not fastened her safety harnesses. She was staring at the ceiling and had fresh blood all around her body, her jaw looked broken and several teeth were missing. Haddad concluded that the unfortunate cadet had been slammed against the metal walls in the crash.

Haddad glanced over her shoulder at Pepito, "I would say that our little rebellion is over. Hsu, Goldsmith, Evart, all of the flight instructors and Seward are dead. Gorski is in prison. Collins and Li are missing. The cadet airfield will certainly be placed on lock down within the hour. Our little group is now stranded in the middle of one of the most dangerous locations in the universe. We are finished."

"Don't count my sister out," Manuel told her as he walked over to where his brother Jorge was sitting. "She is a hellion when she needs to be. I would never bet against her."

"You don't get it, do you?" Haddad had her hands on her hips. "They have superior firepower. They have the numbers and the military tacticians. They have a battle cruiser and control of the lunar base. We have nothing. I like Reynita, she seems like a good person and I am sure she is quite capable. But I fear she will go down in history as another Johann Travis and get all of us killed."

"Who the hell is Travis?" Pepito mumbled as he rubbed his forehead.

Haddad looked at the floor.

"He is a man that was full of ideals and stood up to heavy odds. He died as did his entire group of followers. History is full of men and women like him. Unless we get some hardware and more fighters, we are just as dead. Face it gentlemen, we have been outmaneuvered and out gunned. They will execute Gorski and all of us if they catch us. We are finished."

Manuel helped Xavier to his feet. "You obviously don't know my sister." He knew that Haddad was correct. He felt he had to keep a positive outlook for his brothers as he did not want them to lose all hope and give up. They would need all the faith in the world to do what Manuel suspected would be their next challenge which would be a several mile trek on foot through a dense forest full of man eating creatures. They all needed to be upbeat enough to fight for their very survival just to get back to Clovis City. But once they arrived, if they arrived, they would be arrested, charged, convicted and publically decapitated.

One problem at a time, Manuel Calderon told himself. "Come on; let's check on the pilots and engineers. We are going to need everyone if we stand a chance of getting the ship operating again."

EPILOGUE

Cadet Ann Harcourt had been helping the Frazier's and Daniella Day babysit the dark furred Timber Wolf named Theodora. Ever since Dirk and Therese Fenster had been kidnaped, several cadets that were closest to them had pitched in to help out with his companion timber wolf. Ann had relieved Elektra Frazier of the chore of keeping the wolf company. She was happy to do so. Ann had been an on again and off again lover of Dirk. Their relationship had been one of friendship with sexual benefits. Had he ever asked her to become his steady girlfriend, she would have accepted the offer quickly. Dirk had been good to her in every respect; he was smart, handsome and satisfied her sexually. But he never asked her to consider taking their relationship to a more serious level.

Although Dirk was not considered a player with women, he did have other women that spent time in his company. There had been one of the Day sisters that had a similar arrangement with Dirk and then the Calderon girl who had been killed. Ann wondered how the kidnaping attempt would have turned out had she been there as Dirk's date as opposed to Lupita. Would the kidnaper or kidnapers have killed her, too? She shuddered at the thought as she walked over to Theodora who was sleeping on the carpeted floor of her dormitory room.

She pet the wolf behind her ears and began to work on cutting up meat for her meal. She hoped that Dirk and Therese were still alive. She missed them both, especially Dirk when he would contact her via holo-com for a booty call.

As Ann prepared dinner for Theodora she wondered why Dirk's new roommate, Lu Wang, never volunteered to help out with her. He had been silent about the entire affair. And then there was the most perplexing part of the kidnaping, the fact that no ransom demand had been made. She wondered why. The Fenster family was worth trillions of dollars and could easily summon a load of cash to trade for the lives of the two kids.

Ann rarely used her powers gifted to her as a Child of Athena. But after Dirk and Therese went missing, she scanned Clovis City with her mind reading skills to see if any person had knowledge as to the location of the cadets. She found that whoever had committed the act had left Clovis City quickly. She could not connect her mind to either Dirk or Therese, which meant that they were no longer in Clovis City. Even her fellow Harcourt, Brandon, had tried and he had similar results.

She fed Theodora in silence. The wolf would look at the doorway every time she heard approaching footsteps. No doubt she was hoping that it would be Dirk Fenster returning to claim her. Harcourt did not need to use her powers to read the mind of the wolf to know that she loved Dirk and missed him.

She heard the doorbell ring and the wolf began to growl. She used her powers to calm the wolf as she approached the door. She looked at the security monitor and saw that there were several of her fellow cadets at the door. They each had a look of fear on their faces.

Harcourt opened the door for them. Five cadets rushed inside and hugged her. The first cadet in through the door was computer program major Mandi Nguyen. She knelt down and began petting Theodora. The other four cadets were friends of hers from the computer science section. Ann had never met them, but she knew Nguyen as she was the younger cousin of Mia Nguyen.

"Mandi, why so scared? What is going on?"

Nguyen looked up at Ann and swallowed. She was only seventeen and had an innocent view of the world. At times her statements were jejune at best. But on this evening she had news that shook Ann to her core. "Major Evart was murdered. We have been told that all of his children have a death sentence waiting for them. They killed most of the Goldsmith family, even the little children."

"The lawyer Goldsmith?" Ann asked softly. She had made extra money by babysitting for that family and had good memories of them.

"Yes. That was them. And that is not all," Nguyen went on. "They hung Dean Warren from the flag pole in front of the main administrative building at the Academy. They put Professor Rand in charge of the entire campus and the word is that they killed all of the flight instructors."

"All of them? Captain Upton? Commander Hibbert? Admiral Seward?" Ann called off the names of the instructors she had met over the years.

"Yes, them and all of the others. They are all dead." Nguyen was near tears. "And they locked down the dormitories. They were going room to room and arresting some of the cadets just because they were friends with some of the people that were considered treasonous. Why is this happening to us, Ann? Why?"

"I don't know why, Mandi. How did you five get away?"

"We lied to the soldiers and told them that we were going to a pro Sikorsky rally at the Rattlesnake Soccer Stadium. We came here instead. We knew that Elektra and Arch would protect us. They will help hide us, won't they?"

Harcourt looked at the scared faces of the cadets. She had no heart to tell them that she had no idea where the Frazier's had gone off to. She decided to be reassuring.

"Yes, of course they will help you. I am only watching their home for them until they return. The two spare bedrooms are empty. You all need to go get some rest. Tomorrow we will talk more."

"Thank you, Ann. Thank you."

Nguyen hugged her again and led the other four cadets to the back bedrooms.

Harcourt paced the floor for a few minutes. There were explosions off in the distance as the soldiers of the Royal Family continued their purge of any citizen they felt could be potentially disloyal. The news from Nguyen was distressing. Harcourt was not an astronaut candidate. But she knew that the majority of the flight instructors were men and women of good ethics. They had high standards. They had a code of honor. That was probably what had cost them all their lives.

Harcourt looked out the large windows of the home of Arch and Elektra Frazier. She observed in silence as transport ships were landing all around Clovis City, opening their loading ramps to release hundreds of MI soldiers, Saharakaree and other aliens. She heard Theodora growl and knelt down next to her and pet her.

"I know, girl. I know," Ann whispered to the wolf. "It looks like everything is lost. I pray that they find Dirk soon. I wonder why this is happening to all of us. Why?"

Theodora looked at Ann as if she understood her.

Harcourt hugged the wolf and shuddered. She dreaded what was to come. Humanity desperately needed heroes to rise up. But for now, Clovis City was subjugated and the people would live in fear. The Glorious Leader had won the day.

"How many more of our friends will die today?" Ann Harcourt asked the wolf. She did not receive an answer as she took in a breath of air. The explosions in the distance continued as the Royal Family continued the purge of the citizens deemed disloyal.

Mary Sierra, formerly known as Dulce Maria Reynolds Hernandez Ragnarsson, had developed an attraction for Sean Collins oldest son, Sean. She was a little younger than he was but she was clearly more experienced in the ways of sexuality. She was also trained to be a killer while the young Sean Collins had probably never harmed a soul.

During her time in the Collins mansion, she would flirt with Sean Collins and wondered if his father would object to them having a relationship. Sierra decided that she wanted to see how compatible they were together. Her husband, Dell Junior, had been rough with her and she had endured physical and emotional abuse at his hands. She hoped that cadet Sean Collins would be more loving and romantic.

During the night when everyone in the home was asleep, Sierra snuck out of her room and walked down the long hallway to the room. She stopped in front of Sean Collins door and knocked. She heard no answer. She wondered if the cadet was asleep already. She tried knocking again. This time his door slid open.

Sierra walked into the room and saw that Sean Collins was on his multi-screen three dimensional computer working on some weapons designs for a rocket launcher. He had on a blue t-shirt with the Clovis Academy logo on the front and matching blue sweat pants. He was bare foot as his floors were carpeted. He smiled when he saw her.

Sierra had on a one piece scarlet colored bath robe with matching slipper on. Her hair was down and she had made sure she brushed her teeth and put on some red lipstick to make herself more attractive. As she walked in she noticed that the college student looked her over head to toe.

"Couldn't sleep?" He asked her. He swallowed as she got closer to him. He had found her to be irresistible but had lacked the courage to tell her so.

"No," Sierra said as she stopped a few feet from him. "You?"

Collins shook his head, "I have this assignment due. My professor wanted us to come up with a design to add a new function to the standard issue laser rifle. It could be anything, as simple as a light bulb on the top or something like that. But to get the best grade in the class this assignment is critical. The best and most intricate idea will bring the highest score. So I thought of adding in a concussion grenade launcher on the bottom right here."

He pointed to one of the three dimensional screens and showed her where he was adding the new designs to the laser rifle weapon. "So if I add in the launcher on the top of the barrel it would be feasible for use in actual combat. I am running a program with my computers to calculate the probability of accuracy for the weapon as I designed it and the ease of use for a soldier. I will gather all of that information for my professor to get her input."

Sierra noticed that Cormac was rambling on and on about his project.

"So, do I make you nervous being here?"

He nodded slowly.

"It's just that my dad, he was always pissed off that Siobhan used to sneak Yuri Gorski into her room. He kind of laid down the law on us all to not have girls or boys in our room at night. It was okay when Ginger married Eamon. I mean they were married so it was okay that they shared the same room."

"So, you want me to leave?"

Mary Sierra sat down on his king size bed with black comforter and matching sheets.

"No, I don't want you to leave."

"What do you want me to do?"

"I would like for you to stay," Collins told her.

"Your bed sheets feel very nice, Sean." She smiled and leaned forward. "You know I hate calling you Sean. I refer to your father as Sean. Do you have a middle name or a nick name I can call you by?"

He smiled, "My full name is Sean Cormac Reilly Collins, III. I have never really been called anything else. My older sisters and my closest friends call me Cormac."

Sierra was still smiling and stood up. "So, then, can I call you Cormac? It is a nice name. What does it mean?"

"He was some sort of royalty in ancient history. I never really looked into it. Les Gillis told me what little I know of the name. But, yes, you can call me Cormac."

"You can call me Mary or Maria." Sierra walked over to him and took his hand in hers. "You dated the girl that went to the Blood Moon. Julia?"

Cormac nodded, "We broke up when she graduated."

"So, are there any other women I should know about?"

"None."

"Good," Sierra leaned into him and kissed him. The two began kissing softly and Cormac slowly wrapped his arms around her. The kissing began to grow more passionate. Soon they were moving toward his bed and his assignment regarding the laser rifle was forgotten.

The next morning, Cormac woke up and found that he was alone. Mary Sierra must have been an early riser. He threw on some clothes and realized that it was dawn. He walked down the hallway and down the staircase to the first floor. He saw his father sitting before his roll top desk typing on his holographic computer keyboard. His father must have heard him as he turned his head and smiled at him.

"Can't sleep, son?"

"No, dad. What are you doing?"

The elder Collins turned in his swivel chair and faced his son.

"Cormac, I need you to pay attention to what I have to say. A man named Price came by to visit me late last night. He is an officer in the Marines and a friend. He worked with Gorski and Evart. Price warned me that the new military commanders are going to try and arrest me or kill me, whichever is easiest for them to get away with. They will come soon after the sun rises."

"Then we need to get you out of here, dad!" Cormac said with a panic in his voice.

"The transport is at the end of the cul de sac, we should leave right away. I heard they are trying to arrest all the Evart's and Gorski's but they are in hiding and cannot be found. We should go dad. Now."

"You heard right, the military commanders issued warrants for those families. They killed Major Evart and they will kill all of us if we stay too long. The Wyclyffe and Ward families are gone and so are our friends the Goldsmith's."

Collins stood up and walked out into the hallway. He stood next to the wall outside his study and placed his hand against it. The wall slowly slid open to reveal an arsenal of rocket launchers, armor piercing rockets, laser rifles, laser pistols, knives and some explosives.

"What the hell, dad? Where did you get all that stuff? It's contraband."

"So it is," the lawyer smiled at his son and pulled out one of the rocket launchers and handed it over to his son. "I know you have taken several weapons courses at the Academy and I know they had instructed you on the proper and safe use of this weapon. They will come in large ships, most likely Raumschiff's, and have a platoon or two of soldiers to take me away. We need to be ready. Get Liam up and tell him what is happening. Take a few of the armor piercing shells with you. When they come don't hesitate. Blow their ships out of the sky."

"Dad, we should run."

"We will after we bloody their noses," the elder Collins told his son.

"The problem is that if we run now, they will just shoot us down. You and your brother need to go with your sisters and hide. But if we leave now, the ships that are on their way here will track us. We need to kill them all and then we can escape. But not before then. You understand me son?"

"Yes father," Cormac nodded. "I will wake up Liam now."

Mary Sierra had showered and changed into a black work out set of sweats and tennis shoes. She did not feel bad that she had made love to the young Cormac Collins. She actually felt good about her decision to do so. He had been a gentle lover, unlike what she had been exposed to in the past.

When she was a slave on the Rosenburg Ranch, the men were rough and abusive during sex. Her deceased husband, Junior, had been the same. But Cormac seemed to actually care for her in the way he held her and kissed her. There was no violence or hitting or physical pain. The entire experience had been a mutual pleasure that she had been cheated out of by the rough manner Junior had exhibited with her.

She hoped that they would have more time to spend together and get to know each other better. She was about to dry her hair off when she heard the sounds of approaching space craft. She dropped her hair brush and ran down the stairs. She leaped off the final step and stopped to listen closer to the noise while standing in the living room of the spacious mansion owned by Sean Collins. Sierra then quickly ran to the windows and gazed outside to see two Super Raumschiff space craft landing in the street across from the Collins home. Sierra was certain that she knew what was happening. The new military leadership had been sent to arrest or kill Collins and his family.

Sierra screamed at the top of her lungs for Collins. He came running down the stairs and had two laser rifles in his hands. Without a word, Collins threw one of the rifles to Sierra.

"We will need more than these to fight them off!" Sierra yelled.

As if on cue, Liam and Cormac Collins came running up the stairs from the basement. Liam held a silver and red colored armor piercing rocket launcher over his right shoulder. Sean Collins was carrying two rockets.

"Okay dad!" Liam was breathing heavily, mostly from stress than exertion. "Where do fire them at?"

Sean pointed out the window, "Blow up those ships!"

Without questioning their father, Liam ran to the door as his older brother followed behind him. There were several soldiers in black uniforms jumping off the two Raumschiff space craft from the rear bay doors as the Collins brothers loaded the rocket launcher.

Liam pulled the trigger on the weapon and one rocket was sailing in the air at the nearest Raumschiff. Cormac loaded the second rocket into the launcher and yelled to his brother that he was ready. Liam aimed at the second Raumschiff and fired.

There were several soldiers and Saharakaree leaping from the back exit ramps of their space craft. Some of them did not see the launched rockets that were coming in their direction. They had all assumed that taking the lawyer and his family would be an easy task since he had a reputation of being peaceful and law abiding.

The first Raumschiff erupted in a ball of fire that shook the ground. Metal and torn bodies rose into the air as the heat from the explosion. The red and yellow fireball that accompanied the destruction significantly raised the ambient temperature on the ground. The second Raumschiff exploded seconds later. The screams of the soldiers that were caught in the blast did not last long as they mercifully succumbed to their wounds.

Across the other end of the street, Cara Perez Guerrero was knitting a sweater when she heard the rumble of the approaching space craft. She had purchased the three floor home with her settlement money from the lawsuit she had been a part of against the Rosenburg family. Previously, she had moved in her grandparents, widowed mother and siblings which left about a dozen free rooms. She continued her studies to become a pilot in the Space Command and planned on allowing her family to stay in the home when she eventually received her first assignment.

The neighbors were quiet for the most part. Many of them had enough money to own their own space craft, or maintained employment that supplied them with such expensive transports. Accordingly, she had thought nothing of the noise above as space ships flew over the neighborhood regularly. But when the explosions began she fell to the floor and covered her ears. She heard the sound as the windows to her home shattered from the explosions. She felt her stomach with her left hand and screamed out in pain. She saw blood coming from her side where a piece of shrapnel had hit her. She cried out and began crawling for her holo-com device. She prayed that her unborn twins had not been harmed. She grabbed at her holo-com and flipped it open.

"Computer, contact the ER. I am injured." Perez Guerrero groaned in pain and held her stomach. "Aaaahhh. It hurts! Please hurry."

She looked up to see her mother and one of her little brothers running in her direction. She could see fear and concern in their eyes as they reached her.

"My babies!" She cried out.

"Tranquilo!" Her mother took her hand. "Be calm. We will get you to the doctors."

Mary Sierra and Sean Collins pushed past Liam and Cormac to engage the surviving soldiers and Saharakaree.

Sierra fired her laser rifle three times with distinct precision and blew the heads off of three soldiers. Cormac and Liam watched with their mouths wide open as their father was shooting soldiers down with his laser rifle. Three soldiers charged their father and he had no problem killing all three using a knife in each hand and slashing the three soldiers in the neck and in the abdomen. He fired two more blasts from his laser rifle and split two Saharakaree in half. A Military Intelligence Lieutenant charged at Collins with a knife raised for the kill.

Collins sidestepped the officer and clubbed him over the back of the head with his laser rifle. Collins pounced on the man before he could recover and drove his knee into his chest. Collins then ripped the knife from his hand and then buried the blade into the Lieutenant's chest. The officer screamed as he felt the blade cut through his skin and slice through his internal organs. Collins noticed that the name tag of the dying officer read Rendon.

"A Royal," Collins said softly as he pulled the knife free of the body, rolled off of the officer and turned his attention to the other survivors of the destroyed Raumschiff's.

Sean Collins stood and then charged another soldier that was attempting to take aim at his mansion with a laser rifle. Collins kicked the rifle out of his hands and buried the knife into the right eye socket of the soldier. He threw the other knife at a soldier ten feet away and the man died as the knife buried into his neck. Collins kicked the dying soldier close to him to the ground and began running back toward his two sons and his mansion.

"Dad!" Liam yelled over the sounds of the last Raumschiff crashing to the ground. "What the hell? You never told us you could, you could do that!"

Sean looked at his two sons and his eyes were more serious than either could recall.

"Get your sisters and get out of here! Go to our personal Raumschiff in the Private Docking area on the other end of Clovis City. Get to your cousins in Lynott's Land. Stay there until I tell you it is safe."

"What about me?" Sierra asked as she wiped some blood from her face. She had killed three Saharakaree and seven soldiers in the combat and some of their blood had splattered on her face and clothing. She found she had enjoyed using her skills to kill bad people. It was a nice change for her.

"Go with them!" Collins told her. "Protect my children. They will send more soldiers once they realize that we beat them! Go and hurry!"

Sierra glared at Collins, "You know that I can be of enormous help to you here."

"Yes you could," he agreed with her. "But if they come after my children you can be there to help protect them. I saved you, so I am begging you to return the favor and protect my children. They are everything to me. Please get them all to safety."

Sierra nodded, "Okay. What do you plan on doing?"

"What I should have done long ago," Collins said. "The less I share with you, the better. I will be in touch with you. Cormac and Liam know how to fly the ship and they know where to travel. Go now. Please."

"Dad, we should stay together!" Cormac urged. "Why did they send ships out like this?"

"They wanted to either arrest me or kill me," Collins told them. "I am a threat. They have already killed Sigebert and arrested Nikolai. They need to get rid of me as well. Now all of you get out of here. Hurry up while you still have time."

The two boys ran into the mansion and began retrieving their little sisters. The majority of the younger siblings had slept through the explosions and screams created by the battle. Some were wide awake and cuddled up with their favorite stuffed doll in an effort to find courage in that moment of terror. Cormac and Liam encouraged their sisters to be brave and follow them to safety. Sierra helped them as they all ran to a parked transport ship at a vacant lot at the end of the cul de sac. As they ran, Cormac urged the girls to ignore the wreckage of the ships and the bodies of the fallen. He continued giving the younger sisters the narrative that they were involved in a game and none of what was around them was real.

The craft was hidden in a home that was no more than a hangar in disguise that was owned by Collins. Cormac and Liam had become adept at flying the space craft after many hours of lessons given to them by numerous flight instructors. Liam urged his sisters to fasten their safety harnesses over their shoulders and legs while Cormac began the protocols to warm up the engines and arm the weapons systems. Sierra assisted Liam with the girls and marveled at the interior of the vessel. It consisted of three floors, each stocked with freeze dried food and water, beds, computers, and tables and chairs that were mounted to the lime green metallic floors.

The lawyer watched as Mary Sierra and his children blasted off into the sky.

Alone, Sean Collins sealed his doors shut and ran to the basement area. He ordered the computer system to open the secret room for him. After the thick metal doors slid open, he walked over to the cryo-sleep tubes and stood for about sixty seconds as he wondered if waking the Queen of the Akarzdamedians was a wise idea. After careful consideration he realized he had no choice. More soldiers were coming and they would find her asleep and vulnerable. Collins could not allow that. If she and the others were awake, they would have a fighting chance to survive.

"Computer, wake up all of the Sleepers in the cryo-sleep tubes," Collins ordered.

"All of them, sir?" The computer asked. The previous guardians of the Queen had programmed the computer generations before Sean Collins had the responsibility of watching over her passed down to him. It was as if the computer had more knowledge of the situation than Collins did. "Has the time come?"

Collins nodded and with a resolute tone of voice he answered the computer, "The time has come. It is time for their Queen to live again."

END OF RED JAVELIN

TO BE CONTINUED IN "SHROUD OF CLEOPATRA"